THE BRIT

UNLAWFUL MEN BOOK 1

JODI ELLEN MALPAS

Jodi Ellen Malpas

COPYRIGHT

Editing by - Marion Archer

Proofing by - Karen Lawson

Cover Design - Hang Le

PRAISE FOR JODI ELLEN MALPAS

"Malpas's sexy love scenes scorch the page, and her sensitive, multilayered hero and heroine will easily capture readers' hearts. A taut plot and a first-rate lineup of supporting characters make this a keeper." —Publishers Weekly on Gentleman Sinner

"A magnetic mutual attraction, a superalpha, and long-buried scars that are healed by love. Theo is irresistible." —Booklist on Gentleman Sinner

"Filled with raw emotions that ranged from the deepest rage to utter elation, Jodi Ellen Malpas wove together an incredible must-read tale that fans will certainly embrace." —Harlequin Junkie on Gentleman Sinner

"The characters are realistic and relatable and the tension ratchets up to an explosive conclusion. For anyone who enjoys Sleeping with the Enemy-style stories, this is a perfect choice."—Library Journal on Leave Me Breathless

and still react as if it was the first time. The Protector is a top 2016 fave for me." —Audrey Carlan, #1 bestselling author of The Calendar Girl series on The Protector

"4.5 stars. Top Pick. Readers will love this book from the very beginning! The characters are so real and flawed that fans feel as if they're alongside them. Malpas' writing is also spot-on with emotions."—RT Book Reviews on The Protector

"With This Man took this already epic love story to a whole new, unthinkable height of brilliance." – Gi's Spot Reviews

"Super steamy and emotionally intense." –The Library Journal on With This Man

"Jodi Ellen Malpas delivers a new heart-wrenching, addicting read."—RT Book Reviews on With This Man

"We really don't have enough words nor accolades for this book! It had everything and MORE with added ghosts from the past as well as a surprising suspense. But mostly, it was about a love that proves it can conquer anything and everything placed in its way. A beautiful addition to one of our favourite series!"— TotallyBooked Blog on With This Man

To my sister. One of the bravest women I know.

THE
BRIT

JODI ELLEN
MALPAS

PROLOGUE PART ONE

DANNY

London—Twenty Years Ago

I could smell it. Bacon. Greasy, fatty bacon. It was making my stomach twist harder as I scavenged through the huge bin at the back of the burger joint I raided daily. My frantic hands were digging like my life depended on it, rummaging down and down though soggy chips and bread to find the good stuff. When I moved a cardboard box and the scent intensified, wafting up into my filthy face, I very nearly looked to the heavens in thanks. But I didn't, because if there was a god, I wouldn't have been rummaging through a bin like a tramp.

I was pretty sure bacon had never looked so good, and the piece I'd found had the remnants of melted cheese smothered far and wide. My mouth watered; my tummy growled hard. I shoved it past my teeth and chewed like a child possessed, swallowing way too soon. I should have savored it. Who knew when I'd find another piece of heaven like that, because, let's face it, who took off the bacon on a bacon cheeseburger? It was my lucky day.

Dusting off my hands, I jumped down from the edge of the bin, wincing a tiny bit at the sharp pain in my rib. Pulling up my T-shirt, one of only two I had which was three sizes too small, even for my emaciated ten-year-old frame, I inspected the damage.

"Bastard," I muttered, taking in the colorful patches over my torso, an ugly blend of purples, yellows, black, and blues. I was a dense fool. He'd told me to trust him. He'd promised not to cuff me if I did as I was told and got his beer. The moment I held out the can, he'd taken it and proceeded to pound me with it. It didn't hurt. Never did during the actual beating. It was afterward, when I had escaped the arsehole and was no longer making myself numb, that the pain kicked in. Part of me knew when I took what he dished out without so much as a murmur, it made him angrier. But I learned years before that I got satisfaction in knowing I frustrated him. He'd never see me beg. He'd never see my pain. Never. Not even when he pinned me face first to the kitchen table and shoved his dick in my arse.

I picked up my feet and started strolling down the alley toward the main road. Not even the biting cold affected me anymore. I was hardened. Used to the slow torture that was my sad life. I was wearing a T-shirt, half ripped up one side exposing my scrawny torso. In December. It was minus one degrees, and I couldn't feel a damn thing.

I just made it to the end of the alley when I heard my name being called. The voice should have made me break into a sprint and run away. But instead, I turned, finding Pedro, a boy from the posh estate up the road. He was flanked by his usual crew of five, all kids better off than me. It wasn't a hard feat. Pedro was Italian. His family owned a restaurant on the main drag where I'd often scavenged. The first time I scrounged through the bin looking for leftovers, he caught me. From that day, Pedro made it his mission to make my life miserable. Or even more miserable.

The six boys circled me, and I passed my eyes over each one. I wasn't scared. In fact, I was more in awe of their clean clothes and their brand-new trainers. They were all Italian. Cousins, I think. But Pedro was the leader of the gang, and he was also the largest by a clear foot, both in height and width.

"Find anything tasty, little tramp?" Pedro asked, nodding to the bin I had just crawled out of. His cousins started tittering, like they hadn't heard him ask me the very same question a dozen times before. I didn't bother answering. My reply wouldn't have changed the outcome, and running away would have made the next time he caught me a longer encounter. So I stood and waited for him to approach me, shutting down for the second time that day. His grin was wicked as he leaned in and sniffed me before wrinkling his nose in disgust. "Well?" he prompted.

"Bacon," I answered stoically. "It was better than that shit pasta I find in your family's bins."

His face faltered before he quickly gathered himself and his disgust grew. Sickly, I relished in it, despite the beating I knew was coming. "Cut him," he spat, elbowing the tall lanky boy beside him. I think they called him Bony. I smiled on the inside. He had nothing on me.

Bony produced a flick knife from his stylish jeans, inspecting the blade. I should have flinched. I didn't. Nothing I faced fazed me at that point in my life. "Get on with it," I goaded him, stepping forward. His lip curled, and his arm shot forward. My eyes slammed shut, yet I didn't move anything else, as I felt the blade sink into the flesh of my cheek and drag a few inches down.

The gang cheered, clearly thrilled with today's work, and I opened my eyes, feeling warm dampness sliding down my face, meeting the corner of my mouth. I flicked my tongue out and licked up some blood, reacquainting myself with the coppery taste.

"You're sick, man," Pedro spat.

"Want a taste?" I reached up to my cheek and dragged my finger down through the stream of blood, presenting it to him.

The rage in his eyes thrilled me as he advanced forward, ready to land a few brutal thumps to my face. I was more than ready. Every minute of my life, I was ready. What I endured at home made it easy to take whatever this piece of spoiled shit threw my way.

Pedro pulled his fist back, but the sound of screeching tires halted him in his tracks, and we all turned in unison to see a beat-up old Merc speeding toward us. Pedro and his gang split. Me? I stood and watched as two more cars entered the alley, two other Mercs, but these ones brand new. One raced up behind the old Merc, and one came in from the other end of the alley, blocking it in.

I stepped back into the shadows and watched as six huge, suited men stepped out of the two new Mercs, three men from each car. Despite it being December, they all wore sunglasses. And straight faces. They were all mean-looking motherfuckers. One opened the back door of one of the cars, and then another man emerged, this one distinctly separated from the others in a cream linen suit. He took his time, straightening out the few creases in his jacket before he swept a hand through his hair. He looked important. Powerful. Fearless. Respected. It was obvious to me, even as a ten-year-old, that he'd earned it. He wasn't simply a bully. I was instantly in awe of him.

I watched in fascination as he strolled toward the old Merc and opened the driver's door. Then I heard a plea for mercy.

And then I heard a loud bang. A gunshot.

I blinked a few times, mesmerized, as the cream-suited man coolly shut the door of the old Merc and started to wander casually back to one of the cars. I looked across to the old Merc and saw blood splattered everywhere, a body slumped over the steering wheel.

"Deal with it," the cream-suited man said, lifting his trousers at the knees to get back into the car.

It was then I saw it. A man across the way through some caged fencing, scrambling up onto a high wall that looked over the alleyway. And in his hand, a gun. He looked like bad news. Too tatty and dirty to be with the smart-suited men in the shiny new Mercs, and before I could register my mouth moving, I was shouting, "Hey, Mister. Hey!"

The cream-suited man paused, looking my way along with the other well-dressed men. His blue eyes shone at me. I was a kid, yes, but I knew evil when I saw it. I looked at it most days, though what was staring at me in that moment was a different kind of menacing. My young mind couldn't put a finger on exactly what it was that was different. It just . . . was.

I raised my hand and pointed to the wall. "He has a gun." When I looked back to the wall, I found the guy pointing his firearm down into the alley, right at the cream-suited man. One shot fired. Just one, and it didn't come from the man high up above us. Like a sack of shit, the rogue on the wall plummeted and hit the concrete on a deafening thud, and I stared at his mangled form splattered on the ground, his neck twisted on his body, his head at a freaky angle. His eyes were open, and in them I saw a *familiar* evil. The kind of evil I saw every day.

I didn't look away until a shadow crept over me. Peeking up, I came face to face with the cream-suited man. He was even bigger close up, even scarier. "What's your name, kid?" he asked. He had an accent, just like I'd heard when I'd snuck into the movie theatres. American.

"Danny." I wasn't one for entertaining strangers, but the man demanded to be answered without even demanding it.

"Who did that to your face?" He nodded to my cheek, sliding his hand into his pocket. I noticed in his other he was still holding the gun.

Reaching up to my cheek, I cupped it, feeling my palm slide across the blood. "It's nothing. Doesn't hurt."

"Big, tough guy, huh?" His thick eyebrows raised, and I shrugged. "But that wasn't my question."

"Just some kids."

His heavy brow crinkled a tad, and the evil shone brighter. "Next time they try to do that to you, kill them. No second chances, kid. Remember that. Don't hesitate, don't ask questions. Just do it."

I glanced across to the car that was decorated in blood, nodding, and Mr. Cream Suit looked down my front, turning his nose up at my filthy form. When his armed hand reached forward and lifted the material of my T-shirt with the end of his gun, I did nothing to stop him. Didn't flinch, didn't even move. "They do this too?"

"No, Mister."

"Who?"

"My stepfather."

His blue eyes flicked up to meet my stare. "He beats you?" he asked, and I nodded. "Why?"

Truth was, I didn't know. He hated me. Always had. So I shrugged my skinny shoulders again.

"Your mother?"

"Left when I was eight."

He sniffed, stepping back, and I suspected he was piecing my miserable puzzle together. "Next time your stepfather touches you, kill him too."

I smiled, loving the thought of doing that. I wouldn't, couldn't —my stepfather was five times the size of me—but I still nodded anyway. "Yes, Mister."

I couldn't be sure, but I thought a smile cracked the corners of his mouth. "Here." He pulled out a pile of notes that was held neatly together by a shiny money clip, and pulled off a fifty. My eyes bugged. I'd never seen a fifty before. Not even a twenty. "Get something to eat and some clean clothes, kid."

"Thanks, Mister." I swiped the note from his hand and held it up in front of me with both hands. I was in awe, and it must have been obvious because the man chuckled lightly as he pulled off another.

I watched in wonder as he reached forward and wiped my cheek. With a fifty-pound note! "You're dripping everywhere." He shoved the bloodied note in my hand. "Now, scram."

I darted off with my two fifties, my eyes set firmly on them as I jogged down the alley, worried that someone would snatch them away from me at any second. *Run, Danny, run!*

I heard the familiar sound of a knackered Nissan up ahead, and my feet ground to a halt. My stepfather screeched to a stop and jumped out, stalking toward me with the usual murderous look on his face. He didn't speak first. Never did. The back of his hand collided with my already-injured cheek. I didn't flinch, not even when I heard my flesh tear some more. "Where the fuck did you get them from?" he spat, swiping the fifties from my hand.

It was completely out of character for me, but I yelled and dived at him, trying to win them back. "Hey, they're mine! Give them back."

I didn't want to fight for them or show him I cared but . . . they were mine. I'd never owned anything. I wasn't going to spend them, not ever, and if he had them, they'd be gone before the end of the day on drink, drugs, and a hooker. My sight went foggy when he cracked me square on the jaw before grabbing my overgrown hair and dragging me toward his shit heap of a car. "Get in the car, you fucking shit."

"Excuse me."

My stepfather swung around, taking me with him. "What?"

The cream-suited man had approached, and the evil I saw in his eyes before was back with a vengeance. "This your stepdad, kid?" he asked, and I nodded as best I could with my head partially restrained. Mr. Cream Suit bobbed his head mildly, turning his attention to my stepfather. "Give the kid his money."

My stepfather scoffed. "Fuck you."

Without another word, no second chance or any warning, Mr. Cream Suit raised his gun and put a bullet clean between my stepfather's eyes. My head got yanked back as he dropped to the ground, tearing out some of my hair from my scalp. Just like that. *Bang*. No second chances. Dead.

Gone.

Stepping forward and dipping, Mr. Cream Suit took the fifties from my dead stepfather's hand and offered them to me. "No second chances," he said, simple as that. "You got any family?"

I took the notes and shook my head. "No, sir."

He slowly rose to his full height, his lips twisting. He was thinking. "Two fifties aren't going to get you very far in life, are they?"

At that moment, I felt like the richest kid in the world. But I knew a hundred quid didn't go far. "I suppose not, Mister. Wanna gimme some more?" I threw him a cheeky grin, and he returned it.

"Get in the car."

My eyes widened. "In your car?"

"Yes, in my car. Get in."

"Why?"

"Because you're coming home with me." On that note, he turned and started strolling away, leaving me chasing his heels.

"But, Mister—"

"Do you have anywhere else to go?" He continued walking,

passing his gun to one of his men when he reached his shiny Merc.

"No."

Lowering to his seat, he left the door open, looking at me standing outside his car. "You didn't even flinch when he cuffed you."

I shrugged. "Doesn't hurt anymore. Besides," I went on, feeling my scrawny chest puffing out, like this big, imposing stranger might be impressed, "I would never let him see even if it did."

He smiled. It was a broad smile, and I got the feeling they didn't happen often. "I don't give second chances."

I got straight in the car.

PROLOGUE PART TWO

ROSE

Miami—Ten Years Ago

The pain was unbearable. My whole body contorted, tensing, trying to stem it. My bare back grazed the concrete stones beneath it, ripping at my flesh through my torn T-shirt as I squirmed, clenching my tummy, my cries high and howling. My long, dark, scraggly hair was wet with sweat and sticking to my face. It was suffocating. I thought I'd pass out at any moment. Maybe it would be best. Unconsciousness felt like the only way out of the endless pit of pain. Or death. But I didn't want to die, especially since I finally had something to live for.

I don't know how long I'd been there. Hours. Days. Forever? My life felt like one big hole of agony.

When would this be over?

I rolled onto my side and curled up, making myself as small

as possible. I was alone. Fifteen years old, just a girl, and I was alone.

Always had been. Why now that hurt almost as much as the physical agony was beyond me. I cried. I screamed. Wave after wave of pain kept coming and coming. I couldn't stop it. Couldn't control it. I was helpless, at its mercy.

"You silly girl."

The voice pierced the darkness and my pain, replacing it with fear. I quickly sat up and scrambled back until my back hit the rough bricks of the wall. I don't know why. There was no escaping him.

His expensive dress shoes hit the concrete before me, getting louder, more threatening as he got closer. He bent down, getting my cowering frame in his sights.

And he smiled. He smiled so wide. "Let's get you home, Rose." He stood and clicked his fingers, magically making five men appear. Two scooped me up, just as another wave of pain took hold, bowing my back and having me wail in their arms.

"She's bleeding everywhere, for fuck's sake," one man grumbled, looking at me like I was the most disgusting creature in the universe. I said nothing. Accepted their revulsion. It was ironic that either of the two men carrying me might have been the reason for my state. I was virtually tossed onto the back seat of his swanky car, and then driven back to the place I'd not long escaped. The whole time, my fears started to counterbalance the pain.

When we arrived, I was put in a wheelchair and rolled to a private room. Laid on the bed. Hooked up to machinery.

A nurse hovered over me, as the men who'd carried me in guarded the door, ensuring I wouldn't escape again. I couldn't now if I wanted to. Fear paralyzed me and pain ruled me.

Then I heard it.

Beep.

Beep.

Beep.

I dropped my head to the side and watched a glowing line slowly and consistently jump.

"It's weak, but there's still a heartbeat," a nurse said, looking back to the door when he walked in, joining his men.

He gave me a look to suggest that I'd just dodged death by a whisper. I knew I had. But what about after this nightmare? Would it be worth surviving? And would this nightmare *ever* end?

"Time to push, girl," the nurse said, just as I was ambushed by another contraction, this one worse than any of the others. I threw my head back and screamed my way through it, begging and praying for relief.

It took two pushes before a tiny body was dropped onto my chest, and I looked down, finding a little head covered in blood. Panic soon set in. My baby wasn't crying.

"A boy," the nurse said, wiping at his little face roughly.

"Is it alive?" he asked from the door.

It. My son was an *it*. A nameless lump of life to the cold bastard by the door. To me, he was everything.

The nurse slapped the perfect skin on my son's ass, and then he screamed. He screamed so loud, like a message to the world that he'd arrived. I sighed and flopped back as the nurse cut his cord and lifted him to my breast.

That fifteen minutes of him suckling the only goodness I had from me was the most amazing fifteen minutes of my life.

Then he was ripped from my arms. "No!" I lunged forward to grab him as the nurse wrapped him tightly in a blanket and passed him to the devil by the door. "Please, no." My sobs were instant, despite knowing what was coming. Shock was cutting my heart in two.

"We made a deal, Rose," he said, cradling my baby in his

arms. "You can't take care of him. What kind of life will he have living with you on the streets?"

A deal? You didn't make a deal with this man. You did what you were told or you died.

"He's my only flesh and blood." My insides twisted and yanked as another bout of pain sailed through me. I screamed, clenching my now empty tummy. What was this agony? Grief?

"She's hemorrhaging." The nurse didn't seem in a rush. She sounded calm too. I felt hot liquid pouring from my body, drenching the bed under my ass. "She'll need a transfusion."

"Will she be able to carry again?" he asked from the door.

"Unlikely." The nurse was so blunt. So callous.

My body seemed to drain of life and energy within seconds, and my eyes suddenly felt heavy, my hearing distorted. "Please don't take him away from me," I begged weakly.

"He'll have a lovely home. Loving parents who can give him everything you can't. And in return, you get to live." He looked to the nurse. "Give her the transfusion." I hadn't realized until then that the nurse had stopped working on me. She was waiting for his go-ahead to keep me alive?

If I thought I'd felt pain, I was wrong. Watching him leave with my baby was excruciating. The last thing I saw that day was my baby's tiny hand holding the wicked bastard's finger—the little finger he wore that nasty serpent ring on. It was nearly as big as my son's hand, and the emerald eyes of the snake were as blinding as my pain.

1

DANNY

Miami—Present Day

The walk down the corridor toward his suite feels like miles, the sound of my shoes hitting the solid marble floor echoing around me. Our mansion smells like death. I've smelt death enough to recognize it, except right now it isn't welcome. I feel like I'm walking the Green Mile, though it isn't me who will be six feet under by the end.

The two heavies flanking the solid wooden double doors outside his room look grave. Grief is hanging heavy in the air.

Two sharp nods greet me when I come to a stop outside the door. Solemn nods. They don't open the doors, they know not to until I give them the go-ahead. Until I'm ready. Am I?

"Esther in there with him?" I ask, getting a nod in answer. I swallow and nod in return, taking a deep breath as the doors are opened for me. I wander in, pulling my suit jacket together, looking down my front to check for lint. It's a conscious move, one to distract me, to delay me from looking up at the huge four-poster bed and face what I'm dreading. Grief blocks my throat, but I can't show it. He'll be pissed off if I show it.

The sound of Esther moving around his room pulls my attention up, and I find her emptying his catheter bag. That alone makes my heart clench. The man is proud. Notorious. A fucking legend, feared by everyone in our world. His name alone makes people shudder. His presence injects fear like no other. I always thought he was invincible. He'd dodged dozens of attempts on his life, laughed in the face of the many assassination efforts. And here he is waiting to die at the hands of fucking cancer, unable to take care of himself anymore. Not even in the simplest of ways.

I finally pull my eyes to the bed. My hero, my father, the legendary Carlo Black is half the man he used to be, the disease literally eating away at him. His breathing is loud. The death rattle. It won't be long.

Moving around the edge of his bed, I settle in the chair and take his emaciated hand. "Call the priest," I say to Esther as she folds over the bed covers neatly at his waist.

"Yes, Mr. Black." She looks up at me, smiling in sympathy, and I look away, unable to entertain her silent offer of compassion.

"Now," I add shortly.

She leaves the room, and every second she's gone, his breathing seems to get louder and louder. "It's time, Pops," I say softly, moving in closer and resting my elbows on the mattress, cupping his one hand in both of mine.

He hasn't opened his eyes in two days, but now, as if he knows I'm here and it's time to say goodbye, his lids twitch. He's trying to see me. He knows I'm here. I rest my lips on our bunched hands, silently willing him strength to see me one last time. I don't realize I'm holding my breath until his glassy blue eyes are revealed, the brightness long gone, the whites of his eyes now yellow.

He looks at me, vacant. "Hey," he rasps, following it up with a shallow cough that makes his skinny body jerk a little.

"Don't talk," I say, truly torn apart seeing him so weak.

"Since when has it been acceptable for you to tell me what to do?"

"Since you can't shoot me," I reply, and he chuckles, the sound so welcome, until it turns into another cough and a struggle for air. "Lay still."

"Fuck you." He weakly squeezes my hand. "You come to say goodbye?"

I swallow once again, forcing myself to hold up the front expected of me. "Yeah, and I've ordered you a sending-off present."

"What's that?"

"A nice piece of arse to ride your dying cock into heaven."

"It's ass, not arse, you British piece of shit. All these years . . . been with me. You still talk like . . . like you fell out of Buck . . . ing . . . ham Palace."

"Asshole," I mutter in a lousy American accent.

Another chuckle, this time louder, therefore the cough is even more strained. I shouldn't be making him laugh. But this is us. Always has been. Him delivering tough love, and me accepting it. Every single thing this man has done for me has been because he loves me. He's the only person in this fucked-up world who ever has.

Gazing up at me, he smiles that rare broad smile. I've only ever known him to use it on me. "Never trust anyone," he warns, not that he needs to. He's one of only two people I've ever trusted, and here he is dying, leaving only Brad. But Brad doesn't love me like Pops loves me. "Don't hesitate to kill," he whispers.

"Never have." He knows that. After all, I learned from him.

He takes a moment, trying to fill his lungs. "No second chances, remember?"

"Of course."

"And f . . . fuck's sake, learn how . . . to play poker."

I laugh, the sound pure joy, despite my eyes filling with tears. The sensation is alien. I've not cried since I was eight years old. My dire poker skills have been a bone of contention to my father all my life. He's a pro. Wins every game. No one wants to take him on, but no one has ever refused. Not unless they wanted a bullet in their skull. "If you can't teach me, I think I'm beyond help." I really am. The only reason I win is because the poor fuckers playing me have an invisible gun pointed at their heads. Over the years, my father's reputation had proceeded *me*.

"True," he rasps, his weak grin wicked. "My world is yours to rule now, kid." He pulls my hands to his mouth and kisses my knuckles, then proceeds to remove the serpent ring off his pinky finger. Even the emerald eyes of the snake look dull. Lifeless.

"Here," I say, leaning in to help him, the gold and emerald ring loose, coming off with ease. I slide it onto my little finger, but I don't look at it. Don't want to see it on me. Never have. Because that will make it too fucking real.

"Do me proud." His eyes close, and he inhales, like he's taking his final breath.

"I will," I vow, letting my forehead fall to the pillow. "Rest in peace, Mister."

As I'm pulling the suite door closed behind me, I run into Uncle Ernie, my father's cousin. I have no fucking clue why I call him *uncle*, but Pops insisted, and I always listened to Pops. Ernie is the polar opposite of my dad, and by that I mean he's a law-abiding citizen. He makes his millions legitimately on the stock market, and is an upstanding, respected member of the public. I always wondered how he and Pops gelled so well, given their contrasting ethics and morals. Maybe because Ernie is the only living relative of my father. Their relationship has always been an easy one, but that's only because they had a mutual understanding —never discuss business. The respect and love Ernie had for my father was probably misplaced, given Pops's dealings, but I have many fond memories of them laughing together on the veranda over a Cuban and brandy.

"You're too late."

His shoulders drop, as well as his heavily wrinkled cheeks. Death is embedded into every crevice on his face. "I'm sorry, son. I know how much you adored that barbaric fucker."

I give him a meek smile, and he slips his arm around my shoulders, giving me a half hug.

"You know what your old man always told me?" he asks.

"That you're wasted as a saint?"

Uncle Ernie laughs and releases me, pulling out an envelope from his inside pocket. "Wasted? This saint saved your father's skin more than once."

I smile, remembering a couple of those times. Once in New York when a small-time gangster thought he could jump up the ladder of power if he took out my father. Ernie saw him pulling his pistol and alerted Pops, who ducked in the nick of time. The culprit was tortured slowly by my father's men. I was twelve years old. I watched it, every second of them plucking his nails from his fingers like they could be tweezering unruly eyebrows. Then I watched them carve out my family emblem on his chest and pour acid into the wounds. I smiled my way through it. The arsehole had tried to kill the only human who'd ever looked out for me. So, yeah, he deserved every second of his time chained to that metal chair before he was electrocuted. It was me who turned on the power.

Then there was another time in Costa Rica. I was fifteen. A whore my father was bedding at the time tried to take a knife to his chest while he slept. Ernie disturbed her. Turns out she was planted by the KGB. I never asked what happened to the whore.

Not my business.

"Here." Ernie hands me the envelope. "Your father wanted me to give you this."

I accept it slowly, like it could be a bomb in disguise. "What is it?"

"His last will and testament." Ernie smirks. "He really was a sick fuck." He winks and passes me, heading for my father's room. "It details his wishes for his funeral too. There might be a problem, though."

I look up from the envelope to Ernie. "Why?"

"Well, he insisted on having his send-off in the cathedral, so you may not be able to attend. It's not in good taste to take out an enemy while they're saying their vows, Danny."

I laugh under my breath, remembering the blood bath at the altar just a few months ago. No, it's not in good taste, but it's also not in good taste to groom little girls, and that Irish fucker who was saying his vows in the house of God had a certain fondness for little girls. Fucking animal.

Ernie disappears into my father's suite, and I make my way to the office, opening the envelope as I go. I skim it, jumping over the parts that are likely to dent my emotions, noting my father wants a funeral with all the trimmings. He even details the hymns that he wants sung. I shake my head when I read the list. *I Watch the Sunrise* is at the top. It's for me. *For you are always with me, following my ways.*

"I will, Dad," I say as I open the door to his office and take in the over-the-top space. For six months now I've been running the show, yet I've never been able to bring myself to sit at his desk. It felt too final. Now, he's gone. I look down at my little finger, seeing the eyes of the snake are bright again. Alive. Like he could be watching me. Monitoring me. Making sure I do things right by him. Making sure I follow his ways.

He has nothing to worry about. I have the instinct, and he saw it in me from day one.

"Danny?"

I turn and find Brad at the door, and his face twists when he registers my expression. "Five minutes ago," I confirm, as his gaze falls to the ring on my little finger. I spin it around, finding comfort in the motion, of the feel of it heating my skin with the friction.

"I'm so sorry, Danny."

I nod and force myself to the other side of my father's desk, pulling out his chair. His throne. The second my arse hits the plush leather, I feel at ease. Like he's surrounding me. Hugging me. "Get them in," I order, and Brad nods, going to fetch the men. I haven't got time to mourn. The moment the world heard my father had been taken to his bed six months ago, the shit started to fly, the fuckers mistakenly thinking that with me fronting the organization and maybe distracted by my dying father, holes might appear in our armor. Wrong. More people have died by my hands in the last six months than in the last six years. I take no prisoners.

Brad heads out, and I pull the top drawer of my father's desk open, smiling at the solid gold letter opener lying at an angle on top of his printed stationery. It still kills me. The most feared man in the underworld has pretty gold stationery to send his death threats on. I place the envelope containing his will in the drawer and slide the ring off my finger, setting it on top. Then I collect the letter opener, running the tip of my index finger along the blade until it reaches the pointy top. I spin it until the pressure pierces the pad of my finger, drawing a drop of blood, and I tilt my head, studying it as it swells.

When I hear a knock on the door, I look up as I suck the bead of blood off my finger. Brad leads in ten of my father's men.

No. *My* men.

Every single one of them observes my position at my father's desk and bows their head in respect. "Perry Adams." I get straight to business. "Where the fuck is he?"

"Ringo left an hour ago to give him a wake-up call," Brad answers. "They should be here any minute."

Of all the men Brad could send, he sends Ringo. Good. I'm not fucking about. "He'll think he's having a nightmare waking up to Ringo's unpleasant mug in bed with him." Ringo is one of my finest men. He's also the ugliest. Pitted skin, thin, menacing lips that I'm pretty sure have never smiled, and a nose nearly as big as his bald head. He could make a grown man cry, and I expect Perry Adams is blubbering right about now. With a gun wedged in his temple.

"His nightmare is only going to get worse if he doesn't pull his finger out his ass." Brad says, taking a seat, the only man in my father's office, besides me, who does.

No. *My* office.

"How long until we need to be out of Winstable Boatyard?" I ask.

"The developers start next month. We'll get the next consignment taken care of, and then we're out of there."

I fall into thought. Time's running out. Winstable will be gone, and I haven't yet secured the sale on Byron's Reach Marina. I need that sale, or operations will be severely hampered. Or come to a grinding halt. And Perry Adams, the lawyer for the owner of Byron's Reach Marina, is the man to get me it. He's also in the running to become the mayor of Miami, and that holds benefits far too appealing to me. Which is why I'm funding his campaign. Personality gets you far in politics, but money gets you further and I have lots of the latter. I get the marina, he gets title of mayor. It's a simple deal. Or so he thinks. He'll be a puppet on my strings when he's in power. He'll be fronting the show, but it'll be me ruling Miami.

But for now, all he has to do is secure me the sale of the marina. Shouldn't be too difficult. But, apparently, it is. "What's taking him so long?"

"Fuck knows." Brad sighs, just as the door swings open and the man himself falls over the threshold. In his boxers. The gun is still wedged in his temple, Ringo's finger poised on the trigger ready to take my order. Perry Adams's forehead is slick with a nervous sweat. I'm amused. This guy is famously arrogant, but in that acceptable way that lawyers get away with. His image is everything, from his bespoke suits to his perfectly painted family. And here he is in his boxers, looking like he could have shat himself.

"Morning," I chirp, resting back in my chair as he trembles before me. "You've got news for me." I state it as a fact, not a question.

"I just need another few weeks." He stammers over his words, shifting from one bare foot to the other. "The owners of Byron's Reach, the Jepsons, they're in Dubai on business. A last-minute, unexpected trip. I didn't know they were going until they were gone. I've relayed your generous offer. I have the paperwork ready. It's all set to go. I just need a signature."

"I've given you five million for that marina and ten for your campaign, Perry," I remind him. "You're a heartbeat away from becoming mayor of Miami, yet *I* still haven't got my fucking marina. This was supposed to be wrapped up two weeks ago."

"A few weeks," he murmurs, flicking his eyes to the side where Ringo remains with his gun aimed at his temple.

"You've got a week." I wave my hand dismissively. "Get him out of here."

Ringo removes his gun from Adams's temple and brings it

down heavily across his cheekbone with a nasty thwack, putting him on his knees.

"A week," I reiterate as he's dragged from my office. As soon as he's gone, I stand, fixing my jacket. "Watch him," I order as I pass the men, heading for the door. I don't trust Adams, never have.

My hand pauses on the handle when I hear a mumble from one of my men. I didn't hear exactly what, but mumbles speak volumes. I stop and slowly turn at the door, my eyes zooming in on Pep. I've never liked him. He's been under my father's command for decades, and he's made it clear he doesn't like me, either, though never in front of Pops.

He locks eyes with me, challenging me all the way. Stupid fuck. "Pardon?"

His shoulders straighten, a show of strength in front of my other men. "I don't take orders from a bastard."

I nod, as if in agreement, as I wander back to the desk. It's quiet. Tense. "You don't like me, Pep?" I ask, facing him. "It's okay. The old man's dead. You can say how you really feel about his bastard child."

Pep's eyes flick to the envelope opener in my hand. He doesn't answer. I wander back over to him, casual, tapping the solid gold blade on my palm. I see him back up. "Danny, I didn't mean to—"

No second chances. I cut him off mid-apology with one slash of the blade across his throat. His eyes wide, he grabs his neck as blood spurts through his fingers. I'm surprised how long he remains on his feet. In fact, I get plain fucking bored waiting for him to fucking die. So I plunge the letter opener into his heart, twisting and turning it, before yanking it back out. He falls straight to his knees, twitches a few times, then crashes face-forward to the floor. "Messed up the fucking rug," I grate, bending and wiping the blade on his suit jacket. "Anyone else got anything to say?" I look up, giving each of my men a moment of my attention. Silence. "Thought so." I stand and hand the blade to Brad as I walk out. "Don't let Adams out of your sight." I pass Esther as I head down the corridor, and my eyes immediately drop to the bale of towels she's carrying. "Call Amber and get her to my room," I order, feeling unwanted stress dropping into my cock. There's only one way to alleviate it. Killing someone hasn't touched the burning fury currently blazing inside me. Why did he have to die? The only person in this fucked-up world who ever gave a fuck about me?

I pick up my pace, rounding the corner toward my suite, and my steps falter mildly when I see the doors of my father's room opening. Shannon appears. There are tears in my father's lover's eyes. Not tears of grief. Tears of worry. She spots me as I approach, but I don't stop to acknowledge her.

"Danny," she calls, coming after me. I keep walking, leaving her chasing my heels like the pathetic lap dog that she is. She kept my father distracted from his pain in the later days. That's all she was good for and the only reason I kept her around. But now he's dead. And I know what's coming. The gold-digging whore is transparent.

Her hand rests on my suit jacket, pulling me to a stop, and I look down at her. "What?" I ask coldly.

She smiles coyly. "You must know it's always been about you."

Yes. I've seen the way she looks at me. With lust. Hunger. Pops never missed it, either. "Shame it's never been about you," I reply, short and curt, shaking her hand off my sleeve. "Pack your shit and leave."

"Carlo would never want that," she shouts to my back, panicked.

I stop abruptly and swing around, grabbing her and pushing her against the wall. Rage is instantly heating my veins, cutting through them to a point I think I could bleed out. "Don't fucking tell me what he would have wanted," I hiss. "Don't pretend you fucking know him. You don't. He fucked you. Nothing more." The hard truth makes her face twist. It maddens me. What outcome was she hoping for here? Life-long protection? A house in the suburbs as compensation for riding my old man's dick in his dying days? My father was a predictable man. He didn't love women. He appreciated them, but he never loved them. And he reiterated a thousand times that when he's gone, Shannon should be gone too. He knew as well as me that she was only in his bed for a free ride and protection. "Your time in wonderland is up, Shannon. Get the fuck out." I release her, the fear in her eyes making them watery for different reasons now.

I make it to my suite and yank my tie from my neck as I walk to my bathroom, flipping on the shower before stripping down, leaving my suit in a heap by the sink for Esther to pick up. The man reflecting back at me in the mirror looks the same as he always does. Fresh. Well-kept. The only difference I see today is the devastation hiding behind his blue eyes. Devastation only I can see. Devastation I mustn't let anyone else see. His death is a weight I must hide. It could be a weakness. I'm in this alone.

But I'll be okay. I'll survive this. I can survive anything. Old habits die hard.

I spend some time flexing my shoulders, rolling my head on my neck, trying to loosen my tight muscles. Scrubbing my hands down my face, I sigh, hearing the door of my room shut. And a moment later, Amber is draped over the doorframe of my bathroom. She bites her red lip, eyeing my naked body, her hands twitching at her sides. "You called," she purrs, taking the clip from her hair and letting the blonde waves tumble over her shoulders.

"Your roots need sorting out," I say flatly, turning to face her.

She's not naturally blonde, and today it's obvious. That maddens me too.

She falters, only for a moment. "Where do you want me?"

"On my cock." I stalk forward and push my hand into her chest, forcing her backward toward the bed. "You want that, Amber?" I ask, needing that one word.

"Yes." She never hesitates.

"Bend over," I order, spinning her and pushing her face-first into the mattress. I yank her dress up and pull her G-string to the side. I don't check whether she's ready. I know for a fact that the woman only has to set eyes on me to be ready. I snatch a condom from the dresser and roll it on, then spread her arse cheeks.

"No foreplay?" she pants.

I level up and pound home, and she screams at the hard, sudden invasion of her easy pussy. I breathe in, taking hold of her hips. I don't possess the patience or strength to work myself up. I need to let go, and in my world, this—pussy on demand—is the only way. I pound forward savagely and repeatedly, my head dropped back, my body searching for the release it needs.

"Danny," she yells, making my teeth grit hard.

"Shut up," I growl, forcing her to turn her face into the sheets to help her cope with my wicked drives. The wash of pleasure starts in my head and finishes in my toes, my cock rolling as my climax stalks forward. I groan, swiveling my hips as it churns out endlessly. "Fuck, yeah." I look down at her round arse, spreading her cheeks to watch my dick lunge with each pulse. The relief is instant but will be short-lived. I know that.

When I'm empty, I withdraw sharply, and leave her falling to her front. She quickly spins over, her mouth engaged to speak—maybe to ask why I haven't seen to her. My expression must say it all. "Get out," I demand, leaving her silently incredulous on the bed as I head back to the bathroom.

It's all steamed up by the time I make it there, wet smoky clouds sticking to my skin, doing nothing to warm me.

"I'm sorry about your dad," Amber calls.

She's not sorry. Not many people will be. I've been holding the business up for six months, and I've heard the whispers of relief that Carlo Black was on his last legs.

Stupid fucks.

They might be rid of my father, but they've got me and me alone to deal with now. I didn't earn the name Angel-faced Assassin because I give good fucking hugs. And if they don't know that, they've got no idea what's coming.

I stand on the shore by Winstable Boatyard staring across the water. We've leased this boatyard for decades from an old boy who didn't ask questions and never showed up unexpectedly. He just took his monthly wedge of cash and minded his own business. Until the poor fucker died and his son sold the boatyard to developers in a quick deal done in a matter of days. I suspect the arrangement was in place before the old man snuffed it, which is why I couldn't intercept the deal. I had planned on offering the developer's double what they paid to enable me to retain my operations here. I also planned on putting a bullet in the old man's son's knee for the inconvenience he caused me and my business. And then I had a change of heart. Turns out a college campus is being built here that focuses on scholarships for the unfortunate. Call me sentimental, but I'm all for supporting disadvantaged kids. Besides, Byron's Reach Marina came to my attention, and it's twice as big and even farther off the radar than here. Sealing the deal should have been a breeze. Fucking Perry Adams. I've only got a few more weeks here before I need to move my business. For his sake, he'd better get me that marina.

The water is peaceful, the waves lapping gently at the sandy shore. I watch bubbles pop at the surface, rippling rings appearing and growing before disappearing. I love it here. I'll miss it, but I, of all people, know not to get attached to things.

Brad's phone rings, and I look over my shoulder to him. "Volodya," he tells me before answering. "Yes?" Brad's eyes remain on mine, and then he clicks it to loudspeaker.

I hear the broken English of the man who fronts the Russian mafia. "We need to bring the exchange forward and double the order."

I shake my head, returning my attention to the water. Does he think I just magic this shit from my fucking armpits?

"Not possible," Brad tells him straight. "It's organized for the third of the month for a reason, Volodya. If it doesn't happen then, it doesn't happen at all."

"Where's The Brit?" he asks.

"I'm here," I say to the water. "What's the issue?"

"The Serbians," he rumbles, low and slowly, like the words are being chewed over his tongue. "A rat told me they're buying out of Miami."

"Impossible." I almost laugh. "I'm the only dealer for a thousand miles." I know that for a fact, since my father killed every other one.

"Not impossible if they're buying from *you*."

"I don't deal with the Serbians," I remind him. "Are you questioning my integrity, Volodya?" I look to Brad, whose eyebrows must be as high as mine. Someone's stirring shit. I wouldn't touch the Serbians with a ten-foot pole. I'm selective with whom I do business with, and rapists are at the bottom of my pile. "Now, the third or not?"

"The third," he confirms. "I'll have half transferred. The rest you'll get once the merchandise has been checked by my men."

"Fine," I say, not insulted in the least. We've done dozens of deals with the Russians. We've always delivered. But, as my father always told me, never trust anyone, and don't be surprised when someone doesn't trust me. The Russians and Serbs are enemies and have been shooting to kill for over a decade now. I don't think they even know what they're fighting over anymore, and I couldn't give a shit. They can keep killing each other to their happy, fucked-up hearts' content. It keeps the business rolling. I smile, sinking back on my heels and breathing out.

"The Serbians are buying," Brad says from behind me. "You think someone's moving in on our territory?" He seems more concerned than I am.

"The only way to get shit into Miami undetected is through this boatyard or Byron's Reach. We're here. Byron's is being watched twenty-four/seven. Nothing is coming into this city without me knowing about it."

2

ROSE

He grunts and pants, his stomach slapping against my ass as he clumsily pounds into me. "Yes, Perry. Oh God, Perry. Oh, please, Perry. Harder. Yes, harder, Perry." I can hear myself. I sound convincing, and I must look like I'm in ecstasy. But I feel nothing. I don't even feel filthy anymore. I close my eyes and wish myself away from the luxury of this hotel room and away from this moment. A moment I have no control of, being a woman I hate. But then, in my darkness, I find myself in the only other place I belong. With *him*. The conflict within twists my mind daily, because if I'm not being a pawn—albeit being lavished with gifts, living in luxury, being treated like a goddess—I'm a prisoner. A puppet. A punching bag. A slave to anything he so desires. Whether in hell or sent to some delusion of heaven, it's all out of my control, and that makes me hate each cruel element of my life. Except those stolen moments. The moments I'm not being used as a weapon and he's distracted with business. The moments I can hide away and immerse myself in the luxury of alone time. When I can binge-watch any old thing on Netflix and pretend I'm not me and I'm not trapped in this godforsaken world. When I can soak in the tub, laze around in my robe, eat junk food. When I can let my barrier down and switch off my brain. When I can be the me I like, if only temporarily. Those moments are rare and precious. They are what I live for, along with the memories I keep locked deeply away, safe from the twisted part of my mind. Safe from contamination. But even those tranquil moments snatched in time are tarnished by the knowledge that they are fleeting. Respite. Nothing more than a tease of what could be if I wasn't me. But I am me. Twisted, damaged, and trapped. Beyond hope and help.

I stare blankly at the headboard, the rhythmic pounds of him against my ass zoning me out.

I know the moment he comes. He sounds like a cat being strangled, and I take it as my cue to join him, finding my voice and screaming. And then his body splatters across my back, flattening me to the mattress. "You're a goddess," he whispers in my ear, nuzzling into my neck like a child seeking comfort. I mask my shudder as I laugh lightly, squirming to get him off me.

"I need the ladies'," I tell him, and he rolls off and flops onto the bed, still puffing, panting, and sweating.

I get up and wander to the attached bathroom in the hotel room, pushing the door closed behind me and flipping the shower on. I don't look at my naked form in the mirror, unable to face the woman I am.

"I feel de-stressed already," he calls, following his declaration with a small chuckle. How easily pleased he is. "You're doing wonders for my drive."

I'm giving him what his prim, perfect, wholesome wife can't. Or won't.

"I was meant to find you in that bar, Rose."

Yes, he was meant to find me. But fate played no part. "And I'm so happy you did." I step under the spray and reach forward, pressing my finger to the glass and dragging it across the slippery surface, breaking the solid film of mist, cutting up the perfection of it. Now it's just like me. Ruined.

"I hope you know how special you are to me, Rose." The sound of his muffled voice from the bedroom brings an ironic smile to my face.

I'm special to him. He wants me to *feel* special too. So I'll keep fucking him. But I'm not here to feel special. I'm here as bait. I'm here to seduce him while his wife is off around the world doing charity work to strengthen her husband's campaign to become the mayor of Miami. She's clean-cut. Two-piece suits. Wholesome. A smile that never wavers.

She is everything.

I am nothing.

I clean myself and grab a towel to dry off, hearing Perry Adams talking in the suite. A phone call? I creep toward the door, peeking out, and listen.

"I need to get him that marina or I'm a dead man, and my campaign is nothing without his blood money rolling it. I hate to say it, but I'm broke. I need him." His ass drops to the bed, his hand wiping over his sweaty forehead. By the look of him, I'm guessing he's not feeling de-stressed anymore. "Being in The Brit's pocket isn't ideal, but if he says you're doing business with him, you're doing business with him. That's how it is. I have another six days to get him Byron's Reach Marina or give him back fifteen million. The money's been spent. I don't care what it takes, get the Jepsons on a plane back to the States so they can sign the contracts." He hangs up, and I quietly push the door closed, biting my bottom lip. The Brit? The marina? Perry's campaign is being bankrolled by Danny Black? I've never seen the man. Wouldn't want to either. He's notorious. Deadly. Kills for sport. The son of Carlo Black is, apparently, heading the mafia family while his father recovers from an unknown illness. Nothing much surprises me these days, but Perry Adams, the respected, likable lawyer, in bed with a man like Danny Black?

I shoot to the mirror when I hear him making his way to the bathroom, picking up my toothbrush and shoving it in my mouth. The door opens. I look at him in the reflection. He's trying to hide it with a dazzling smile, but he looks troubled.

"Rose." He puts himself behind me, his chin on my shoulder. "I have to leave."

I pout, feigning disappointment. This suite is luxurious and all mine when he's not here pummeling into me like a depraved sex-starved animal. I'm free to indulge. But I'm never really alone. Never really free. "When will I see you again?" I ask, because that's exactly what I should do.

"I'll be back later this evening."

My jaw tightens. "Perfect." I turn into him and lay a kiss on his cheek. "Look forward to it."

He leaves the bathroom, and I hear him close the suite door behind him a few moments later. Now would be a perfect time to seize one of those rare and precious moments. To draw a bath. Pig out on the in-room dining. Scroll the channels and watch something mind-numbing. But . . .

I head into the bedroom and settle at the desk, plucking the camera from behind the lamp. Then I call him.

"Rose." His voice has my tongue thickening in my mouth and my throat closing up on me.

"I have more videos."

"We have plenty of videos. What I need is information. You've been there for two weeks and have nothing but footage of him fucking you, which I can't use without breaking your cover. Go out with him. In public."

"He's too careful. He won't risk being seen."

"Find a way."

"I ca—" There's a knock on the suite's door, and I swing around on my chair. "I think he's back."

"Answer the door, Rose. I sent you room service."

I stare at the wood, breathing out my nose quietly so he doesn't hear the fear escaping me. Room service? *Sure.*

Not since the day this man *bought* me has he ordered me room service. He's done nothing for me without a personal motive. That's never going to change. I stand, holding my towel to my body, and make my way to the door, opening it to find a trolley cluttered with platters and silverware. "Thank you," I say down the line, looking up to the guy who's delivered my *room service*. I stare him straight in the eye as he draws his fist back, and then I turn away as he launches his punch, sinking his fist into my back. The air is knocked out of me, and my body folds in instinct rather than to stem the pain. For ten years, I've been at the mercy of the man on the phone. Bruises, cuts. Pain has been my constant companion. Physically? I'm not sure how much more I can take. Mentally? Mentally, I've been a nonentity for too long to know. There is only hopelessness.

I straighten and return forward, knowing that's what's expected of me. A sick sense of gratitude or something equally ludicrous. "I heard him on a call," I say down the line. "He spoke of The Brit and a marina. Black is funding Perry's political campaign."

"That's more like it," he says, his voice dark and deadly. "Let's keep up the good work." He hangs up and his minion turns and walks away, leaving the trolley behind.

I lift the lid from a platter.

And stare at a photograph of a boy. *My* boy. He's riding his bike in the park. It's a reward for my compliance. But then I see him. The black-suited man in clear sight. *He's not alone. He's not really safe.* My boy's security is an illusion—a reminder that he controls me. And as long as I conform, my son will be safe.

As if I needed reminding of why I'm in this hell.

I fold to the floor and hug my knees, trying to stem the pain. The mental pain.

3

DANNY

It takes me a week to read his will. A week to find the strength. I still haven't got the strength now, but the half bottle of Scotch has helped.

His coffin should be oak like the doors in our mansion. The inside of the lid should be engraved to match the wooden swirls of his office door. If he's dead, he wants to stare at his office door when he's dead. He wants to feel like he's at home.

He wants me to carry him into the cathedral. Brad, Ringo, Uncle Ernie, and me. I'm to take the front right. He wants the Lord's prayer to be recited. Twice. Once at the beginning of the service, once at the end. I'm to ensure that every single person in the cathedral says every word. Both times. If they don't, I'm to put a bullet in their head. I can hear him telling me, "No second chances." The bastard. *God, I miss him.*

Apparently, I get to warn the congregation in advance. If Uncle Ernie so much as smiles at the irony, I'm to put two bullets in him. One in his gammy knee, the other in his temple. I laugh to myself, knowing Uncle Ernie has read all of this.

He wants me to speak. Say a few words. And he wants me to give the church one hundred grand after the service. If any FBI agents show up, he wants me to stab them in the heart with a crucifix. I turn the page and read on. He wants to be buried in the cathedral's graveyard with one hundred peace lilies surrounding his headstone. I laugh. Awkward fucker. That graveyard hasn't seen a burial in over fifty years.

But reading on, I note that arrangements have already been made with the priest. My father was many things, and prepared was one of his best traits.

Everything is left to me. His empire, his assets.

His deadly reputation.

It's all mine.

I look up, dropping the papers on my desk, as Brad walks in. "It's been a week." He tells me what I already know, taking a seat in the chair opposite me. He looks hungry, ready for a killing spree. My right-hand man is a close second to me in the animal stakes. He's the only man left in this world who I can trust. The bloke is a rock, has been by my side from day one. Now he's my only family, my cousin, son of my father's dead sister. He's been a loyal friend to me, even as kids when we barely knew what loyalty stood for. He took the rap when I beat the shit out of a boy five years my senior, because Brad knew if the cops got hold of Carlo Black's son, they wouldn't let go. He's a good friend.

"Actually"—I look down at my Tag Heuer—"he has one minute left."

"I don't think Perry Adams is gonna make it from Vegas to Miami in one minute." Brad tosses a stack of photographs on my desk, and I pick up the pictures, browsing through the first couple, seeing the corrupt prick laughing at a poker table. Has he forgotten that he's got a cold-blooded killer to satisfy? His head is tossed back where he sits with stacks of chips in front of him. "Looks like he's having a whale of a time too," I muse, dropping the pictures and leaning back in my throne, stroking my cupid's bow in thought.

"He's avoiding my calls." Brad adds to Adams's list of wrongs. "What's his game?"

"I don't know," I admit, wondering how any man could be so fucking stupid. He's been falling all over himself to get me Byron's Reach and take my money to fund his efforts to become mayor. And all of a sudden he doesn't give a shit?

"We need that marina." Brad hates anyone stating the obvious, so when I raise a brow at him, he rolls his eyes. "We should go straight to the Jepsons."

"You can't legally buy land without a lawyer. Besides, I want Adams in power too. I'm fifteen million down, and so far I've got fuck all to show for it except a thirst for his blood." I want to slam my fist on the desk. But I don't. *Never show your frustration.* Looking down at the pictures, I ask, "When were these taken?"

"A few hours ago. He's still there. Had it confirmed by the Aria's security."

I stand, fixing my jacket. "Get the jet ready."

4

ROSE

The dress isn't my taste, but it's what he likes. Short. Revealing. Strapless. Nothing like his wife would wear. Or *could* wear.

The style is a far cry from what my tall body feels comfortable in, because at five foot nine, a short dress is shorter on me than the average woman. Not that I'm here to feel comfortable. I'm just here. In a tarty red dress. I hate it. It screams whore. But that's what I am.

The fire red is definitely me, though. I'll keep telling myself that. It's a way of accepting something that's out of my control. My whole life is out of my control, but this red? I would have picked this color. Against my tan skin and mahogany hair, the shade looks like it was made for my coloring. It may well have been. Perry Adams is nothing if not lavish with his money when it comes to me. But I don't want his money. I don't want his gifts or his attention or his sweaty body pounding into me. I don't want to be here, and as soon as Nox has what he wants, I'll be out. Well, away from Perry Adams, anyway. Who knows who my next target will be. Now he's brought me to the US, the possibilities for him are endless.

"You look gorgeous, Rose."

I look up to the mirror as I secure a diamond in my ear, calling on the smile he loves so much. "Thank you." I turn and rest my backside on the dresser in Perry's hotel suite of the Aria. He's wearing one of his signature navy suits. His power suit, that's what he calls it.

He approaches, and I quickly locate the invisible barrier and pull it down so that when he touches me, I won't shudder. The tip of his finger rests on my forearm. "I'm not sure how I feel about you out on your own while I'm taking care of business."

Perry Adams is not a stupid man. He insisted I accompany him to Vegas where he's gambling with the best of them, rubbing horns with other political types, however, outside of this suite, we won't be seen together. But he needs to know I'm close. Needs to fuck me to make him feel even more powerful after he's been busy fighting legal battles by day and aiming for mayor of Miami by night. And maybe I'm here because he's possessive. He doesn't want me back in Miami where there's no one to watch me. Where I could potentially meet someone closer to my twenty-five years. Someone single. I laugh inside at the very notion. It's a ridiculous notion. If I ever feel like drowning with a weight tied to my ankles, I might entertain the idea of meeting someone off my own back. I long ago accepted that this is my life. Looking pretty. Doing what I'm told, because I don't have a choice. It's the only way I have to survive, to function, and now it's all I know. My life isn't my own anymore, but at least I'm still breathing. And at least my son is safe.

"I love you," Perry whispers, pressing his chest into my front, his lips on my neck. "I had no idea that I needed you in my life until I found you all those weeks ago. And I hate that I can't be with you properly. But you understand, don't you, Rose?"

"I understand." I close my eyes while he sucks and slaps wet kisses all over my throat. "We don't want to make you late for your game." If there's one thing I've learned about Perry Adams, it's that he's a stickler for promptness. He has ten minutes to make it to the casino floor.

"I love how you know me so well."

Because it's my job to know you so well, I think, but say, "Of course," pulling a lavish smile from nowhere. For a man who is supposedly in love with me, he doesn't know *me* very well. He doesn't realize the smiles are fake. The orgasms are fake. There's no way he'll ever know my whole fucking life is fake. That I'm simply a tumbleweed, the wind controlling where I go. A powerful wind . . . an invisible force. *The Devil.*

"Terrance will walk you down when you're ready." Perry pulls away and takes my hand, kissing the top. "And no taking the stairs." He cocks an eyebrow, reaching for my back and rubbing at the bruise there.

"I'm just a little clumsy." I smile mildly. "It's nothing."

"You knocked yourself up pretty bad. It's been a week and you're still black and blue." He gives me another kiss before taking a call and strolling out of the swanky suite. "We have a new investor," he says as he goes, piquing my interest. *He does?* "They're getting me the cash to pay back Black. The Brit can go fuck himself."

Perry has a new backer? The moment he's gone, I look around for my cell, thinking I need to call through this news. But Terrance coughs, winning my attention, and motions to the heels by my feet. *Later*, I tell myself. Call it in later.

I slip them on, taking me nearer to six foot. Perry Adams is playing with fire, and it seems I am not the only flame. Danny Black can go fuck himself?

When we make it downstairs, I'm escorted to the bar and handed a glass of champagne. The good stuff. I see Perry in the distance at the blackjack table being lavished with attention by various men, all obviously politicians. He's smiling, lapping it all up—the smacks on his back, embracing the onslaught of well wishes. Word has it he's practically won already, the past few weeks campaigning being a huge success. Miami loves him. But if Black can go fuck himself, who will be funding him now?

"Don't go far. He'll want to see you when he's done," Terrance grunts, and I look up at him. He's not scowling at me, but he's not exactly showering me with friendliness. He doesn't like me. The feeling is mutual. It's fascinating how those watching their bosses choosing to cheat on their wives always blame the whore. It's *never* the man's lack of self-control or respect of vows that's questioned.

Terrance disappears into the crowd, leaving me on my own. I could go for a wander. Go see some sites. But that's not part of my job. Being in public isn't helpful, because I can't be seen with Perry without risking his race for power, or pissing him off. But I can wander, observe, remain in the background. I need *something*. Well, I have something—Perry apparently has a new investor— but I need more. I need to be out of Perry's life. God, how long will Nox have me playing the smitten mistress? Adams makes my skin crawl. I've gotten Nox pictures and video footage. I've told him what I've heard.

I start a slow wander toward the table where Perry is sitting, but I'm soon pulled to a halt by Terrance's hand around my wrist. "Not too close," he warns. I sigh, casting my eyes around the space. It's bustling. Loud. Almost hectic. The casino floor of the Aria is deafening.

And suddenly, it isn't.

Suddenly, you could hear a pin drop.

Suddenly, it's like someone pushed the pause button on life.

Everyone falls silent. Everyone stills. Everyone looks in the same direction.

And everyone visibly tenses.

I frown with my glass at my lips, following their stares until I find what has their attention. My spine rolls until it's straight, my glass lowering a fraction.

He's flanked at every angle by heavies, four of them, and I swallow, letting my stare wander all over his tall, suited frame. His body is nothing short of lethal. His aura is nothing short of a warning. Sharp, dangerous, icy-blue eyes scan the space as the crowd moves to allow him through. It's like the parting of the sea. The homecoming of Christ. And his face . . .

"Fuck," Terrance says from beside me, pulling my attention to him. He yanks his cell urgently from his jacket and dials. "The Brit's here," he informs whoever's on the end.

The Brit? My eyes shoot back to the man who has everyone's attention. The Angel-faced Assassin? Danny Black? With the confirmation of who he is, I know I should be doing what everyone else in the vicinity is doing. Trembling. Yet I'm not. It's been a long time since I allowed myself to be frightened, and if the man before me now can't scare me, nothing ever will. I've heard whispers about Danny Black. His influence. His power. His ruthless and brutal approach to business.

But no one ever said he's beautiful.

I look down at my champagne, noticing it's splashing up the side of the glass. I'm well aware that this isn't because I'm suddenly shaking with the fear that was absent. I should be certifiably quaking in my heels at his presence, along with everyone else. But instead, I'm rapt. Trembling for a whole other reason.

I exhale shakily, looking up through my lashes. I study him as he approaches Perry, and a quick glance at my lover confirms that he, above everyone else here, is shaking the most.

The Brit comes to a stop, one hand in his pocket, the other extended toward the man I'm fucking. Perry looks like a rabbit caught in the headlights. *Danny Black can go fuck himself?* I laugh on the inside. With Terrance distracted, I move forward, keen to hear what's about to go down. What's going to be said? My God, if I deliver something truly monumental to Nox, I may get more than a photograph of my boy this time.

"What a surprise," Perry says, glancing around as he takes The Brit's hand.

"A nice surprise, Perry?" The Brit is cool. Way too cool. It's a dangerous cool.

"Of course." Perry ushers him to the side and they speak for a few moments, Adams looking downright terrified, The Brit looking nothing short of impassive. I've been around these kind of people long enough to know what I'm seeing. I'm seeing a man in fear of his life and a man who wouldn't hesitate to take it. I edge as close as I can without being obvious, listening.

"I'm getting impatient," Black says, his jaw tight.

Perry flinches, and my eyes fall to their clasped hands. The Brit's hold looks brutal, Perry's flesh white from lack of blood flow. "I'm afraid I can't do business with you anymore," Perry says, trying to sound confident, but I know. I just know. "I have to go legit. I don't have any choice. I'll pay you back every penny," he says, prompting Black to pull his hand free and turn it palm up. "No, no," Perry says, shaking life into his hand subtly. "Not here. Not now."

"I want it now."

"I don't carry around fifteen million in my pocket."

"I don't think you heard me." Black bends a little, surely so Perry can see the deadliness of his stare up close. "I want it now."

"I . . . I don't . . . I don't have it now. Not at this precise moment."

The Brit nods, thoughtful, seeming to ponder something as he rises to his full, intimidating height. I conclude he's calculating how many pieces he's going to cut Adams into. "Then we should play for it."

"What?" Perry looks plain horrified.

Black motions to the poker table, and I notice one of his men smirking. "We play." Slapping on a big smile, he gestures for Perry to lead the way. "Straight-up, good old-fashioned gambling. You win, your debt is wiped here and now. No more business. I win . . ." He bends again, pushing his mouth against Perry's ear.

My lover turns white. If he loses, he dies.

"But you're renowned to be a terrible player," Perry mumbles. Fear is embedded on his face. Pure, raw fear. And if I wasn't seeing it for myself, I probably wouldn't believe Perry Adams was capable of that look. He's a shark as a lawyer and has no problem lording his success over his subordinates. Always cocky. Always confident. Except right now.

"Then you have nothing to worry about." Black makes his way to the table and gets comfortable, and Perry can barely walk straight as he follows, a curious crowd building around them. That crowd now includes me, and I'm making the most of Perry's and his men's distraction. They clearly have bigger problems on their plate right now than a little whore like me. But then Perry finds me past the throngs of people, and when I expect him to warn me away, he gives me a small smile instead. Like, *he's got this. Don't be worried.*

I'm not worried. I'm fascinated.

The manager of the casino swoops in, attentive and welcoming of Danny Black and his crew. Something tells me it's not because a lot of money is about to be bet.

I slip around the other side of the table for the best view. Of him. His forehead is heavily lined. He has a scar running from just under his eye to the top of his lip. His gaze is shrewd and piercing.

And utterly spellbinding.

He's the most stunningly dangerous-looking man I've ever seen.

And as if he's sensed someone is studying him, he looks up. I take a step back when his eyes meet mine, and my dead body seems to come alive. Then my arm is virtually yanked out of its socket by Terrance, and I look up at him, a little vacant. "I told you to stay away," he snarls, but we both know he can't drag me away without causing a scene. So he leaves me, stalking off toward Perry. Danny Black's presence has caused a massive panic in the camp, and I can't help but smile about that.

My eyes snap back to the table. He's still watching me, his stare roaming all over my face as he plays with a chip, rolling it between his index and middle finger. My body goes up in flames. I swallow as his blank face slowly turns away from me, his hand reaching for the cards that have been dealt before him. The loss of his eyes does something odd to me. It's not like they're warm eyes. In fact, they're the coldest eyes I've ever seen. Killer's eyes.

My legs feeling a little weak, I take a seat on a nearby stool, watching as the game starts and Perry continuously flicks nervous eyes to Black. He tries to spike banter with him. He tries to crack a few jokes. He's trying to thaw the stone-cold killer. It isn't working. Danny Black remains stoic, playing his hand without a word.

Throughout the entire game, Black's expression doesn't crack, but Perry's becomes more and more worried with every hand he plays. Perry is wiping the floor with Black, but each time the dealer pushes The Brit's chips toward Perry, his nerves seem to get worse, his forehead becoming slicker with sweat. The crowd is looking on, for the most part silent, except when the hands are shown. Each time the crowd see the cards, there are mumbled gasps when The Brit loses. Each time, he takes a cool sip of his drink. And each time, Perry wipes his brow.

And every second I'm watching Black being hammered at poker, I barely take my eyes off him. Because I can't.

When the game ends, Black stands and collects his drink,

seemingly unperturbed by the mountains of chips that have changed from his side of the table to the other. Perry is quickly out of his seat too, scuttling around the table to Black as the crowd disperses. For a man who just won, he doesn't look too pleased to still have his life.

"So that's it? We're square?" Perry asks.

My intrigue grows as Black stops, throwing his drink back as he faces Perry. "Square?" he asks, pointing his glass at him.

Perry looks back at the table. "I won."

"Of course you won. I'm shit at poker." The Brit moves in close, virtually snarling. "You think you can walk away from me just like that? Without consequences?" The venom in his tone is cutting. "You still owe me fifteen million, Perry." His British accent makes me shudder, every word spoken clearly and concisely. Threateningly. He makes a threat sound like a well-spoken promise to look forward to. "I just lost another ten. That ten just turned into twenty." Black points to the table, where his chips still remain on Perry's side. "We'll call it inconvenience money, because it's been mighty fucking inconvenient for me to fly to Vegas and remind you of your obligations." His eyes take on more of a dangerous edge. "You now owe me thirty-five million. Have you got thirty-five million?"

Perry's eyes widen. "No. God, no."

"Didn't think so." Black accepts another drink from a tray. "I want the fucking marina, Perry. And no one walks away from me unless *I* release them."

Perry's eyes close briefly, his situation hitting him hard. Whatever was he thinking getting involved with Danny Black? Adams is a respected lawyer. Or, he *was*. "The marina." He swallows. "It'll happen. Please, just a bit more time."

The Brit smiles. It's fake, almost evil. "Sure, I'll give you time." Another casual sip of his drink as Perry visibly deflates in relief. I don't know why. Even I know there's a catch coming.

"Thank you." Perry smiles, and it's all I can do not to yell at him for being so fucking dumb. That's why I'm here. Because he's fucking dumb.

The Brit slaps Perry's shoulder. "No problem, my friend." Then he points his tumbler at me, his eyes landing on my body with a lethal boom. My insides twist as he drinks me in. His iron gaze frightens me and thrills me. His scar is pulsing, as if his deadly mood brings it to life. The way he's watching me now, I feel the most naked I've ever been. "The woman," Black says, his accent rich and smooth. "Who is she?"

I still, my glass in my hand threatening to crack under the force of my grip. Perry turns to me, his relief disappearing. "Her?" He looks at me like he doesn't know me, which shouldn't injure me, because he doesn't. "Never seen her before."

"Then you won't mind if I take her." Black keeps his eyes on mine, the coldness of his stare eating away the material of my dress, reaching my skin. But my flesh doesn't go cold. It burns.

The Brit starts toward me, and despite my mind demanding my feet to back up, I remain where I am. Immobile. Paralyzed by his eyes.

When he reaches me, we're virtually chest to chest. My mind rolls. My insides clench. Still no fear. Just complete and utter awe of the dangerous, beautiful killer before me. I lift my chin to keep my eyes on his, and I detect a small lift on the side of his mouth where the scar ends just a fraction before his lip line. He has otherworldly lips. Lips that have ordered thousands of deaths, and lips that I imagine could kiss a woman until she died of pleasure.

I lift my chin higher, and his mouth twitches farther. He's read me. Sensed my attraction. My jaw tightens, annoyed that I've revealed my thoughts.

He wants to take me? Why? I've sat here, silent, in the distance. I've given no clues to suggest I'm in bed with Perry Adams, that I'm of any use to Black. Or . . .

I glance across to Terrance, finding his nostrils flaring. This is on him. He grabbed me, threatened me, and Danny Black didn't miss it. The stupid idiot. I can't go. It's more than my life is worth. But, then again, no sane person refuses Danny Black.

Eyes still on mine, Black seizes my wrist with a brutal force I'm all too used to, clawing his fingers into my flesh to the point I know I'll bruise. I don't wince. I show no scrap of pain. Judging by the snide leer painting his gorgeous lips, he finds my lack of a reaction amusing. "Come." He starts pulling me away.

Perry is suddenly before us, and so are four other men. All Black's men. They all rest their hands on their hips, where I know their weapons are hiding behind their expensive suit jackets.

The Brit cocks his head. "You don't know her?"

"I do," Perry whispers, his eyes darting around. "I do know her."

Black leans in, getting his face close to Perry's. "The marina. Until then, *I'll* be getting to know her."

Perry is yanked from our path by one of Black's men, and I'm pulled through, Black's hold of my wrist now loose, though still firm. We make it to the elevators, surrounded at every angle by his men. I'm not struggling with him. I'm unsure why. Maybe because I've learned the hard way not to fight with forces out of my control. Danny Black is definitely a force out of my control. He's a force out of *everyone's* control.

I look down when he moves his grip from my wrist to my hand as we board the elevator. Then up when I feel his eyes on me. The cold blue stones sink in deep under my impenetrable skin. "No fight?" he asks. It's the first time he's spoken to me directly, and his British accent does nothing to slow down the fluttering inside my tummy. I'm morbid. Must be. My fucked-up life is the only answer to why I find this animal attractive. I'm so fucking angry with myself. I've always worked hard to force attraction, to fool people. Now I'm working hard to fool a man into believing that I'm *not* attracted to him. This is a fucking disaster.

I rip my eyes from his and stare at the back of the man in front of me, saying nothing as the elevator carries us to the very top of the hotel. We exit, still surrounded by his men. It's a carefully executed operation, every man here knowing their place. *Everyone* knows their place. Except me. What am I supposed to do?

Only when we're in the safety of his suite do they disperse, heading to a room off the main space, leaving me alone with Black. I watch him as he wanders over to a cabinet and pours himself a drink. I hear the ice hit the glass. The sound of the liquid meeting the tumbler. The hypnotic clinking of the ice mixing with Scotch as he swirls his drink, turning to face me. Now, in the harsh light of the room, he isn't just dangerously handsome. He's deadly handsome. His black hair and pale blue eyes are a stark contrast, but a perfect combination, his tan skin is dusted with even, dark stubble, and his scar is more prominent. Deeper. His eyes seem dead. Cold and dead. But beyond the frostiness, I sense heat. White-hot fire.

Walking casually toward me, he continues to swirl his drink, holding my gaze. Then he's close again, and I feel my jaw tightening once more in determination to remain as cool as he is. He takes a sip of his drink, forcing me to look away from his taut throat. But I can only convince my eyes to move a few inches up to his, finding him studying me as he rolls an ice cube around in his mouth. Hot and cold. Fire and ice. Two very different things that come together so perfectly. He is fire. And he is ice.

Then he crunches the cube, the sound deafening in the silence. "You remind me of someone I used to know," he says, his voice low and penetrating.

"Who?"

He moves so fast, I miss his hand sailing through the air

toward my cheek until his palm connects with my face, delivering a brutal slap. My head jars, and for the first time since I can remember, it hurts to be struck. Not that he would know because I don't cry out. I don't flinch or grasp my burning cheek. I just stare him down, watching as a knowing smile creeps onto his face. This smile is genuine. It's a smile that you would never know this hard face was capable of had you not witnessed it for yourself. And something tells me not many people have.

He nods mildly, taking another swig of his drink. "Slap me," he commands, full of demand and authority that only a mad person would ignore. So maybe I'm mad, as well as empty.

I shake my head, and he dips, bringing his lips close to my ear. "Slap me," he whispers, the quiet sound not lacking any of the demand in his previous order, but also sounding like the most erotic order ever murmured.

"Why?" I breathe, closing my eyes as he blows subtle breaths into my ear. Every exhale seems to seep into my mind and ignite every other sense I possess. I'm hyper-alert. God, I feel more alive now than I ever have, and it's absurd for me to feel this way. The man has death painted all over him.

He pulls back and places a fingertip on my blazing cheek, drawing a line through the fire. "Because I told you to." Taking a step back, giving me the perfect range, he raises his glass. "Do it."

I don't know why, but I don't think he's tricking me. I don't think he'll beat me black and blue if I strike him. He's figuring me out. So, I do something I've never dared do before. I hit a man, and I do it without one concern that I might be brutally punished in return. My arm moves as quick as his, my strike accurate and hard. It's like a lifetime's worth of stress lifts from my shoulders, a million slaps saved for this moment. It's as if he knows I needed it more than I realize myself.

My slap is deafening, my palm against his skin exploding. And not because it stings. But because . . . contact. He hardly moves a millimeter. It's like hitting a brick wall, and he has the exact same reaction as I did when he slapped *my* face.

No reaction at all.

Retracting my hand, we stare at each other for a while, until he eventually downs the last of his drink, never taking his eyes off mine. "Just like someone I used to know," he murmurs.

His riddle frustrates me. Yet I do what I'm so good at: hide my emotion. Although my curiosity can't be held back. "Why do you want the marina so bad?"

"That's not your concern."

"Since you've taken me as security, I'd say it is my concern." I have no idea where this boldness has come from. I'm playing the devil's advocate.

His eyes flash, as if hell could be right there in their depths. It probably is. "I don't discuss business with the latest whore I'm fucking."

I barely hold back my inhale. "You haven't fucked me," I point out, doing nothing but making him smile. It's probably not escaped his notice that I didn't refute his other label. Whore. *That*, I am.

"You want to change that?" he asks.

"No."

"Liar." His hand is around my throat in a split second, and a second after that, I'm pushed against a wall with his gorgeous lips practically brushing mine. Not reaching forward and tasting them takes more willpower than I ever thought I'd need in my life. His hold of my neck isn't hard. I can breathe perfectly well.

But I can't.

He flexes his hips forward, making sure I feel his condition past his trousers. "How would Perry feel if I plunged my cock into that sweet cunt of yours?"

Fuck.

He's solid. Throbbing.

My stable mind scrambles for a few moments, trying to remember what he just asked. How would Perry feel? Devastated. He thinks I'm his. But I'm not. And I can't be Danny Black's either, not in *any* capacity. No matter how turned on he has me. It's fucked-up. He's callous. Cruel. I've never lusted after a man. Never wished with every fiber of my being that a man would fuck me because I wanted him to. It's always been done out of necessity or because I was forced. But now. Oh, now. It's backward. Of all the men I've encountered, I should be scared of this one the most. But the only fear I feel anymore is fear for my son. I only know how to survive and to ensure his survival. And I *will* survive.

I'm unintentionally reacting to Black. Not just externally for him to see, but internally for me to feel. I don't *feel*. I don't know what to do with *feelings*. I'm trying to hide it, yet I've no doubt he's detected my swallows against his palm where he has me pinned by my throat.

He eventually releases me, stepping away, giving me space I didn't ask for. Then the slow formation of a smirk spreads across his face before he turns and walks out. I'm left staggered that he manages to leave, because I'll be damned if I could have. He paralyzed me. The energy between us was . . .

No.

I look around the room, wondering . . . *what now?* My answer comes quickly. I open my purse and get my phone to let Nox know that Perry, apparently, has a new funder and Black has him held to ransom. Oh, and that I've been taken as security until Perry delivers on the marina.

I find *"Mom"* in my cell contacts, but my thumb doesn't make it to the call icon before my phone is snatched from my grasp. I look up and find Black glaring down at the screen, and my heart starts beating a mile a minute.

"Mum?" he asks. "Will she be worried about you?"

"No," I answer truthfully.

He spends a few moments going through my phone, glancing up at me every now and then. My face remains straight. I'm not worried. He won't find anything. Then he slips it into his pocket, and I'm suddenly *very* worried.

"You're taking my phone?" *Shit*. No, he can't. "Am I your prisoner?"

He moves in closer, breathing down on me, and my stomach cartwheels like crazy. I swallow. I move back. And he closes the distance I've gained, his face coming closer and closer and closer.

"No," I whisper, shaking my head.

Black immediately halts his advancement, eyeing me with . . . I'm not sure what. Then he turns and walks away, and I exhale, my usually stable nerves shot. "Let's call you my guest." He takes the handle of the door and strolls out. "Sounds more humane."

The second he's out of sight, I flop down onto the bed.

Fucking hell. What on earth happens now?

5

DANNY

Fuck, this wasn't part of the plan. No second chances, and taking his lover is a second chance. I'm blaming it on grief. And the fact that I need that marina and Adams in power. Good God, Adams has had more chances than all the men who have wronged me put together. But I *need* that marina.

I sink back into the chair on the terrace, trying to focus on business and not her. I don't even know her fucking name. The moment I sat at that card table, I felt eyes on me. It's not unusual for many eyes to be on me, but this time I didn't sense fear in a stare. My skin wasn't cold. It was blazing. I sensed something other than fear. I sensed fascination. And that only fascinated *me*, more so when I found the source of the stare.

Her.

"Business," I growl to myself. Perry Adams is trying to worm his way out of my clutches, and something tells me it isn't because he wants to go legit. And the stupid fuck thought I'd just let this go? I should have shot him across that fucking card table. Probably would have, had something else not got my attention.

Her.

She moved gracefully. She glided. Her legs go on for days and carry her body with a beautiful elegance. Not forced. Not practiced. It was natural and spellbinding. She could have been floating, and it's ironic since she's so obviously weighed down by something. Her face, however impassive, radiated a cruel beauty that made me pause what I was doing for a moment and try to absorb it. Forcing my eyes back to the table took an inner strength I've never had to call on before. And then Perry's man fucked up and grabbed her violently, and she didn't move a whisper. I saw the brutal hold from meters away, saw his fat fingertips puncturing her delicate flesh. She was completely unmoved by it. Untouched and unbothered.

And I know it wasn't only because her attention was rooted on me. I started that card game knowing I was going to lose. I started knowing what I was going to take when I lost. Perry's wife. I had men lined up to fetch her from her charity trail in Cambodia, just to help her stupid husband along the path to sense. Things changed the second I saw how he looked at *her*. Perry's in love with another woman. The feeling isn't mutual, that's very clear from her complete lack of reaction to Perry denying he knew her. *Ice princess.* Regardless, she'd be useful. A pawn to me. A means to get what I want.

I toast my conclusions on another swig of my drink.

When the door on the terrace slides open, I look up and find Brad. He closes it behind him and joins me, handing me a cigarette. "At the risk of you shooting me, what the fuck?"

I smile, only because Brad is the only man on this planet who I *would* hesitate to kill. "We need the marina, and I want that twat in power."

"But the woman? You know the rules, Danny. We don't deal

in anything that clouds our judgment. Drugs and beautiful women cloud our judgment."

"Only if you develop an attachment or addiction."

Brad glances at me, not saying anything but saying everything. "So, what now?" he asks.

"Now we watch Adams. No one suddenly decides they want to go legit, especially when they've taken my money." I light the cigarette and pull in a long inhale, staring at the stick as I blow out a cloud of fumes. I need to fucking quit. I can hear Pops in my head warning me. Threatening me with my life. "Watch him while he's here. We'll head back to Miami when Adams does. We have the shipment coming in next week to the boatyard. We need to be ready."

Brad nods, twiddling with his cigarette between his fingers.

"Spit it out," I prompt, hearing his mind racing.

"It's been over a week, Danny," he says tentatively. "The priest is asking about the funeral arrangements."

The priest. A man of God. A man who is an advocate of the seven commandments. We're sinners. Not saints. My father wasn't religious. Part of me wonders if his wishes are a sick goodbye joke. And another part of me wonders if the money he's churned into the church over the years was his way of gaining absolution for his sins.

"Everything my father wants is listed in his last will and testament. I'll send it to Father McMahon."

Brad nods and stubs out his half-smoked cigarette. "Get some sleep, Danny. You look like shit."

Sleep. What's that? I haven't slept properly for six months, passing the night hours watching over my father. He's not here to watch over anymore. But I'm still not sleeping. I growl under my breath, frustrated by the pang of hurt in my dead heart. That damn man is the only person who can make me feel anything in the muscle that keeps me alive. It beats. Steadily. Always has. But it doesn't feel.

My thoughts drift back to her. It didn't beat so steadily when I had her against the wall.

I sink deeper into the chair, bringing the cigarette to my mouth and watching the end burn away as I pull a long drag. The glow of amber feels like the only color in my fucked-up black world. And on that thought comes another. Her red dress. Against that olive skin of hers, it looked like the most perfect color combination I've ever seen. Her dark hair is almost alive with shine. Her lips like rosebuds. Her cheekbones high. But her eyes? Those dark blue eyes were dead. Her reaction to Perry's man grabbing her sealed it. If I was any good at cards, she might have put me off my game. It's true what I told her. I've known someone like her before.

Me.

Taking her phone from my pocket, I hit the screen. No picture. No photo. Just the standard factory setting screen saver. Who doesn't have a picture saved as their home screen? Everyone has someone—their kid, their lover, their mother. Everyone except her.

And me.

The screen prompts me for a code. I need to get one of the men to unlock it. Flicking my cigarette butt off the balcony, I stand, sliding the phone into my pocket, but it chimes, stopping me. I lift it back out. A text. From "Mom."

> How are you, darling?

I swipe left and get the option to reply or clear. So I reply.

> Good. You?

I keep it simple, and I don't add a kiss, since her mother hasn't. The response is quick.

> Good. Call me when you can.

"She will," I say to myself as I slide it back into my pocket and head into the penthouse. When I make it through the lounge area to the bedroom, the woman isn't where I left her. I'm not concerned; she'd have to be Houdini to escape this suite. I follow my feet to the bathroom, hearing the tap running. I don't knock, striding straight in.

Her eyes flick up to the mirror where she's standing, her hands halfway through securing her long hair into a ponytail. Her position exposes the tanned flesh of her neck. My eyes root there.

"Some privacy, please," she says, turning to face me. She's taken off her heels, exposing red toenails that match her dress. Why I'm noticing this trivial shit is beyond me.

I ignore her and walk to the toilet, unzipping my trousers as I go. I pull out my cock slowly. I see her gaze drop to my groin. I hear her breath skip.

And I piss, one palm resting on the wall behind the toilet, the other holding my dick. I take my time, casual, aware that I'm being studied. And when I'm done, I wipe, flush, and turn to face her, still holding my cock, her gaze stuck there. I can hear her breathing. It's shallow as I stand, exposed to her, watching her take me in. The girl has some high walls up, but I know she couldn't turn away if she wanted to. And she doesn't. For the first time *ever*, I'm amused. She's going to be fun to play with. To torture.

Her hands meet the vanity unit behind her as I walk forward, pulling a stroke down my thick shaft. Her aroused condition only enhances mine. I'm firming up in my hand.

When I reach her, I take one of her hands and wrap it around my solid cock, and I don't feel one hint of resistance. She inhales. I do too. But I say nothing, starting to instigate her strokes, my body wanting to instantly spin her, bend her at the waist, and fuck her brutally.

Her hand. My dick. *Fuck.*

Her mouth goes slack. Her tongue dashes out, sweeping her bottom lip. For someone trying to convince me that she finds me repulsive, she looks and feels pretty turned on right now. I could take her. She wouldn't stop me. She'd fucking love it. *I'd* love it.

But she's not here to enjoy herself. And she's not here for me to enjoy, either. Would I? Enjoy her rather than feel like I'm scratching an itch? "Feel good, baby?" I ask on a whisper, and her eyes narrow a little, her gaze never leaving mine. Her hand flexes a little, getting a firmer grip, and my lips part, my breaths shallow.

"I don't know, does it?" she counters, licking her bottom lip.

No. I thrust her hand away and tuck myself in, backing away, ignoring how fucking hard it is to do that. That vanity unit is calling for me to bend her over it. Every muscle I possess is straining with the pressure to withdraw. But though her eyes are begging, she is not.

Yes, this is going to be fun. Or fucking kill me. "You'll sleep in my bed," I tell her, watching in amusement as her stoic façade falls and her eyes widen, just a tiny bit. "Naked," I add.

"And you?" she fires back.

"I'll be right there beside you, baby."

She somehow manages to keep the shock of my declaration contained. She's good. "You're not touching me."

"Who says I want to?" I force my lip into curling, looking her up and down.

I see hurt in her eyes. It throws me for a moment. Until she speaks again. "Good, because I wouldn't let a murdering bastard like you touch me if my life depended on it."

Bastard.

Heat flames in my veins, and before I know it, I'm across the room with her neck in my palm, my face close to hers, my lip curling. "I'd rethink that claim." I release my tongue and lick slowly across the seam of her lips, and her chest presses against mine, her soft breasts pushing into my hard pecs. "Because your life actually *does* depend on it." I slam my mouth on hers and kiss her hard. No tongues. Just hard, forceful lips, and she whimpers. Not in pain. She whimpers in want. And just as I feel her open up to me, I pull away. It takes everything in me and more. *And that's not acceptable.*

She's panting when I reach for her ponytail and fist it, tilting her head back. "You're not much of a challenge when you're so easy."

"Fuck you," she breathes, jarring her head, instigating a brutal yank of her hair. Then she smiles. It's full of satisfaction, and I return it. It's in that moment I realize that I'm not only a challenge for her.

She's a challenge for me too.

A challenge to resist.

6

ROSE

The gravity of my situation suddenly hits me. I've always been pretty fucked up, but now I feel utterly *fucked*. Just *fucked*. I'm the *guest* of Danny Black. I couldn't fuck him if I wanted to, which I don't. If I did, I'd be jeopardizing everything. Risking everything.

I have no phone. I'm supposed to be with Perry Adams, and Nox will be waiting to hear from me.

There's only one way this is going to turn out.

Messy.

My stomach rolls with dread. I will be punished. I can take the beating, always do, but the pictures of him that I know will stop? They keep me going. They remind me why I'm in this hell. What will I do without them? Without seeing his face and marveling at how much it has changed since the last time I was rewarded with a photograph. Granted, those rewards aren't frequent, but knowing they could come at any time drives me. "God, Rose,

64JODI ELLEN MALPAS

what have you done?" I should have kept my eyes to myself.
Should have stayed well away. I slowly slip out of my dress.

Danny Black's physique is intimidating fully clothed. Naked?

I push my panties down my thighs and drop them on a nearby
chair with my dress. Then I brace myself to climb into the huge
bed. The irony doesn't escape me. Of all the hard things I've done
and still do, getting in this bed is one of the hardest. It's massive.
We could probably go the entire night without touching. Yet I
know he's going to make that impossible. He's going to torture
me in a way I've never been tortured before. And I've been on the
receiving end of some pretty brutal punishments in my time.

It's going to be a long night.

But I'll survive it. It's what I'm best at. Survival. As well as
screwing.

Screwing. What would it be like to screw . . .

No. It would never be worth the risk, even if I know beyond
doubt that fucking Danny Black would be an experience worth
enduring. Because I'd be fucking him and wanting to.

"Jesus, Rose." I quickly realign my thoughts. The man's a
killer. I need my head checking.

I settle and pull the sheet over me as the door opens and he
enters. I close my eyes, escaping the magnificent vision. How
attractive he is, how attracted to him I am, only makes me hate
him more. He doesn't know it yet, but he's pretty much signed my
death sentence.

"Open your eyes." There's demand in his tone that I know I
shouldn't ignore. So I do what I do best. What I'm told, though
with Danny Black it's a challenge when it should be easy, given
his reputation.

His face is impassive when I find him, his long, thick fingers
on his shirt buttons. He's going to make me watch him undress. I
hate him more. Every inch of his skin that's revealed takes more
and more of the air in my lungs until he gets to his trousers and

I'm left holding my breath. His torso is impossibly hard. His thighs are impossibly thick. His legs are impossibly long and lean. He's a fucking masterpiece. A deadly masterpiece. I breathe in deeply.

I have to sleep with this.

I despise him.

He walks to the bed and pulls the covers back, exposing my naked form to his eyes. My body has never been my own so if he's expecting me to try and hide, he'll be disappointed. Yet I see no disappointment on his face. I see nothing, actually. Not even appreciation. His expression is blank, and that strips me of the little power I have in my life. My body is my only weapon, and he seems immune to it.

Sliding in smoothly, he lies on his back. There's a foot between us, but it feels like just a millimeter. I'm on fire. I can't stand it. I can't stand the insane, uncontrollable, mysterious pull. Why? I should be overjoyed that some feelings have been uncovered. Overjoyed that I'm apparently not *completely* emotionally dead. But all these reactions are for a man I should not be reacting to. The strange mixture of wariness and desire is playing havoc with my mind.

I flip myself onto my side, my back to him, staring ahead at the wall. And then there's suddenly no wall to look at. Just darkness. He's turned off the lights.

I'm so tense, there's not a hope in hell of me getting any sleep. Not when he's in bed with me. How long will I have to be here? How long before I'm taken back to where I belong? How long until Nox finds me?

The mattress beneath me dips, and my body rolls with it. He's moving, and I hold my breath, waiting for . . . what?

Will he touch me? Climb on top of me? Force me? And will I fight him if he does?

His bare foot brushes mine. It's just a foot, but his skin on mine isn't a simple touch. It's an inferno, raging and screaming. My tense body swiftly shifts into brittle territory. I'm going to break. He slides his foot across mine, and no matter how desperate I am to whip mine away, I don't. I'm not sure whether it's that thing ingrained into me to do what's expected of me, or the fact that I like his skin on mine. I like the inferno. I like the burn. Those thoughts have me pulling away before I can stop myself, my mind in meltdown. Of all the people on this planet I could chose to defy or be attracted to, Danny Black should be the last on the list. Yet my natural instinct to comply is shifting. It also might save my life. As long as Black doesn't kill me first.

"You don't like me touching you?" His voice is soft yet hard, and it has me clenching my eyes and burying my face in the pillow.

Yes. I hate it because I love it.

"No."

"Liar," he claims, not for the first time. "So if I put my hand here." His palm lands on my naked hip, and I squeeze my eyes closed into the pillow, battling my way through the torture. "You don't like it?"

"Get your hands off me," I spit, and he does. It surprises me. It also disappoints me.

"Remember I told you that you reminded me of someone?" His question, which is soft and quiet, has my anger shrinking and my body slowly turning over to face him. I can see him, not clearly, but he's looking at me, his eyes shining in the darkness. "Yes."

"That person was saved." Without warning, he moves, pushing me to my back and spreading his body all over mine. He doesn't pin me down, simply lays his palms over my arms that are above my head. The weight of him is intimidating and exhilarating all at once. Every naked piece of him is touching me. My body isn't the only thing to go up in smoke. So does my mind.

"You haven't been saved," he whispers, his nose skimming mine. "Yet," he adds, knocking me further off balance with a grind of his hips. "What's your name, baby?"

"Rose." I deliver my answer on a mere whisper, and I sense more than see his smile.

"Get some sleep, Rose." He dips and kisses the corner of my mouth. "You're going to need some energy to keep resisting me."

And then he's off my body.

And I'm missing the feel of his sinful weight immediately.

7

DANNY

You haven't been saved. Yet.

And what? I'm going to save her? I shake my head to myself
as I lie in bed next to her, watching her. She's curled up on her
side, as far away from me as she can get, her back to me. One
poke in her shoulder would have her tumbling out of bed.

The dark waves of her hair fan the stark white pillow; her hair
tie is loose and has nearly worked its way to the end. I reach
forward without thought and pull it free. I see her shoulders rise,
just a fraction, and I smile to myself. She's awake but pretending
not to be. The kid in me that never really existed appears from
nowhere, showing up to the party years too late. I take the sheet
that's pulled up under her arms and peel it down her body, slowly,
softly, exposing the full length of her spine. The morning light is
dusky through the blinds, hazy and slight, but I still see the nasty
bruise. And my morning mind is a little foggy, but I still feel rage
fuzzing my head. The black mass stretches from one side of her
back to the other, just above two cute dimples that sit a fraction

above her arse. It's not old, not yellowed or purple. It's solid black. Fresh.

I reach forward and glide a soft fingertip across the battered planes of her lower back. She tenses, and I look at the back of her head. Who did this to her? *What the fuck do I care?* She's a whore with a mouth on her. *Doesn't mean she should be fucking beaten* . . .

I quickly take back my hand and swing my legs off the bed, sitting up. I need to get in the gym and burn off some of this . . . weirdness.

As I stand, my phone lights up on the nightstand. It's 6 a.m.

Swiping it up, I pull on my boxers. "Morning, Perry."

"Please don't hurt her." He gets straight to the point, not ashamed to hide his feelings now he's not in public. "She's delicate."

I have to force myself not to laugh. Delicate? She might look it, but the woman in my bed is as hard as nails. A warrior. That bruise, though. Adams? Did he do it? The American public think he's the perfect, enviable family man, but I know otherwise. He's a shrewd businessman, isn't scared to dip a toe in the darkness to get what he wants, hence his association with me. But would he beat a woman? I don't think so. "Don't tell me what to do, Perry. Besides, look at it like this. I'm doing you a favor. "

"How?"

"You want to be mayor. I want you to be mayor. Parading around with your whore a few paces behind in public, Perry? That's a sure-fire way to fuck it all up, you dumb arse."

"I'm careful."

"Really? How do I have her then?"

He's silent for a few moments, probably regretting calling me now, at the same time wondering how the fuck he got in this mess. "It's just . . . she dreams." He breathes out. "I don't know what about, but she's restless."

Restless? "She slept pretty soundly in my bed last night," I say, reaching the door and swinging it open. I look back over my shoulder and find she's sat up in bed, the sheets a messy puddle around her waist. She's watching me through her sleepy eyes. "Are you going to want your precious girl back once I've pinned her down and fucked every hole she has?" Rose's face doesn't falter, but Perry gasps, and I smile wickedly, knowing he believes a callous arsehole like me is capable of such a thing. I'm not. It's the only thing people have wrong about me. I would never take a woman against her will. I'm depraved, but I'm not a fucking monster. "You know, I've had a change of heart," I go on. "Take your time with the marina. I've got something to keep me busy." I hang up and back out of the room, keeping my serious eyes on hers until the wood comes between us.

I hit the hotel gym, but not before the whole place has been cleared out by my men. Generally, most people don't need to be asked to leave. They take one look at me, then my entourage, and decide they've suddenly burned enough calories for the day, making a swift exit. Then you get the odd twat, like the man currently using the bench press. As if to make a point, he adds a further 50 kilos to each end of the bar before resuming his reps. And to make *my* point, I pull the Glock from Brad's holster and aim it at his head. "I work out alone."

Poor bastard nearly crushes his big, meaty chest when he loses his focus, almost dropping the bar mid-rise. For a giant, he moves fucking fast, shutting the door behind him. "Better." I hand Brad back his gun and pull my T-shirt up over my head as my men move to all the doorways, ensuring my peace is maintained. "Joining me?" I ask my right-hand man, taking the fifties off the bar that the gorilla just added. I'm strong, but I have no point to prove.

Brad motions down his suit. "I worked out at five. I thought you'd skip it this morning given the circumstances."

I lie on the bench and grasp the bar, lifting it from its resting place, straightening my arms. "And what circumstances would they be?" I take the bar down steadily, appreciating the instant strain on my tight muscles.

Brad is standing over me now, looking down at me as I push out fifteen reps, each one smooth and consistent. "Fresh pussy in your bed."

"I didn't fuck her."

"Why?" His question is quick, and it catches me off guard.

I replace the bar and take a breather. "She's not here for my pleasure."

"But it wouldn't hurt to take some, right?"

"I don't want any."

"Do I look like I'm buying that?"

"You should."

"Or what?"

"Or I'll put a bullet between your motherfucking eyes." I take the bar again as Brad chuckles. He doesn't stop laughing the whole time I'm pushing out another fifteen reps.

"I think for the first time in your life, you haven't a fucking clue what you're doing," he says in a tone laced with humor that makes me want to smash his fucking face in.

"I know exactly what I'm doing. I'm doing everything I can to ensure we get that marina and Adams in power. That's what I'm fucking doing, and the woman is going to help make that happen. I don't know what the fuck Adams was thinking, risking his campaign by dragging his whore around town with him."

"How about what the fuck was he thinking trying to fob you off? Or is the woman trumping that? Like I said, I don't think you know what you're doing."

"I know what I'm doing."

"And how the hell is *not* fucking her gonna change that?"

"Shut the fuck up, Brad," I grate, wondering the very same thing. It's a game. One I can't help playing with her. Women always want to fuck me. Whatever their reasons are, I couldn't give a fuck. Money, power, protection. They get none of those things. Rose is going out of her way to prove that she doesn't want to fuck me. And that turns me the fuck on. Like nothing else.

"She's refusing you," Brad says quietly, knowing my story, the only person alive who does. He knows I would never take a woman against her will.

"Her mouth is. Her body isn't."

"Be careful, Danny." He knows the game I'm playing is dangerous. Women only make our hazardous world more deadly. For many reasons, least of all because they make men easy targets if they show a woman even a scrap of compassion. Just like Adams, and now he's paying for it.

"She's bait. That's all," I affirm, getting on with my session.

Over the next hour, I smash ten ton of shit out of the punching bag, sprint 10 kilometers, and push weights until I feel like myself again. I grab the towel and wipe over my wet chest as I'm walked back up to the penthouse by my men. When I get to my bedroom, I hear the shower running and smile to myself, pacing to the bathroom and entering the steam-filled space. But no matter how foggy the air is, I still see her. Fuck, do I see her.

That wasn't a hitch of my breath I just felt. That was simply my heart rate trying to get back to normal after my mammoth workout. But I have to admit, the body currently under the spray is something of a vision. Wet. Firm. I rest my shoulder on the doorframe and watch as she swipes her hands through her wet hair. Her long waves conceal her bruise, but not those cute little dimples at the base of her spine. One on each side. Perfectly even. My eyes drift down, over her pert little arse to her legs—legs that go on for fucking days. Her face is pointed up to the spray, her eyes closed. She turns a fraction, revealing dark nipples that are soft under the warm water. And she's humming. She's humming like she could be happy. She's fascinating me more every minute.

Reaching forward, she flips the shower off and proceeds to squeeze the excess water from her hair, pulling it over one shoulder. The urge to demand she wipes the screen of all the water drops to better my view is hard to push back.

She sees me. Stops humming. I expect her to lunge for a towel and cover herself. She doesn't. She's too distracted. I look down at my wet chest and smirk to myself. It seems I'm not the only one rapt.

Pushing myself off the doorframe, I collect a towel from the wall-hung warmer by the shower and wander to the vanity unit, resting my arse against it.

She steps out of the shower and faces me, bold and unabashed. And she just stands there. Wet and naked. I take my time, dragging my eyes over every inch of her tall, slender frame. She's well groomed, the small patch of hair between her thighs a perfect dark strip. I didn't expect anything less. On the outside, she's perfection, yet I sense that on the inside she's shattered. All this is a front, just like she's fronting for Adams too. She's young, beautiful. No wonder she can't seem to control herself around me. I'm a stark contrast to that middle-aged, balding man she's currently screwing.

After an age of staring me down, making her point, she eyes the stack of towels within her reach. She could grab any one of them, but she won't. She's going to prove another point. Her dainty feet pad across the marble floor toward me, carrying her graceful body as elegantly as I've come to expect, and my dick pulses with every step she takes until she stops in front of me.

She doesn't take the towel in my hands. She's waiting for me to cover her. I keep my face straight and devoid of the amusement I'm feeling. She fucking hates me and desires me all at once. Good.

Then she licks her lips and my cock twitches behind my shorts like it's been electrocuted. "Turn around," I order, and she does, lifting her arms a little and resting her chin on her shoulder to look back at me. I wrap her in the towel and push my chest into her back, grazing her shoulder with my teeth, inhaling. "You smell like me." She's used my body wash, and, fuck me, if it doesn't smell gorgeous on her.

"I have nothing here, so I had to borrow yours." She's tense, though trying her hardest not to be. And then as brash as can fucking be, she subtly rolls her hips, compressing her arse into my groin. I hiss, unable to stop it.

"Thank you." She breaks away from me and strolls off, and in a moment of pure fucking weakness, I take hold of the sink and talk down my wayward cock, breathing my way through it. Fucking hell, if anyone could read my mind right now. Cold, ruthless killer being affected by a little woman. Where the fuck has she come from?

With a quick swipe of my hand down my face, I follow her into the bedroom, finding her shimmying her black lace G-string up her legs. I swallow, my jaw tensing. For fuck's sake. What the fuck am I doing to myself?

I walk over and grab her hand, hauling her naked form out of my room. I expect resistance. I get none. She follows obediently, despite only having a small scrap of material covering her pussy.

All the men look up as I yank her through the suite toward the office.

"In here now," I order them, positioning her at the side of the desk facing the door. On full show. Her hands hang by her sides. Her wet hair splays her shoulders. Her perfect breasts rise and fall with her even breathing. Steady breathing. Completely unaffected breathing.

The men all enter, Brad the last, closing the door behind him. None of them look at her. It pisses me off. What, do they think I'll have a problem with that? They know better than anyone that women mean shit to me. I shove her phone in her hand. "Call him. Tell him I'm in the shower."

She looks up at me through her lashes. "And what?"

"Tell him you want to go back to him. Beg him. Tell him to pay the money he owes me so you can go back."

Her frown is slight, though I know Brad's will be heavy as fuck. He knows I don't want that money. What I want is results. I reach for the gun sitting on the desk and disengage the safety, pushing it into her forehead. "Do it." She doesn't bat a fucking eyelid, and that just angers me more. Why the hell isn't she scared? Why the hell isn't she having an epic meltdown while I'm displaying her naked body for all my men to see? Adams worships her. Really, that's fucking obvious. He wouldn't hurt her; it's not his style. So what the fuck happened to her to make her so fucking impenetrable? And where the fucking hell did that bruise come from? "Cry," I order.

"I don't cry." She bores holes into me with a suddenly steely gaze. "Not for anyone."

I'd slap her face if I knew it'd have the desired effect. She doesn't cry. The woman is iron. I move the gun to her mouth and force it past her lips, taking her throat with my spare hand. "Sound convincing."

What she does next has me caught between admiration and fucking fury. It has my dick screaming and my mind ready to explode. She pulls back, letting the gun slide from her mouth slowly and seductively. And eyes on mine, she kisses the tip. I hear the sounds of feet shuffling nervously behind me, all of my men probably talking down their hard dicks.

Just like I am.

With a salacious smirk tickling the edge of her mouth, she dials and puts the phone to her ear. I snatch it away and click it to loudspeaker while I take my gun back to her forehead.

"Hello?" Adams voice is hoarse and tired.

"Perry, it's me," she says, eyes on mine. "I have to be quick. He's in the shower." She reels it all off like she could be reading from a script. Auditioning for a role she'd die for. There's urgency in her voice that almost has me believing her too. Jesus, she's good.

"Oh my God, Rose, sweetheart," Adams gasps. "What has he done? Has he touched you? The bastard. I'll kill him. I swear, I'll kill him."

I look over my shoulder to Brad. There are three things in his short spurge of words that have assisted in white-hot rage turning my veins to ashes. First, of all the things he could have called me, he calls me a bastard. Second, he'll kill me? The man just hung himself. Just as soon as I've got what I want, I'll cut every organ out of his body and feed them to the Dobermanns that guard my mansion back in Miami. Those two things are enough. But hearing him call her *sweetheart* has the gun vibrating in my hand. She must be able to feel it.

"You have to get me out of here." She keeps her eyes on mine. They're devoid of emotion, but her voice is not. "Please, just get him what he wants or pay him back. I'm begging you. He's an animal, Perry."

I cock my head in question at her choice of word. Animal? She can't hide her secret smile.

"Rose." Adams sounds defeated, and it has my attention. "I'm so sorry for getting you in this mess. I'm doing everything I can. My contact will help. He'll sort this out, I swear."

His contact. I look at Brad again, and he nods his understanding. He's in bed with someone else, and whoever it is must have been making it more worth his while than I was. And I was making it pretty fucking worth his while. *Ten million dollars'* worth his while. What have they promised him, and what has he promised them? But more to the point, who are *they*?

As I cast my eyes back to Rose, I just catch the falter of her steely expression. I can't figure out if it's hurt or worry.

"But I can promise you one thing," Adams goes on.

"What?" she barely whispers.

Yes, what?

"Danny Black is a dead man."

Her eyes widen. And what do I do? I smirk. A death threat? Is that all he has? I hear Brad sigh his tiredness. I can virtually hear Rose's heart pound harder.

"How?" she asks, surprising me. Oh, nice. She wants the gory details of my apparent demise?

"Just trust me. Hold on in there, sweetheart. I'll get this sorted out and you'll be with me in no time."

I pull the gun from her forehead and swirl it in midair before her nose, my way of telling her to wrap it up. I've heard enough. Enough to know that Adams is trying to turn me over. It's the last thing he'll ever do.

"I have to go," she breathes. "I just heard the shower shut off."

"Okay. Make sure you delete this call from your recent call list. He's a shrewd man. Doesn't trust."

"Okay."

"I love you," Adams says, with so much softness, I believe him. *The stupid fuck.*

"I love you too," she replies, with so much resolution, I'd believe her too.

If I wasn't looking into her dead eyes.

I disconnect the call. "Hold on in there, sweetheart," I say quietly, taking my gun and running it down the center of her naked breasts. Her chest concaves. Her nipples pebble.

And I smirk wickedly.

I turn to the men, ready to debrief them, but fuck if they're looking at me. They're staring at Rose. I clear my throat, and they all get their eyes under control. I look back to Rose. Her blue eyes darken. And she subtly pushes her chest out and widens her stance a fraction, spreading her thighs, giving my men more to feast their eyes on.

What the fucking hell? A switch flips in me, taking my body temperature to burning levels. I grab her harshly, yanking her toward the door. The men, alarmed, move from my path, all dropping their eyes to their feet. And Brad? He just shakes his head at me. I snarl at him as I steam out, looking out the corner of my eye, seeing Rose's breasts bouncing, her wet hair slapping the perfect globes as I manhandle her back to the bedroom.

Fuck!

I push her through the door and throw the gun on the bed before I go on a shooting spree. Then I shove her up against the wall aggressively. The back of her head hits the plaster with a thwack. And she smiles a sick, satisfied smile. I could explode. "Who is he dealing with?" I gasp in her face, my fury leaving me breathless.

"I don't know." Her chest heaves as she pulls air into her lungs. "He doesn't talk business around me."

"If you're lying to me—"

"I'm not lying."

"How do I know that?"

"You think I want to protect him? He's nothing to me but a new pair of shoes each week and fancy hotel rooms wherever he wants to take me."

Her face. Stone cold. I see a similar sight in the mirror every day. "How does it feel to know he's left you at my mercy?" I ask.

"About as good as it feels knowing I'll be sleeping with you again tonight."

My lip curls. It's another face-off. They're both electrifying and frustrating. This woman fucking frustrates me. Why? Because she challenges me. The weak woman who asks how high when she's told to jump is challenging me. Me. Danny Black. Does she have a death wish?

I'm about to ask her that very question when her eyes fall to my lips. And in answer, mine drop to hers. I could take her here and now. Fuck her black and blue. Make her scream my name. Shit, I could do with the relief. She wouldn't stop me.

Without any prompt, my lips move in toward hers. They brush. She moans. "You want it, don't you? You want my big dick pounding your sweet cunt." My cock pleads for her to confirm it as I lick the seam of her lips, grinding our hips together.

She hums, sounding dazed. "I'd rather you kill me."

"Maybe I will."

"You need me."

She's right. And I'm starting to need her for another reason—one that doesn't involve business. My tongue leaves my mouth, skimming the tip of hers. I groan roughly. She whimpers softly. "Go on," she whispers, goading me. Giving me the okay? She bites my bottom lip, tugging the flesh. "Kill me."

Fucking hell.

I move my mouth across hers, hoping to taste fear, but instead I taste nothing but sex. It's intoxicating. Mind-blanking. "Fuck," I whisper, and I feel her smile around my mouth.

The door swings open, Brad appears, and I'm yanked back from the brink of a dangerous moment. Perfect fucking timing. His gaze moves from us to the bed. Where my gun is. Not in my hand. Not tucked behind my back.

Shit. I push Rose away and compose myself under the suspicious glare of my right-hand man. "We just got confirmation of Adams's dinner reservation at Hakasan tonight," he tells me.

"Who with?"

"Some lawyers and governors. Sounds boring as shit."

"But still . . ." It's business as usual for Adams, then? Cheeky fucker. I look at Rose. She's motionless, quiet, eyes on mine. And she's still naked. I grab a towel and thrust it in her chest, a demand to cover herself. "Looks like you and I are going on our first date this evening, *sweetheart*," I inform her, taking myself to the shower.

8

ROSE

Our first date. Or rather, the first round of Perry's torture. It'll be a show. A demonstration.

I'm driving Black wild, and I can't help getting satisfaction from that. But it feels so good to have a little control, even if it's a twisted psychological control.

I haven't seen Black since this morning. He's been holed up in his office with his army of men, though he made sure one guarded the door to the bedroom so I couldn't escape. I found that out when I actually tried to escape, peeking out the door to check if the coast was clear. It wasn't. The guy smiled at me, a knowing smirk full of laughter. And I spilled some crap about needing a drink. There's a perfectly furnished mini bar in the bedroom. He knew my game.

I'm getting desperate. I'm not supposed to be here. I'm supposed to be with Perry Adams. He has a new investor. I need to share that information with Nox, need to tell him where I am, but I can't so much as sneeze without Black finding out. He's having me watched constantly. And to make matters worse, I'm lying to him. Bare-faced lying. He thinks I'm a gold-digging whore who's latched onto Adams for financial benefits. I wish.

The outcome of this mess is becoming clearer and clearer.

Me.

Dead.

The question is, *who* will kill me? Nox or Black?

I fiddle with the towel wrapped around me, trying to focus on my boy and my reason to live, at the same time trying not to think about how Black paraded me in front of his men naked, and then clearly regretted it.

The joy I felt in that moment floored me. And scared me. He couldn't stand another man seeing me naked. So what would he think about another man touching me? Or violating me? I sickly smile to myself. There it is again. Joy. *No, Rose.* Joy isn't an emotion I should get used to. I feel it from time to time, once in a blue moon when I get a glimpse of my boy. And then, moments later, the inevitable heartbreak when my reality sinks back in.

I need to get out of here, or I'm a dead woman. I might not feel much, but I still have a survival instinct, and I want to live. Even if I'm a prisoner in my own life. It still means someone else is free. My mind momentarily wanders to places I always forbid it to go, before I quickly pull myself back from the brink of feeling. Feeling would be pointless. It wouldn't change anything. I need to focus on getting myself out of this mess. But tonight, I have a date. I also have another problem.

I look at the red dress on the floor, the only item of clothing I have here. I hate myself with a vengeance for wanting something else to wear. Something I picked. Something undeniably me. I can't remember the last time I wore something because I wanted to wear it, not because someone else wanted me to wear it. In fact, it's never happened. As a little girl, I didn't want to wear the rags that were the only clothes within my reach. And as a woman, I've never wanted to wear the clothes I've been made to wear to make me look like the enticing piece of meat that I am. But I have. Because that's what I do. Because I have no choice. It's the times when I'm alone, when I can lounge in a pair of pajamas, that I feel most like me. I cherish those times. Have to, because they are a rarity.

I sigh and stand, pulling my towel in and going to the bathroom. I find a hairdryer in the vanity unit and start blasting my hair. I have no makeup, no perfume, no anything. And I hate myself again for wishing I did. Because I want to look nice. Not for him, but for myself. Because it'll enhance the power I'll feel when I'm holding my own with Danny Black.

Another sigh.

I flip my head upside down, blasting my hair from every angle. One thing I'm blessed with in this miserable life is thick, wavy hair and even a rough dry will give me something smooth and manageable. I spotted some men's hair product earlier that I can use to gloss if necessary. *His* hair product. His shower gel, his shampoo.

Tossing my hair back, I look up to the mirror. And freeze. He's standing in the doorway watching me, and I'm quickly so thankful he can't hear my thoughts. He's in a suit. A three-piece. A light gray three-piece suit. Designer. Bespoke. It makes his hair look blacker, his eyes bluer.

He's trimmed his stubble, making his scar more prominent. He's fixed his hair, making it almost too perfect for his sharp, angry features.

I've been looking at him for far too long. I quickly gather myself, feeling the towel loosen around my chest. I don't stop it from falling, letting it hit the floor as I switch off the dryer and blow my hair out of my face. His facial expression doesn't falter in the slightest. I'd wonder if he's becoming immune to the sight of my naked body—Lord knows he's seen it enough—but I sense his determination to remain unaffected by my brazenness. I confuse him. He can't hide that. I imagine every woman falls all over herself to please him, whether that be because of lust or fear. The latter is wasted on me. The former I will go to the end of the earth to contain.

Without a word, he comes to me, taking my wrist and pulling me from the bathroom, ever the gent. He stops us by the full-length mirror in the bedroom, placing me in front of it and taking up position behind me. Unashamedly, he looks me up and down in the reflection, his chin virtually resting on my shoulder. "What will you be wearing for our date?"

He knows damn well I only have the red dress. "Whatever you tell me to," I reply evenly.

He nods approvingly. "I'm telling you to wear what's laid out on the bed."

My eyes dart to the bed beyond his reflection, seeing a floor-length gown. It's a muted silver satin, a lovely off-the-shoulder piece cut on the cross. It's very me. It's just what I would choose. It's not tarty or suggestive. It's elegant and beautiful and . . . him? Obviously. Is The Brit trying to transform me from a whore into a lady? I chew my lip as I try to slow my whirling mind.

"You hate it," he says, and it's the first time I've heard him sound unsure.

My gaze finds him, seeing his eyes look unsure too. It makes the monster seem vulnerable, and I soften a little on the inside. Does he actually care whether I do or not? "Do *you* like it?"

"Whether I like it isn't the question. I want to know if *you* like it."

I'm so fucking confused. Why the hell does he care? "I love it."

He nods sharply and moves back, revealing a shoe box too, as well as a basket full of makeup. "I didn't know what cosmetics you use, so I had them send everything."

Where's this all come from? Is he being kind? "Have you ever bought a woman a dress before?"

His persona seems to change in an instant, the veil of evil falling. "I don't spend my money on clothes that are going to be ruined when I rip them off." He turns and walks away. "We leave in fifteen minutes. Be ready." The door slams.

The man is well protected. That much I've learned, and it's really not surprising. I shudder to think how many people want him dead. Me included. We walk from the limo to the hotel door, the staff falling over their feet to greet him, smile, ask if he needs anything. He doesn't acknowledge one of them, pulling me along beside him, his grip of my hand solid.

I can't ignore the fact that I feel the loveliest I've ever felt. The dress, the Dior strappy heels, and the makeup. The fact that I'm wearing four-inch heels and he still towers over me is a novelty. My hair is roughly pinned up, my makeup perfect.

I've gone to too much effort. But for the first time in my life, I made an effort because I wanted to, not because it was expected. The reason why is something I need to cast aside. Though when I stepped into the room where he was waiting with a brandy in his grasp, I saw the squeeze of his chest from his inhale. The tremble of his hand as he lifted his drink to his lips. The stirring beyond the fly of his gray trousers.

It was the same reaction I had when I set eyes on him in his three-piece.

Wonder.

And, like me, he tried to hide it.

"Mr. Black, what a pleasure," a man says, falling into stride next to us. "Anything you need, please, just ask."

Black continues, not even blessing the man with a glance. But then he pulls to an abrupt stop, forcing every one of his entourage

to stop too, all of them clearly confused. "Actually"—Black uses
his free hand to go to his inside pocket, then turns to the man—
"your chopper. Have it on standby." He releases my hand and
flips off at least a dozen hundred-dollar bills and passes them over
before claiming me again. "I might feel like a sky tour of Vegas
after dinner."

"Of course, sir."

A helicopter? Just like that? "That's a bit spontaneous," I say
without thought as he moves us forward again.

"I don't do spontaneous," he replies flatly, releasing my hand
and taking it to my lower back. My teeth bite down together, as
his big palm splays the entire width, his touch burning through the
silky material of the dress. Danny strokes the area gently, and I
can't help but wonder if he's mindful of the bruise he's seen there.
"Spontaneous gets you killed," he adds quietly.

"Wasn't this dress spontaneous?"

"Yes, and it might get me killed." His face is deadly serious
when I shoot a surprised look his way. "After you," he says,
opening the door and letting me go through, but not before three
of his men.

I see Perry immediately. He's at a table of four, throwing back
shots rapidly. He looks troubled. Very, very troubled. I feel
Danny's mouth at my ear, and my body rolls. "I hope you're
looking forward to this evening as much as I am."

"I would rather walk on broken glass."

He laughs softly as we're led to a table mere feet from my
lover. A romantic, cozy table set for two. Just two. Two places
laid side by side. Not opposite each other. They're next to each
other. This is going to be more of a spectacle than I anticipated.
Danny Black is about to torture me throughout dinner, and
appearing disgusted rather than turned on under Perry's watchful
eye is going to be hard.

One of Danny's men indicate the seat, and I sit, placing the silver purse that's a perfect match to the dress on the table. Black takes a seat beside me. He's close. Too close. His men move away, not too far but far enough to give us privacy, not that this dinner is going to be private. Nowhere near.

I know the second Perry sees us. I know because Black curls his arm around my shoulder. And then I feel the heat of his mouth moving in on my cheek. My body does what it's so good at doing when he's this close. It trembles. I flick my eyes to Perry, seeing a horrified stare pointing my way. I try to pass my shakes off as a shuddery cringe, closing my eyes as if struggling to endure Black's closeness. I should be quite convincing, because I really am struggling. Thank God Perry can't see my thighs clenching under the table.

But Danny can feel them when his hand lands on my leg. I sense his wicked grin spread across my skin as his lips linger, my cheek set to burst into flames with the rest of my body. We've been here a few minutes. How will I ever get through the entire evening?

"I think you've made your point," I say quietly as the waitress pours us wine.

"On the contrary." His big hand squeezes my thigh, his rough palms bunching the luxury satin fabric along with my flesh. "I haven't even started yet."

"Why don't you just fuck me on the table and be done with it?" I say stupidly, my own words making me shift uncomfortably in my seat. I've never been turned on. I've pretended to be and always done a stellar job, and now I have to pretend *not* to be.

Don't be turned on, Rose!

I just know I'm not very convincing. Maybe to everyone surrounding us, but to Danny Black who's touching me, feeling me, I'm not fooling him. How can you hate someone and lust for them at the same time?

Black's face doesn't crack as he stares me down. "Something tells me you'd love that."

"Never."

Taking his glass of wine, he guides it to my lips, forcing me to open. The crisp, refreshing white wine slides down my throat, and Black slides closer. "You have some here." Leaning in, he licks from one corner of my mouth to the other. Slowly. Softly. "Never," he mimics me, full of knowing. My heart begins to pulse as I silently weigh the merits of giving in to the madness of my body's wants. Just to get it done with. Just to rid myself of this helpless feeling of desperation. For the first time in my adult life, I feel scared. I don't like it. But as I keep reminding myself, I sleep with who I am told to sleep with, and I haven't been told to sleep with Danny Black. I hate myself for wishing I had. But none of this matters, because Danny Black takes what he wants. I would never be able to stop him, and that terrifies me. I wouldn't want to stop him. That terrifies me more. Yet there have been plenty of moments in the past twenty-four hours when he could have forced me. But he hasn't.

"Why haven't you fucked me?"

He pulls back, his face hovering a mere inch away from mine. "You sound disappointed."

"Here on this table. Me screaming for you to stop. Wouldn't that be the biggest fuck you to Perry?"

"I'm many things, Rose, but I am not a rapist."

"Oh, would that be a step too far into animal territory?"

His quick hand grabs my jaw, squeezing it firmly, and his eyes cloud, darkening, a thunderstorm rolling through their depths. I've touched a nerve. "We'll find out if you continue to push me."

He doesn't mean that. A veil of bricks just fell into place, a protective shield. "I don't want you to rape me," I murmur, unable to stop my mind from casting back to the most hideous moments in my life. I unwittingly flinch, looking away so he loses his hold, but my jaw is quickly reclaimed, and my face is pulled back.

His eyes jump to mine, suddenly unsure. And he stares at me, deeply, trying to read what's in my eyes. Has he clicked? Read me? Figured it out?

Black drops my face and puts distance between us, his jaw tight as he throws back his wine, looking across to Perry. He raises his glass, pulling an evil smile from nowhere as he toasts the air between them. The mask is back in place. "Lovely evening for it," Black calls, putting his arm around me again and tugging me close. "Enjoy your meal, Adams. I know I will."

It's hell. Pure, painful, burning hell. Acting has always been a natural ability since my life depended on it. Hiding my feelings and true emotions came instinctively. Holding up that front in the presence of Danny Black doesn't come so naturally. It's an effort, and it's wearing me down bit by bit. I endure him sporadically feeding me throughout our appetizers and main course. I hold my breath countless times when he touches my leg. And I cling to my wine glass like it's a life jacket when his touch slips between my thighs, stroking over my begging core.

Black doesn't miss any of it, at one point peeling my fingers from my glass and smiling. At another point, he squeezes my hand in an odd move to reassure me.

Perry watches it all. I know it, can feel his eyes on me throughout the entire performance, and Danny Black relishes every second. I'm eating everything being put in my mouth by him, swallowing hard each time, praying my twisting stomach doesn't revolt and send it back up.

By the time he's cleared my plate and placed the fork neatly to the side, I'm full, exhausted, and feeling infuriatingly emotional. While Danny's had an amazing time, apparently, I feel like I've been dragged through erotic hell. I'm silently begging him to take me back to his room so I can sleep off these alien feelings and wake feeling my usual self.

"I enjoy feeding you," Black says quietly, resting his hand on mine gently.

I look into his eyes and quickly dart them away, wishing the hardness back. They're currently soft. "Why are you being nice?"

"Because the best fuck you to Adams is him watching you fall deeper and deeper under my spell. And it seems I don't have to work too hard to achieve that." He drops his napkin on the empty plate and slides his palm onto my neck, tugging me forward until his exhale of breath supplies my inhale. "If I kissed you now, would you fight me?"

I breathe in shakily, unsure of his motive. "Will you kill me if I do?"

He smiles a little. "No." Then he slowly drops his mouth to mine and simply rests our lips together. My shakes are instant. And so are his. He doesn't move, doesn't try to gain access to my mouth. He's testing me. I'm not fighting. I really don't know *what* to do. Perry is only a few feet away. I'm supposed to be finding this kiss the most disgusting thing ever, but, in truth, it's the most consuming ever. Just our lips touching. His lips. Soft lips on a hard face. My tongue is aching with the effort it's taking me to hold it back. I desperately want to advance our touching lips, but when he moans, I'm snapped from my weak moment.

I pull back, flustered, and he smiles.

"Now, I've made my point." He takes my hand and helps me to my wobbly feet, and I glance up, across the restaurant.

And freeze.

It's dark, but I would know his menacing face anywhere.

Nox.

And as quick as he's there, he's gone. I come over freezing cold, scanning the space frantically for him. Oh my God. He's here. He's seen I'm with Black. He's seen the spectacle that was our dinner.

I'm pulled two paces before Black brings us to a stop at Perry's table. His arm slides around my waist and pulls me close. I keep my eyes down, afraid I'll reveal my desire, and not just to Perry. I'm not stupid enough to know that if I can't see Nox, it doesn't mean he can't see me. I can feel his evil presence lingering, can hear his threats whirling through my mind.

"I hope your meal was satisfactory," Black says, and I hear a few low mumbles from Perry's dinner companions. But not from Perry. He *cannot* react in front of these men, especially not in public. He can't risk the backlash of social media and its daily scrutiny of whether or not he's the best candidate as mayor. But is his silence terror or false bravado?

"I'm taking dessert in our room." Black drops a kiss on my cheek before I'm led away.

"Madam!" someone calls, and Danny stops us, his men quickly moving in to surround us.

I turn and find the waiter who served us throughout dinner holding out my purse, looking a little alarmed by the wall of men blocking his way to me. "Your purse," he murmurs.

Brad claims it and silently passes it to me. "Thank you," I say quietly as Black escorts me away.

"Have you had a nice evening, Rose?" he asks, stroking the base of my spine.

I nod in reply. It's all I'm capable of with the heat of him touching me burning away my power of speech, and the fear of Nox's presence knocking my confidence.

When we reach the elevator, we're approached by the casino manager again, his distance being kept safe by Black's men. "Will sir be requiring the helicopter?"

"Keep it on standby until the morning," Danny says, nodding to Brad who hands over more notes.

We enter the elevator and the doors slide close. The small space is suffocating, and not because of the four big men surrounding us. I can't breathe. Can't think. I'm in up to my neck.

"Rose?"

I look up through my lashes, the backs of my eyes stinging. The concern on his face only makes it worse. He frowns, and I quickly look away, feeling a bead of sweat tricking down between the center of my breasts. I need to hold it together. *Just hold it together.* "Too much seafood," I murmur, exhaling when the doors slide open, blessing me with air and space.

When we make it into the suite, I hurry away, taking myself to the bathroom. I hear one of his men say something as I go, though I don't catch what, and I hear Black mumbling something in return. I feel sick. Terribly sick. I practically throw myself over the sink, running the tap and dousing my face with cold water. The relief is instant, but it has nothing to do with the cool water on my skin and everything to do with the distance I've gained from Black. He can't see me like this.

But that distance doesn't last long, yet I've stolen enough time to gather my nerves. He enters the bathroom, pulling at his tie before unbuttoning his suit jacket. "So, dessert?"

I slowly turn, ready for more of his games. The reset button has been pressed. I should've known Nox would find me. Would know my every move, whether I chose to make it or was forced to. "I'm full."

His eyes drop to between my thighs. "You sure?"

"Very." I walk past him, brushing his arm as I go. I expect to be grabbed, manhandled to a wall, and tortured some more. But much to my shock, he lets me leave. I reach to the back of my dress and feel for the zipper. I pull it down, letting my dress drop and pool at my feet, and I step out of it, leaving my heels buried in the mass of material, unpinning my hair as I walk to the bed.

Then I crawl in and turn onto my side, closing my eyes and

wishing for a clean outcome to this horror movie. But Nox knows. Fuck, what will he do? I know what. I can kiss goodbye to my updates.

When the bed dips beside me, I open my eyes and find him sitting on the edge in front of me, his torso bare. His beautiful, hard chest. The shadows between each raised muscle hold my attention. "I'll take that as a no." He rests his finger under my chin and lifts my face to meet his eyes. Then he places a soft kiss on my forehead. "Sleep well, Rose." He leaves.

And my meltdown begins.

9

DANNY

I take myself to the office, pour myself a hard drink, and slump in the chair, opening the drawer and taking out her mobile phone. I check the screen. Nothing.

My head pounds as I spin it in my grasp, my head falling to the back of the chair. She is fascinating me more by the minute, no matter how hard I'm trying to force my mind into line. I want to know her history. I want to know every fucking thing there is to know.

I also *don't* want to know.

Knocking back my drink, I savor the burn as it works its way down to my stomach. Brad walks in, taking off his jacket and tossing it on the chair, joining me for a drink. "Quite a show you put on tonight." He rotates his wrist, swirling the Scotch so it coats every bit of the glass. Then he raises it. "Assuming it was a show."

I eye him as he sips his drink, rather than knocking it back like me. He can't need it as much as I do. Brad holds my stare, waiting.

"There's something about her," I admit, doing what I've never done before. Confiding in someone. Truth be told, I've never had to confide in Brad. He reads me like a book. Like now. I've never entered into a discussion with him on anything other than work. That's just the way it's been since we were kids. I think it stems from us both fearing that any show of emotion would render us less capable in our deadly world. With my father mentoring us, it's understandable why we took that angle. But now he's dead. And I need to get this off my chest. And though my father always said trust no one, he knew I trusted Brad.

Brad takes a seat, resting his glass on the arm of the leather chair. "There's something about her," he muses quietly. "You mean those insanely long legs, flawless skin, and perfect breasts that are the starring role of any man's wet dream?"

I give him a tried look. "Her assets aren't helping matters," I admit. The woman is a goddess.

"We've had many pretty women in our beds. What is it about his one?"

"I see something familiar in her."

"What?"

"Me."

Brad falters a beat, a flash of worry washing over his rugged face. "You, how?"

"Lost. Trapped." I swig more of my drink. "Dead."

He looks wary. Probably should be. There aren't many people —only two in fact, Pops and Brad—who know my history before Carlo Black found me. Brad's mother, my father's sister, took me in as her own, just as Pops did. Brad respected his mother, listened to her, and we soon became best friends, as well as family.

"She's the mistress of an upcoming politician," Brad says.

"She's not trapped. She's with him because she's a gold-digging whore like the rest of them. And she doesn't look very dead to me."

I let his analysis of Rose go over my head, ignoring that his detrimental label riles me. "There's more to it," I say, getting up and pacing the room. "Her back's bruised as fuck. Like she's been punched in the kidneys by a pretty solid fucking fist."

"She's not your concern. She's here for a reason, Danny. Remember that."

I breathe in and pull myself together, if only to try and convince Brad I'm thinking straight. I'm not. "Tell me the deal."

"Adams leaves tomorrow. Back to Miami to pick up his campaign, though how he's going to do that is a mystery since his bank account is dry."

I eye Brad with caution. "Completely?"

"All gone."

"And he hasn't asked for more," I muse, looking out across the skyline of Vegas. "So who's bank rolling him now?"

"Whoever it is, we need to ask if they knew you were bankrolling Adams first. Because if so, we're dealing with braver men than I knew existed."

"Or Adams has kept my contributions to himself, leaving his new investors in the dark."

"The Russians?"

"The Russians and the Blacks have an agreement. They wouldn't break it."

"The Romanians?"

"The last time the Romanians tried to move in on the US, most of them ended up dead, remember?"

Brad smiles. "I remember."

Pops didn't wait for them to come to him when he got word of their plan from the Russians. He went to them. Killed the problem, namely their leader. What was his name? Ah, that's right.

Dimitri. Marius Dimitri. His men scattered like ants and haven't reformed since. I was fifteen at the time. Pops took Brad and me along for the ride. It was the first time I held a gun, and I was forced to use it. Not because Pops made me, but because one of the Romanian fuckers had Brad. Stupid fuck was so busy watching the grown-ups, he missed me in the car. I took the greatest of pleasure blowing out his brain. Pops smiled. Brad, slightly shook up from staring death in the face, swore he'd repay me, and he has. Tenfold.

Brad sighs. "The Mexicans?"

"They don't have the resources, or the balls."

"You sound sure."

"I'm sure of nothing. Check them all out." Nothing more needs to be said. "The shipment?"

"Half the money is in the bank. We need to be ready for the exchange next week."

"And the goods get here . . ."

"The day before the exchange."

"Have the men check it all before the Russians arrive."

"Done. So we're leaving tomorrow?"

"In the morning."

"And the girl?"

"She comes with us." I wander over to the desk and slide her phone across to Brad. "Have one of the men get into this." I knock back my drink and slam the glass down. Conversation done.

The next morning, I stand at the edge of the bed watching her. She looks like Sleeping Fucking Beauty. So peaceful and serene. I almost don't want to wake her.

Almost.

Yanking the covers back, I expose her in all her naked glory, at the same time abruptly waking her. Her sleepy eyes blink rapidly until she eventually glares at me. "Get ready. We're leaving in an hour." I make my way to the shower to wash off the sweat from my morning workout.

She's in fast pursuit. "Where are we going?" Her panic is obvious as I kick my shorts off and step into the stall. She's doing nothing to hide her nakedness, standing as bold as I know her to be on the other side of the screen.

I keep my stare up. "To my home."

Her eyes widen. "What? No, I can't."

My hands pause on my head as it cocks. She's getting herself in a state again, just like last night in the elevator. The barrier is slowly crumbling. "Yes, you can."

"What if Perry doesn't get you the marina or pay you back? What then? You keep me forever?"

I hum to myself, as if considering that. "Yes," I answer, going back to washing my hair.

"I need to go back to him."

"Why?" I ask, straight up. "Come on, Rose. You don't love him. And it can't be the fucking money, because it turns out he doesn't have any now."

Her face falters, confusion mixing with the fury. "And why are you so desperate for that marina?"

I don't entertain her question, taking myself under the spray and rinsing my hair. "Stop staring at me and go pack."

"I have no fucking clothes, you bastard."

I'm out of the shower like a bullet, pushing her back into the door. "Call me what you fucking like, but *never* call me a bastard."

She whimpers, and for a second I feel something odd. Guilt. Then it hits me as I breathe down on her, staring into her deep blue eyes. She's not whimpering in fright. Her nipples pierce my chest, and it registers. We're both naked.

Breaths.

Deep, restraining breaths. "Be ready in ten minutes." I yank myself away, resisting the pull of her magnetic body, and grab my black dress shirt down off the back of the bathroom door. "Wear this."

She catches it when I throw it at her. "And nothing else?"

I look down at those long legs, inwardly groaning. Those fucking legs. What do I care if they're on full display? Grabbing a towel and wrapping it around my waist, I stalk through to the suite and find Ringo. "Call the concierge. Have them send up some women's jeans from one of the stores. Size two."

He's on it quickly, and I pace back to the room, finding her still in the bathroom, though now her top half is covered with my black shirt. It's a minor consolation. "Some jeans are on the way."

"My hero," she mutters.

I glare at her. I could strangle her. Quite easily. And then she smirks. It's sexy as fuck.

Shit.

I grab her arm and manhandle her out of the bathroom, away from me, slamming the door behind her.

Fuck.

My forehead meets the wood.

My mood hasn't improved when I'm ready. And it takes a further nosedive when I find Rose waiting at the door with my men. Not because they're looking at her. They're not. But because in those skin-tight jeans, my black shirt, her silver strappy heels and matching purse from last night, she looks a perfect, beautiful mess. Her hair is in a haphazard ponytail. Her face free from makeup.

She spends only a brief moment sizing me up, taking in my more casual look of jeans and a T-shirt. Then she defiantly looks away.

I take her arm and push her toward the elevators. She doesn't say a word the entire ride down, doesn't even look at me. Neither does she wriggle in my viselike grip, which I'm pretty sure must be hurting her. Why the fuck isn't she protesting, even if only to defy me?

When we exit, the men lead us to where the limo is waiting to take us to the private airfield. Ringo pulls the door open, and just as I'm about to thrust Rose into the back seat, I hear it.

A scream.

Then all fucking hell breaks loose.

"In the car!" Brad bellows to me, pulling his gun and firing immediately, no hesitation. I look across the roof of the limo, just as a man drops, his brain spraying the concrete. There's a gun in his limp, dead grasp. Another shot, but this one isn't Brad. I feel the bullet sail past my ear, and I turn to see one of my men jolt before grabbing his shoulder and cursing. The chaos gets worse, bystanders screaming, people running for cover as more shots fire around me. I catch Brad's eye as he dives for cover. "Get in the fucking car!"

I reach out to grab—

Where the fuck is she?

I whirl around, searching the sea of heads for her. People are being carried by the charging crowds, some diving to the ground. I pull the car door close to shield my body as Brad bends down by the back wheel, a few feet away, reloading his gun. I flinch when the rear window shatters, raining down broken glass all over him. "Fuck," he curses, smacking the bottom of his magazine and peeking up over the car. No sooner has he raised to half height, he dips back down, a bullet just missing him. "Motherfucker."

I reach into the car and flip open the glove compartment,

pulling out a Glock. I'm just in time to catch a man in the crowd aiming at Brad's head. I fire, taking him down before he has a chance to engage his trigger finger. "Who the fuck are they?" I ask, taking another scan of the crowd.

"Fucked if I know," Brad yells. "Get in the fucking car."

"Where's Rose?"

"I couldn't give a fucking shit where your whore is, Danny. We're being fucking shot at."

I lose my shit, lunging forward and thrusting the barrel of my gun in my oldest friend's face. "Call her a whore again, I'll put a fucking bullet in your skull myself."

His eyes say everything. "Got it." He aims and fires without looking away from me, catching a man to the side of us with a tidy-looking Heckler in his grasp. "She's in the car."

I yank the door open and find Rose sitting there calmly like there isn't a fucking shoot-out happening. Then I get to her eyes. Wide eyes. She's scared, and it's a fucking relief. I was beginning to think she was a robot. "You okay?"

She swallows and nods, letting me pull her from the car.

"We're clear," I hear Ringo yell, and I slowly rise to full height, taking in the carnage. There are five of them, all dead. "Search them." I glance around the space, looking for cameras. "And have the cameras wiped." My men disburse, following my orders. One scoops up Rose's silver purse and hands it to her, and she thanks him, her voice scratchy and broken.

I turn to Brad when he doesn't acknowledge me, finding him staring forward, forcing me to pivot and check what has his attention.

I find a gun.

Being held to my forehead. *What the fuck?*

The feel of Rose's hand constricting around mine forces me to return it, telling her we're fine. *Fine?* I'm literally staring down the barrel of a 9mm. I tug her hand, silently ordering her to move behind me. I can hear her strained, panicked breathing. I can hear Brad cursing behind me.

"Shoot," I order the man before me, curling my lip, pushing my forehead into the end of his gun. "Fucking shoot me."

"No," Rose screams, just before I jerk back, knocking her out of the way. I hear the shot fire and blink a few times, waiting for my body to hit the deck. It doesn't. I'm still standing. But the man before me drops, and I turn to see Brad, his arms braced in front of him. "Any time," he grunts, quickly turning to his left and pulling the trigger again. "Get out of here, Danny."

This time, I listen. Maybe because I now have Rose with me. I grab her hand and yank her up, pulling her back into the hotel. I head for the lift, my men following, firing bullets all over the fucking place. "Get in," I order, shoving her into the lift and backing in, all of us holding back the three men advancing on us. We don't lower our weapons until the doors are closed, bullets bouncing off the metal beyond.

"In motherfucking daylight in the middle of fucking Vegas." Brad falls against the wall and looks at me, his shock clear. "Who the fuck is that bold?"

I glance at Rose, wondering if she's thinking what I'm thinking. "Black's a dead man," I murmur, getting no acknowledgment from my repeat of Perry Adams's words. But would he risk Rose's life? No, I don't think he would. Which means whoever Adams is in bed with now knows for certain he was in bed with me first. And that makes them serious players. I'm fucking astounded by their boldness.

I say no more, pulling Rose from the elevator when it opens. The chopper blades whirl loudly, and she looks up at me, eyes wide. "I'm never spontaneous," I remind her, jogging us to the door and lifting her in.

"You k-knew . . . you knew something would happen?" she asks as I belt her up and Brad gets comfortable up front.

I check that she's secure before taking a seat next to her. I can feel her eyes on my profile as we take off. "I'm always prepared for something to happen."

That's a lie.

I wasn't prepared for *her* to happen.

10

ROSE

I could have run. Amid the chaos, I could have bolted, and Black would never have noticed until it was too late. Yet, I didn't. I also should have wished the gunman aiming at Danny Black's forehead had pulled the trigger before Brad got to him. But I didn't. In that moment I was truly terrified, and it's utterly shocked me. Nox is in Vegas. Was that his attempt to get me back? Because if it was, it was a mega fail. That man doesn't fail. Would he be so careless with my life?

I don't know, but Danny Black winding up dead would surely be the best thing to happen. But in that moment, it felt like the worst thing that could happen. I heard him threatening to kill his man if he called me a whore again. The whole scene played out just beyond the car door where I'd found myself while men fired guns left and right. That's why I didn't run. Because I was stunned by the words he roared at his man. And then when he found me, and then found a gun aimed square between his eyes, he pulled me back, covering my body with his.

No one has ever protected me before. I don't want to like it. Liking something makes it more painful when you no longer have it, and protection isn't something I can keep.

The entire flight, I sat there playing the whole scene on repeat in my head, searching for another logical explanation for Danny's behavior. Of course, there is one. Maybe I'm that valuable to him. Maybe he really does need me. But I keep coming back to the words he yelled at his friend.

Call her a whore again, I'll put a fucking bullet in your skull myself.

Does he see . . . me?

When we were guided from the helicopter to a private jet, the questions circled as Danny gathered his men in the next galley, most splattered with blood, one sporting a bullet wound to the shoulder. It was carnage, but nothing like what they left behind. I didn't recognize any of the men that laid dead, but that wouldn't be unusual. Nox has men everywhere. I heard Brad ask who would do this. And I'm afraid I know exactly who. He saw me with Black in the restaurant last night. I know he watched the whole dinner act play out. Nox knows me well enough. I may have fooled Perry that I find Black abhorrent, but I would never have fooled Nox.

When we land, we're whisked away in a limo back to a mansion on the outskirts of Miami. Hidden behind a ten-foot wall that has guards stationed regularly, the building is like nothing I've seen before. We're greeted by a woman. Esther. She's an attractive lady, but completely stoic, giving me nothing as she takes me away from Danny the moment he barks the order at her. She shows me to a huge suite, and the whole way through the colossal mansion I remain dazed, confused, and worried.

Sitting on the edge of the bed twiddling my thumbs, I glance around, taking in the space. I rise to my feet and wander to the wall of wardrobes, finding them empty. I step into the elaborate bathroom but none of his cosmetics are here. This isn't his room.

I go to the curtains and pull them across, revealing enormous French doors that lead to a terrace. There's a jacuzzi, a couch, and a fire pit. It all looks over the most well-primped garden. Topiary trees cut into all kinds of weird and wonderful shapes are precisely placed between the dense flower beds, pillar lights line the cobbled paths, a gazebo dripping in lavender, and an impressive infinity pool is to the right. It looks like you could swim right off the edge and tumble down the cliff side. It's beyond paradise. It's heaven. Nothing like the hell I feel I'm in.

I pull the doors open and step out onto the balcony, closing my eyes and relishing the warm sun on my skin, catching a rare and peaceful moment. I cast my eyes right and spy another terrace separated from this one by a glass pane. It's for the next room. Another guest room? Is that what I'm in?

I'm a guest, not a prisoner.

"Were you worried about me?"

I swing around, finding Black on the threshold of the terrace wearing a pair of gray shorts hanging low on his hips. Why? Why does he always feel the need to present himself to me half-naked?

"No," I answer with grit.

He wanders across to one of the glass panels, leaning his elbows on the metal balustrade and looking out across the garden. His bare feet cross at the ankles, his tall body bent at the stomach, enhancing the stupidly defined muscles of his back. "Why didn't you run?"

My brain spasms. I've been asking myself that question repeatedly, but I never anticipated *him* asking. "Shock, I suppose."

He turns a smile onto me. It's that genuine smile. The rare one. "You? Shocked? Pull the other one, Rose. You're steel."

Shit.

"Where would I go?"

"Back to your lover," he suggests, casting his eyes out to the landscape again "Not that you'll have one once I've blown his brain out."

He's wrong. I'll still have a lover. It might not be Perry Adams, but I'll have a lover. I just don't know who yet, or why I'll be in his bed.

Taking a packet of cigarettes from the pocket of his shorts, Danny offers me one. I've never smoked in my life. I've heard it's a relaxant, and I could do with relaxing a bit. I scoot over and pull one from the pack, twisting it between my fingers as he slips another between his full lips. He lights it, illuminating his face. His gorgeous face. Then he holds the flame toward me. Nervously, I slip the cigarette between my lips and suck.

And cough.

Fucking hell, I'm choking. The sound of me hacking all over the place drenches the air. And beyond it, I hear him laugh.

It's a rich sound, full of lost happiness. My choking to death makes him happy. "Come here." He turns me away from him and proceeds to smack my back lightly until I've gathered myself. And then it's quiet. And we're close. His hands rest on my hips. The cigarette falls from between my fingers, and I pull in air, trying to be discreet. Impossible when he can see the rise of my shoulders. I turn to face him, his hands sliding across my midriff as I go. I find him shielded by a cloud of smoke, the cigarette resting lightly between his lips. His eyes shine. His scar glows.

"Smoking's bad for you," he grunts, releasing me and taking a drag. "Get some sleep." He flicks it off the terrace, turns, and leaves.

I stare at his back as he goes, a little . . . lost. I just saw another glimmer of softness. And then, as if he realized he was

being nice and it's forbidden, he switched. Or is he simply
playing an asshole's game?

I hardly slept a wink, my mind rolling with so many contradicting
thoughts. He didn't sleep with me. I don't know why, but it bothered me. Almost as much as his swaying mood. He bounces from
cold and aggressive, to showing small hints of a caring nature.
I'm not sure which I dislike the most. The former, I know better
how to handle. The latter instigates a whirl of emotions in me that
aren't familiar or welcome.

Lust being one of the most frustrating.

And even more frustrating . . . I feel that lust with whatever
side of his personality I get. He might awake unusual stirrings of
desire within me, but mostly it's . . . awe. He could have thrown
me at the man with the gun to his head. He could have left me and
ran into the hotel. *You're steel.* It had sounded like admiration.

I stare at the bedroom door from where I'm sitting on the edge
of the bed, naked. I can hear activity, the passing of people, the
calling of names, the sounds of cell phones ringing. He hasn't
come to get me. Am I supposed to sit here until he does?

I'm contemplating the question for another half hour before I
finally throw on his black shirt, pull the jeans up my legs, and
pluck up the courage to venture from my room. I take the handle
and turn, cautiously peeking down the hallway. I can still hear
people, but I can't see them. I wander down the wide corridor on
my bare feet, taking in the art that hangs between every door,
elaborate abstract prints in vivid colors hung on plain cream
walls. There are a lot of doors. The one to my suite is double,
wooden, and heavily engraved, as is the next door. That's Danny's
suite. His scent is leaking through the wood. The room next to
mine is his. The terrace next to mine is his.

The rest of the doors are single, all closed. I count a dozen on each side of the long corridor, until I break out onto a gallery landing. The marble steps sweep down to the right, the balustrades gold and sparkling, reflecting pretty twinkles of light from the crystal, low-hanging chandelier suspended from the high ceiling above. My warm soles hit the cold marble, my hand taking the railing, but quickly retracting, not wanting to smear the shiny metal with my sweaty palms. The front doors, towering and white, are at the bottom of the stairs, each side flanked by huge urns bursting with palms.

When I reach the bottom, I instinctively take a right, following the voices until I reach a pair of double doors that are wide open. The giant room seems small. Because it's full of men, all standing. And sitting at a desk in front of a set of glass doors that lead into the garden, is The Brit. The Angel-faced Assassin. He looks like a king showing his army the battle plan, pointing to something on his desk, moving things around. I hover on the threshold, just watching him looking all kingly and listening to him as he talks, his voice that of a leader. And deep, and raspy and . . .

"They'll come in from here." He indicates whatever it is on his desk and the men move in closer. "We'll have a boat here, keeping watch. Anyone drifts into the space, get rid of them, preferably without raising any alarms."

"What about the Coast Guard?" Brad asks. "They have a habit of showing up when they're not wanted."

"If they do, they'll be distracted. Ringo's gonna be here." He points to something else. "Both when we take delivery and when we do the exchange with the Russians. I have a feeling that dodgy engine in that shit-heap boat of his is finally going to fail."

"I've been meaning to get it fixed." A man, Ringo, I presume, shakes his head in feigned despair. He's a beast of a man, tall and slim, and extremely scary looking. "Thought I'd get one more fishing trip in first."

"Don't get burned, will you?" Danny asks seriously, making a few of the men chuckle lowly. "Don't want to ruin that pretty face of yours."

More chuckles, and I have to force my own back. Ringo is probably one of the ugliest men I've ever laid eyes on, and I've seen some pig-ugly guys in my time. His pitted skin is like leather, his nose big enough to land a small jet on. I've not spent much time with him, but I've figured his personality isn't exactly winning either. Poor guy hasn't got much going for him. Except, maybe, the ability to kill from a mile range.

Ringo sniffs back the insults, but says no more, leaving Danny to go on. "We have an hour tops turn around. Get the consignment off, in the containers, checked, and we're out of there. Then we wait for the—" Black's head snaps up, finding me at the door, and I don't mistake the flash in his eyes for anything less than fury. His fists ball on the desk. His men all turn and look at me.

I back up, not saying a word, and make a hasty retreat, heading back the way I came. I've seen his eyes in various states of fury, but never have I seen them burning that hard. I'm just about to hotfoot it up the stairs when I hear my name being called. But not by him. I turn toward the woman's voice, finding Esther, the dark-haired lady who showed me to my suite last night.

"You must be hungry," she says, indicating to her right. "I was just about to bring breakfast to your room, but since you're here . . ."

It's the first time she's spoken to me. She's English? She's a very attractive lady, maybe late forties, with a slim body and clear complexion. She's wearing the same as last night—a gray maid's uniform. It's plain. Boring. I look back toward Danny's office, torn.

"He wants you to eat," she says, winning back my attention. "The kitchen is this way." Turning, Esther wanders away, and I resolve myself to follow, perhaps because she's the only other woman I've seen since I arrived. It's someone to talk to.

Entering the kitchen, an enormous space with more glass doors leading to the garden, I take a seat at the island. Esther doesn't speak as she putters around, wiping the sides, emptying the dishwasher, putting a fresh pot of coffee on. The silence is awkward.

"How long have you worked here?" I ask, trying to make idle conversation.

"Long enough," she says over her shoulder, swirling the coffee pot as the machine drips fat drops of caffeine into it. Long enough. That sounds like too long.

"You run the house?"

"I do as I'm asked to do." She pours the coffee into a cup and passes it over, and I accept on a small smile. "You'll do well to do the same."

I say nothing but think plenty. Everyone does what Danny Black asks them to do. I should heed her advice.

"Bagel? Toast?" she asks, reaching into a cupboard.

"Toast, please."

She loads the toaster with two slices of bread and presses the lever, sinking them. Then she goes about her chores again, as if I'm not here. I spin my coffee cup, wondering if she's even curious about me and how I've come to be in her boss's mansion. "I hope you don't mind me ask—"

"You can leave, Esther." Danny's voice hits my back with force, sounding as angry as his eyes looked when I fled his office. I don't turn around, and instead watch Esther scuttle off without another word. Dropping my eyes to the speckled gray and black marble counter, I start studying the various patterns, trying to make shapes and pictures out of them. I know he's getting close. Every hair on my nape is standing to attention. I shudder, tense.

And then his hand rests on my neck. But rather than tense more, I relax.

"Never listen in on my work conversations again."

"Okay." I don't apologize, and I don't try to explain myself either. It would be a waste of my energy.

His grip tightens. "You're hungry." I nod. "Thirsty?" I simply raise my coffee cup, and his grip tightens a little more. You would think with my compliance he would be softening. But his hold of me is getting harder. And I know why. He's looking for a yelp, anything to show my discomfort. He won't get it.

"Harder," I spit without thought, setting my coffee cup on the counter and placing a hand over his on the back of my neck. "If you're going to do it, do it properly." I push down, egging him on, and he moves in, his groin pressing into my back.

Dipping, he bites my lobe, grazing it harshly through his teeth. I close my eyes and force myself not to allow our contact to dent my resolve.

"Coffee?" I ask, completely out of the blue. It's stupid, but there's a method in my madness. Get him off me before I do something I regret. Like swivel and unzip his fly.

He chuckles in my ear, the sound soft and light.

Just like that.

From growling, angry bear, to cute little cub.

"Please." He releases me, and I jump off the stool like a rubber ball, taking myself to the safe side of the island as I shake myself back to life. He takes my stool, cocking one foot on the rest and leaning his elbows on the counter, watching me as I find my way around. I prepare his coffee, at the same time talking myself down from the edge of a deadly cliff. I also try to think of something else to say that doesn't include anything I may or may not have heard while hovering on the threshold of his office. Unwanted Coast Guards. Consignments. Distractions.

I'm not surprised by my newfound knowledge. I'm curious,

and curiosity in this world gets you killed. Luckily for me, I have a desire to breathe, even if I'm not technically living. "Sugar?" I ask, turning to face him.

"Obviously, I'm sweet enough."

I scoff, and I don't apologize for it. Danny Black is about as sweet as hell is cold. "Here." I slide the cup across the island, and he takes it before I have a chance to remove my hand, pressing my palm into the hot ceramic, keeping it there while holding my eyes. His are blazing. Fire and ice swirl in their depths. I let my stare fall to his neck, where a dusting of hair pokes out the top of his open-collared shirt. And then they drop farther south to our hands on the cup. The heat sinking into my flesh is there, but it's not there. Nothing is really there when I'm touching him. Close to him.

"Thank you." He releases his palm and watches me as he takes the cup to his mouth. "I think something's burning."

My senses are hyper-alert, but my sense of smell is too busy appreciating his cologne to notice the other potent scent in the room until he pointed it out.

Then I see smoke.

"Shit." I dart across to the toaster and press every lever on it, trying to eject the smoking bread. No luck. My breakfast continues to burn, the smell intensifying. I glance around the area, searching for anything to dig it out. There's nothing. "Damn it." In desperation, I shove my hand in and flick it out, worried I might set all the fire alarms off.

I throw the burnt toast on the plate and stare at the pile of charcoal. "I hope you didn't kidnap me for my culinary skills." I look up and find Black with his coffee resting to his lips, still and quiet, watching me. His face is impassive. No amusement whatsoever. We stare. It's silent. My eyes begin to roam every inch of his face, and his roam over mine. His breathing deepens. Mine becomes strained. I see a million sins in his eyes. And I wonder if he sees the dirt of my life in mine.

The lever on the toaster pops up. It makes me jump, and my eyes snap away from his. I realign my thoughts quickly and take the plate, ready to dump my breakfast in the bin.

"Put the plate down."

I freeze. Look up at him. "What?"

He slowly places the cup on the island and rounds it, taking the plate from my hand and setting it aside. Then he presses the lever down on the toaster again. "I haven't put any more bread in it," I tell him, reaching for the loaf that Esther left. My hand doesn't make it. He seizes my wrist firmly, stilling me.

Then he guides my hand toward the toaster. The heat on my flesh is instant. So is my confusion. His eyes drill holes into me while he slowly takes my hand down until my palm meets the red-hot heat of the metal. I feel nothing. Am I hardened? Stupid? I don't know, but I don't feel what I'm supposed to feel. *Pain.*

"If you pull away, I won't stop you." His statement must trigger something inside of me. Alertness. My nerves spring to life, and suddenly the pain is there. But I don't pull away, my teeth gritting instead as I endure his torture. It's nothing in comparison to other cruelties I've faced. Nothing compared to other punishments I've suffered.

But he's not punishing me. He's trying to figure me out.

And me him.

I engage my spare hand and reach blindly for his, our eyes glued. Danny makes it easy for me to find, actually placing his big hand in mine. I bring it over the toaster too. He doesn't stop me. I press his palm down on top of the metal, right next to mine.

His face doesn't crack, but his eyes go from simmering heat to a full-blown inferno, his jaw now as tight as mine as we stand there torturing each other.

He won't pull away. I won't pull away. What point are we trying to prove to each other?

Then the toaster suddenly decides enough is enough and the lever springs up. The heat dies. And Danny suddenly jerks us both away, both of us gasping. Turning our hands palm up, he looks down, studying the matching welts. "We're the same," he whispers, bringing my hand to his mouth and kissing the burn.

Soft Danny.

It's then realization slams into me, so hard, he must feel my body jolt. He returns his fiery eyes to mine, as if he's heard the bombshell drop into my brain.

I remind him of someone.

Him?

It doesn't add up. He's the son of Carlo Black. Rich, powerful, feared. My eyes fall to the scar on his cheek. It seems to be glowing at me now, highlighting its presence and stirring the pot of questions in my tangled mind.

"Let's fix you up." He breaks into my thoughts, cutting off the questions before I can ask, and something tells me it's tactical. I'm in a trance, unmoving, paralyzed by curiosity. I snap out of it the second my feet aren't keeping me anchored to the ground anymore. He picks me up and sits me on the countertop next to the sink, flipping the faucet on. Then he takes both our burned hands under the cold stream together, turning them over in the water. I stare down at them, his skin next to my skin, the same tanned tone. His manly hand and my dainty one. "Did you sleep well?" he asks, not looking up at me.

I hum my response, unable to kick the questions back. I should, since his actions now are warning me in every way not to ask. Then why spike my intrigue with moments like that?

Turning off the water, Danny grabs a towel and pats at my skin, inspecting the damage. The center of my palm is red raw. He looks up at me, the front of his jeans brushing my knees.

"I'll dress it for you."

"There's no need." I pull my hand from his and try to slip down, but I'm blocked, my hand reclaimed.

"I will dress it for you," he repeats, this time sterner.

I press my lips lightly together to stop another refusal flowing as he places my hand gently on my lap and moves across the kitchen, pulling something down from a cupboard. I see it's a small first aid kit when he makes it back to me. He takes my wrist and pulls me down, walking me to the island. "Sit." Brusque Danny is back.

I perch on the stool and watch as he goes about dressing my hand, but first he rubs some cream into the sore, spending an age making sure every bit of the white lotion is absorbed before he meticulously wraps my hand in a white length of material. He does a very neat job, leaving me with a perfectly bandaged hand.

I flex it a little. "Thank you," I say, as he starts putting the things back in the box, ignoring me. "What about your hand?" Something deep and misplaced inside of me wants to take care of his wound too.

He shoves the box back in the cupboard. "My skin is thicker than yours," he grunts, striding to the door.

"What now?" I call, making him stop a few feet from the exit. Is it me, or is he in a rush all of a sudden?

He doesn't look back. "What now *what*?"

"Well, what am I supposed to do?"

"You wait until I tell you what to do. In the meantime, show yourself around. Use the amenities. Whatever." He takes two more steps and stops again, still not looking back. "But if you try to escape, I won't think twice about killing you." And with that final warning, he disappears.

11

DANNY

"The men had nothing on them. No ID, nothing," Brad says as we walk the maze of paths on the grounds of the mansion the next evening. I've been holed up in that office all day, finalizing plans for the delivery. My head's ringing with logistics. I needed to escape. Some days, I just need to walk. To feel my feet. To breathe in air and look at the color blanketing the beds of the garden. To remind myself there is something other than blackness in my world.

Sometimes, I just want the pressure to fuck off from my shoulders so I don't feel so heavy anymore. Then I remember who I am. What I do.

"Ringo took these photos." Brad hands me a phone, and I look down at the faces of the dead men. I recognize none. "I had Spittle run the faces through his system—"

"Nothing," I finish for Brad, handing back the phone.

"Nothing," he confirms. "And Spittle was seriously pissed off."

I bet he was. A bloodbath in the middle of Vegas will be a headache and a half. My relationship with Spittle is frosty to say the least. But the bent FBI agent owes me, and he couldn't pay me back in three lifetimes. "Fuck Spittle." I slip my hand into my pocket and frown, pulling it back out and looking at the blister.

"What the fuck did you do to your hand?" Brad asks.

"Argument with the toaster," I grunt as we reach the rockery, where water tumbles down the ragged stone into the stream that leads to the pool. I watch the water for a time, thinking. It's no good asking who wants me dead—the list is too long. But there's someone who specifically stated that I was a dead man. Adams is in bed with someone else, and I won't let him get out of *my* bed. Desperate men do desperate things, but would he ambush me like that to save himself? *And with what cash?*

"I spoke to Voladya," Brad continues. "The Mexicans are lying low and the Romanians are still disbursed after Carlo's last vacation to Romania."

I chuckle at his dry wit. "Have a couple of men look deeper. I want answers."

"Well, look what we have here," Brad says, amusement in his tone. I follow his gaze to the garden house across the lawn, finding Rose's back plastered against the wood. She's as still as a statue. And before her? Two growling Dobermans.

My secret smile is wicked. "They just want a kiss," I call, making Brad chuckle from beside me. "With tongues."

"Asshole," Rose manages to spit, without even moving her mouth, making my two girls snarl more.

I stroll over casually, my hands deep in my trouser pockets. Her eyes remain on my growling dogs. "Go on. Just a peck," I tease.

"I'd take the mutts over you any day of the week."

My grin is epic, and Brad snorts from trying to contain his laugh. "Wise. They're less deadly than I am." I whistle, the

familiar sound gaining their attention. They know better than to
take their eyes off a possible threat until they hear my call.
"Heel," I order, and they rush over to me, sitting at my feet. I
smile and give them some love, encouraging them to start
jumping up to try and lick my face. I laugh on the inside. *Yeah,
yeah, love you two too.* "Away," I order, gentle but firm, and they
dart off toward the back of the grounds, barking as they go. Rose
relaxes against the wooden garden house, her hand coming up to
her chest, her eyes narrowed on me. My grin doesn't falter.

"What happened to your hand?" Brad asks Rose, stepping
forward and pointing at the bandage I carefully wrapped her
wound in yesterday.

She looks down at it, stalling. Then she shrugs. "Had an argument with the toaster."

I manage to hide my smirk, feeling Brad's accusing stare
rooted on my profile. He sighs. "Sounds like the only deadly
thing around here is the fucking toaster," he mutters, heading back
to the house.

Rose purses her lips. "Did I say something funny?"

I shake my head.

"Then why are you smiling?"

I shrug.

She sighs, exasperated. "I have to go." She passes me,
following behind Brad. "I'm busy being bored in my ivory
tower."

I say nothing as I watch her stomp off, the bump of her arse
quite the view. My lack of a retort must piss her of, because she
halts abruptly and swings back to face me. Her expression is
beautifully strained. Annoyed.

"Just how long do you plan on keeping me here?"

I shrug again, unable to stop my silly need to rile her.

"Oh my God, you're infuriating."

Another shrug.

She yells, frustrated, and steams toward me, her hand locking and loading. I catch her wrist as her palm sails toward my face, and she stills, her enraged eyes burning into mine. "If you slap me, I get to slap you back," I warn.

She jars her wrist in my hold, her way of telling me it's not a problem for her. "The person who I remind you of"—she breathes in my face, anger getting the best of her—"who is it?"

"The person who raped you," I retort, moving in close, sliding my palm onto her hip. "Who was it?" I saw her face at dinner when it came up, heard her tone. I'm slowly figuring her out, and I know she's doing the same with me. Should I mention that I want to kill whoever violated her? Should I mention that it would be the most brutal of deaths?

"You know nothing," she whispers.

"I know everything."

My reply causes a hitch of her breath. A shudder of her body. Her blue eyes shine, and past their stunned state, I detect . . . hope? She sees my curiosity and snatches her hand away, her jaw tight as she moves back, gaining some personal space.

"What's your surname, Rose?" I ask, placing my hands back in my pockets.

"Fuck you."

"Rose *fuck you*?" I muse, thoughtful. "Has a nice ring to it." Brushing past her, I make my way to the house. "You need feeding."

"I'm not one of your fucking dogs."

I smile at my feet, keeping on my way. The woman makes me smile. I can't help it. "Esther will prepare something for you," I call, hearing her indignant huff. "And stay away from the toaster."

"Danny!" Her shout sounds urgent, and I pull to a stop, something inside of me kicking. My name on her lips. It's good. I look over my shoulder. "Cassidy," she says quietly, her bare feet padding the grass. She's nervous to tell me her name. "It's Rose Lillian Cassidy."

I nod mildly, watching her for a few too many pleasurable moments, as she nibbles on her bottom lip anxiously. A beautiful name. A beautiful woman. A beautiful mind. "Get something to eat, Rose Lillian Cassidy," I order softly, returning my attention forward and walking away, pushing back all thoughts of her.

Or, at least, I try my fucking hardest.

When I make it to the office, Brad and Ringo are looking over the map of the coastline, Brad removing pins and pushing them into other sections of the sea. "What's going on?" I ask, rounding my desk.

Ringo turns his big nose up and takes the pin back to the original point "No. It has to be here. I can see all three possible routes to the boatyard from here. If the Coast Guard turns up either during the delivery or when we do the exchange with the Russians, I'll send my boat up in flames to distract them."

"And what if they get distracted by us on the shore offloading?"

"They won't."

"How'd you know?"

Ringo turns his ugly mug slowly toward Brad. "Because I'll make sure of it."

I take a seat and watch them having a face-off. I know many things about Ringo. I know he's the son of a dead hooker. I know he's never touched alcohol or drugs. I know he respects women. And above all that, I know he went above and beyond for my father, and now he'll do it for me too. If Ringo says he'll make sure of it, then he'll make sure of it. "Ringo stays in the original spot." I put the debate to rest and write a quick note on the leather-bound pad before me, tearing it off and handing it to Brad. "Look into this name for me."

Eyeing me with suspicion, he takes the scrap of paper, not even looking at it. He doesn't need to. "Why?"

"Because I told you to," I reply coldly, giving him a stare that suggests he'll do well not to question me. "Any news on her phone?"

"Nothing." Brad takes it from his pocket and tosses it on my desk.

I frown, taking my mobile and dialing a number that'll surely have the owner staring down at the screen in dread. But he'll answer. Of course he'll answer. "Black." His voice is harboring all kinds of caution. Rightly so.

"I have a phone I need you to look at. I want records."

"I have a job I'd like to keep," he retorts on a small laugh. "A man of your caliber doesn't have the staff to get him phone records?"

"Oh, I do." I kick my feet up on the desk. "I have you, Spittle." Ringo smiles, the expression doing nothing to soften his features, and Brad takes Rose's phone from my desk and sets about packaging it into an envelope. "And that job you speak of is still only yours because of me," I remind him.

"How long are you going to hold me to ransom with those fucking pictures?"

"How long do you plan on working for the FBI?" I ask, dropping my feet from my desk and strolling over to the framed Picasso hanging over the fireplace. I hold the phone to my ear with my shoulder as I lift the art down, revealing my safe.

"I'm sixty next month," Spittle says. "Retirement is looming. What you gonna do when I'm not around to blackmail anymore?"

I spin the dial and open the safe, pulling out an envelope from beneath a semi-automatic. "But you're around now. And these pictures are still as fresh as they were five years ago." I slide one out and smile down at Spittle snorting a line of cocaine off a woman's pussy.

"You planted those hookers."

"They weren't hookers, Spittle. They were honeytraps. Totally different ballgame. Not that the public would know. And I had nothing to do with the coke. You know I don't dabble in that kind of shit." I stuff the images back in the safe and shut it, motioning to the Picasso for Ringo to re-hang. "Do your FBI magic with the phone. Tell me what you find." I hang up and bring my mobile to my mouth, chewing the side thoughtfully.

What's Rose's story?

12

ROSE

It's like trying to get blood out of a stone. Esther is impenetrable. I'm tentatively nibbling at the corners of a croissant as I watch her move silently and efficiently around the kitchen, an awkwardness hanging in the air. Three times I've tried to strike up a conversation, and three times I've been shot down with a simple yes or no. So I try something other than a closed question. I clear my throat and set down my croissant. "How is Danny's father doing? I've heard he's been ill."

Her movements stall, and she looks over her shoulder at me like I could be a two-headed beast on the loose. It makes me sit up straight on my stool. "Mr. Black's father passed away last week." She doesn't sound in the least bit sorry about that, turning away and carrying on about her business of scrubbing the burners. "It would be wise of you to avoid prying."

His father died last week? I would hazard a guess that Danny's dark mood could be a result of that, but I dismiss that notion quickly. Danny Black is dark, period. "Prying with you or Danny?" I ask, starting to pick at the pastry on my plate.

Esther sighs and turns to face me. "Both. It's a sore subject, as you can imagine."

"Maybe I could offer an ear," I reply quietly, trying to keep the conversation going before it's cut dead. "Try to ease his pain." What am I saying? And how do I plan on easing his pain?

"Mr. Black isn't interested in your compassion, child. He's interested in what you . . ." She fades off, quickly turning away. She's said too much. "Mr. Black doesn't feel pain, so you have nothing to fear there."

"Emotional pain or physical?" I ask, pushing my luck.

Once again, she turns to face me, giving me a look that could turn me to dust . . . if I could feel anything at all. "Both." She holds me in place with her glare for a while before returning to her chores like she might not just have silently threatened me. "I think it's time for you to retire to your room."

"Right." Like a naughty little girl for asking too many questions. I slip down from the stool and snag the remainder of my croissant from the plate, leaving the kitchen. "It was nice talking to you, Esther," I say sweetly, with a little bit too much sarcasm. "Have a lovely evening."

I hear voices from Danny's office, but think better than to listen again, heading up through the otherwise quiet house to my room, finishing my croissant on my way. I shut the door behind me and strip out of the jeans I've worn for two days, tossing them on the chair in the corner. Unbuttoning the shirt as I pad to the bathroom, I shrug it off and drop it into the laundry basket, collecting the plush white robe off the back of the bathroom door and slipping it on. The marble counter is bare except for the toothbrush and paste that I found there this morning when I woke. There are certain things I need if I'm going to be kept here against my will. Cosmetics, for one. I head back to the room and collect the silver purse Danny gave me in Vegas, taking it to the sink. I pull out the compact face power and set it by the tap, followed by the lip balm and the miniature bottle of *Viktor & Rolf* perfume. As my hand reaches in for more things to decorate the counter with, just to make it feel a fraction like my own, I frown, pulling out a cell phone. A small disposable one.

Nox.

I don't bother asking how he got this into my purse in Vegas. It would be pointless—the man has capabilities beyond my comprehension. My heart rate increasing isn't avoidable as I stare at the cell. I turn it over and remove the back, looking for the final clue that'll tell me Nox is responsible. The small chip looks back at me. He can track me with this phone. And the bug means I can't use it to make calls or texts, other than to him and the random dummy numbers he's saved to it.

I replace the back and switch it on, and the screen soon asks me to unlock it. I know what the code is. It'll be the same code he programs into every cell phone he gives me. My fingertip punches in the four digits and the screen illuminates.

As expected, there are dozens of fake contacts and easy-breezy text messages, all for show, just in case it falls into the wrong hands. I go straight to *Mom*, dialing and bringing the cell to my ear, closing my eyes and bracing myself for the sound of the voice that'll always remind me of my place in this world. How am I going to explain what happened in Vegas? He was there watching me. He knew the moment Danny Black took me.

"And how are you settling in at Casa Black?" His serious question has me closing my eyes and quietly inhaling.

"Did you try to kill him?" I scold myself the moment I've asked. Never ask questions. *Ever*.

"Excuse me?" The malice in his tone cuts deeply, and my mind casts back to the photo served on a silver platter right after I was served with a brutal punch in the ribs.

"I'm sorry," I say softly, looking up into the mirror above the sink. *Dead*. My blue eyes look hollow and dead.

"What do you know?" he asks, and I frown. Marinas, boat-yards, consignments, the Coast Guard. It's all I can hear in my head, and for the life of me, I don't know why the words aren't forming on my tongue for me to speak them. To tell him what I've heard. Then, as quickly as I question myself, I remind myself of the consequences if I don't do what this bastard asks me to do. "I heard him talking about a consignment. I don't know what it is. There's an exchange happening. He talked about Coast Guards showing up and a decoy to distract them. I don't know any more than that." Every single word that passes my lips feels wrong. So, so wrong. "Adams owes him millions," I go on. "I think Perry's getting money from someone else now, but Black won't release him."

Nox hums, thoughtful. "And this consignment, where is it coming from?"

I pull up, thinking. Wait a minute. Why ask where it's coming from? Why not ask what it is? I start doing the math in my head, working backward and putting things together. What I come up with forces me to take hold of the sink for support. "You're Adams's new backer," I breathe, looking at the open bathroom door into the suite. Good God, Perry is in a mess. He has two malicious killers on his back. "The marina, you want it." And I know why. Of course I know why. There's only so long Nox can get away with smuggling women into the States in containers and offloading them in the dead of night at the docks. My mind races. The marina Black is buying is a cover for whatever Danny deals in, and obviously the perfect location if anyone wants to smuggle things into Miami. "You want Adams in power too."

"You've always been smart. Carry on being smart. Find out when the consignment is being delivered to Black. He will be selling on, to the Russians, I expect. I want to know when."

"Selling what?" I cringe the second I've asked. *Just do as you're told.*

"I'm not sure America suits you. I might take you back to my homeland."

I breathe in. No. I can't go back there. I may still be a prisoner, but at least I'm back in *my* homeland. At least I'm in the same country as my boy. It's not a comfort, it's more psychological. I'm of more use to Nox in America, and he knows it. He's run out of people to blackmail in Romania. There are limitations to the power he can achieve. "Maestru," I murmur, defeated.

"Better. Get to work."

"You're leaving me here?" My brain has seriously short-circuited.

"You're of better use to me there."

"What about Adams? Does he know I work for you?" *Oh my God.* "Me being here, it was all part of your plan, wasn't it?" He's set Black up. "Why would you ambush Black in Vegas if you need all this information? I can't get it if he's dead."

"Just rattling a few cages, Rose. And I'll keep rattling. It would be convenient if Danny opens his mouth to my whore, would save me time and patience, but it's not life or death to me if he keeps his mouth closed." He chuckles. "It's life and death to you, Rose. I'll get what I want eventually, with or without you. Can you say the same?"

I'm silent.

"Can you?"

I close my eyes, my face looking to the heavens for a god I wished I could believe in. "No."

"Get me the information. Do whatever it takes. A întelege?"

I turn and lean against the vanity unit, my fingertips pushing into my forehead in dread. "Da," I say quietly before hanging up. I let my hand drop, limp and heavy, and look at the bathroom door. I'm dead if I don't get what Nox wants, and I'm dead if I do. One way or another, my time is up.

On a lumpy swallow, I glance around the bathroom, searching for somewhere to hide the cell phone. I switch it off, pull out the drawer in the vanity unit, and tuck it behind.

As I rise, I hear the door to the suite open. My stupid breathing diminishes to nothing, and I swing around toward the mirror and quickly pull my hair tie free, shaking out my mane. I need something to do with my hands, something to focus on, so I start gathering up the waves again and re-tying them. My mind is ticking a hundred miles a minute, my situation becoming more dire with each run-through of the facts I have. All hard facts. Scary facts.

"How are you settling in?" Danny's tone is rough, magnetic, but I keep my eyes on my own in the mirror.

"You mean in my prison?"

"Quite a luxurious prison, if that's what you want to call it."

"Pretty it up all you like. I'm here against my will, and that makes this my prison." I'm done tying my hair, so I start fussing with the ponytail for a continued distraction.

"You trying to look nice for me?" he asks, a certain humor to his tone that has my hands faltering for a split second before I yank out the tie and start all over again. What the hell am I going to do? How do I play this horrific game? Like I'd normally play would be the obvious answer, but Danny Black isn't like my normal targets. Not for the first time in my adult life, I'm in up to my neck. But unlike all those other times, the rules of the game are blurring. I've been told to do what it takes to get the information Nox wants. What will it take?

I jump a little, startled from my thoughts, when his palm wraps around my wrist, halting my mindless hair-tying task. Our gazes collide in the mirror. Our touching skin sizzles. My poor brain could explode with the mixture of conflicting thoughts currently holding my body hostage. "I'm sorry about your father," I say without thought.

"Are you? Have you lost a parent?"

I very nearly blurt out that I have no parents. But I stop myself in the nick of time, remembering that he has my other cell phone, and there are many convincing messages from my *mom* on it. "My father." Another lie. I've told millions of lies, but this one I question. And that makes my brain hurt even more, the conflict growing.

"I'm sorry," Danny murmurs, relaxing his grip on my wrist and lowering it to my side. Releasing me, he takes the tie from my hand and moves in close behind me. I watch him silently as he carefully and meticulously gathers my hair into his big palms and fixes it in a ponytail.

My insides turn and swirl and jolt. *Seduce him.* That's all I have to do. Blow his mind and loosen his lips. Gain his trust. I'm an expert at all those things. It's all I have to do to get out of this mess.

I slowly turn to face him, looking up into his pale blue eyes as my hands lift to the waist of his jeans. He doesn't stop me, just stands quietly—deathly still—watching me as I pop the first button of his fly. *Seduce him.* My hand skims his flat stomach, the hairs tickling me. I pull in air nervously, moving to the next button. My mouth is dry, my swallows thick, every nerve I have thrumming. The next button. His astute eyes darken, his hands still motionless by his sides. The next button. I have to clear my blurring vision, and Danny subtly bites down on his bottom lip.

Our eyes still locked, I take the sides of his jeans, pushing them down over the swell of his ass. His skin is fire. His eyes are wild. His lips are calling me. And then he licks them, taking one small step into me, closing the space, silently telling me to kiss him. This kiss is going to be the death of me. Literally.

I reach up on my tiptoes and slide my hand into the front of his boxers, my fingers skimming the hard, taut flesh of his erection. Our lips meet. Just touch, and my hand circles his thick girth. I inhale sharply. This isn't the first time I've touched him so intimately. I know he's well endowed. But a faint breathy gasp still escapes, and Danny swallows it down. "You don't want to do this," he says against my lips, his arm circling my lower back.

"I do." I so do. Even with a million strands of guilt and doubt blitzing my head, I know I really want this. I *need* this.

His mouth leaves mine, his palm moving from my back to my wrist and seizing it harshly. "No, you don't." Pulling my hand from his boxers, he steps back, breaking all contact, his eyes paling again. Icey. "Every time we're close or touch, I can feel your lust crawling all over my skin," he says quietly. "But just then, all I felt was fear. You're scared."

I look away. "You're the Angel-faced Assassin. Of course I'm scared."

He takes my jaw harshly, pressing the tips of his fingers into my flesh. "You're not scared of me. You're scared because you really, *really* want me to fuck you. Hard. Ruthlessly." A wicked smile ghosts his lips. "And that fear I can feel is because you know you'll love every second," he finishes on a whisper.

I pull myself free and push myself back into the vanity unit. "I need to take a shower," I tell him, desperate to get him out of the bathroom so I can compose myself and rethink my approach.

"Help yourself." He sweeps his hand out toward the stall. "Don't tell me you're suddenly shy."

If only to prove a point, I shrug off the robe, dropping it at his feet, before I step into the shower and turn it on. The water is cold. Good. I need something to shock me back to life.

"I have a dinner meeting this evening." He pulls down the seat of the toilet and lowers himself, resting his elbows on his knees as he watches me wetting my hair. "You're coming."

"Perry?" I ask, more dread falling. I don't think I can handle another spectacle like our romantic dinner in Vegas. And now I know Nox is lurking in the shadows, hiding my desire is paramount.

"Not Adams." He smiles when I exhale my relief, standing and walking out of the bathroom. I watch his back disappear on a small frown, and moments later, he's back, a bag in his hand. Placing it on the vanity unit, he pulls out a bottle of shampoo and conditioner, followed by some shower gel. "As much as I like you smelling of me, I thought maybe you'd prefer something more feminine." He approaches the stall and sets the bottles on the shelf in the shower. "Be ready for seven." Plunging his hand into my wet hair, he hauls me forward until our faces are close. "Use plenty of the shower gel," he whispers. "I can *smell* fear on you too." He drops me and leaves, and I have no choice but to sink to my knees when my wobbly legs give, my breathing erratic and strained. He sees me. Has from the first time our eyes locked. And he's right. I *am* scared. I'm scared of my attraction toward him.

After finally convincing my legs to work, I shower and wash my hair using the products he left. All rose scented. As I'm drying my hair in the mirror, I realize I have nothing to wear. I haven't seen the silver dress since I took it off in his Vegas hotel suite, and the jeans and shirt I've been wearing are hardly suitable for dinner.

Placing the dryer down, I slip into the white robe and make my way out, set to go and position my problem to Danny. I make it to the door when I hear something from outside on my terrace. His voice?

Intrigued, I back up, edging toward the open glass doors. I see him through the glass panel that separates this balcony from his. He's sitting in a large wicker chair smoking a cigarette, staring out over the garden. He's in his boxers. Slumped back in the seat.

Legs extended before him, straight and crossed at the ankles. His hair is wet and falling into his eyes. Staring is easy, and I rest my shoulder against the doorjamb. This is a side of Danny I've never seen. Relaxed. He looks . . . peaceful?

"I know you're there," he says to the garden, taking his cigarette to his lips and pulling a long drag.

I pull my robe in and step out onto the terrace, having to squint a little when the sun shines in my eyes. "I have nothing to wear."

He casts me a sideways look as he exhales, looking me up and down. "You look good in that."

I let my shoulders drop. "You want to take me out in this?"

"I'm not taking you out. You're accompanying me."

"Whatever," I snap. "I'm sure you'll want me to wear clothes."

He flicks some ash in a tall ashtray next to his chair. "You sure about that?"

My head tilts, my lips purse. "After your performance in your suite's office in Vegas in front of your men, yes. Yes, I'm pretty sure you don't want to parade me around naked."

His jaw instantly tightens, and I find a smile creeping up on me. *Power*. I feel powerful all of a sudden. Pushing himself up from his chair, Danny wanders over to the glass panel and takes another pull of his cigarette. "There are clothes for you in the wardrobe."

I withdraw in surprise, looking over my shoulder to the wall of closets. He bought me more clothes? Do I thank him? I'm pondering that question for far too long, but just as I decide that some appreciation wouldn't hurt, a woman walks out of his bedroom pulling on one of his shirts. My words of thanks shoot to the back of my throat with an inhale and nearly choke me, and my reaction forces Danny to glance over his shoulder to what has my attention.

The woman is taking me in, looking me up and down, her pretty face curious. She's not a natural blonde, but, of course, she's gorgeous. I rip my bitchy eyes away from her and find Danny poorly concealing a sly grin. So he walked out of my bathroom with a solid cock and had himself relieved by someone else? This woman here? Why? Why not me? And why the fuck am I injured by that?

"Hello," I say as evenly as possibly, straining something close to a friendly smile. I get nothing in return. No acknowledgment. No smile. No words.

"This is Amber." Danny takes another hit of nicotine. "Amber, this is Rose." His smirk is growing by the second.

Suddenly, Amber slaps on a smile and comes dancing toward me. "Nice to meet you." She offers her hand over the glass, and I take it, holding my smile in place.

"You too."

Danny puts his arm around Amber's shoulder, pulling her in close to his naked torso. She looks up at him in surprise but goes with ease, settling against his skin. My strained smile is going to crack my cheeks soon.

"I'll leave you two to it." I swivel on my bare feet and head back inside.

"Please do," Danny calls, and I turn when I get to the doors, catching him walking Amber back into his room, one hand in her hair, the other still holding the cigarette. I don't mean to slam the doors. It just happens, creating a deafening crash. For a moment, I half expect the glass to shatter. "Probably bulletproof," I mutter, going to the closet and yanking it open in a temper. My grievance is forgotten the second I'm facing the contents. Dozens of items grace the rails—dresses, sweaters, pants, tanks. Glamourous, casual, smart. My eyes drop to the shoe stand, where there are various pairs of sneakers, heeled pumps, and flip-flops. He's covered every wardrobe eventuality. What's going on?

I start browsing through the pieces and soon realize that every single item is something I would choose for myself. None of it is tarty. None of it screams whore. It's all tasteful and classy. *Which means I have no armor.* I pull out a cream dress with gold stitching on the hem and sleeves. There are gold-heeled pumps to match. Appropriate for dinner? Yes, I think so.

I get myself ready, before applying some makeup that was left on the dresser too. And the whole time, I'm silently stewing over what could be happening next door while I'm in here getting ready to *accompany* him to dinner. Then I hear a collection of bangs. And a definite roar of pleasure. My jaw tightens, and my hand gets a little too vigorous as I swipe my lipstick across my bottom lip, painting it thickly in the bright red shade I wore the fatal night Danny Black took me. *Whore* red. I smack my lips and stand back from the mirror. And I stare into my empty eyes for the longest time as I slowly pin my hair into place, assessing myself. Perfect.

Grabbing my purse, I slip my feet into the heels and make my way downstairs, not looking at his door as I pass. Is she still in there? I shake my head and my thoughts away, hitting the stairs, my heels clinking on the marble. The sounds distract the group of men at the bottom, and they all turn and look up at me as I descend, my hold of the rail tight, my chin high. I make it to the bottom, and the ugly guy, Ringo, looks past me. I turn and see Danny at the top of the stairs, watching me.

I hold his eyes, my jaw solid, my mind ignoring the vision of his tall, hard frame looking fine in another expensive three-piece, this one navy. The deep blue makes his eyes pop, even from down here.

He takes slow steps down, fastening his tie as he does, his eyes never leaving mine. Defiantly, I stare him down, refusing to look away. My grit amuses him. When he reaches the bottom of the stairs, he passes through a few men until he's before me. The silence is heavy. He finishes fastening his tie and holds out his hand. Brad places something in his palm. I don't know what. I refuse to take my eyes off his. Then he moves in, lifting his hand to my face, and wipes a handkerchief from one side of my mouth to the other, dragging off my red lipstick. My look must be pure indignation, but I say nothing, licking my dry lips once he's done.

"You didn't like the red?" I ask.

"Not today." He slides his palm onto my neck and turns me, leading me out of the door by a firm hold on my nape. "Glad you're back to your normal self," he muses, opening the back door of a shiny Mercedes.

I stop and look up at him, my face impassive. "My normal self?"

He smirks, dipping and kissing my cheek. "Fiery," he whispers, his tongue licking the shell of my ear.

My inhale is loud. My body still. My skin erupts, my resolve becomes rickety.

"Get in the car, Rose." Danny pulls back, and I slide into the back seat, my heart hammering, catching sight of Amber standing in the doorway, now dressed. Her face twists in displeasure before she can correct it. And for reasons unbeknown to me, it thrills me.

The restaurant is an Italian in the center of Miami, old and traditional. It's also empty when we arrive, and I'm not sure whether that's intentional or whether it's not popular.

We're shown to a table at the very back, near a corridor that leads to the kitchens and restrooms. Six of Danny's men take a table at the front of the restaurant as he pulls a chair out for me and takes my hand, helping me down. "Is it always this quiet?" I ask, looking around the restaurant.

Danny settles to my right of the table for four, unfastening the button of his suit jacket as the waitress places a bottle of water down. "We're early by Italian standards." He orders wine and takes my cloth napkin from my place, flapping it out and laying it across my lap.

"Who are you meeting?" I ask.

"A local businessman."

I falter a second, studying his profile as he pours some water for me. His scar looks especially silver today, and not for the first time I wonder how he came to have the nasty wound. "So you'll be talking business." I accept my water when he hands it to me.

"We will."

"I thought you don't discuss business in the presence of the latest whore you're fucking." I bring my glass to my lips and take a small sip, watching as he holds back a faint smile.

Collecting his own water, he turns in toward me, resting his elbow on the table. "I believe what I said was, I don't discuss business *with* the latest whore I'm fucking." A small sip around another small smile. "And, as you've pointed out yourself, I've not fucked you."

I pout a little, severing our eye contact to have another gaze around the restaurant. There's too much satisfaction in his words, his tone, his eyes. Back at his mansion, I moved in and he pulled away. Then he went to his room and fucked that Amber woman. And what about the fact that he doesn't like me being called a whore?

"Why are you frowning?" he asks, and I look at him, wiping all evidence of said frown away.

"I'm not frowning."

"You were frowning," he persists, nodding to the waitress when she places a bottle of wine down.

"Would you like to try, Mr. Black?" she asks, turning our glasses up the right way.

"No." His answer sends her on her way without her asking if he would like her to pour. Danny returns his attention to me.

"I wasn't frowning," I confirm before he has a chance to challenge me again, because I just know he was going to.

"Okay."

"Okay," I mimic. "And thank you for the clothes."

"You like them?

"Yes, but why?"

"Because I can't very well take you anywhere with no clothes on."

Ah. So it *is* a problem if I parade around naked. "Maybe don't take me. Or maybe you could return me to my rightful owne—" I snap my mouth shut as Danny cocks his head in question.

"Owner," he finishes softly. "Right now, Rose Lillian Cassidy, *I* am your rightful owner."

"How many women do you own?" I ask, bracing myself for the answer.

"Just one." He takes the wine and pours each of us a glass. "You," he adds, in case there was any need for confirmation.

"Then what about Amber?" I wince as soon as I've asked, wondering where on earth that question came from. He makes me behave stupidly, makes me say stupid things. I take refuge in my wine, downing half the glass.

His smile is truly epic, the sparkle in his pale eyes blinding. "Amber is the latest whore I'm fucking."

What's that pain in my stomach? "But you don't care for her?"

"Do I look like the kind of man who would care for a woman?"

No. He looks like the kind of man who doesn't care about anyone at all.

I look up when I hear the door to the restaurant open, seeing a middle-aged man in a black suit and a briefcase stroll in. He nods to Danny's men, his movement jerky and nervous, and then makes a beeline for our table, his short legs working fast.

"Danny." He dumps his briefcase on a chair and takes the other, wiping his brow with a handkerchief as he does.

"Gordon." Danny swirls his wine casually, taking in the flustered mess of a man before us. "This is Rose." He motions to me with his glass, and Gordon nods at me in acknowledgement, though he doesn't make eye contact. One would think he had a nervous disposition, but, then again, he's in the company of Danny Black. "Do you have my money?" Danny asks.

Gordon's eyes jump across the floral tablecloth. "It's just—"

"I'll take that as a no." Danny lifts his glass to his nose and smells, closing his eyes. It's condescending and aloof. And the atmosphere just shifted from slightly uncomfortable to borderline unbearable. I glance over to the table where Danny's men sit, each looking this way. "I lent you a lot of money, Gordon."

"And I'll pay you back." For the first time, he looks at me, and I see the fear in his eyes I expected. "Things haven't gone as planned."

"Yes, I've heard." Danny's glass meets the table and he reclines in his chair, completely relaxed. He's the only one. Why did he bring me here? "I had a pleasant little chat with Spittle."

Gordon's eyes widen, and I look between the two men, my discomfort increasing. *Who's Spittle?*

"Oh, you didn't know we were acquainted?" Danny asks. "Of course not. Why would an FBI agent be in contact with a criminal like me?"

"Let me explain." Gordon wipes his brow once more, his throat swelling with each swallow.

"No need. Spittle gave me a rather comprehensive rundown of your latest endeavor, Gordon." An edge of menace makes it into Danny's tone, though he does a good job of keeping it from his expression, which remains stoic. Leaning forward, he gets closer, forcing Gordon to retreat. "You told me my money was for the extension of your pharmaceuticals business. For medical research."

"Please, Danny."

"Do. You. Have. My. Money?"

A mild shake of his head, a face full of dread. "No."

It happens so fast, I don't have the chance to look away or cover my ears. Danny pulls a gun from his lap and fires, and I jump and then still, watching as Gordon's head jerks back on his neck before he slumps forward in his chair, his upper body crashing onto the table. I stare at the back of Gordon's head, frozen in my seat, watching as blood seeps into the threads of the tablecloth, growing rapidly to form a perfect circle.

"I think we need a new table," Danny says calmly, holding his gun out to the side. Brad takes it, and Ringo, along with another man, whose name I don't know, make quick work of ridding the chair of Gordon's dead body.

Raising his hand and clicking his fingers, Danny summons the waitress and indicates the mess of blood. "Another table, please."

"Of course, Mr. Black. This way, please."

I watch, utterly stunned, as Gordon is carried out the back of the restaurant and the waitress doesn't bat an eyelid. The feel of Danny taking my hand doesn't pull my attention away or have me standing. "Rose?"

I look up at him blankly, and he smiles. It's a mischievous smile, like he could have just stolen my last piece of candy or passed a rude comment. But he's done neither of those things. He just killed a man. In front of me. No warning. No apology. I know he does this often, it's a sport to him, but why in front of me? "Are you trying to make a point?"

His lips push together in silent contemplation. It's as patronizing as could be. "Yes, I am. I'm pointing out to Gordon that he's gone against the terms of our deal and in doing so, there are consequences."

I slowly stand, though I can't deny my legs are wobbly. It's not like I haven't seen endless horrific things in my time. I'm not shocked by what I've seen. I'm shocked that he's brought me along to watch. "But how can he appreciate the consequences?" I ask. "He's fucking dead."

"And I feel much better about that."

"Why? Now you don't get any of your money back."

"Maybe not, but I can guarantee no one will delay a payment to me in the future."

"So you're making an example of him?"

Danny laughs lightly, placing his palm in the small of my back and applying pressure to get me moving to a table near the front. A clean table. One that isn't splattered with blood. "I make an example of *many* people, Rose. But that's not the only reason I killed Gordon." He helps me down to another chair and takes a new bottle of wine, pouring me a fresh glass. Placing it in my hand, he kneels before me, cupping my knees with his palms. I look down at him, still stunned. "I loaned Gordon one million dollars to extend the research program of a cancer drug," he explains gently. "I found out that he used two thirds of that money to pay off his personal debts. To add insult to injury, his personal debts were amassed from sex and drugs. I despise both."

My eyebrows furrow as I stare into eyes that are now soft. "You despise sex?" It just falls out of my mouth, but . . . he despises sex? My only thoughts now are that of a tragic nature, and they don't involve death or bloodshed. Inappropriate, yes, but still. He despises sex? That is going to make my task to extract information extremely tricky. My body is all I have to get what I want. *He despises sex?* But I've seen him hard. I've felt it too. God, is he a monk? A monk who battles his morals each day to not give into that sin called desire? My thoughts are running away with me. Of course he's not a monk. He's just left me not a few hours ago to find relief elsewhere.

A smile breaks across Danny's face, deepening his scar, and the beam of his pearly white teeth snap me out of my mental debate. "I should have chosen my words better." He squeezes my knees. "Gordon was partial to females of a certain variety."

I'm frowning again, and Danny reaches up to my forehead and starts rubbing at the lines, trying to smooth them out. I'm lost. "Females of a certain variety?"

"Girls," he says, the one-word clarification hitting me like a boulder in my stomach. I feel my body convulse, my mind being blitzed with unwanted memories. It's Danny's turn to frown, and I look away, certain that every image in my head is screening in my eyes for him to see. "Then I'm glad he's dead." I need to shut the hell up.

Danny's hands slide up to my thighs beneath my dress, and I look out the corner of my eye to him. My expression should warn him not to ask. And, thankfully, he doesn't. With one knowing flex of his grip on my flesh, he rises and takes a chair opposite me. I notice the waitress go to the restaurant door and unlock it, and so I glance over my shoulder to see the table we just vacated is now freshly laid. You'd never know a murder just happened there.

"So," I say, returning my attention to Danny and taking a much-needed sip of my wine. "Do you kill here often?"

His mouth drops open momentarily, and then I'm left absolutely stunned when he bursts into uncontrollable laughter. Like the falling-apart, belly-clenching, body-spasm kind. He's in pieces across the table from me, eyes watering. I'm not sure what to do with it, so I look across to his men, seeing they're all having a similar reaction to me. Surprise. I shrug at them when they all look at me as if to ask what the hell has gotten into their boss. "Are you okay?"

Danny wipes at his eyes, sighing repeatedly, chuckling more, jerking constantly. "Oh, Rose." Reaching for his wine, he takes a sip around another cute giggle. I'm surprised, yes, but I'm also awed. Danny Black having a laughing fit is irrefutably one of the most amazing things I've ever seen. Five minutes ago, he was a menacing, murdering devil. Now, he's an hysterical, chuckling god. Shaking his head to himself, he lays his forearms on the table, smiling across at me. "I kill here quite often."

My smile can't be held back. "And the owners just accept that?"

"The Italians like me."

"Why?"

"You find it hard to believe that someone could like me?"

"Maybe," I admit.

"I keep them in business." He shrugs. "The local government wanted to kick the owners out when the lease expired five years ago. The restaurant has been here since 1902. I appreciate history and sentiment, so I bought the building."

"And in return, they let you kill people in their establishment?" I ask, and he shrugs once again, passing me a menu.

"Technically, it's *my* establishment."

I accept the folder detailing the cuisine and set my wine down, but not before another quick sip. "Do you enjoy killing people?"

His smile is gone now, and I hold my wine in my mouth for a few seconds before swallowing hard. "I only enjoy killing people who deserve to die."

Oh? "And how do you determine if they deserve to die?"

"I make executive decisions based on what I know to be fact. My instinct helps too."

"Sounds like a well-thought-out process," I muse quietly, scanning the endless pasta choices, all of which sound mouth-watering.

He reaches over and points to a seafood linguine on my menu. "Maybe I should adopt the same protocol when it comes to the women I fuck."

My eyes jump to his, finding a glistening, almost playful stare. I'm reading between the lines. Is that what he's doing with me? Thinking hard? "Maybe you should," I reply, staring him down. "Are you saying you're easy?"

"No, I'm very hard." He shifts in his chair, cocking a cheeky eyebrow. He's *really* playing. Is this his idea of a wind down after a kill? Chill-out time, so to speak? The indignant side of my female mind wants to cast his suggestive move aside. After all, he rejected me a few hours ago. But the sensible side of my female brain, the strongest side, realizes that this is exactly where I need him to be. My foot twitches under the table, wanting to lift and place itself around his groin area. Too much?

"We'll have two of the seafood linguine," Danny says to the waitress when she approaches, not taking his eyes off mine. "And oysters to start."

My lips stretch unstoppably. I like suggestive Danny. I like the playful side of the cold-blooded killer. "You like oysters?" I ask as the waitress leaves us.

"No, hate them. Do you like them?"

"Not really. I never know whether to chew, suck, or swallow."

Lifting his fork, he taps the end of the prongs, his lips pouting. "All except chew. Suck and swallow to your heart's content, but for Christ's sake, don't chew." He peeks up at me, a smirk growing.

Laughter rises up from my toes and my head falls back, my amusement pure and real. I've never heard myself laugh before. Not real laughter. Not the kind that is overwhelming and rich and warming. Laughter sounds good on me. I drop my face and take more wine, unable to stop myself from relishing the sight of Danny's soft features. Soft on hard. Happy on evil. "You're quite nice when you're funny."

He lifts his glass. "Does that mean you like me?"

I tap the side of my glass to his. "I'm not allowed to like you. You're keeping me against my will."

All amusement vanishes from his face, stripping it of the softness. Now, he's serious and regarding me carefully. "Am I?"

I tilt my head, thinking hard before I speak. "Are you telling me I could get up and walk out of here?"

"Do you want to?"

I feel like he's testing me. Playing a game. Had he asked me the very same question this morning, I would have been gone faster than he pulled that gun on Gordon. Now? Now I'm in touch with Nox. That thought has me glancing out of the window, scanning the people in my sights. It's stupid. If he's there, he'll make sure I can't see him. "Do I want to?" I mimic on an exhale, refocusing my attention on my new target. My next move should be considered carefully. Say yes, then he might actually let me leave, and I can't leave, not now. Say no, and that might rouse doubt in him. How could I go from wanting out to wanting in within a few hours? I ponder, weighing up each option while he watches me closely. I place my glass down. "I'd like to leave."

"Then go." He doesn't hesitate a beat.

Uncertainty plagues me as I slowly rise from my chair, feeling all his men watching me too. I've said it now. I have to follow through or risk provoking suspicion. Because, why the hell would I want to stay?

Danny's jaw is so tight it could pop, his body solid and still, his eyes now cold again as he watches me. I round the table and focus on the door, using all my strength to put one foot in front of the other. Fuck, how did I get myself into this? I need to stay. I need information. My head is in chaos, my body moving against my mind's will. The door is close but miles away. But freedom isn't beyond it. It's just an extension of my prison. What's beyond that door is punishment. Consequences. Hell.

I reach the door and take the handle, pulling it open. And then jump when his hand comes over my shoulder and slams it shut again. My heart works its way up to my mouth and wedges itself there. "But if you leave," he whispers against my cheek, forcing me to close my eyes and find air. "You will be dead before you make it to the curbside."

I exhale, feeling all the stress drain from my body. It's crazy, since he's just threatened to kill me, but Danny Black seems to do crazy things to me.

"So I suggest you get your arse back to the table."

I hesitate for a second, just long enough to appear to have thought about it. Does he think I deserve to die? Would he kill me? I actually think not. But when he finds out I'm here to betray him . . .

I move, facing his ominous frame crowding me. After a few seconds of him making sure I see the threat in his eyes—a threat I'm not sure is real—he moves aside and lets me walk back to the table. I retake my seat, and Danny joins me. Any light and easiness that was with us before is a distant memory. Now, I'm faced with the real Danny Black again.

I'm glad. This guy is easier to handle. I'm better equipped to deal with threats. And his sinister side seems far less dangerous to me than the wickedly charming Brit.

I picked my way through the seafood and skipped the oysters altogether. There's been no conversation, just a thick, horrible silence, which leaves room for my mind to go to wild places. He's angry. He told me to leave and didn't think I would. So he threatened to kill me if I did. It's one way to keep a woman, I guess. Or is it his way to keep *me*? Either way, I'm still here, which is good because I need to be.

The restaurant is now full, every table around us occupied with families, couples, friends. Everyone seems to be enjoying their meal and company. Except me. I've spent the past hour avoiding his eyes, all my muscles tense, and my head is beginning to ache from thinking too much. I've felt him watching me throughout as I've silently contemplated what he may be thinking and how the hell I'm going to break him down and get what I need to survive this mess. "Excuse me," I say, dropping my napkin on the table and standing. "I need the ladies'."

Danny clicks his fingers, and the guy who helped Ringo carry Gordon's dead body out of the restaurant motions the way. He's not as ugly as Ringo, but he's a close second. His jet-black hair is too long and secured tightly at the nape of his neck, and his lips look like they're constantly sneering. "Watson will accompany you," Danny says.

I don't question it and start walking, Danny's man following. He holds court outside the ladies' while I use the toilet and check myself in the mirror, giving my cheeks a few smacks to get some color back into them. I look like a ghost—pale, troubled, and stressed.

I get back to the table to find the bill has been paid and Danny is standing, waiting for me. "No dessert, then?" I quip, slipping my purse under my arm.

"We'll get dessert at home."

"I've suddenly lost my sweet tooth," I mutter, ignoring the heat of his hand on the center of my back as he guides me out.

"Who said anything about it being sweet?" Danny stops me just before the door, looking across to a table of three men. "Wait."

Quickly, Brad is beside us, as well as Ringo and Watson. "What's up?" Brad asks, slightly bewildered, his hand moving to underneath his suit jacket.

"An old friend." Danny redirects us toward the table, bringing us to a stop at the edge. Their meal interrupted, they all look up at us. I expect them all to balk in horror by who's approached, but they just look blankly at Danny, and a quick peek out the corner of my eye tells me Danny doesn't seem surprised by this. "Pedro?" Danny says, smiling. It's not a genuine smile. This is a fake smile. A dangerous smile. Like the smile he gave Perry that night in the Aria before he took me.

"Yeah . . ." The guy sets his beer down, clearly thrown. "Sorry, you are?"

"Danny." His hand extends across the table to Pedro, whoever Pedro is, and he takes it and shakes.

"Of course, Danny. Good to see you, my friend." The delight on Pedro's face is as fake as Danny's smile. Pedro doesn't have a clue who Danny is, and something tells me he should. And he should also probably be shitting himself.

"What are you doing in Miami?" Danny asks, keeping his smile fixed.

"Just visiting family. Back to London next week." He stabs at his dish and lifts a piece of ham. "We were told this is the best Italian in Miami."

"It really is." Danny takes my hand and pulls me close, forcing me to snuggle into his side. The three men all take me in, and I smile nervously, as bewildered as they are. "We just finished, and it was sublime." Danny looks down at me. "Wasn't it, sweetheart?"

Don't scowl, don't scowl. "Stunning," I confirm, matching his false beam. "And now we're going home for dessert," I add.

Danny laughs lightly. That's false too. "It's fate, Pedro. You here in Miami, us in the same restaurant."

Pedro nods around a mouthful of pasta. "It was good to see you." That's a polite way of ending a conversation, if ever I've heard one, and I inwardly shake my head at Pedro. Silly man really doesn't know who he's speaking to. But how does Danny know him?

"And you," Danny says quietly, menacingly, and starts to tug me away.

"I don't think he recognized you," I murmur, looking back over my shoulder, seeing Pedro shrugging at his friends, clearly still clueless.

"He soon will." Danny opens the door and takes my neck, directing me onto the sidewalk.

A nasty feeling comes over me as I'm led to the Mercedes and helped into the seat. Danny shuts me in the car and walks off, turning down an alleyway a few yards up the street with his men in tow. My hand reaches for the handle of the door and pulls. It opens. Why would he leave it open? Just leave me here unattended, free to run if I choose?

But I can't run.

I get out and walk to the entrance of the alleyway, finding Brad standing quietly to the side with five more of Danny's men. Danny's eyes are on the concrete under his dress shoes, his fists opening and clenching by his sides. Rage is building, polluting the already stale air in the alley. He looks up and spots me, and he slowly shakes his head. He's telling me to go.

Brad sees me and comes over, trying to usher me away. "What's going on?" I ask.

"Fucked if I know, but he doesn't want you here."

Brad is halted from trying to shift me when Ringo appears, dragging a bewildered-looking Pedro with him. "What the fuck, man?" Pedro yells, stumbling along.

Danny's eyes jump from me to his old friend. And he smiles. Wide, bright . . . and one thousand percent deadly. Brad's spare hand goes to his hip, resting on his gun, ready to draw.

"Pedro," Danny sings, arms extended in front of him, as if inviting him in for a hug. "I'm just so fucking pleased to see you."

Pedro still looks clueless, his worried eyes bouncing between Danny and his men. "What is this?"

Danny steps forward, and Pedro starts to retreat, only getting a few paces before he backs into Ringo. "I'm just gutted you don't remember me." Danny reaches for his cheek and draws a line down his scar. "How could you forget me, Pedro?"

My lungs drain, my hand coming up to my mouth to try and push back my gasp.

"Oh fuck," Brad breathes, confirming what I think I know. He moves in front of me, blocking my view. No. Something sick and disgusting inside me wants to see this. I step to the side, bringing Danny back into my sights. His blue eyes are dancing, pure joy mixed with hatred. The penny has dropped for Pedro. His eyes are wide. His body tense, ready to fight. I pity him.

"We were kids, Danny."

"Just kids." Danny nods, pulling something from his jacket pocket. A switchblade. He releases the blade and inspects it. "I think mine's sharper." He looks up and smirks.

Pedro's hands come up, his body moving back until Ringo shoves him forward. My eyes are burning with the need to blink, yet they refuse, as if scared they're going to miss it. But I'm forced to turn when Pedro's friends crash into the alleyway. They skid to a stop. Take in the scene. Then hold their hands up, backing away when Brad pulls his gun out. "You should have stayed in the restaurant, boys." Brad nods to Ringo, who moves in, along with a few more of Danny's men.

"No, wait," one guy says, tripping up a trash bag as he backs away. The other turns to run and gets no farther than the end of the alleyway. Both men are seized, and I watch in silence as they're held against the wall by guns to their foreheads.

"Come to watch?" Danny asks, pulling my attention back his way.

"I'm sorry," Pedro whimpers.

"I'm not." Danny steps forward calmly and lashes the blade across Pedro's forehead, opening up his flesh with one long slash.

The squeal of pain is piercing, his hands shooting up to his head. Another slash, this one across the back of his hand, slicing through muscles, tendons and probably even bone. His hands drop and Danny's arm moves so fast, it's a mere blur, though accurate, slicing up Pedro's face from his chin, through his nose, his eye, and crossing the gash on his forehead. He drops to his knees, screaming, his bloody hands slipping across his face. And still, I don't take my eyes off the gruesome sight. Danny rounds Pedro's kneeling frame, coming in close behind him. Taking his hair, he yanks his head back so he's forced to look the man who's about to kill him in the eye. Danny's face is a picture of pure evil. Pedro's is a picture of pure fear.

"Please," he sobs.

The smirk that crosses Danny's face multiplies that evil by a million. "I was ten. I didn't cry, and here you are, a grown, dribbling man, begging for it to stop." He bends and gets up close. "I've dreamt of this moment for years. I've imagined all the ways and all the places I'd cut you." Holding him in a headlock, he takes the blade to his cheek and starts carving a circle while Pedro screams and begs for mercy. I don't realize my feet are moving forward until Brad takes hold of my arm, stopping me, and I look up, seeing him shaking his head mildly.

"What is he doing?" I ask, casting my eyes back to Danny, who's now flicking the knife out from the edges of the circle, like he could be adding flashes of color to a painting.

"He's carving the family emblem," Brad answers.

Pedro is quiet now, and when Danny releases him and he falls face-forward to the concrete, I realize he's passed out. Danny wipes the blooded knife across the back of the lifeless man's jeans and slips it into his pocket, pulling his suit jacket in before turning and striding toward us. "Finish it," he says to one of his men as he

passes, collecting me from Brad. "And get rid of the witnesses."
With his hand in the center of my back, he guides me back to the
car. I'm quiet and willing, constantly checking his deadpan face
for any hint of emotion. There's nothing.

Brad gets in the car, along with Ringo, and starts the engine. I
hear a gunshot in the distance as we pull away, and two more just
as we round a corner.

"Feel better?" Brad asks, looking at Danny in the rearview
mirror.

Danny doesn't reply, but he takes my hand from my lap and
puts it in his, holding it as he stares out of the window.

And I wonder what it must feel like to put an end to someone
who has affected you so terribly.

"The person who raped you . . . who was it?"

"You know nothing."

"I know everything."

I couldn't look away from him as he took the power back.
Vengeance. He *does* know. Maybe not everything, but he understands violation. He understands destruction. He knows hate.

And tonight, while he fought hate, I was there silently
cheering him on. And when he sought me, I let him take my hand.
He took comfort from me.

13

DANNY

A weight has lifted from my shoulders. One that has sat there for years and pulled me down, no matter how hard I tried to ignore it. A weight on one's shoulders suggests the presence of a problem. For me, it's always represented a need. A need for vengeance. A need to look that motherfucker in the eye and know in that moment he felt how he wanted me to feel all those years ago. It doesn't matter that I was never scared. It doesn't matter that he couldn't hurt me. The point is, he wanted me to feel scared. He wanted to hurt me. He wanted me to look in the mirror every day and remember how I got my scar. The latter is the only one he achieved, and unlucky for Pedro, it just made his death more brutal.

When we pull up at my mansion, Rose still hasn't murmured a word. I'm thrown that she didn't bolt having been given the perfect opportunity. Instead, she came into the alleyway and watched me calmly carve that man up. And when I was done, I found she was rapt. Riveted. I could almost hear her silently encouraging me. I could sense her . . . peace. For me?

Brad opens the car door for me, and I get out, looking down at my hands. They're stained red, as is my shirt. "I need a shower," I tell him, climbing the steps to the door. "Meet me in the office in half an hour. Have the men there."

I start to pull my tie loose as I ascend the staircase and work the buttons of my shirt as I wander down the corridor. By the time I've made it to my room, I'm bare-chested. Dropping everything I've stripped off into a heap by the door, I kick my shoes off and head for the bathroom, removing my trousers as the water warms.

The spray has never felt so good, and I stand under it for an age, arms limp by my side, head dropped, watching the red-stained water swirling around my feet as the last of that weight is washed from my body and pours down the plughole. His face, the fear, the moment he realized who I was. *Magic.* I close my eyes and see my father's face on the day I met him. The tiny smirk he gave me when I proudly boasted it hadn't hurt when Pedro's side-kick sliced my cheek open. How Pops looked into my eyes and told me the next time I see Pedro, kill him. *Well, I did, Mister. You brought him into my path, and I did what you told me to do.* And it felt good. Right.

Final.

I'm still lost in my thoughts when I hear movement behind me, and I slowly cast my eyes over my shoulder, finding Rose is naked by the door. Her clothes are in a pile at her feet.

I've killed two men today. One quickly and cleanly, the other I made a bloodied mess of. She saw both and hardly twitched. She's fucking immune to my world. She also had a chance to escape in between each kill. Yet she didn't. I don't have the energy right now to try and figure out what that means. The woman is a fucking enigma.

Turning back to face the tile, I continue relishing the water raining down on me. It's still not clear around my feet, red tinging the water. "Come to clean me down?" I ask, feeling her closer. My voice is rough, short, and unfriendly. Not that it will penetrate Rose's thick skin.

I feel her hand slip between my hip and my arm, reaching for the shower cream on the shelf before me. Her cheek meets my shoulder as she stretches, her wet breasts pushing into my back. The temperature in the stall goes from hot to scorching, and I reach for the wall before me, resting some weight on my braced arm.

I hear the lid of the bottle flip, the squirting of some cream into her palm. Her hands. All over me. "I have a washcloth," I tell her.

She says nothing, massaging the soap into my skin. Air is suddenly hard to find. So is my sense. Resisting her is a challenge like no other I've faced. She wants me. That's been proven more than once. I've had a yes, even if she's not actually said it. So what the fuck is stopping me now?

Fear.

I've never been scared, yet this woman frightens me. How resilient she is. How fearless. How she tells me I'm the devil but looks at me like I'm a god. How she isn't scared of me. How fucking beautiful she is. For the first time in my life, I'm fucking scared. Because she could be my ruin. My Achilles heel. My weakness. Everything I've fought for could be wiped out the second I give in to my desire. I never truly appreciated how powerful desire is. I've had the desire to fuck a woman. I've had the desire to kiss one. But never have I had the desire to want to *know* one.

The circling motions of her hands across my back seem to be raising my body's heat a degree with each rotation. My insides are blazing, and when I look down, I see the heat has woken up my dick. The urge to wrap my fist around it is strong. So is the urge to turn and face my biggest nemesis. But no. Stare ahead. Ignore the feel of her working her hands all over my skin. Or, better still, tell her to get the fuck out of my room. Why haven't I done that?

"Get out," I say quietly, turning to face her. Her hands, covered in suds, are now on my pecs, her arresting eyes gazing up into mine. Tiny drops of water hang from a few of her lashes, and one from the end of her perfect nose. Her cheeks are deeply flushed. Her perfect skin perfectly flawless. Her nipples are wide awake. Her body is wonderfully naked and wet.

But . . . no.

"I said, get out."

She backs up, showing rare wariness. But she doesn't speak. Twice in one day she's practically laid herself on a sacrificial stone for me to take. And twice I've denied her. Twice I've forced myself to reject her. Twice I've ignored my body's craving. Twice I've fought my mind's demands to take her.

I won't manage a third time. I need to send her back to Adams, because this game isn't a funny distraction anymore. It's getting dangerous.

I open my mouth, set to order her out of my home, as well as my life, but she turns and walks away before I can muster the words. When she makes it to the door, she looks back at me as she scoops up her clothes. "You should have sliced the asshole's throat too." Then she's gone before she has a chance to see my reaction.

Which is to fall back to the wall and gather myself before I stop her from leaving and fuck the fucking daylights out of her.

"Drink?" Brad asks as I enter my office a while later. It's taken me an hour of standing under the spray to gather myself.

"Do I look like a need one?" I take my chair and run my hand through my wet hair. That move alone answers my question, and

Brad hitching a brow tells me he caught it. Although if he thinks my stressed form has anything to do with me bludgeoning a man tonight, then he's wrong. I won't correct him. "Where's Adams?"

Brad points to my phone, just as it starts to ring on my desk.

"Clever," I quip, answering the call. "You have good news for me, don't you, Perry?"

"How's Rose?" he asks immediately, ignoring my question. Brave man. The fucker has some explaining to do, though pointing out I heard his threat on my life will also point out that I heard his conversation with Rose. Firstly, he can't know that I know he has another *investor*. Secondly, I need him to trust Rose.

"I didn't take your call to talk about your whore," I say calmly, ignoring Brad's poorly concealed look of incredulity at my reference to Rose. "I asked you a question. You have good news, don't you, Perry?"

"Not exactly," he says nervously. "We have a problem."

"I don't like problems. They make me cranky."

"I managed to get the Jepsons on a plane back to the States."

"Good."

"To finalize the deal."

"Good."

"They took off last night."

"Good."

"The plane went down in the Pacific."

"Not good."

"They're dead."

"Really not good." I flick my eyes to Brad who's already on his mobile checking out Perry's story. Someone up there seriously doesn't want me to have that marina. "So who's in charge of the estate?"

"Their son."

"Good. Then have him sign."

"It's not that simple."

"Don't piss me off, Perry," I warn. The thrill of my recent kill is disappearing by the second. "Why?"

"Well, first off, he was on the private jet too. He's alive, but he's in a coma. Second, even if he makes it, he's ten years old and the estate is held in a trust until he's twenty-one." The second Perry finishes, Brad gives me the nod. His story checks out.

"Motherfucking God," I breathe, landing Brad with disbelieving eyes. It's one fucking disaster after another. "Then let's hope he doesn't make it," I say without thought, earning a stunned look from Brad that I ignore. "I'll check in again soon." I'm about to hang up when I hear Perry blurt my name, panicked. "Rose is surviving," I tell him before he can ask. "Just."

"What have you done to her, Danny?" He's between anger and emotion. It's quite sweet. Shame she doesn't feel the same way about him.

"Nothing she didn't love *and* beg for."

He inhales, the sound whooshing down the line. "What happens if the Jepson kid makes it?"

I nod toward the cabinet across the office, deciding I do need that drink. Ringo has one in my hand quickly, ice and all. "Then you'd better get creative, because you're not getting Rose back until I get that marina, and even if I do release her, you won't get to indulge in her perfect pussy again because you'll be dead." I hang up and down my drink in one fell swoop, gasping in appreciation. "I want every detail from the crash investigation."

"Got it," Brad confirms. "Do you think he had anything to do with Vegas?" he asks as I study the side of the crystal tumbler.

I keep coming back to desperation. Adams is in the shit, would do anything to get himself out smelling of roses. But with Rose in the line of fire? No, not Adams, but that doesn't mean his contact wouldn't. Perry's up to his neck, caught between me and .
. . who? I don't know, but he's a brave fucker. And a light

reminder to Perry that I'm the greater of two evils won't be missed. "Send Adams her little finger."

Watson, the sadistic bastard, has his knife out before I've even registered my own words, and I momentarily frown, wondering what the fuck he's doing. "You sure about that, boss?" Brad must have caught my confusion, his probing eyes watching me across the table.

"Yes, I'm sure." I stand and approach Watson, taking the knife from him. "But I get the honor." I leave the office, feeling Brad's worried stare rooted to my back, and pace through my mansion, spinning the blade in my grasp as I go. What better way to prove to anyone, including myself, that she means nothing to me?

My breathing is labored as I pause outside her door, my hand on the knob. My palm's sweaty. My heart is thumping. My fucking head could explode. *Just do it.* If anything, it'll truly make her hate me. It'll halt these insane moments of rhapsody that are quickly followed by reality. It'll show her that she's here for one reason alone. I push my way into her room, determined, the knife poised . . . and freeze when I find her sitting on the edge of the bed in her underwear, a razor blade plunged into her forearm.

My head that was feeling like it *could* explode, goes right on ahead and detonates. I see red. Rage sails through my body like fucking wildfire, unstoppable and damaging. Like nothing I've felt before.

She finds me vibrating by the door and quickly gets up, running to the bathroom. I'm in pursuit quickly, flying after her. She goes to slam the door in my face, but it hits my foot and bounces back open. Fucking hell, I feel out of control. She walks cautiously back, a fear in her eyes that I've not seen before. And I'm not surprised, because I must look beyond my usual murderous self.

Her hands go behind her back, resting on the vanity unit.

"Don't you know how to knock?" she murmurs, her pathetic question doing nothing but turning my already burning blood into rivers of lava in my veins.

I can't even speak. All of my focus is centered on helping me to breathe through my fury. The drops of blood hitting the tile floor are deafening. I stalk forward, my whole face aching with the tenseness of my tight jaw. She can't even look me in the eye. Her head's dropped, focusing on anything except the psycho slowly closing in on her.

When I make it to her, I push my front to hers, if only so she can feel how madly my heart is pumping. "Give me your hand," I grate, looking down at her. She shakes her head, refusing to look up at me. "Give. Me. Your. Fucking. Hand." Another shake of her head, and further defiance by keeping her face down. I seize her jaw, squeezing hard, probably too hard. I know she feels it because she flinches, trying to pull away. That's a novelty. She *actually* feels something. Without moving, she fights me with all she has, pulling against my pushing, but I win. She's heaving by the time I get her eyes, the blue pits to her soul overflowing with anger. "Give me your hand, Rose."

"Fuck you, Danny," she mumbles through her squeezed lips.

I reach behind her and grab her hand, squeezing it tightly into a fist as I pull her arm around her front. Now, she doesn't flinch. She doesn't cry out. She doesn't try to pull away. I look down and see blood seeping out the cracks between her clenched fingers, and I damn myself for feeling brutal and cruel.

I pry her hand open until I'm staring down at the razor blade, the metal glistening with blood. Her blood. The only blood I've ever seen and wished I hadn't. I breathe in, trying to gather the will to speak. I can't. This woman, at every motherfucking turn, strips me of normal capabilities. I tip her hand, sending the blade to the marble floor with a little ping. It's a ludicrously pretty sound for something so ugly and damaging. Taking in oxygen, I turn her arm over until I have her forearm, where a neat slice stretches across her perfect skin, blood bubbling from the opening on her flesh. It's only now I see them. Maybe a dozen white lines marring her tan skin. All neat. All clean. All done on purpose. I look up into her eyes, eyes that are welling. Not because she's hurt. Not because she regrets hurting herself. But because I've found her doing it. I've found a weakness. Or it could be a strength. It could be her way of dealing with things. But dealing with what? The unknown is a true killer. It physically hurts me. It's slowly driving me mad, and I'm astounded by my lack of ability to know what to do. I'm fucking stumped. Instinct is all I have, and before I register my moves, I've stepped back, away from her, and placed the blade I took from Watson on my forearm.

Her eyes snap from the knife to me. "Tell me why," I demand, the blade resting on my skin.

She shakes her head.

So I draw the knife slowly across my arm, opening the flesh, and her mouth falls open as blood trickles toward my wrist. "Tell me why," I repeat.

Another shake of her head.

So I move the blade and drag it through my flesh again, parallel to the first slice. "Tell me why."

She swallows, her eyes wide and haunted. And another shake of her head.

This time, I yank the knife violently, and the collection of blood from my three wounds gathers and swells and starts dripping to the floor. "Tell me why," I say again calmly, setting the knife on a fresh piece of my arm.

"No," she says, eyes batting back and forth between my face and my arm.

I slash once more, my arm now drenched, pouring with blood. "Tell me why."

"Danny, please."

My jaw's going to snap, the muscles becoming tighter with each refusal she gives me. Another cut.

"Danny," she whimpers.

Another cut. "I'll keep going, Rose," I promise. "This doesn't hurt me." I cut myself another two times until she lunges forward and seizes the knife, tossing it to the floor and grabbing my arm. I make to retrieve it, not taking her horror as anything more than that. She still won't tell me. Which means my arm is going to look like a patchwork fucking quilt very soon.

"No!" She kicks the blade away, out of my reach, and yanks my body upright.

"Talk," I grate as she grabs a towel and wraps my arm, applying pressure, looking uptight and stressed. She has nothing on me.

"I haven't done it for years." She takes her hands away and moves back, and I can see her intention to walk away, her gaze passing back and forth between my arm and the door. No. I block the doorway and yank the towel off.

Looking up at me, she shakes her head mildly again, as if she thinks I'll accept her silent plea for immunity.

"So why now?" I kick the door closed and rest my back against it.

"Why do you care?"

Her question throws me. It's a damn fucking fine question, one I hadn't asked myself. "I don't."

She laughs, quietly and disbelievingly, and I can't blame her. "You don't care?"

"I care that you're alive for me to use as bait."

"Liar," she whispers, stepping forward. "You're harboring so many demons and—"

"Now you're one of them," I say, and she recoils. I look away, unable to face the questions in her eyes.

"Am I?"

I stare at the blood-soaked towel on the floor and dip, scooping it up and tossing it in the shower stall. "You are a demon, Rose." I glance up at her and reach back for the door handle. "I don't care why you're hurting yourself. I care that you're doing it in my home. I don't care that you're drawing blood. I care that you're spilling it all over my fucking carpet. I don't care if you want to kill yourself. I care that it'll fuck up my plans if you do." I yank the door open, watching her nostrils flare with hatred. "I don't care about you." I'm so fucking dumb, I deserve a medal for supreme stupidity. I look down at my slashed arm and close my eyes. Instinct screwed me over this time.

I make to turn but get stopped by the feel of her hand on my hip. I look down and see her bloody palm spread on the waist of my jeans. "What if I told you that I care about you?"

"I'd say you are either stupid or suicidal."

"Maybe I'm both."

"Maybe I don't give a fuck." I try to shake her off, but she stands firm, moving in front of me until our chests are compressed, her bra-covered breasts pushed into my T-shirt. I don't have much willpower left.

"I call bullshit." She slides her hand onto my shoulder. "I say you're scared."

"Of what?"

"Me."

I can't argue with that. But I should. "I've never been scared of anything."

"Me neither. Not for a long time." She reaches up on her tiptoes and pushes her mouth to my cheek. I swear, every time her mouth touches a part of me, a little bit of something good sinks into me. "Until you."

My head loses all strength, dropping until my mouth meets her bare shoulder. She still smells of me. I can hear my father bellowing at me, reminding me of my obligations and of the weakness women present. He nearly fell into that trap once. "You're not scared of me," I point out. "And that's what scares me." Breaking our contact, I move away. The simple step is harder than I've ever found it to end a man's life.

Finding some vigor, I bend and collect the razor blade from the floor, wrapping it in tissue and flushing it down the toilet. Then I grab a towel and wrap her arm in it, keeping my eyes on my task, feeling her watching me. "Be wise, Rose," I say, collecting the knife, turning, and leaving the bathroom. "I'll have a doctor come sort those cuts." I ignore the pull trying to take me back and virtually throw myself out her bedroom door.

I bump into Brad, and his eyes fall to my arm. Any normal man would assume she'd turned things around and attacked me. But it's Brad.

"You need stiches," he says, grimacing at my mess of an arm.

"And my head checked," I tell him as I head to the office. I don't know what that woman's game is. I don't know why she's not scared of me. And I know I shouldn't want to know. But why the fuck did she take a blade to her arm? *It wasn't a suicide attempt.* She wasn't trying to escape me.

Was she punishing herself?

I can't shove aside my desire for knowledge. It's almost as powerful as my desire for her.

Almost?

Nowhere near.

Either way, I'm fucked.

14

ROSE

The feeling of guilt is twisting my head. My sense of regret is turning my stomach. If I didn't know better, I would think Danny's suspicious of me. Being around him is getting harder by the hour. I need to get out of here before I lose my mind. Seducing him should be easy. Especially given I can see how much he wants me. I've never failed to get what I want from a man. It's always been clean and easy. This time, though, it's messy and hard. I've been told what I need to do, but I'm meeting resistance. I would say he's the sensible of the two of us. But he's not the one straddling life and death. I don't want to trick him into confiding in me. I don't want to share his secrets. It's beyond me why, but I don't want to betray him. Every time I think about it, my stomach flips, and not because I realize he'll kill me if he finds out. It's just . . . I don't know. Maybe it's a warped goodness in him I see glimmers of. Or maybe I've finally lost my mind.

Yet I have no choice. My life depends on it, and so does my son's. As long as I play ball, my boy retains his happiness and freedom. As long as I do as I'm told, I get drip-fed pictures of him growing up. I get proof that he's alive. That he's happy and safe from the debased world I'm in. It's never been a difficult decision to play ball.

Until now.

Everything about this feels wrong, and it has nothing to do with Danny being a murdering bast—

"Asshole," I say to myself as I lie on the lounge chair on the terrace. I look down at my bandaged arm, and for the first time, I regret hurting myself. Not because I didn't get that release of pressure I so desperately needed, but because he caught me doing it. He saw me in a moment of weakness, and I hate that. But more than that, I hate his reaction. Why? Why would he do that to himself? And what happens now?

I swallow and close my eyes, feeling exhausted. I didn't sleep one wink last night, asking myself those questions. Why? What now? I see glimmers of a man somewhere close to human. Then flashes of a man somewhere close to a monster. I see a lightness in his eyes when we've verbally sparred. Then blackness when those moments abruptly end. He is a paradox.

I sigh and try to enjoy the sun on my skin, trying to clear my mind of those lingering questions before they drive me mad. Or am I already there? Now, this moment, alone with the bright, warm sun, would usually be something I'd seize with everything I have and make the most of. Quiet is a rarity in my world. Alone time even rarer. Except I'm not alone and it's not quiet, not with my mind screaming at me, my questions and fears running circles in my brain. "Goddamn it," I whisper, opening my eyes and staring at the clouds. They roll through the blue sky, free and wild. There's nothing but open air, endless space.

But I'm still a prisoner. Whether with Danny, Nox, or Perry, I'm trapped.

Voices from the garden below drift up to the terrace, and I

prop myself up on my elbows, craning my neck to see through the glass panels. Danny's down there with Brad, looking like an evil god post-workout in a pair of sweatpants, his T-shirt draped around his neck. I curl my lip in disgust. Then my eyes fall to his arm, seeing it wrapped like mine.

"It's all offloaded and checked," Brad tells him, and I watch closely, seeing him scrolling through his phone. "It's all in the containers at the boatyard ready for the exchange."

Danny dips and ties the laces of one sneaker, looking up at Brad. "We'll go to the boatyard later this evening so I can check the consignment before the exchange with the Russians."

I fall back to the lounge chair when Danny rises, his head turning toward the terrace. I remain still, holding my breath.

"I need to let off some steam," I hear him say, the collective sounds of their feet crunching the graveled path muffling their voices.

But I still hear Brad's reply. "Call Amber, for fuck's sake."

"I will," Danny replies.

"Of course you will," I whisper to myself, dropping my head to the side to look through the glass of the panel that separates this terrace from his. And I'll be expected to remain in here, listening to him letting off some steam? *No.* I have to get something for Nox, and I have to do it fast. I can't bear this place, can't bear *him* any longer. He's going to the boatyard this evening. Will all his men go too? Either way, I need to get into his office.

Then, I'm out of here.

I get up and head for the bathroom, feeling around the back of the drawer for the cell phone. I turn it on and punch out a quick message to Nox.

> A consignment arrived at his boatyard. He's going there this evening to check it. I'll get into his office once he's left.

I click send and replace the phone, then wrap my arm and take a shower, leaving my room before the sounds of Danny letting off steam start to torment me.

By five o'clock, I'm restless again. I roamed the garden, wandered the house, and when I knew it would be safe to return to my room, I did just that. All signs of mine and Danny's massacre are gone. At least, the blood is. The wounds, especially his, will take weeks to heal.

I know Danny's not left for the boatyard yet because I've been watching Brad play tennis from my terrace for a few hours now, and he wouldn't go anywhere without Brad. But then Brad leaves the court, and I dash into my room. My ear is soon pushed up against the wood of the door, listening for any sign that Danny's leaving his mansion.

I hear footsteps, a soft padding of feet on the plush carpet outside my room. *Shit*. I dart across to the bed, falling to my back and closing my eyes. How juvenile. But still, no contact. No engagement. I hear the door open, followed by an impatient grunt.

"Up," Danny orders, and my face muscles strain with the need to curl a lip, or at the very least throw a filthy look at the asshole. But I remain still and quiet, hoping he'll fuck off and leave me alone.

I'm outraged when he grabs my arm and shakes me. "Up," he snaps curtly, manhandling me to my feet. *What the hell?*

"Get your fucking hands off me," I yell, not at all sleepily, tossing my elbow out to the side in an attempt to shrug him off, but his face is low and . . .

Crack.

My bony elbow collides with his nose, and it seems to explode, blood pouring over his lips. Danny flinches and blinks rapidly, caught off guard, his eyes watering madly in an instant.

"Motherfucker," he breathes, taking his hand to his nose before inspecting it. It's a blood-stained mess. Oh shit. He looks like he's going to launch me into outer space with his fist, his knuckles going white with the force of his clenched hands. Then his bloody nose starts pouring all over the carpet, and he curses, holding it while he paces to the bathroom. For some strange reason, I follow him, finding him bent over the sink, big fat drops of blood hitting the porcelain in consistent light thuds, splashing up the shiny white enamel.

I have no idea what possesses me. No idea at all. "Did that hurt?"

His eyes lift and look at me in the reflection, his face blank. It did hurt. I can tell. He was surprised, and his watery eyes suggest pain. "No." His lips don't even move, his snappy answer delivered through clenched teeth.

I can't help it. My cheeks start to pull, and as hard as I try, my smirk can't be held back. I'm forced to reach up and pinch my nose, feeling laughter rising from my toes. I mustn't laugh. He'll likely strangle me if I laugh.

His shoulders rise, he wipes his nose roughly, and he slowly turns to face me, not in the least bit impressed. He's twitching violently, and I just know it's because he doesn't know what to do. Well, actually, he does. Kill me. But he won't. I'm no good to him dead.

I rein myself in and step back, seeing his muscles engaging. My face straightens quickly, my own muscles becoming alert, ready to fight.

His nose is still dripping. His jaw solid. His eyes wild. Then he's coming at me fast, and I try desperately to locate the shield that always keeps me safe, that protects me from my life—from the pain, the grief, the plain awful. His arm draws back as he approaches. My shield can't be found. I close my eyes and brace myself for it.

"Arhhhhh," I scream, flying into the air and landing on something hard. I'm disorientated, brushing my hair out of my face as I bounce up and down. No sooner have I figured out that he's flung me onto his shoulder, I'm in the air again, this time landing with a thud on something soft. The bed?

My ankle is seized, and I'm yanked to the edge where he stands. He still looks like a psychopathic killer, but that doesn't stop me from trying to kick him. He catches my other ankle too, and I wriggle and buck like a mad woman, vehemently trying to fight him off. Then in a quick move, he crosses his arms, therefore my legs too, and I'm spun onto my front, his hand on the back of my neck, applying pressure in a small spot that effectively paralyses me. I actually cannot move, my cheek squished into the pillow.

His face appears, his knee in my back, his entire body holding me in place, but it's his touch on my neck keeping me still. He looks like he's been ripping apart a fresh kill, his nose smeared with fresh blood, more still dripping, making a mess of the bed sheets. "I want to fucking kill you." He brings his face down, closer, allowing me to see the murder etched across it.

What kind of woman ever smirked at such a threat? And from a man like Danny Black? Me. That's who. I'm certifiably in-fucking-sane. "Then kill me," I breathe. "And make it slow and painful."

"What the hell are you?" He's completely stunned.

"I'm a heartbeat," I reply simply, staring at him. "I'm nothing, Danny Black. And you are God." His hold on my neck flexes, but he doesn't release me. He just gazes at me while he continues to pour blood all over the place, including me. "You're going to ruin the bed," I whisper.

"Fuck the bed."

"You're going to ruin my clothes."

"Fuck the clothes."

"You're going to ruin *me*." I hold my breath and watch as he lets my statement and its meaning sink in. I know it has when he blinks rapidly, as if pulling himself from a daze. He releases me, being quite gentlemanly about it, and pulls me up, before grabbing a pillow and pulling off the cover, wiping his nose.

"You can't ruin something that's already broken, Rose." His words are soft, not cutting, but they still hurt. And he's wrong. He could destroy me completely. But I don't challenge him.

Pointing to the wardrobe, Danny takes backward steps toward the door. "Get ready. We're going out."

"Where?"

"My boatyard." He opens the door and leaves, and I remain where I am, my mind racing. He's taking me? I hurry to the bathroom, flipping the shower on. Then I stare at the drawer for an age, torn. I decide against it. It's not like I have anything to tell him, anyway.

You can't ruin something that's already broken, Rose.

He just has no idea how broken I actually am.

Jeans and a sweater. It seems like a suitable wardrobe choice for a boatyard. The jeans are Armani, low-rise, and hug my ass tightly, and the gray sweater has the Union Jack on it. Very . . . British. Like him. I can only imagine Esther is responsible for my new wardrobe. Who else?

I slip my feet into some tennis shoes and pull my hair into a ponytail as I make my way downstairs, and I nearly tumble down the damn things when I spot him. In a baseball cap. Danny Black in a baseball cap? It's sounds so very wrong, but it's looks *very* right. He's in jeans too; his are an easy-fit as oppose to my skinny things, and he's also wearing a sweater. His is navy, emblazoned with the Union Jack too. He looks casual. Relaxed. It suits him. I discreetly pull my British sweater away from my chest to circulate some air as I approach him, my feet careful on the marble steps. I can't help but wonder if the flag on the front of my sweater, the sweater he had put in my wardrobe, is The Brit making a point. But what point? This is all very . . . couplesy.

I can see Danny's subtly taking me in as Brad talks to him, pointing at his slightly swollen nose. When I'm close enough, Danny clasps the top of my arm, just above the bandage under my sweater, and leads me out to the car. "I can tell this is going to be a romantic date," I quip, falling to the back seat once he's opened the door for me.

He ignores me, gets in, going straight to his phone, and that's where he stays, engrossed in the screen the entire way.

The sea smells good. The breeze feels good. Loose strands of my hair whipping my face feels good. I stand by the car, looking back at the dirt road that led us down to this little haven. A station wagon pulls up behind us, a trailer hooked to the back. And on it, a jet ski. A surfer type jumps out and starts toward one of the huge containers set to the left. I frown, continuing to take in the boatyard. The name suggests a few rickety sheds, maybe a jetty and a few old boats thrown into the mix. But there's none of that. A huge log cabin is by the shore with a raised decking area that juts out over the water, supported by stilts. There are endless huge metal containers, and a sandy shore leading to the water. We're in a cute cove. It's all really very pretty and idyllic . . . if it wasn't for the noise.

I cast my eyes across the water and see jet skis. Lots of them, zooming across the sea, circling, spraying water when they sharply turn. Endless jet skis bob on the water on the shore, and endless people in wetsuits are milling around.

"Coming through," a man shouts, hanging out his truck window as he reverses his trailer down to the water. I move aside and get an endearing wink. "Come for lessons?" he asks as he rolls past.

"She's with me." Danny moves in and takes my hand, pulling me toward the cabin.

"Hey, Danny." The guy smacks the side of his truck, a cheerful smile on his face. "It's busy out there today."

"European competition season is on the way," Danny says, only further deepening my frown.

The guy's trailer hits the water and a few more men in wetsuits start unstrapping the jet ski from the back. "I'm confused," I admit as we approach the wooden steps of the cabin.

"What are you confused about, Rose?"

"This place. It's yours?"

"Everything except the land it's on."

We enter the cabin, and I come to a stop in the doorway, unable to grasp what's going on. There's a massive café to the right, a shop stocking all things water sports to the left, changing rooms up ahead. And virtually everyone is wearing wetsuits. "Jet skis," I say to myself as Danny passes me, heading for the serving counter of the café.

"Yes, jet skis." He looks back as he pulls his phone from his pocket. "Drink?"

I join him and scan the refrigerator. "A coconut water, please."

Danny orders, while I spend more time absorbing the space. My presence hasn't gone unnoticed, many people—men and women—looking this way. He hands me a carton and I'm left to follow him out onto the decked terrace looking over the water. It's stunning. But . . . "Jet skis?"

Pulling out a chair for each of us at a table at the far side, right by the railings, we sit, and Danny spends a while gazing out across the water. The noise is loud but bearable. "I deal in them," he tells me without looking at me, unscrewing the cap off his water.

He deals in jet skis? I'm at a loss. The consignment, the deal, the handover. It's for jet skis?

"This part of the bay is a prime location. Still waters, good depth, plenty of space." He takes a swig and leans back in his chair, pulling off his baseball cap. "The top competitors train and practice here."

"Oh." It's all I have.

"We offer lessons, sell the equipment, and import the top performing machines for sale."

I laugh under my breath. The cold-blooded killer deals in jet skis. With my coconut water at my lips, I look across the water, squinting from the sharp sparkles reflecting back at me from the low sun. "Is that another boatyard?" I ask, pointing to the other side of the bay. I can just make out a ramshackle of a marina in the distance.

"That's Byron's Reach." Danny sounds thoughtful as he tells me. "I'm in the process of buying it."

Ah. So that's the marina he wants. "Why?"

"They're developing this land soon. We have to be out in a few weeks."

"Well, what about this building? And the beach and this deck?"

"I'll rebuild it all across there." He cocks his head, indicating over there. "It's a much better location. Bigger. More potential. More secluded."

"This is pretty perfect." I shrug, thinking it's a shame that all of this will no longer be here soon. "It'll take you months to rebuild all of this. Can't you keep this place while you build?"

"Sadly not." Danny stands, downing the rest of his water before setting his empty bottle on the table. "Had I secured Byron's Reach a month ago like I'd hoped, then maybe. Unfortunately, buying it hasn't been as smooth as it should be."

"Yes, I heard." I smile cheekily when he raises his eyebrows.

"But just think, had you gotten your marina easily, we wouldn't be having all this fun together."

Danny smiles on a shake of his head. "And what a travesty that would be," he muses, flipping his baseball cap on and pulling his phone out when it rings. "I have a few things to sort out. Don't go far."

I roll my eyes and kick my feet up on a chair, happy to sit here and smell the water, breathe in the fresh air, and soak up the sun. I shouldn't enjoy it, but in my world, a moment's peace, any moment I can grab, should be cherished.

But . . . jet skis?

A while later, the noises are no more, the sun is beginning to set, and it's even more beautiful out there, the water calm and still. I stare across the sea, an odd sense of tranquility blazing through me. Despite everything, I've sat here this whole time without that lingering familiar sense of foreboding. I've not been on the edge of my seat. I've not dreaded this moment ending or being disturbed by my real life. It defies reason, since I'm still very much a prisoner, but . . . why? I shouldn't be feeling peaceful. I should be more afraid than ever. *It's him, you fool. He's as fucked up as you, and you find comfort in that.*

I look over my shoulder to see the café is now empty, and a quick scope of the shore below tells me that's empty too. I drop my feet off the chair and stand, groaning as I stretch my muscles. God, that feels amazing.

As I wander through the cabin, I browse the rails of wetsuits, as well as the glass cabinets that are full of goggles, sunglasses, and sports watches. At the back of the shop, I spy a workshop, where a few jet skis are in parts. He fixes them too. What a wonderful notion. To be fixed. Repaired. To be made as good as new.

Making my way out to the front, I scan the deserted space. No one. Nothing. It's like a ghost town. I must have been relishing the sun and peace for longer than I thought. I take the steps and follow my feet to where his car was parked. It's still there. No Danny. No *anyone*, in fact.

I'm about to call out a hello when I hear a loud clatter from one of the containers. My spine straightens, and I follow the sound of voices. Danny's and Brad's voices. As I creep closer, I hear Ringo too. All of them in a big metal container? Then I remember: the consignment arrived. They'll be checking the order.

"All looks good, yeah?" Brad says.

"Yeah," Danny replies. "Very good."

I edge around a corner and stop abruptly in my tracks on a lumpy swallow, not sure I'm seeing right. Danny's holding a machine gun in his hand, inspecting it closely, as Ringo pulls out another, this one a rifle, from underneath a jet ski, handing Danny that one too. Guns? *Oh my God.* I cast my eyes across the endless jet skis, counting twenty of the big machines in total. Are they all packed with guns? "Get them all loaded back inside," Danny orders, handing the gun back to Ringo. "I want them spread across all the containers."

I quickly back up before I'm spotted. Guns?

"Who's watching the girl?" Danny asks, and I freeze, listening.

"I thought you was," Ringo grunts.

There's a bang, the sound of a container door shutting and then the slide of a big metal bolt engaging. "I can't watch the girl *and* count fucking bullets."

I'm moving quickly, tiptoeing across the ground as quietly and as quickly as I can, practically throwing myself up the steps to the cabin. I've never moved so fast in my life. I land in the chair that Danny put me in earlier, and just about get my breathing stable and my feet up when I hear urgent thumping footsteps coming through the café.

I look back as he falls through the doors onto the decking, his face a little red, his breathing shot. He thought I'd be gone.

"Okay?" I ask, visions of machine guns rolling through my mind. Not just machine guns, either. Bullets, rifles, grenades, and all kinds of other weaponry, all hidden in the bottoms of jet skis. My brain is currently an arsenal fit to kick off a world war. This place, it's a cover. That's all. I should laugh at myself for stating the obvious. Of course it's a cover. I knew that. Danny Black owns it, for God's sake.

His whole upper body rolls and relaxes, his hand coming up to the doorjamb to support him as he finds breath to talk. "Yeah," he exhales, looking over his shoulder. I hear the stampede of more steps and see Danny shake his head, silently telling his charging men the panic is over. He's found me.

"What's going on?" I ask, acting totally dumb.

He sighs and comes forward, gazing down the length on my legs stretched out before me on the chair. "You've been here the whole time." It's not posed as a question, more of a statement. Like he's telling himself.

"It's peaceful," I say without thought. "Besides, you told me not to go anywhere."

He takes my feet and lifts them, sitting on the chair and resting them back on his lap. He's thinking. What's he thinking? "And you listened to me?"

I nibble on my lip, unable to read the way he's looking at me. It's almost . . . pensive. "You'd find me and kill me," I whisper.

"Yes, I would." His eyes narrow on me, scrutinizing my reaction. I have no reaction. Yeah, he'd find me, but he wouldn't kill me.

"Then I'm sensible, yes?"

"Not obedient?"

My smile is unstoppable. "Never."

And so is Danny's. "Ever been on a jet ski?"

I slowly shake my head.

"Want to?"

No, not if I'll be riding on something harboring enough grenades to destroy Miami. Thank you very much. "I don't think it's my thing."

"Fraidy cat," he says quietly, starting to stroke over my shins. Denim is thick material. Not thick enough. I subtly shift in my chair and pull my feet down off his lap, but he puts them right back and continues with his torturous strokes, smiling innocently at his hands. Innocent? Nothing Danny Black does is innocent. Everything is thought out, that much has become glaringly obvious.

"I'm not a fraidy cat," I whisper.

Looking up at me, he loosens his smile, making it more of a cheeky grin. "Then prove it."

Prove it? Haven't I proved it enough? "By riding a jet ski?" I ask, and he nods. "I wouldn't know how to."

"You don't need to know how. You'll be with me."

Stuck to his back? No. I don't think so. "Thanks, but I'll respectfully decline."

"Respectfully?" He laughs, finally putting my feet back on the ground. "What are you afraid of?"

A grenade exploding underneath me.

Actually, no. *I'm more afraid of you.*

My eyes climb his body as he rises and looms over me, holding out his hand. "I'll take care of you."

Those words, those simple words, are like tempting a dehydrated dog with water. My hand's in his before I've thought about it, and my body is stuck to him a second later, his tug pulling me up smoothly and quickly. My heart is going crazy in my chest, and I know he's felt it because he glances down between our pressed bodies and smiles to himself. "You *are* scared." Eyes back to mine, his smile falls. "But not of jet skis. And not of me."

"I am scared of you."

"Not in the normal sense of the word, Rose." His hand reaches for my cheek and caresses it, before sliding his palm onto my nape and massaging gently. Again, he's right. I'm not afraid of his violent nature, his business, or his reputation. I'm scared of the rush of blood to my head when he touches me. I'm scared of my kicking heart when I look into his insanely blue eyes. I'm scared of the backward sense of security I feel being his prisoner. I'm scared that he clouds my purpose. I'm scared that I hate him for all the wrong reasons. Not because he's callous and cruel. Not because he says wicked things. But because I know for me, it's all a front. I close my eyes and sink into his touch. "Feel good?" he whispers.

I hum and let him massage away . . . everything. My thoughts, my tension. I'm putty in his hands. It's only when a small moan slips free that I open my eyes. And as soon as I meet the intensity of his stare, I look away.

But I caught the look of knowing in his gaze. And the satisfaction. "Come," he orders softly.

We walk through the café, where his men now all sit with beers in their hands, and into the shop. Danny pulls down a black and pink wetsuit and leads me into the men's changing room. "Put this on."

I stall, looking at his outstretched hand. "This is the men's changing room."

His arm drops, a flurry of mild amusement creasing his face. "So *now* you're shy?"

"I'm not shy." I snatch it from him and proceed to strip down until I'm in my underwear, and he smiles the whole time, collecting his own wetsuit from a nearby locker and undressing himself. Every godforsaken muscle on his torso undulates as he pulls his sweater up over his head, revealing the bandage. He shouldn't get his wounds wet. "Your arm," I say, a misplaced sense of concern coming over me.

"*Your* arm," he counters, holding up some protective bags and moving in. He wraps my arm carefully to protect it from the water before taking care of his own wounds. His bandage is stained, the blood having seeped through, and I turn away feeling . . . guilty. I did that. His wounds are because of me.

I step into the wetsuit, reaching behind me for the cord that'll get the zip up.

"Here." He moves in, and I move away.

"I've got it," I say, feeling around, finding nothing.

My hand is knocked away and the zip dragged up my back slowly. "All done," he murmurs, taking my ponytail and pulling the ends out of the neck. I shudder and take one cool step back into my personal space, and when I turn around, his wetsuit is only pulled up to his waist. *Good God.*

"How long have you rode jet skis?" I ask, blinking back my wonder as I gather up my pile of clothes and set them on a nearby bench. *Do you ride them? Drive them?*

"Since my father built this place fifteen years ago."

"Your father built it?"

"Yes." He walks away, and I follow, my eyes rooted to the wide expanse of his bare shoulders.

"Aren't you sad to be leaving it then?" I ask, watching him toss his baseball cap on the shop counter and replace it with some wraparound shades on his head.

"It's business. No smart man gets sentimental over business." He makes sure I'm in his sights as he articulates every word clearly.

Of course. I'm business. "And you sell all these?" I motion to the line of shiny new jet skis in the store.

"I do." He goes to a sliding metal door and takes the handle with both hands, leaning back to pull it across. More rippling muscles. I force myself to focus on them and not on his arm.

"And which jet ski will we be on?" I turn away, trying to sound nonchalant, when on the inside I'm wondering what on earth I'll do if he leads me to the container full of loaded jet skis.

"One of these." He points into the room he's just revealed, and I peek inside. There are two jet skis strapped to trailers, both sparkling clean, both huge, and both black. Completely black, except for the gray writing down one side that says SEA-DOO. Every other jet ski I've seen today has been mostly colorful. "This one is mine." He slides open another door, and Brad pulls up in an old Jeep. "And that one was my father's." He nods to the other jet ski.

"Your dad rode a jet ski?" I blurt without thought, and he smiles, starting to hook up the trailer to the jeep.

"Before he was ill, yes."

I wander down the side of his dad's jet ski, my hand stroking the black paintwork. I crouch when I reach the rear, running a finger across some small print. "Mister," I say quietly, biting my lip as I glance at Danny.

"I used to call him that."

"Mister?"

"Yeah, like a term of endearment." He points to his jet ski, and I bend to look at the back. "And he called me *kid*."

Mister and kid. I look at Danny. There's that softness again, the part of him he keeps hidden behind the monster. "That's kind of cute." I say, and he huffs a small burst of laughter as I straighten.

The Jeep pulls away, reversing down to the water edge, and Danny starts pulling the top of his wetsuit up his torso. His muscles are doing crazy swelling and tensing stuff. I exhale my relief when his bare chest is finally hidden from my sights, as well as his mutilated arm. I turn away from him and head for the water, shielding my eyes from the setting sun.

"You need some glasses," Danny says, joining me and handing me a pair of black wraparounds. "Put them on."

I do as I'm bid, covering my eyes. "Isn't it a bit late to be going out on the water?"

He wades into the sea and negotiates the jet ski from the trailer. "Sunset is the best time on the water." Danny jerks his head, summoning me on as he pulls his shades over his eyes. He looks out of this world in a wetsuit. Out. Of. This. World.

"It's just us?"

He gazes around, prompting me to do the same. The place is deserted, and Brad's now gone too. Into the café, I assume. It's just me and Danny. "Just us," he says, an edge of something unrecognizable in his tone. "The wind in your hair, the salt spray on your face. You'll love it."

I'm sure I will, it sounds amazing, but all this has thrown me, more than the discovery of hidden firearms. "Are white-knuckle rides all part of my stay at the pleasure of Danny Black?"

"White knuckle?" He pouts, and, damn him, it's kind of adorable on his murderous face. It's mischievous. Playful. "You want white knuckles? Because I can think of a much better way of achieving that."

I sigh. "How? When I'm gripping your bedpost?" That's all good and well, but I've given him plenty of opportunities to give me white knuckles, and he's not taken them. Now he wants to take me on a jet ski. He's also being mildly sweet this evening. He's even talked about his father. The man has a split personality.

He shakes his head on a small smile. "Get that arse down here, Rose."

It's the way he says ass. It's something else that sets my insides alight. I bat down the heat and wade into the water. "Fuck, it's cold," I gasp, tempted to dash straight back out.

"You'll be used to it in no time. Come on." He makes grabby hands, and I soon find myself up to my waist. "Wait there." He mounts the jet ski like a pro, and then offers me a hand, pulling me up onto the big padded seat easily. "Comfy?"

"Where do I hold on?" I ask, looking around for something, anything, other than him.

He reaches back and takes my hands. "Here." And guides them around his front. I squeeze my eyes closed and shut off my sense of smell. His back is so broad. So hard. With my cheek pressed to him, I clench my thighs around the seat. "Relax," he says on a laugh.

I ignore him and focus on remaining still and holding on tight, the roar of the engine drowning out the remnants of his amusement.

Danny pulls away smoothly, the sound now a comfortable purr, and I open my eyes. We're chugging along at a leisurely pace, and Danny points to a yellow buoy. "We can pick up speed once we're past that marker."

"Great," I quip, my hold constricting. And the moment we're past that buoy, the engine bellows, and I jerk on a girlie squeal, starting to bump on the padded seat, as he goes from zero to one hundred in a few hair-raising seconds. "Shit," I yell, squeezing the life out of him. "Oh my God, Danny!" The asshole. He's doing this on purpose, trying to scare the shit out of me. It's working. "Slow down," I scream, and he laughs wickedly, continuing at an insane speed across the cove. Salty water is hitting my face, despite him shielding me, and my hair is flying all over the place. Love it? Nope. Can't say I do. I'm sure if I were to loosen my hold of him, I'd fly off the damn thing. "Danny!" He takes no notice, zooming across the open water like a madman. I'm incensed. So fucking mad, I'm prepared to risk falling off just so I can hurt him. I release one arm and feel down toward his groin, locating the delicate flesh on his inside thigh. And I pinch him through the rubber of the wetsuit. Hard.

"Fuck." We immediately start to slow, and he looks over his shoulder.

"Did that hurt?" I yell over the rush of water.

"Yes," he grates.

"Good."

He releases the throttle and we eventually slow to nothing until we're bobbing on the water. "Are you telling me the warrior woman is afraid of something?" he asks.

"Are you telling me the Angel-faced Assassin just felt pain?"

He huffs a light bubble of laughter. "You caught me by surprise."

"I know how that feels," I murmur, settling into his back. "Is that why you've dragged me onto this stupid thing? To make a point?" So I'm not too keen on flying across the water at one hundred miles an hour. Forgive me.

"I have no point to make, Rose." He flexes the throttle a little. "Shall we go slow?"

"Please."

"Don't hold me so tightly. You're more likely to fall off when I take a corner."

"Then don't take a corner."

His laugh. Oh, his laugh. "I need to take a corner, or we'll wind up in Cuba."

"Then do it slowly."

"I'll do it slowly," he confirms, his tone pacifying. "If I get too fast, pinch me."

"Don't worry, I will." I leave my hand on his thigh in readiness . . . and maybe because it feels good there. I'm thinking Danny must think so too, because he surrenders one of the handlebars and takes it, flattening my palm and holding it down. I swallow a few times and turn my face the other way, looking out to the Atlantic as we drift along at a comfortable speed.

The water is calm, my heart is calm, my life, in this moment, feels calm. He's weaving his fingers through mine, feeling them, twiddling with them, stroking them. I close my eyes, forsaking the incredible view, and channeling all of my energy into savoring how good it feels. To be this close. To be touching. *Without being forced to.* Enjoying. *Without pretending.* Is this what other women enjoy regularly? Would they consider this . . . romantic? I know that will never be part of my life, not permanently, but I can enjoy this glimpse . . . can't I?

But more importantly, should I?

"Shit!" Danny's hand is quickly off mine, and I startle, loosening my hold of him. I shouldn't have. My body lurches off the back, and I'm suddenly sailing through the air, Danny's yell traveling after me. I hit the water with a slap, sinking quickly before I register the need to kick my feet. *Fucking hell.* I break the surface on a gasp, my head snapping left and right, my limbs working madly, panic feeding the adrenalin in my muscles.

"Rose!"

I blink the water from my eyes and see Danny diving off the jet ski, swimming toward me. When he makes it, he's out of breath, his arm slipping around my waist and pulling me to his body. "What happened?" I splutter, clinging to his shoulders and naturally wrapping my legs around his waist, anything to keep afloat without draining too much more energy.

"A log in the water," Danny puffs, treading water calmly, keeping us both afloat. "I saw it too late. Turned too quickly." He reaches forward and pulls my wonky sunglasses up, resting them on my head.

"Goddamn it, Danny." I heave against him, splattering my chest to his and letting my head flop onto his shoulder. And then I laugh, chuckling into his neck as we bob on the calm water, wrapped around each other. I see the jet ski a short distance away, rolling with the swell of the rippling waves. Neither of us make to break away from each other. One of his arms is under my ass, the other around my waist. I'm quite comfy, my heavy head settled against him, my eyes taking in the vast, still expanse of water stretched out before me. My shock has passed. That feeling is back.

Peace.

Calm.

Comfort.

"Rose?" Danny's quiet calling of my name sounds unsure. Tentative.

I remain where I am. "What?"

"I'm sorry."

My forehead bunches, my fingers clawing into his back. Something tells me he's not apologizing for throwing me off the back of his jet ski. "For what?" I ask, my eyes now darting over the sparkling water.

I feel him move, pulling out of our cozy embrace, forcing me to relinquish my resting place on his shoulder. Removing his glasses, he slides them up into his hair. And he stares at me. He doesn't gaze. It's not soft or uncertain. He stares. A hard stare. An angry stare. I feel my lungs slowly shrinking. He looks truly remorseful. I almost don't want to ask. "What are you sorry for?"

His hands move from my waist and crawl onto my face. "This." His mouth finds mine . . . and I'm gone. Lost. Consumed. Overwhelmed with every feeling imaginable.

Anger for loving it.

Hurt for feeling it.

Guilt for not stopping it.

Pain for the aftermath.

My mission is suddenly all I can think of. My imminent betrayal. "Danny."

"Shut up, Rose." His palms press down on the side of my face, his wet mouth working over mine like he's been there a million times and knows it like the back of his hand. I stop myself from opening up to him for only a second. But then his tongue slips past my lips, and I'm quickly past the point of return. My arms cage him in, my thighs tighten around him. His mouth is salty but wonderful, his lips soft but firm. His hand moves to my hair and clasps my ponytail, fisting it hard, but our kiss remains controlled, our tongues moving smoothly and steadily. Never in my life have I been taken away from the cruelty of my existence. Never have I been swallowed whole by passion. I'm drowning. Struggling for air. Fighting to keep my head my own. Our moans are mingling, loud and gratifying, and Danny consistently nips at my bottom lip, pulling away from my mouth long enough for me to find more air before he finds my lips again and explores every bit of my mouth.

I find his hair and grip it, pushing him closer to me. Something tells me this is it. He's lost his battle to resist me. I've won.

Or have I lost?

"Have you ever imagined how amazing something would be?" He talks around my lips, unwilling to give them up, devouring me between each word.

"Only once," I admit, and he breaks our kiss but keeps our faces close, our fingers still knotted in each other's hair. Now, he's gazing at me. Truly gazing, eyes full of awe that I'm feeling myself. This hard, evil killing machine makes me melt. He's discovered emotions and feelings deep within me. Not lost feelings. They were never there in the first place to be lost. These are new feelings. Alien feelings. My body seems to know how to deal with them even if my brain does not.

"Only once?" he counters, scanning my face. "Now?"

I nod, just a fraction, probably not enough to be seen. But with his hands in my hair, he feels it.

He looks sad for a split second, his chest compressing against mine as he breathes in. "I have to get you in my bed." His mouth falls to mine again, his tongue lapping slowly.

"Worried you'll change your mind?"

"No." One hand leaves my hair and finds my breast, his touch molding me through my wetsuit. "We need to continue this somewhere private."

"I don't see anyone," I tease, feeling him smile around my lips as he starts to swim back to the jet ski, me still attached to his front. I'm not letting go. Of him, or his mouth.

"Me either. But I haven't *seen* anyone else since I laid eyes on—"

Boom!

I'm thrown skyward on a scream, the force carrying me high, the sky illuminated with red and orange. The heat radiating through my body is instant, my ears pierced painfully by the unbearable sharp sound. Disorientation and shock render me incapable of figuring out what's happened as I'm thrown like a rag doll, landing in the water with a silent splash, all sound drowned out by the echoing roar of noise.

I plunge deep into the water and start kicking my legs wildly, but I just keep sinking deeper and deeper. I can't breathe. Can't see. My lungs fight against my instinct to draw air, but my desperation to breathe wins. I inhale and choke on salty water, every part of my body and head in a panic, my limbs flailing to get me out of the water, my mind battling to find instruction.

I'm going to drown.

A strange peace comes over me, my fight to survive leaving me for the first time in my life. I feel weightless. I've never felt so light before. Giving in to the pull of the current and letting gravity do what it will, I let it drag me down, everything in me settling. Accepting. If I'm dead, they can't threaten him anymore. He won't be at risk. He'll be left to live his life, to be happy. Not that he knows it, but he won't be living on the edge of evil anymore. They'll have forgotten him sooner than I'm dragged out of the sea. He will be of no use to them anymore. I die. But he gets to live.

I close my eyes and let my arms float out to my sides, my panic now gone, acceptance replacing it.

My body meets something. The seabed. And then I'm moving, feeling like I'm being pulled. My eyes open, and through the murky water, I just see his eyes before he pushes me up from beneath and I'm quickly shooting up through the water toward the surface. The sight of him brings me back to life. My legs start kicking, my arms working against the force of the water, my lungs screaming.

I break the surface on a rush of air and immediately bring up water, coughing as my lungs squeeze. My head feels like it could burst from the pressure of my heaves, my body out of control. It could be daylight. The space before me is illuminated, bright and clear. Then I hear the roaring sound.

I turn in the water, coming face to face with a ball of fire, the flames red-hot and wild, touching the sky. "Oh my God." I circle, searching the glowing water for him. "Danny!" I yell, feeling frantic and panicked. More alien feelings, and I can't stop them. I can't see him. "Danny!" I hold my breath and immerse my face, trying to see beneath the surface. My lungs are shot. I can't hold my breath for long enough to find him, and I resurface, my head snapping back and forth, looking for him. He didn't come up. After he made sure I made it to the surface, he didn't come up. "Danny!" I scream over the sound of the raging flames, spinning when I hear something, another roar, except this one is from a boat. A speed boat. I throw my arms into the air, seeing Brad and Ringo on board. They spot me, both of their faces riddled with worry, with shock.

"Rose," Brad yells. "Stay there." He shuts the engine off when they're a good ten feet away and start floating toward me steadily. He leans over, ready to pull me up.

"I can't find him." My voice breaks. I feel like I've swallowed something large and hard and it's trapped in my throat. "I can't find Danny."

"Fuck," Brad curses, leaning out as far as he can, stretching his arm for me. "Take my hand."

Just as our fingers brush, I hear something behind me. I abandon Brad's hand and fly around, my eyes darting across the water wildly. I see his eyes before I see anything else. I hear my heart pounding its thanks before I hear his coughs and splutters, followed by a curse. His hands go through his hair, pushing it back, and he searches the water. Something inside me bucks. Something profound and demanding. Something that will not go ignored. And then our eyes meet, and I realize in this moment . . .

I'm in more trouble than I ever comprehended.

Trouble that scares me more than death. More than Nox, but not more than what I know he can do to me. Yet . . . will that stop me from being so reckless?

My arms and legs start moving of their own volition, taking me to him, rather than accepting Brad's hand and going to safety. I'm swimming toward him. Toward the flames. Toward the heat.

Toward the danger.

Danny starts swimming too, and when I make it to him, our bodies crash together, and I curl every limb around him, hiding my face in his neck, feeling like I'm drowning all over again. "You're okay," he says against my throat, holding me tightly as the fire continues to blaze just a stone's throw away. "You're okay."

Tears come. More feelings, more emotions, more madness. He saved my life. He's the only person who has ever deemed me worthy of being saved.

I hear Brad yelling in the distance, calling for us to swim to him. "We should go," Danny encourages me from his arms, but stops me before I can turn my face away. He says nothing as he takes me in. Just gently wipes under my eyes. I don't bother telling him that it's sea water. He knows. The warrior has had her armor destroyed.

I'm suddenly exhausted, all of my adrenalin gone, so Danny has to hold me while he swims us to the edge of the boat where Brad is waiting, his face grave. He takes my hand and pulls as Danny pushes me up, and I'm caught on the other side by Ringo. He gathers my wet body into his arms and puts me on the soft bench, and I start to shake, not that I'm cold or anything. I'm just . . .

"Shock," Ringo grunts, taking a fleece blanket and wrapping it around my shoulders. "Have some water." A bottle is thrust into my hand before he joins Brad and helps get Danny up, and once he's in the boat, the three men stand and look out to sea, watching the fire blazing.

"Another life down," Danny quips, looking at Brad. "Someone really wants me dead."

Like a volcano, realization erupts, and my shakes take on new levels. As Danny turns toward me, taking in my vibrating frame, I look away, shame eating away at my trembling flesh. All I can see in my head, glowing and bright on the screen of the cell phone, is my text message to Nox. I close my eyes and feel Danny settle beside me, his arm coming around my body and hugging me close. I don't deserve his comfort. This is my fault. I told Nox he would be here. He just didn't expect *me* to be too. "You're cold," Danny murmurs, and I nod into his chest, because I can't possibly speak until I've found air to simply breathe. "Rose?"

I can't look at him. Can't face him knowing it's me who nearly got him killed. Taking my chin lightly, he applies only a little pressure, not forcing me to look at him, but making it clear that he wants me to. When I find his soft eyes, my guilt triples. "I'm sorry," he breathes.

I can only shake my head, hoping he translates that to "*Don't be*." This is all on me, though I could never confess that. Danny saved me. He thinks I'm sitting here shaking like a leaf because I'm shocked and terrified. I'm both of those things, but not for the reasons he believes. He smiles and rests his chin on top of my head, cuddling me into his solid side. "We'd better go before the Coast Guard shows up," he says. "And when the police come knocking, we tell them the jet ski was stolen."

The engine of the boat kicks in, and I'm forced into Danny's side more when Brad gets us moving. And I stare at the fire until it is a mere dot on the horizon.

Today, Danny Black saved my life.

Today, he discovered the life that was there to be saved.

Today, he also signed my death sentence.

15

DANNY

I can see Brad is itching to launch into a verbal tirade on our way back from the boatyard, the tightness of his jaw evidence of how hard he's biting his tongue. I get it. My mind is reeling too, but for the most part, I'm watching Rose stare blankly ahead at the back of Ringo's seat, her shakes getting worse the closer we get to my home. I pull her close, try to hold her tight to stem her trembles. She doesn't even cast me a look. From the second I met Rose Lillian Cassidy, I wanted to pierce her defenses. Hurt her, if only to prove to myself that she could be hurt. And perhaps find some comfort in that. Seeing her like this has had a profound impact on me. This wasn't my fault. But I still hate myself.

We're still in our wetsuits after having made a speedy departure from the boatyard, and when we pull up outside my mansion, I'm forced to gently coax Rose from the car when she shows no signs of moving, lost in her trance. I guide her up the steps, rearranging the blanket around her shoulders as we enter. Esther is waiting in the entrance hall, and her face falls into a frown the moment she catches sight of us.

"I've got it," I say, passing her with Rose's shoulders in my palms, directing her up the stairs. She's like a zombie. I'm pretty sure she'd drop like a rock if I let go of her.

"Danny?" Brad calls, and I look back, seeing his hands palm-up, facing the ceiling. "Shouldn't we be getting our asses in the office to discuss?" He's desperate to offload the fucks he's held back in the car. He'll have to wait. I'm cutting him short at every turn recently. The state of my arm, my bruised nose. He's not got anything out of me, and it's seriously pissing him off.

I give him a death stare. "Have a drink ready for me." I keep moving, just catching the shake of his head as I turn. Fuck him. I couldn't leave her if I wanted to.

I don't question why I stop short of her suite. One whole room short. I open my bedroom door and negotiate her inside, kicking the door closed behind me before walking her to the bed. I strip her out of the wetsuit until she stands only in her underwear, her back to me, and then remove my own, watching her motionless body as I do. I frown when I turn her around to find glassy, empty eyes. I miss the fire in them already. Cupping her cheeks with my hands, I pull her face up to mine. She looks straight through me.

"Rose?" I jiggle her, starting to worry. Should I call a doctor and have her checked out? It's like shock has paralyzed her. I get no response, the pupils of her eyes huge. I just need her to tell me she's okay. Desperation has my lips falling to hers, my kiss firm but chaste. I pull away and see it. The spark of life in her eyes. So I kiss her again. Once more, firm and chaste, pulling away to search out the flames. They're there, burning in the back of her blue stare.

The blacks of her pupils shrink, and she blinks, focusing on me. And I kiss her again. This time, I linger for a few seconds, feeling her body firming up against me. And I hear a little whimper. But her hands remain dead by her sides.

"No." She steps away, dropping her gaze to our bare feet. "You shouldn't kiss me."

I'm not the kind of man that gets confused. My life is too clean-cut. There's no room for misunderstandings. So now, I'm a little stumped. "Why?"

"You just shouldn't." She makes to turn, but I grab her wrist, stopping her. There's no question that I should let her leave, but an odd sense of entitlement wants an explanation. There's a simple one, of course. She nearly died, but fear isn't something that goes hand in hand with Rose. She's made that obvious from day one, so what's changed? "Let me go." She's begging. It makes me more suspicious.

"No," I reply, no anger or frustration entering my tone. It's just a simple no.

Looking up at me, she fights to control her wobbling lip. "You need to send me away, Danny."

"Fuck, no." I laugh, but nowhere near amusement. "You forget why you're here, Rose."

"Yes," she yells, violently snatching her arm out of my hold. "Yes, I have forgotten. So remind me." Her palm is sailing toward my face before I register she's moved, and though I still have time to avoid her aim, I don't. I let her slap my face with force, her anger fueling the power. I know what she's doing. She wants me to hit her back. To remind her. I don't hit her. Won't. But I do take her neck lightly and back her up to the nearest wall. I'm angry, yes, but not because she's slapped me. I'm fucking mad because she's backtracking. I finally gave in, and now she's taking it away. I won't fucking let her.

I thrust her back into the wall and flex my fingers around her throat, pushing my face up to hers. My snarl is very real. My blood is very hot. I can feel her swallows against my palm, her face tight with indignation. I spin her around and push her front forward into the wall, holding her by the back of her neck with one hand, sliding my thumb into the edge of her knickers with the other. She inhales sharply but doesn't fight me off.

"You want a piece of me, Rose?" I spit, ripping her knickers off and tossing them aside. She cries out, her head falling back on her shoulders. It gives me perfect access to her neck, my mouth falling there naturally. I lick the column of her throat. She tastes like salt. Salt, sea, and fucking heaven. "The real me?" I bite down on her flesh hard, reaching for her tits and yanking the cups of her bra down. I feel no resistance. I hear no refusal. Consent is dotted over every inch of her body in the form of fire. My cock swells behind my boxers, lurching against the material, straining hard. I pull down the waistband and free it, groaning when the tip skims the crease of her arse. "Tell me you want it." I take hold of my dick and trace lines across her arse, leaving trails of pre-cum as I go. "Tell me you want my thick cock smashing into your desperate pussy."

Her fists come up to the wall and slam hard, my teeth sinking into the flesh of her neck again.

"Tell me." Suddenly, I need that verbal go-ahead. I need her to beg.

"No." Her breathy refusal isn't telling me I can't fuck her. But I still won't. Not until she gives me the magic word. It takes everything in me, but I drop my cock, drop her body, and drop her neck from my mouth, moving back. "No," she screams the moment I'm no longer touching her, slumping against the wall, her fists going mad, bashing against it.

If I wasn't so fucking frustrated, I'd smile. But smiling is beyond me now. Way beyond me. "Fuck off out of my room," I snarl. "Get the fuck out of my room before I throw you out." I either throw her out or fuck her blind without the okay I need. I can't do that. I refuse to do that, no matter how much she wants me to. No matter how much I need to.

She rolls against the plaster, showing no signs of obeying my command. It fuels the fire inside me, both the desire and the anger. I steam forward grabbing her arm and manhandling her to the door. She fights me, just as I expected, trying to pry my fingers from her flesh, hitting and smacking me as I drag her to the door. It would be easy to lose my cool. Easy to knock her to the ground with one slap. I've never had the urge to lash out at a woman, and not even my lack of control in this moment will change that. I swing the door open and turn toward her.

And get knocked back by a fist square on my jaw.

I stagger back in surprise, blinking through the stars in my vision until I can see her. Fuck me, she's got a stellar right hook. I flex my jaw, practically cracking it into place. The look in her eyes tells me she's surprised too, her form frozen once more. I don't know what to do with this. "You just fucking punched me." So I state the obvious like a moron.

She backs up, wary, her eyes wide. She thinks I'm going to return the favor. Oh, I am. I lunge forward and grab her, spinning her until her back slams into my chest. I take her wrists and cross her arms over her front, immobilizing her, disturbing the bandage on my arm as I do. I ignore the flash of pain when I brush the cuts against her flesh and walk her to the wall. My mouth at her ear, I whisper, "Say it." And she nods. "Say yes, Rose," I demand, leaning into her, pushing her against the wall. My cock reloads.

"Yes," she whimpers, sounding like she could burst into tears at any moment. I exhale and slowly release her arms. Her stance widens. My palms come up and rest either side of her waist. Her face turns to the side. Her arse juts out in invitation. "Yes," she repeats, this time evenly.

I look down at my cock. The damn thing is weeping. Reaching

forward, I take her hair tie and pull it free, releasing her damp waves. My hand slides onto her scalp and clamps down, my body moving in. When the tip of my dick meets the crack of her arse, my body folds in anticipation for the pleasure it knows is coming.

I. Am. So. Ready.

Desperation is going to lead this. "Tell me you're on birth control," I order, tracing a line up her spine with my fingertip, flipping the catch of her bra as I pass. She nods. "Tell me you've always used protection before me."

"Always. Now you tell me the same."

"Always." Taking her hips, I yank them back, stepping out, widening my stance to get level. My dick needs no guiding in. It knows exactly where it wants to be, and I push past her entrance on a stifled growl. My teeth clench. My muscles tense. My body spasms with the pleasure of that first deep plunge.

She goes listless in my hands, her torso collapsing forward, her finger clawing the smooth wall. "Danny." My name is broken, cracked by pleasure. I have no desire to kiss her. To caress her skin or go slow. She's starved the animal. I've starved the animal too. So there's only one way.

I draw back and slam forward on a curled lip, moving one hand to her neck and clawing my fingers into her nape over her hair. Her scream is just what I need. My cock rolls against the walls of her pussy as I pull back, and I look down, admiring the vision of my taut shaft slick with her arousal. I clench my teeth and pound into her again, delighting in her consistent grunts that quickly roll into moans. I must be hurting her with the brutality of my advances. I smile. She'll never admit it. Heat pricks at my skin as I admire the sight before me. I have her pinned in place like an animal. It's carnal and inhumane.

I should do the gentlemanly thing and warn her that I'm about to let loose. I should. But I won't. She asked for this. Hard. Fucking. The vulnerable woman in the sea who I kissed is gone. *My Rose is back.*

My hips buck, my control faltering for a split second, and she cries out, her forehead rolling across the wall. I move my hold from her neck to her hair to pull her head away, groaning when I catch a brief glimpse of her drowsy eyes. My veins pump harder. I've teased her enough, primed her enough, given her enough time to adjust to my length and girth.

Rearing back, I take in air and brace myself.

The gloves are off.

I rocket forward on a roar that could crumble the house, slamming into her wickedly, and I give her no time to prepare for the next thrust, pulling back and launching forward again. Sweat instantly beads my skin. Pleasure rapidly cripples me. Want for more takes over. I let go completely and fuck her like I've never fucked a woman before. Harder than I have before. Faster than I have before. With more frustration and purpose fueling me than I ever have before.

Rose's body absorbs my blows, each drive dislodging another scream from her hoarse throat. Her hands feel around the wall for something to hold on to, her head jerking limply on her shoulders. Every time I enter her, I feel like I'm going deeper and deeper, and each time I withdraw, I feel like I could lose my mind with the desperation to get back in there. All this just makes my hips piston faster.

I've lost control. Blood is pounding in my ears, my hearing a whoosh of nothing, my shouts, her screams, just a distant, muffled sound. I'm out of my body, but so very much in it.

She comes before me. I feel it in the solidifying of her body, hear it in the change of pitch in her screams, and then the extended moan and the limpness of her body. Not that I need it, but it's the invitation I want to another world.

I breathe in deep and close my eyes, letting the pleasure take over and spark, igniting the start of my release. It builds slowly at first, but when it hits my balls, it erupts, surging forward at a rate I'm not equipped to cope with. I gasp, my body folding over her back, my knees wobbling with the intensity. I'm held on the cusp for just a few painful seconds as I draw out one last time, and then sink in slowly as my cock explodes and has one hand reaching for the wall to hold me up. I snake my other around her stomach, seeing she's struggling to remain on her feet too. My roar is suppressed. My body out of control.

I shake and tremble, staring down at her back as I fight my way through. It seems to drag out forever, the pulses of my dick going on and on. Rose is breathing heavily beneath me, creating a wave with my body as it follows the rolls of hers.

Release. Somehow, we both achieved a release, but it wasn't enough. An angry, hate-filled fuck should have satisfied me. Sated me. And yet, I'm just empty.

Tasted heaven, but feel like hell.

I pull out on a quiet hiss and head for my bathroom, flipping on the shower. I should feel better. Relieved. I don't. I just feel like an arsehole. My back meets the tile, and I stare into the steam, mentally beating myself up. But she asked for it. Made it that way. I flex my jaw, feeling the ache from her perfect punch. And I look down at my arm, ripping the bandage off. The cuts are weeping. *Motherfucker.*

I wash myself down, realigning my thoughts to more important things. Like who just tried to blow me up. I brush my teeth, pull on the jeans that are hanging on the back of the chair in the corner of my bathroom, and make my way into the bedroom.

She's gone.

Good.

After finding a bandage in the kitchen and doing a piss-poor job of redressing the wounds on my arm, I head for my office. I ignore Brad's curious look when I enter. "The ice has melted," he says, placing the tumbler in my hand as I pass. I ignore his subtle observation of the time it's taken me to get down here, slumping down in my chair. I also ignore the fact that it hasn't escaped his notice that I have a tidy blemish on my cheek. But he doesn't mention it. "Didn't you have time to get dressed?"

I look at my chest that is missing one T-shirt. "Fuck off, Brad. Tell me what's going on."

"You tell me, Danny. Your arm is shredded, your nose looks broken, and to top it off, some fucker just tried to blow you up."

"My arm and my nose aren't your concern. Let me worry about that." I glare at him across the desk. "They're getting closer." I neck my drink and immediately hold up my empty glass. Ringo grabs the bottle of Scotch and refills it while Brad settles in a chair opposite and the rest of my men move in. "How the fuck did they get a bomb in my jet ski?"

"Monroe's been on watch down there for the past two days." Brad sighs, rubbing at his head, which is undoubtedly aching. "I've got him speaking to the staff. Checking the bookings, the deliveries. With no CCTV, we're kinda fucked. You should reconsider having it installed."

I get up and start pacing, needing to feel my feet. "CCTV is more of a risk than a gain. The police come sniffing around, they'll see too much of what we don't want seen." I neck the rest of my second Scotch and this time refill it myself. Whoever did this is getting too close for comfort, and I don't just mean to ending my life. We operate out of the boatyard. I can't have that being exposed. "Someone was watching us." I look at Brad, who's frowning. "There was no trigger on the jet ski that set the bomb off. I wasn't on it. The engine cut when I dived in after Rose."

"What are you saying?"

"I'm saying someone watched me ride out from the boatyard. I was too far out to be seen from the shore. They detonated the bomb assuming I was still on the jet ski." Rose catapulting off the back was a blessing in disguise. "Any news on the Mexicans and Romanians?" I ask.

"Badger checked in earlier. The Mexicans are in Mexico and Romania has a new small-time organization making waves."

"Waves?"

"Amateurs. Drugs, hookers, petty crimes. With Dimitri gone, it was only a matter of time before some wannabe gangster tried to make a name for himself."

"No threat?"

"They can barely coordinate an orgy. No threat."

I sigh, trying to breathe through the building frustration. *Then who, for fuck's sake? Who?*

"Listen, about your dad's funeral."

I look at Brad in disbelief. "Do I look like I want to fucking talk about my dad's funeral?" I get up to leave, grabbing the bottle of Scotch as I go. I fucking miss him, but I haven't had a minute to stop and grieve. *Don't trust anyone. No second chances.* I want more than just those words to deal with this fucked-up state I'm in. I should go on a rampage. Shoot to kill. Wipe out all the fuckers. I'm pretty sure that's what my father would have done. I'm forced to shove my bottle of Scotch under my arm when my phone rings from my pocket. I look down at the screen and up to Brad. "Adams." I reverse my steps and place the Scotch on the desk, answering on loudspeaker. "Tell me."

"The Jepson kid woke up this afternoon."

"Fuck," I spit, closing my eyes and wondering what other obstacles are going to be thrown in my way. "And?"

"And he got off lightly, considering. Should be out in a week or two." He sounds beaten.

Brad dramatically slumps back in his seat. I would too, if I was sitting. Instead, I pour myself another Scotch and sink it, preparing myself for what needs to be done. "And Byron's Reach is in a trust until he's twenty-one?" I ask, needing to hear the situation loud and clear one more time before I take action.

Adams is quiet for a few moments. This isn't just shitty news to me. This is shitty for him. Because he's not getting Rose back until I get that marina. "It'll be released in ten years and seven months."

"Sort it."

"How?"

"I don't know, but can you wait eleven years to see Rose, Adams?" I ask, as much malice in my voice as I intended.

"You can't keep her."

"Fucking watch me." I see Brad's disapproving head shake, and rightly so. I need Rose around about as much as I need to be blown up. "And thirty-five million will turn into forty if I don't see results soon." I push myself off the desk, practically hearing Adams wince, and stab at the screen to end the call, feeling the pressure building in my head. "Find out what hospital the kid is at," I order Brad. Kill the kid. Send Rose back. Get the marina. Find the motherfucker who's got a target on my head. Simple shit. Or, it should be. I look up at Brad.

"What are you going to do, Danny?" he asks.

"I'm going to get rid of an obstacle."

"What the fuck? Let's just get Adams here and torture the fucking information out of him. Find out who's moved in on him and get this shit done with. Send the girl back. Get on with our fucking job."

"You don't think whoever's pocket he's in will be waiting for that? I've got millions at stake. The second Adams is in this office denying shit, I have to kill him." *No second chances.* "Have Adams watched. Send Len. Get his phone tapped. Get his bank accounts looked at. I want to know who he's talking to and what he's spending. As soon as I find out who wants me gone, and I can guarantee my money and the boatyard, he's dead."

"And the woman?"

"She'll be dead too. The hospital. I want to know what hospital the kid is in."

"Danny," Brad begins, his tone worried. "Seriously? A kid?"

"I need that fucking marina," I say calmly, but I'm far from feeling it. I pace out of the office, the bottle at my lips.

16

ROSE

He's slumped in a chair at the far side of my room, an empty bottle of Scotch in his hand. He looks troubled, even in his sleep. Has he been there all night? I prop myself up against the headboard and bring my knees up, circling them with my arms and resting my chin on the tops. I'm sore between my thighs, heavy and uncomfortable. It's not an unusual feeling. It's a feeling that goes hand in hand with my job. Or rather, my daily torment. But now, the source, the circumstances, it feels all wrong on me. Last night, Danny fucked me against the wall like he hated me. It didn't stop me from coming, though. Fury, frustration, and guilt only seemed to intensify my orgasm. I was at his mercy before he even got me against the wall. I'm at his mercy with or without the complexity of the circumstances surrounding my involvement with him. Not that Danny knows any of that. To him, I am just a whore. *No smart man gets sentimental over business.* Translated: you're business.

He has no idea.

I sigh despondently as I edge my way to the side of the bed and settle my bare feet onto the carpet. The squidgy fibers feel good between my toes, a softness in this hard, rotten world.

Making my way into the bathroom, I take only a second to look at myself, turning away from the mess that reflects back at me. My skin still smells salty, my hair is matted, and my eyes look more haunted than ever before. I close the door and lock it, going to the drawer and feeling around the back for my cell. I pull it free and stare down at the screen, torn. The guns run circles in my head, the information I've learned tormenting me. But not for long. The consequences of withholding information soon supersedes my doubt to betray Danny.

I turn on the phone and dial Nox, turning on the shower to create some background noise. It's time to tell him about the guns. It's time for me to be out of this conflicting space of heaven and hell. I need to go back to what I know, familiarity, and Danny Black isn't familiar to me.

It rings and rings before clicking to voicemail. It's not his voice. It's the standard automated voicemail message. I hang up, knowing the rules when it comes to leaving voice messages. Then I dial again, my hands beginning to tremble a little. I need to offload the information before I do something stupid like change my mind. It's not like there's any going back. I've already given Nox information on Danny's movements, resulting in the carnage last night at the boatyard. Does Nox know yet? Does he know I was there? Once again, it goes to voicemail, and I cut the call, staring at the cell.

My head snaps up when I hear a thud from beyond the door, and a second later, the door handle is rattling. I shoot toward the vanity unit and push the phone into its hiding place. "Coming," I call, quickly composing myself before breathing in and opening. His hands are braced on the doorframe, his body leaning forward. He's holding himself up. He looks like shit. With a cold stare, he takes me in, up and down. "What?" I ask, short and curt. He's set the standard, and it makes what I'm going to do a little more bearable. At least, it should do.

"I'm going out of town." His biceps flex as he pushes into the frame, straightening himself up. "I'll be back this evening." He turns and walks away. Just like that.

"Where are you going?" I ask, pacing after him.

"Out of town," he says without turning back, keeping up his stride to the door. "Esther and some of the men are here if you need anything."

"What might I need?" I spit, getting angrier as I follow him.

"Well, it's not me, obviously." He stops abruptly in his tracks the second he's spat out his statement, forcing me to stop too, or crash into his back. There was hurt in his tone. He didn't mean to say that, or sound so indignant. But he's wrong. I feel like I do need him, but I can't have him. This is for the best.

"Obviously," I confirm, taking one step back. "When can I leave?"

Danny turns, slowly revealing his hard, cut face. "Now."

I recoil, his answer unexpected. Now? I can go now? His face tells me I heard him right, his eyes drilling into me with ferocity. "I want you gone before I get back." He walks backward toward the door, never severing our eye contact. A horrible pain pinches at my heart. A nasty ache turns my stomach. This is it, and though I've begged for it, I'm all in a muddle now. And it has nothing to do with what Nox will do. Besides, I'm pretty sure I have the information he wants, anyway. My boy is safe. But Danny Black is not. No more rattling cages. Next time . . .

I swallow down more lumps in my throat, feeling them hit my stomach hard. "Okay," I say simply, ripping my eyes away from him as I turn and head for the shower. With every step, the pain intensifies, until I reach the bathroom door and look back.

He's gone.

. . .

An hour later, I'm still sitting on the shower floor, bunched up neatly in the corner, hugging my knees. My skin is wrinkled, my body squeaky clean. Forcing myself to my feet, I turn off the shower and dry myself, pulling my wet hair up into a high knot. I can't be bothered to dry it. I should just go.

Call Nox and have his men collect me. Not that I have an address, but I have no doubt Nox will know.

I leave the bathroom tidy and find my red dress, the one I wore the night Danny found me. I slip it on, grab my purse, and head for the bathroom to get the cell phone, turning it on. As I look down at the screen, I dawdle, my thumb hovering over the dial icon. An image of a boy is what has me pressing down and taking the cell to my ear. Every picture I've ever seen of him flashes through my mind, serving as the best reminder. It rings twice. Then I hear his voice, and before I think better of it, I hang up and start hyperventilating, having to take a seat on the toilet to gather myself.

I start to rock myself back and forth, my torso folding in over my knees. I can't think clearly here.

I jump up and head out, jogging through his mansion until I reach the stairs. A man is standing at the bottom. I recognize him. *Watson.*

"Danny said I could leave." I drop my shoes to the floor and slip them on.

"Yeah, I know." Watson slides his hands into his pockets, tilting his head, looking me up and down. I should laugh. He wouldn't have dared do that in Danny's company. "Want a ride?" There's a sinister edge to his question that puts me on my guard.

I straighten and pull down the veil of hardness. "I can take a cab."

His dirty brown eyes take a quick scope of the entrance hall.

He's checking we're alone. I back up and immediately damn myself for it. So I stop, pushing my shoulders back. In this dress, I should feel at home. My armor on and my hardness ready to take anything thrown at me. But I'm in Danny's house, and I'm feeling like I've never felt until I met The Brit. *Vulnerable.*

"How about a parting gift?" he suggests, advancing toward me.

"You want me to fuck you?" I ask, looking him up and down, a curl to my lip. "No thanks. Even a whore like me can do better." I see it coming. The slap that'll put me on my ass. He wallops me with a force I've dealt with more than once, but now it hurts. I stagger back, tumbling to my backside. "I still don't want to fuck you," I sneer, throwing my hair back and looking up at him.

"You little whore." He grabs my injured arm and yanks me to my feet, shoving me into a nearby wall. I hit it with force. That hurts too. Why the hell is everything hurting all of a sudden? I go to dart to his left, but my path is quickly blocked by a big arm braced against the wall. I pin myself to the plaster and hold my breath, fighting to find the shield that'll protect me. Watson leans in, breathing all over me, his palm slipping up my inside thigh under my dress.

"No," I murmur before I can stop myself, trying to slap his hand away. I feel dirty. Wrong. This situation isn't unusual— assholes taking advantage, and usually I would oblige, knowing it was for the greater good. Knowing I got to keep my life if I just let it happen. Not now. Now, I can't think of anything worse than another man's hands on me.

"Oh, you're shy?" He nuzzles my nose, and my stomach churns, my face turning away. "I've seen that fine body of yours. In Black's office. You weren't shy then, were you?" His fingers slip past the seam of my panties, and I tighten my thighs, trying to make access as difficult as possible. "You're not wet," he hums. "We'll soon see to that."

My dress is quickly yanked up to my waist, and I cry out. "Stop!"

"I'll stop when I've got what you've been teasing every man in this house with since you arrived." He yanks at my panties, and the move brings last night flooding back. Danny was rough, but he didn't make me feel like a whore. He didn't make me feel this cheap. *But I am. This is all I am. I just forgot for a few hours.*

No!

I muster strength from somewhere and shove him back, darting for the front door. Watson yells and throws himself in my path, blocking me. So I swing around and retreat up the stairs, running as fast as my heeled feet will carry me. I fall into my room and rush to the bathroom, locking myself inside.

I can hear him on the other side of the door. He tries it once, jiggling the handle. Then he laughs and leaves.

I curl up in the corner on the floor, pulling my dress back into place.

And . . . I cry.

17

DANNY

I step out of the car, Brad and Ringo in tow, and look up at the face of the building, pulling off my shades. I've felt off all morning, and while I'd love to put it down to the bottle of Scotch I sank last night . . .

I want you gone before I get back.

Her surprise. The hard, determined look in her eyes. Her . . . acceptance.

I pause at the door of the hospital in Fort Lauderdale, my hands clammy. *Just do it. Get this shit sorted and the deal wrapped up.*

The electric doors open, and I scan the entrance hall.

"You sure about this?" Brad asks, speaking up for the first time since we left Miami.

"No."

"Danny, the woman."

"What about her?"

"She's distracting you. Affecting you. You're making stupid decisions."

"What, like killing the boy?" I get moving, striding through the hospital. "Where's his room?"

"He's in the gardens getting some fresh air," Ringo says, pointing the way. "I have eyes on him." We round the corner and find a set of automatic doors leading out into a vast green land-scaped garden, where dozens of people mill around. I put out my arm, stopping Brad and Ringo at the door. There's too many people. "Cameras?"

"Off." Brad practically sighs as I turn to Ringo.

"I'll text you your command. Meet us back at the car."

"Got it," Ringo confirms, and I make off down a brick path, ambling casually, looking discreetly around the area. It doesn't take me long to find the boy. He's by the pond in a wheelchair, the nurse handing him bread to toss to the ducks. I come to a stop, watching them, the boy expressionless, the nurse trying to coax a smile. She's trying in vain. The kid has woken up and been told that his parents are dead. He probably wants to be dead himself. I can put him out of his misery. End this for him. Do us both a favor.

Something tugs in my heart, something unwanted.

"You got any family?"

I took the notes and shook my head. "No, sir."

"Two fifties aren't going to get you very far in life, are they?"

"I suppose not, Mister. Wanna gimme some more?"

"Get in the car."

"In your car?"

"Yes, in my car. Get in."

"Why?"

"Because you're coming home with me."

And he did exactly that. Gave me a home. I was saved from my misery. And I realize in this moment the kid has everything to live for. I look at him and see me. A boy with no hope. No future. No love.

Fuck, what the hell is wrong with me?

I pull my phone from my pocket when it vibrates and answer Ringo. "I see him. I have a clear shot," he tells me, and I whip my eyes across the pond to see my man up on the roof. His gun is poised, aimed and ready to fire. My eyes cast back to the boy. He's smiling. It's faint, but he's smiling.

"Stand down," I order, shaking my head at the same time.

"What?" Ringo sounds confused.

"I said, stand down. Don't fire. Mission aborted. Understand?" I turn my body toward Brad and find his eyes. "Stand. Down."

He smiles mildly, nodding. Yes, I've come to my fucking senses. Let's not make a big deal of it. I shake my head to myself, hanging up. The boy is out of the equation. And now I've told Rose to get out, so is she. I'll think of another way to get the marina. I'll find out who the power of attorney is and convince them to sell it to me in the best way I know how. Threats. Blackmail. Death.

I stand for a while, just watching the kid. I don't know how long for, but it's enough time for Ringo to make it down off the roof, and just when I'm about to tell them the new plan, one that involves Brad's suggestion, torturing Adams, a sharp bang sounds out, followed by a high-pitched scream. I jump, as does Ringo and Brad, all of us ducking, the sound familiar to us.

Gunfire.

"No," a female voice screams, anarchy breaking out around us. Everyone starts running for the doors into the hospital, causing a stampede of panicked people.

"What the fuck's going on?" Brad asks, scoping the area, his hand automatically going to the back of his trousers. Ringo does what's natural to him and grabs me, pulling me out of the open, but I shake him off, rising to my full height, my eyes shooting toward the pond. The boy is alone, a sitting duck in his wheelchair.

"Fucking hell." I break into a sprint toward the kid, hearing Brad yelling at me. When I reach him, I scoop him up out of the chair, flinching when the sound of a bullet ricochets off the metal of his chair. *What the fuck?*

"Danny, you stupid fuck," Brad roars, and I look over to him as I cuddle the kid close to my chest, finding him frantically searching around the garden, his gun ready to fire. "Run!"

My brain engages, and I sprint across the garden with the kid, wincing when I hear him cry out a few times, his healing body jerking in my arms, hurting him.

I make it into the hospital, Ringo and Brad close behind, guarding us, and pace toward the nearby desk. "Some assistance," I yell, stopping a nurse and pretty much dragging her over. The boy's staring at me in shock as I lay him on a nearby gurney. "Take care of him," I order before I walk away, passing between Ringo and Brad, their eyes everywhere.

Brad stops me just shy of the door, his hand in my chest. "Ringo will get the car and meet us out back."

I can't argue with sensibility, and since I seem to be short of it recently, I'm listening, no matter how eager I am to get out of here and finally fix this shit. "Fine." I back off and let them do their thing while I wonder what the fuck just happened.

When we pull up outside the mansion, I remain in my seat, staring ahead at nothing in particular. I have not a fucking clue what's going on, and not for the first time, I wish Pops was here to help me figure this shit out. I pull the lever of the door and step out, my mind homing in on my office and a brand-new bottle of

Scotch. I need peace. Quiet. Alcohol. It'll help me untangle all this shit.

Esther appears, stopping me in the hallway. Her face. It's not an expression I've seen on her before, though I'll be damned if I know what it is.

"What?" I ask, as short as ever, my patience diminished.

"It's Miss Rose." She flicks her eyes to Brad and Ringo behind me, and it's now I realize that her expression harbors fear. Esther has been here for ten years. For ten years, she's accepted my brusqueness without a word. For ten years, she's watched me become more like my father every day, and she's accepted it, no questions. I know she hates what we do here, and it begs the question why she sticks around to watch. Why she indulges my every demand. Why she watches me with a mixture of admiration and disappointment.

"What about her?" I ask, steering away from the direction of those thoughts. I'm angry enough already. "If she's still here, I'll throw her out myself."

"She's still here." Her lips purse. "In her suite."

A rage like no other consumes me. "It's not her fucking suite."

"I delivered tea to her a while ago."

What? "Is this a hotel?" I bark, taking the stairs fast and stalking down the corridor to her suite. *My* suite. I can smell her, the sweetness of her scent stuck to every wall, every door, every fucking piece of me. It would be sensible of me to stop for a moment and calm down before I do something I truly regret. Unfortunately for Rose, I've had a bad day, and she's just made it a whole lot fucking worse. I steam through the door and find the suite empty. The bed is made. The terrace doors are closed. My eyes fall to the bathroom. The door's shut. The ten paces it takes me to reach it doesn't give me the chance to cool my temper. Nothing could. I take the handle and push, meeting the resistance of the lock. With my teeth clenched, I pull back and ram my shoulder into the wood, and the door flies open, hitting the wall behind.

"I told you to get the fuck—" My scathing words die on my lips when I see her huddled in the corner, her face tear-stained, black trails of mascara painting her cheeks. She's in the red dress she wore the night I met her, her feet bare, her purse and shoes in a pile by her side. When I find her gaze, her eyes well and overflow, and she buries her face in her knees, hiding from me.

My anger is dowsed in a second. Her shoulders jerk from her suppressed sobs, her fingers and toes curling, like she can't make herself small enough. I approach her quietly, as if sneaking up on a wild animal, scared it'll bolt. I drop to my haunches before her balled body and rest my palms on her shoulders. I expect her to flinch. She doesn't. I expect her to shrug me off. She doesn't. What she does instead is move her hands and lay them over mine, a silent message that she's glad I'm here. And, God help me, I am too. I drop to my arse and bend my legs, spreading them and shuffling forward so I frame her body, and she crawls into me, entwining every limb around me, holding me with a force like I've never been held before. And she settles. And for the first time today, for the first time in my life, I feel that too. Settled. My arms hold her to me as I sit on the hard floor with her wrapped around me, and I let her be, holding back my questions until my arse starts to go numb.

I push one hand into the floor and get myself to my feet, not disturbing Rose who remains clung to my front. I take us to her bed and settle against the headboard, and she never leaves my neck the whole time.

"You want to talk about it?" I ask, drawing circles across her back with my palms, feeling her shake her head into me. "How about if I don't give you a choice?" Another shake of her head, and I think, wondering what my next move should be. With anyone else, usually a gun to the temple will fix the problem. But not with Rose. "Tell me." I decide to ask nicely, nudging her. "Please." She doesn't move, remaining quiet and still against me. I can't deny that she feels good there. Warm, soft, and calming. But I need to know what's wrong. She was fine when I left—resolute with my order to leave, her usual spitfire self. This isn't the Rose I know and love.

I roll my shoulder to coax her face from my neck, looking down, my chin on my chest. "Talk to me, baby."

I feel her take a few controlled breaths, and then she slowly reveals herself to me, her hands on my shirt where her fingers twiddle. "I tried to leave." Her voice is rough and croaky. How long has she been locked in the bathroom? And why?

"And you didn't." Everything inside of me wants to believe she's still here because she wants to be, but there's something more, and it's making me feel uneasy. Her eyes drop, but a quick hold of her chin soon brings them back to mine. "What's going on?"

"I tried." She homes in on my scar, taking a finger and tracing the full length of it, from my eye to my lip. "I didn't want to go, but I tried."

She didn't want to, but she *tried*. "So why are you still here?"

She shakes her head and swallows, looking away, and I feel my patience start to fray. I take her chin, my hold harsh, and bring her face close to mine. "Tell me what the fuck is going on."

"One of your men . . ." She fades off, and I recoil.

What. The. Fuck?

My bloodstream is already on its way to boiling, and I haven't heard much yet. "One of my men what?"

Her bottom lip wobbles. "I know I'm a whore. I know what I am and what I'm good for."

I'm starting to heave, her body moving up and down on my thighs. "Shut up, Rose," I spit. "One of my men, what?"

"He wouldn't let me leave before—"

"Did he touch you?" I breathe in slowly, dizziness distorting my vision.

Rose looks away. It's all I need.

Holy fucking shit, I'm burning. I try to swallow, to breathe, to talk myself down. Fail. I get up and set her on her feet. "Who?" I demand, bending and getting up in her face. "Tell me who the fuck touched you?" She flinches when I grab her jaw, threatening and desperate.

"Watson," she whispers, reaching up and taking my clawed fingers from her face.

I straighten, searching for some calm and reason in my chaotic head. No calm. No reason. I grab Rose's hand and pull her out of her room.

"What are you doing, Danny?" she asks, jogging to keep up with my long strides. I can't talk. Can't focus on anything other than making my feet move. "Danny!"

We reach the stairs and Brad looks up to us as I pull Rose down them, halting his conversation with Ringo. His eyes jump from me to Rose, his forehead heavy. "Everything okay?" he asks, following our path as we round the bottom.

"Where are the men?"

"Playing cards in the dining room," Brad answers, coming after us as I stalk off, sweating pure rage. "Danny, what the fuck?"

I shove the double doors open and find five of my men sitting around the table, each with playing cards fanned in their grasps. My eyes zero in on Watson. "Stand up," I order, aware of the confused looks being tossed around by everyone here. Everyone except Watson. He knows.

Slowly, he rises to his feet, tossing his cards on the table. "She was asking for it." He throws Rose a curled lip, and my anger ramps up, feeling Rose moving behind me, like she can hide.

"Did she *actually* ask for it?" The other men sit back on their chairs, moving as far away as possible without fleeing the room, and Brad curses under his breath from behind me.

"She didn't need to." Watson's initial hard front is denting. He must be able to see my unbridled rage.

"Did she say no?" I drop Rose's hand and approach Brad, reaching past his suit jacket and pulling his Glock free. He doesn't stop me, but his eyes ask me if I know what I'm doing. I know exactly what I'm doing. I turn, and Watson starts backing up the second he sees what's in my hand. "Whoa, Danny." He laughs shakily, nervous as shit.

"Did she say no?" I repeat, releasing the safety.

His hands come up in surrender. "I don't remember."

I look at Rose. She's staring blankly at me, her eyes empty. "Did you say no?" I ask her.

She nods.

Watson curses loudly. "You're gonna believe a whore over a man who's worked for you for ten years?"

I lift the gun, aim at his leg, and fire. Watson squeals and drops to his arse, clenching at his splattered kneecap. "Call her a whore again," I demand. "Go on. Call her a fucking whore again." He starts dribbling with the effort it's taking him to keep his painful cries back. I put my hand out to Rose without taking my eyes off Watson bleeding all over the floor. "Come here." I feel her hand lay in mine, and I pull her toward me, positioning her in front of my body, facing Watson. Sliding my hands under her armpits, I hold the gun in front of her.

"What are you doing?" Watson tries to scramble to his feet, but his knee fails him, sending him back to the carpet in a heap.

"Danny?" Brad's tone is warning. And ignored.

"Take the gun," I order Rose, claiming one of her hands and placing it on the Glock. Her other hand comes up with no instruction from me, both her small hands holding the gun, her arms braced. I direct her aim, getting it as close as I can without holding the gun myself. Then I release her, placing my hands on her hips. I bend and rest my chin on her shoulder. "Kill him."

"Danny, for fuck's sake," Brad barks.

"Shut the fuck up," I spit, watching as Watson turns pleading eyes onto every man in the room, looking for someone to save him. "Kill him," I say again, before kissing her cheek softly. I feel her willowy frame tighten, her finger squeezing. Her jaw is like rock, her tenseness making her shake. She's terrified. I reach forward and frame her arms with mine, steadying her. "You said no to him, Rose. No means no."

Bang!

She drops the gun the second she's fired it, swinging around and hiding in my chest. She can't watch, but me? I take the greatest pleasure watching Watson's eye socket explode, Rose's aim slightly off, missing his forehead. He drops, screaming—the ear-piercing, shrill, painful kind of scream. The death scream. It makes my fucking ears bleed.

Dipping, I pick up the Glock and aim. With Rose held to my chest by one hand splayed across her back, I fire, putting Watson out of his misery and relieving my ears of his irritating cries.

Now, the room is silent, though a thousand words are being spoken through the eyes of my men.

They all know better than to speak those words. I engage the safety on the gun and toss it to Brad. He catches it, and a mild nod of his head tells me he understands. Although I spell it out, just so the others can hear. "When someone says no, they mean no." I cast my eyes around the room. "I don't associate with rapists."

I scoop Rose up and get out of there, passing Esther on my way up the stairs. Her expression is another I'm unfamiliar with. A smile, albeit tiny, but perfectly detectable on her usually impassive face. I give her a nod of assurance. "She'll need to eat soon," I tell her.

"Just let me know when." Esther makes no big deal of my

softness, continuing down the stairs. She knew. She knew why Rose was locked in the bathroom.

"Esther," I call, and she turns back, waiting.

"Thank you."

Now, she doesn't hide her smile, nodding again before disappearing into the kitchen. I look down at Rose nestled into my chest. Vulnerability doesn't suit her, but part of me likes it. Part of me loves the notion that I can protect her. The other part of me hates seeing my little warrior so utterly bared. Because it's gone. Her shield. Her unassailable strength. Ferocity. *Gone.*

Carrying on up the stairs, I automatically go to my room, setting her on her feet by my bed. She looks up at me, uncertainty in her eyes. That red dress looks all wrong on her. Reaching back for the zip, I unfasten it, taking the material and sliding it down her body until the dress hits the carpet. Better. So much better. Then I catch sight of a tear in the lace of her knickers. I swallow down my anger before it clouds me, taking her hands and guiding them to my shirt buttons, silently demanding her to unfasten them. She begins without question while I shrug my jacket off and pull my tie free. On the last button, she pushes the tails of my shirt aside and gazes up at me as she lowers her lips to my chest. I look to the ceiling, my hands coming up to my face and dragging down my scratchy cheeks. Lord, have mercy, my skin burns under her lips, the fire spreading over every inch of my flesh. I sink my splayed fingers into her hair and massage her scalp, my whole body relaxing under our contact. Dropping my head, I pull her mouth from my pec and lift her from her feet so our eyes are level.

"Yes," she says before I can ask, her palms holding my face. Her mouth meets mine and instigates the kiss that'll lead to what will be a pivotal moment for both of us. I hug her to me, our mouths working steady and slowly, as I walk us to the bed and lower her, coming down above her. Her hands go to my trousers and start working the fly, and I lift, allowing her to push them over my arse with my boxers, kicking off my shoes and socks. Our kiss becomes clumsy while I try to wriggle free from the material, being forced to relinquish her mouth and look at what I'm doing. I calmly free myself of the material, and once I'm naked, I lean over her, one fist pressed into the mattress, the other hand taking the top of her knickers. She inhales, and I drop my mouth to her hip and kiss my way down her legs as I draw the lacy material to her feet. A soft moan, a subtle arch of her back. The sight of her calmly writhing under my touch is fucking stunning. I work my way back up her body, dragging my lips everywhere I can. The juncture of her thighs meets my nose, and I place a hand on each knee, spreading her wide open.

"Danny." She whispers my name so softly, her fingers sliding into my hair. My nose circles the small strip framing her special place, my lips dotting kisses between her thighs. Her breathing becomes louder, her hips flexing. I've never smelled anything like her. Blood booms in my veins, need possessing me. *Slow*. I want to be slow this time. Appreciate all of her. Savor every inch and every second. My tongue is hungry and eager, licking slowly up her center, and her hands tighten in my hair, her body bowing violently this time. I hum, circling her clit, breathing her scent into me. She is like nothing else. I kiss her everywhere, plunging my tongue deeply inside, greedy for her wet flesh all over my mouth. If there is anything more delicious than this, I'm yet to taste it. I introduce my fingers, mixing plunges with licks, bites, sucks. "God, Rose," I mumble, the tip of her clitoris buzzing with need.

"I don't want to come," she croaks, pushing her arse into the mattress, escaping me. "Please, I want to come with you inside me."

I slip a hand under her arse and lift her back to my mouth, sealing my lips around her and sucking hard. She cries out, the sound drifting into a moan. She can have both, I'll make sure of it. "You're going to come so many times tonight, Rose, you're going to need me to carry you everywhere for the next week."

She looks down at me, and I can tell by the sparkle in her eyes that she likes the idea of that. "You would do that? Carry me, I mean."

I smile as I kiss her inside thigh, looking up at her. "Would you let me?" We're both outside our boxes here. She nods, subtle but clear. "Then I will," I confirm, returning to feasting on her magnificent, wet, begging pussy. Her body stiffens under me, and I place my palms on the insides of her thighs, pushing them wider as I work her up and up and . . .

"Ohhhhhhh . . ." She fists my hair brutally and tugs, her head rolling from side to side, and I pull back, blowing a cool stream of air over her clit, seeing it twitch before my eyes, before I go in for the kill. A gentle kiss. A light bite. A deep, long suck. She stiffens, pulls my hair, looks down at me with fire in her eyes, and then she moans, dropping her head back to the pillow, tilting her hips, pushing herself onto my mouth. I flatten my tongue and apply pressure where it counts, helping her work through it. My cock is pulsing where it's wedged between my stomach and the mattress, dying for some airtime.

But this. This now. It's magic.

Pleasuring her.

Hearing her.

Watching her.

It's new.

It's addictive.

She settles and finally finds it in herself to open her eyes, and I watch her slowly drop her lazy gaze to mine, her grip relaxing in my hair. The passion and need staring back at me pierces my hard heart.

She's so beautiful.

So graceful.

So . . . empty.

I get to my knees and crawl up her body, kissing each breast as I pass, and settle between her legs, caging her head with my arms resting on the bed. I stare down at her. "Promise me that if anyone ever hurts you again, you won't hesitate to kill them. No second chances, Rose." My voice is gruff with pleasure.

"I promise." She doesn't waver for a second. "But I won't need to because you'll do it for me."

The sureness in her makes me smile. Because she's right. "No hesitation." I lift my hips, and my cock falls to between her thighs.

Her breath stutters. "What if it's you who hurts me?"

I close my eyes and sink into her, the pleasure stripping my muscles of all strength. I settle my weight and swivel, choking a little as I inhale through the incredible feeling of her welcoming me into her body. "I won't hurt you." I look up and kiss the corner of her mouth, licking the seam of her lips. "I'll never hurt you." Never have I said something with so much conviction. In the haze of lust-driven thoughts, I know this is unprecedented. I know my father would say I'm an imbecile. *But this is right.* She's . . . right. Her watery eyes and the gentle bite down on her lip spells relief. "I'll only ask once. Do you want to be mine?"

"Yes." *No hesitation. No second-guessing.* Yes.

I drag my mouth over hers, moving slowly, owning her. Her hands leisurely roam my back as I start to rock gently into her. I'm blinded by the rightness, consumed by the feel of her accepting me in every way imaginable. I'm sure our bodies were made to fit together, every part of her molding to mine. And our souls. We're both damp, both slippery, both getting steadily breathless. Passion, a connection, anything remotely meaningful during intimacy with women, has always eluded me. Now, in this moment, a lifetime's worth of feelings are pouring down on me, and it feels good. So fucking good. I'm making love to a woman. It's my first time. And I know it's her first time too.

Every advance and retreat makes me shudder, the strength to keep my eyes open zapping my energy. I want to last. I want to last all fucking night, but my body has other ideas. I can feel the start of my climax getting ready to hijack me, and I roll to my back, bringing Rose with me. Her arms go ramrod straight, bracing on my chest as she breathes through the deeper penetration. Her pink nipples point at me, and I reach forward, gently circling one while she gathers herself. "Take your time."

"So deep," she gasps, juddering, and I smile, sitting up and holding her around her back. I bend my knees and let them drop out, leaving her room to move when she's ready. She covers my mouth with hers.

"You can't handle me?" I ask as she starts to sway, controlling all the movements.

"You know I can handle you."

I do know. And that's why I adore her so much. Strong, full of fire, and not fazed by me in the least. It's staggering, and seeing her in pieces earlier—the devastation, the torment—makes me appreciate her more. And now I know, I would do anything to keep that fire in her belly.

She sighs into my mouth and languidly sways back and forth, stroking my cock perfectly. Her kiss becomes firmer when she starts building, her body pushing farther into mine as urgency takes over. I channel all my efforts into getting myself there at the same time, my hips beginning to buck. Our teeth start to clash, her pants into my mouth coming with cute grunts. I feel my balls tighten, and my pace picks up, my hand moving to her shoulder and gripping. She yells and pulls free from my mouth, tossing her head back, and my face falls straight to her breasts, nuzzling into the soft flesh, sucking her nipples hard.

"Fuck." I convulse, feeling electric sparks going off all over my skin. "Rose, I'm there, baby."

Her head drops, and her eyes find mine. Fire. Red-hot fire. Her jaw tight, she grabs my face and pushes her forehead to mine, her gaze burning through me. She nods, and I thrust upward one last time, throwing us into a bottomless pit of pleasure. I'm clinging on for dear life as she bites into my shoulder, whimpering loudly as she vibrates all over me. "Shit," she puffs, stroking at the hair on my nape, limp against me. We're one big pile of sweating, heaving bodies.

And it's fucking perfect.

I collapse back, and she splatters on my front, her wet cheek on my chest. I toss my arm on the pillow above my head and hold her with the other. My eyes are heavy. I could sleep for a fucking year.

Reality leaves me. My purpose leaves me. My life leaves me.

Right now, there is only Rose. I feel like I've been born again. And even though I secretly swore to save her, I'm now not sure who's saving who.

18

ROSE

He wasn't being gallant. There was no gain for him in his actions, only loss. He lost a man. Before that, he had already won me, and I think he knew that deep down before he put a gun in my hand and told me to kill Watson. He was proving a point to me. He was also proving a point to his men. No one can touch me if they want to continue breathing.

It felt good. For someone to have my back, it felt so good. But with the elation comes guilt. And worry. But if there is a man who can fix my mess, it's Danny. First, I have to hope he forgives me for betraying him. I also have to build up the courage to tell him I'm not who he thinks I am. But that's a problem for another day. Maybe tomorrow. Maybe the next day. I know time isn't on my side, but while he's currently spooning me, his body curved perfectly around mine, I can't bring myself to ruin this moment. He's still inside me, though soft now, and has been snoozing with his lips in my hair for a while. It's 7 a.m. He only finished blowing my world apart again and again a few hours ago. I'm sticky, the scent of sex hangs thick in the air, and I'm aching perfectly everywhere, the best between my legs. I've never felt so serene. So at peace. It defies reason with so many consequences hanging over me.

Taking his hand on my stomach, I weave my fingers with his and melt further into his body, closing my eyes and concentrating on feeling him on every inch of my skin.

"I dreamt of you." His voice is hoarse with sleep, his breath hot against the back of my head. I open my eyes and stare forward, waiting for him to go on. But he doesn't, and I start to turn over, hearing him hiss a little when he finally slips free from me.

I shuffle over with his help until I'm mirroring him. His hand finds my hip, and he props himself up on his elbow. He is gorgeous in the morning. All sexed up, his eyes drowsy. "What did you dream?" I ask as he circles his fingertip on my hipbone. A flurry of tingles pitter-patter over my skin, reaching my nipples, and he smiles at the stiffening of them, leaning down and brushing his lips across one. I exhale and roll to my back, letting him crawl onto me and spread his body over mine. My hands delve into his messy hair while he splits his attention between each breast.

"I dreamt about these." He bites down on my nipple, making me solidify beneath him. "And this." His hand sinks down between us and cups me, his long, thick finger slipping easily inside of me. "And these." He moves up to my lips and indulges my mouth for a few, mind-spinning moments while he works me up once again. It's easy affection, and it's wonderful. "I dreamt it was all mine."

"And is it?" I ask. "All yours?"

"There's no question." His grin is wicked as he goes back to my chest, devouring each breast hungrily, his one finger turning into two. "My father always warned me that women make you vulnerable." He works his way down to my stomach and brushes his nose across my skin, studying the expanse of flesh. I prop myself up on my elbows to look down at him, watching him drift lower and lower. My blood whooshes with anticipation.

I breathe his name, spreading my thighs wider for him. He replaces his fingers with his mouth and licks me softly, kissing me gently between each sweep of his tongue. *Good God.* I drop to my back and sink my hands into my hair, searching for control.

"That good, baby?"

My internal muscles begin to contract, my shakes rapidly taking over. My heart booms faster, my temperature swiftly rises. His tongue is magical. And when he slips two fingers inside me again, doubling the sensations and pleasure, it's my undoing, my legs hardening as I come all over his face in sharp, rolling waves. I sink deeper into the bedsheets, electric shocks stabbing at the swollen cluster of nerves in my clit. My cheeks puff out, my body dazed from the fast onslaught of pleasure. I'm sated and hot as he kisses me gently, pulling his fingers free, trailing his mouth across my skin as he crawls back up my body. "Morning," he whispers, shifting his hips and driving straight into me. His move has my fading orgasm rebuilding.

"Morning," I sigh, hugging him, letting him take me to a place far better than this world. His drives are deep and exact, his grinds steady and firm. I've lost count of the amount of orgasms we've shared throughout the night, and more are on the way. He's right. I won't be able to walk properly, but it's okay. Because Danny will carry me wherever I need to go. Which isn't far from him. I smile to myself and stick my lips to his shoulder, stroking across his upper back as he sinks into me consistently and precisely, stripping back my breathing to shallow pants. He's a surprisingly masterful lover. Gentle, selfless, and utterly consuming. I'm totally taken by him, everything about him. His ethics are questionable. He's probably killed as many people as women he's fucked. He's cruel, callous, and he slapped me within an hour of meeting him. It's backward for me to feel anything other than hatred for him. But I don't hate him. I admire him—admire the state of mind he has me in. I admire him for being as fucked up as me. I couldn't tell you if the ache in my heart is love. I couldn't tell you whether the sting in my eyes when I think about his absence is love. I couldn't tell you if the butterflies in my tummy each time I look at him is love.

But I fear it is. Because it's the same ache I feel whenever I'm blessed with a picture of my son.

I close my eyes and breathe his sweaty skin into me, turning my face into his neck, squeezing him that little bit tighter. If I want to be his, then I am. But there's so much he doesn't know about me. "Danny," I whisper, my voice broken by the over-whelming sensations invading every piece of me, of the feel of him moving inside me. Just tell him. Spit it out. The longer I stall, the worse it'll become.

His head lifts so he can get me in his sights, and I fear for a moment that he'll see all of my sins in my eyes. He continues to thrust gently and slowly. "What is it?" He dips and kisses me, holding his mouth on mine as he keeps up his dizzyingly expert pattern of drives and grinds.

I lose my nerve, fearful of the reprisals. I'm not scared that he might hurt me. Not physically, anyway. I'm scared he'll turn his back on me, and this tranquility will be stolen from me. I swallow and shake my head, distracting him from pressing me by cupping the back of his head and plunging my tongue into his mouth, sweeping through hungrily. Sparks start to fly, my world starts to spin, and when Danny grunts under his breath, I naturally start to thrust up into his plunges. My fingers claw. He starts to shake. "Shit, Rose." His hips jerk, and on a drawn-out mumble of nonsense, he sinks his face into my neck and bites down gently, pushing me higher and higher with each drive into me. Stars start to hamper my vision, my pulse in my ears distorting our moans of ecstasy. Our bodies become frenzied in the search for their releases, our voices louder.

My climax is there, right there, just waiting for me to seize it.

But it seizes me. It grabs me and tears me apart with the force, and I cry out into his shoulder, my body hijacked by stabs of merciless pleasure. I gasp, I choke, my eyes fly wide open as it savages me. "Oh my God," I pant, blinking rapidly, my nerves sizzling. The pull of my walls around him is natural and unstoppable, milking him on and on as he growls his way through his release. I'm dizzy, my world spinning crazily. Never before has helplessness felt so good.

Exhaling loudly, he rolls off me, falling to his back and throwing his arms to the pillow above him. The cool air that blankets me is bliss, but nothing like having him swathing me. I move onto my side and place my finger on his tummy, drawing over his abdominals, counting them as I do. Not that I haven't mentally done it a dozen times. Eight. Danny Black doesn't just have a six-pack. He has an eight-pack. I smile as my finger draws lines in the shadows between his muscles. "Can I ask you something?"

His head drops to look at me. "No."

I give him a feigned filthy look and pinch the flesh over his ribs. Of course, he smiles. It's beautiful. I might be pushing my luck, but that seems to come naturally with him. "Why are you unkind to Esther?" If I were her, I would have told him to go fuck himself. "She does everything for you. Washing, cleaning, cooking, and you're so clipped with her."

His face falls into impassiveness. Coldness, a coldness I'm familiar with, but now I get a strange vibe from it. It tells me he's wondering whether he should say what he's about to say. He inhales. "Isn't washing, cleaning, and cooking part of what a mother should do for their child?"

For a second, I'm thrown by his statement, my brain unable to compute the connection. Then, like a lead balloon, realization drops. I recoil, my hand leaving his stomach. Esther is his mom? "I don't understand," I admit, floored by confusion and shock.

"She's my mother."

No. I'm clearly missing something here. "But you treat her so terribly." I've obviously said something wrong, because warning falls like an iron veil over his soft eyes, hardening them. I retreat, heeding the threat, keeping my mouth under control before I unwittingly say something else to anger him. But I know him well enough now to know that these flashes of anger are actually pain.

I can see perfectly well that he's working hard to contain his irritation, and though I wish it wouldn't, it just makes my curiosity heighten. Eventually, he rips his steel stare from mine and breathes in. "My mother abandoned me when I was eight years old," he says softly, though resentment burns the corners of his quiet voice. Something tells me that this isn't something he's talked about much, if at all. I honestly don't know what to do, so I do what's natural. I take his hand and hold it. My move, thankfully, loosens him up a bit, and he cracks the straightness of his mouth with a small curve, lifting our held hands to his lips and kissing my knuckles. "Carlo Black isn't my biological father."

My mouth falls open. "He isn't?"

"I'm British, Rose. Carlo was American. How does that work?"

"Easy. Your mother could be British." I frown. "Which she is." I'm stumped.

"Come here." He sits up and pulls me onto his lap, arranging my legs on either side of his hips while I continue to frown. "Remember I once told you that someone saved me?"

"Yes."

"The person who saved me was Carlo Black." He smiles at my shock, taking my hands and holding them on his stomach. "I was ten. It was two years after my mother abandoned me and left me at the mercy of her piece-of-scum boyfriend. It was the day this happened." Danny points to his cheek with our hands, and my stunned eyes fall onto the beast of a scar that dominates his right cheek. "I'd been beaten black and blue for four years, starved and ra—" He stops himself, his gaze unlocking from mine. He looks past me into nothingness.

"Raped." I utter the vile word, winning back his attention. "He raped you." I feel sick. So fucking sick, I have to swallow down the bile building. Look at this strong, beautiful man. Just look at him. *Raped?*

The flash of vengeance in his blues is raw. And I get it. "So, you see, when Carlo put a bullet in my stepfather's head, I didn't shed a tear. I was mesmerized by Carlo—his crisp cream suit, his American accent, the two fifties he slipped me, and most of all, I was mesmerized that he had just killed my problem. Just like that. Gone. No hesitation." Light flickers in his hard eyes, and though it seems inhumane to take pleasure from the death of a person, I can't help appreciating how good it must have felt. I had a problem in Watson. And Danny killed the problem. In that moment, I felt a burden lift, and now, more than ever, I can't help the hope building. The hope that Danny can erase all of my problems.

"He asked me if my stepfather caused the bruises on my ribs," Danny continues. "And I told him yes. So he shot him." He laughs a little. "Then he told me to get in his car. I didn't hesitate. I got right on in there with a perfect stranger, a killer, and never looked back. My mother had abandoned me, and the monster I lived with was now dead. I had no one. Carlo brought me back to Miami. He fed me, watered me, made sure I was clean. He hired a private tutor and demanded I relay everything I learned each day. It didn't make much sense to me, but who was I to argue? Then one day, on my eleventh birthday, I finally plucked up the courage to ask him why he'd saved me."

"And what did he say?" I press, swallowed up in his story, eager to hear more of how Danny Black came to be.

"He said he wanted a son." He smiles. "He wanted a son and he didn't want a woman. So he took me. Simple as that. He told me that a kid who'd had half his cheek sliced off and didn't cry about it was worthy of the status of being his son. He gave me a new birth certificate. Had my name changed to Black, officially adopted me, and I became an American citizen. I have not a fucking clue how he did it, but I never questioned him. I trusted him. Because he saved me."

Given who Carlo Black was, it's insane for me to think that Danny won the jackpot. But he did. "And your mom? How come she's here now?"

"Because Carlo found her and brought her here." His sweet reminiscent tone has gone and resentment is back. "I thought I wanted to find her. But when Carlo tracked her down, I looked at her and felt nothing but hatred. She chose drugs and prostitution over me. She left me to slowly die, and I will never forgive her for that."

But she's here. It's Danny's way of being cruel and kind all at the same time. This man, this killing, formidable, merciless man, isn't as hard as the world thinks he is. He can't turn his back on her completely.

I bite my lip, astounded, but especially that he's told me. Confided in me. Esther serves a purpose. Danny's giving her the chance to do all the things she didn't do when he was a boy. "And now Carlo's world is your world."

Danny nods, though something in his expression tells me he's not as pleased about that as he feels he should be. "And what about you?" Danny asks.

Me? I clam up. We are not having that conversation, and I'm ignoring the wretched guilt I'm feeling after he's told me his story. I shrug as nonchalantly as I can. "Nothing to tell."

"Rape."

I naturally flinch at the word, feeling myself crawling into my shell. I don't know what to say, so I say nothing, flexing my hands in his until he releases me. I rest my palms on his bare chest and lean in, giving his scar a light kiss, before I get up off the bed.

"Where are you going?" he asks.

"To get my toothbrush." It's all I can think of to get me out of the room to compose myself. As I step away, he seizes my wrist stopping me, and I silently beg him not to press. "Rose?" I look over my shoulder tentatively, so nervous he's going to demand answers. He studies me for a few moments, obviously taking in my sudden discomfort. "Don't be long." He lets go and edges down the bed until he's lying again.

Relief. It nearly floors me. I take his shirt from the floor. "Mind if I borrow this?" I push my arms through the sleeves before getting his answer, then find my panties and pull them on. He watches my every move until I pull his bedroom door shut behind me. Then I stand on the other side, staring at the wood, my head thumping. All the words, every confession, are all on my tongue ready to be spat out. I just don't know where to begin.

I hustle back to my room and find the phone behind the drawer, and I don't think twice about texting Nox to tell him I have nothing to report. That's the first step of my plan complete. The easiest step. I quickly replace the cell, scrub my teeth, and hurry back to Danny's room, but when I make it there, he's not in bed. I look across to the glass doors and see him on the terrace, his long body naked. My eyes root to his back as I creep up on him, slipping my arms between his and hugging him from behind. "You realize the panels are glass, don't you?" I ask.

He moves so fast, it's all a blur, and then I'm swiftly in front of him, my ass pressed up against the glass panel, Danny caging me in.

"It is?" he says, taking the bottom of the shirt I'm wearing and pulling it up to my waist. "Oh dear."

I purse my lips and peek over my shoulder. It's silly. If there was anyone in the garden below, Danny wouldn't be exposing my ass to them. Returning my attention to him, I shrug and he wrinkles his nose, rubbing it with mine. Everything—the jet ski incident, Watson, last night, now, it's all building a pile of rightness, telling me that what I'm doing is the best thing. "Can we have dinner tonight?" I ask. I'll tell him then. It'll give me the day to figure out where to begin and how I'll explain bit by bit.

Pulling away, he cocks a questioning head. "Dinner? Like a date?"

What is that heat in my cheeks? "If you want to call it that."

His lips twist, as he clearly tries to wrap his morbid mind around the concept of a normal date. I suddenly feel stupid and for a brief moment I waver on the edge of uncertainty. "A date," he muses.

"It's easy," I explain. "Do what you've done the past two times you've taken me for dinner, just don't kill or threaten anyone during," I quip, trying to make light of what he clearly thinks is an odd suggestion.

"Okay." He starts bending his arms against the rail behind me, bringing his face down to my neck. He presses a kiss on my throat before straightening them again, pushing away from me. Then he bends again, dropping down and placing another kiss on my chest before straightening his arms.

"What are you doing?" I ask, as he continues to bend and straighten his arms, like he's doing push-ups against the railings, me trapped between his muscled limbs. Another kiss, this time on my cheek.

"I missed the gym this morning because of you." He drifts away and my eyes fall to his biceps bulging. They are truly sigh-worthy, and an appreciative wisp of air leaves me.

"I think three sets of twenty will do." I pout as I stroke down the length of his swelling arm, happy to admire him while he has a quick workout.

"You gonna count?"

"One," I start as he slowly lowers toward me again, looking me in the eye as his lips land on my chest.

"Open the shirt," he orders, pushing himself up straight again. I do as I'm bid and expose my front to his eyes as he slowly descends again. This time, he goes lower, kissing me between my breasts.

"Two," I breathe, resting my arms on the metal railing and leaning back, making the distance between us greater. Not that it fazes him. With each press, he kisses a different part of my body, and with each flex of his toned arms, his muscles swell more, the blood pumping in more than one place. I'm so lost in the mesmerizing sight of him before me, I lose count, my mind only willing to focus on his mouth meeting my skin. By the time Danny finishes, there's not an inch of my torso or neck that doesn't have his lips imprinted on them.

His final descent brings his mouth down onto my forearm. My dressing is gone—Esther said the wound needs air—and he brushes a delicate kiss across the cut. Regret captures me again, and my eyes fall to Danny's arm, where a bandage still covers his wounds. Not just one cut, but many cuts, all much deeper than my single slice. I swallow and lay my hand over the white dressing. "Why did you do that?" He pulls his mouth away from my arm and looks up at me, searching my eyes.

"Why did you?"

"Release of pressure. Something I can control." My admission surprises me more than it surprises Danny, his face remaining straight. "And because sometimes I hate myself."

He swallows. "I did it because it was me or you."

"What?"

"Enough people in your life have damaged you, Rose." He eyes me closely, and I swallow. He has no idea. "I didn't want you on the list of people I want to kill."

He wants to kill everyone who's ever hurt me? That list is a long, *long* list. And my hope just soared, yet I can only manage a meek smile.

Danny circles my nose with his. Pushes his lips to mine. "After our date, where I promise not to kill anyone, will you join me in bed again?"

"Yes."

"Good. I'm done with pushups." He slips an arm around my waist and hauls my breathless body into his arms. "Ready for some thigh work?"

"You or me?"

He smiles mildly and carries me to the bed, sitting me on the end and shoving my legs apart. "You." His rough voice could make me come all by itself. "Squeeze," he demands, and I strain to close my legs. They don't move a millimeter, not with his palms keeping them where they are. "Harder, Rose."

I grit my teeth and fight against his resistance. I get nowhere.

"I think three sets of twenty will do."

"What?" I choke, alarmed, as he abruptly pulls my panties aside, burying his face between my legs. My eyes roll in the back of my head and my back plummets to the mattress. "Three sets of twenty," I breathe, smiling when he bites the tip of my clitoris. It doesn't take him long to get me fisting the sheets, my legs squirming around his head. I pull the sheets over my face, relishing the coolness of the cotton on my blazing skin. It's coming, I'm there, it's . . .

I hear a loud bang in the distance, and Danny is quickly out from between my legs, looking lost between drunkenness and alertness. My building orgasm is swallowed up by worry as he jumps up and paces to the door. "Stay there."

I quickly cover myself as he swings the door open, completely naked, and looks down the corridor. On a curse, he slams it and finds some boxers, pulling them on and grabbing his phone from the nightstand. "What is it?" I ask, getting to my feet and fastening the buttons of his shirt down my body.

The door to his bedroom flies open, and Brad falls in, looking harassed. Ringo follows on behind. "What's going on?" Danny asks as Brad fights to get his breath back.

"Explosion by the front gates." He makes his way onto the terrace with Ringo.

Danny follows, his eyes raging holy hell. Every muscle on his back protrudes with uneasiness. "Fuck," he curses, and I look past him, seeing smoke rising in the distance, a dense, dirty gray cloud that symbolizes ruin. I walk out onto the terrace, my nostrils immediately picking up the smell of burning rubber.

"Get the men together," Danny orders, brushing past me and retrieving some jeans, tugging them on while I stand on the terrace with Brad and Ringo, watching the smoke ball growing.

I step forward toward the edge, setting my hands on the metal while Ringo and Brad back up into Danny's room, talking urgently. Their voices morph and muffle as I stare across the grounds toward the main gate. I see a few men running through the gardens, guns poised, shouting panicked orders and instructions as they go.

Apprehension engulfs me, as grim and destructive as the swirl of smoke still rising.

This is my fault.

The shoot-out in Vegas, the jet ski, this. It's all happening because of me. I swallow, searching for the courage I need to tell Danny. I can't wait. I need to do it now. I turn, finding him pulling a white T-shirt over his head as Brad talks into his cell and Ringo throws Danny's boots at his feet.

"Danny," I say, and he looks up. I expect him to dismiss me, to tell me he hasn't got time for me right now. But he doesn't. He comes to me. Kisses me. And looks at me in a way that tells me everything is going to be okay. And then he walks away. "Danny," I blurt, and he stops at the door, turning to look at me standing motionless on the terrace. A faint whistling sound infiltrates my thoughts, and I try to push it back, focusing on mentally running through my confession, straightening it out in my head before I speak. The sound grows louder and louder. I can't find the words. Where are the words? I stare into his questioning eyes, digging deep for the courage.

Then Danny looks past me, his eyes growing wide, fear creeping in from the edges.

I frown as the whistle transforms into an ear-piercing screech, and slowly turn to look behind me, to see what has his horrified attention.

"Rose, move!"

I see something black coasting through the sky toward me, growing by the second. By the time I realize what it is, it's too late.

The whole house shakes, my eardrums feel like they burst, and I scream, grabbing the railings on the balcony as flames billow in front of me. I'm grabbed from behind and hauled back, the terrace disappearing from under my feet, crumbling away in huge chunks. "Rose!"

My body jolts painfully, my arm feeling like it's been ripped from its socket. It takes me a while to figure out why. Then it hits me. I look down calmly. There's no terrace under my feet, just a sheer drop to the ground where the remains of the terrace lays in a pile of bricks, rubble, and smoke. I'm hanging over the edge, one hand in Danny's, death staring me in the eye.

How easy it would be to let go of him. To be rid of my problems and the consequences attached to my choices.

My boy will be okay. He'll be safe if I'm gone. Because I

don't think I can fight this battle now. The war is over. I can feel my hand slipping from Danny's. Nox won't take any pleasure in hurting my boy if he can't hurt me.

I look up into Danny's eyes. They speak to me amid the chaos of fire, destruction, and panic, and all I can think in this moment is how much more destruction there will be if I *don't* let go. More death. More hurt. Clarity hits and sticks. I was deluded. Mad to think this mess can be sorted out. Mad to think I could spill my sins on Danny and think it'll all be okay. It won't be. How can it be? Danny won't kill me for betraying him, yet his rejection will feel like death. But Nox *will* kill me. Call me stupid, but I'd rather call the shots on how I go. It'll be the first time in my life that I've ever made a decision for me. I can't be with Danny. That's my cold, hard reality, and now, in this moment, I don't want to live if I can't be. I've lost too much already. I can't lose him too.

"Don't you fucking dare let go," Danny growls, releasing his spare hand that's holding on to the mangled metal doorframe and dropping to his stomach, extending it to me. "Take it. God help me, Rose, take my other hand."

I find myself shaking my head, flexing my sweaty hand in his, trying to free myself from his grip.

"No," he yells, scrambling to reach for my free, swaying hand. "Rose, I'll fucking kill you myself, I swear."

I stare at him. Silent. My world is mine again.

"Rose, for fuck's sake," he pants down at me. "I didn't just spill my fucking heart out, tell you my whole miserable fucking story, for you to bail on me now. Take my fucking hand. You don't get to die now."

I'm dead either way. I yank my hand free and feel gravity claim me, pulling me to my death.

"No!" Danny lunges forward, seizing my wrist and roaring as Brad grabs the waist of his jeans to stop him falling over the edge with me.

"Fucking hell, Danny," Brad bellows, breathless.

"God damn you, Rose." Danny looks me straight in the eye, his face awash with fury as he starts shuffling back with the help of Brad, dragging me up over the edge, my thighs and chest scraping on the rough, jagged concrete as I go. "What the fuck?" he yells, shoving me to my back and flopping on top of me, his breathing shot. I stare at him, dazed. I've seen anger on Danny Black before. On countless occasions. But those times pale in comparison to what I'm seeing now. Pure, raw, burning rage. And it frightens me. For the first time, he's frightening me. I look away from his fiery eyes and get yanked back to face him. His mouth is twisted violently, his scar deep and glowing. "I didn't make love to a woman for the first fucking time in my life for her to end this." He virtually pushes my face away. "But at least I know where I stand." He gets up, his look pure filth, and he keeps it on me for a long, painful time.

"We need you downstairs," Brad says, edging out of the room.

"On my way." Danny grabs my hand and pulls me to my feet, giving me a quick once-over before pulling me toward the door. I stagger along mindlessly, my head ready to burst, my mind in tatters. The chaos extends into the main house, men running everywhere in a panic. We meet Esther at the bottom of the stairs, and I'm handed over to her like a piece of discarded trash. "She's covered in cuts. See to it." Danny disappears out the door, and I look down my front. I'm filthy, dirt and soot smearing me. My hand rests on my stomach over Danny's shredded shirt, and Esther moves in quickly, opening one of the buttons to reveal a mess of scrapes and raw grazes. It doesn't hurt. Nothing hurts.

Except my heart.

19

DANNY

Fucking carnage. As I stand amid the rubble, slowly circling on the spot, I question for the first time in my existence what my purpose is. We've lost one man. Freddie. He was on the gate when it was hit. My personal suite has been ripped apart, and the police are swarming my property.

I dip and shift a lump of brick, reaching past it and pulling at a piece of material that's buried. The silver dress I bought Rose. An image of her face flashes through my mind, a face that screamed defeat as she hung from my hand off the edge of the terrace. Moments before that, she was gazing adoringly at me as I swirled my tongue through the slickness of her addictive pussy. Something shifted between us during the night, and it's shifted right back. I was distracted. While I was lost in her, my men were dying and my house was being destroyed. I nearly lost her too.

Brad lets out a sigh, crouching down beside me, looking around to make sure we're out of earshot. "Len checked in earlier. I was on my way to tell you, but the bomb . . . " He picks up a piece of wood and looks it over before casting it aside on another sigh. "Adams is taking calls from a burner phone. Untraceable. His bank accounts are bone dry. All of them."

"We didn't tell Adams we were going to the hospital," I say out of the blue, gazing around at the carnage. I can feel Brad's questioning eyes on me, so I go on. "Whoever was at the hospital wasn't there to shoot me. They were shooting at the kid because he's in their way too. So whoever Adams has breathing down his neck wants my marina, and, like me, they want Adams in power. They want Miami." It's like the explosion didn't only light up the sky, it also lit up my mind. "They know I won't release Adams. They probably haven't got thirty-five million to pay me off, plus whatever more cash they need to continue bankrolling Adams, so the only way for them is to see me dead. It's easy. Cheap. The question is, who and what are they planning on getting into the country through my boatyard?"

"Easy? To kill *you*?" Brad almost laughs. "You're still standing, Danny. Just."

I hear him. He's telling me, in an indirect kind of way, that I need my wits about me. I always need my wits about me. Pops was right. Women are nothing but a distraction. "Get Adams here. It's time for some torture tactics."

"With fucking pleasure." He's off, heading back to the house. Keen, eager.

I've put Brad through a hell of a lot of shit in his life. And in this last month, more than he's used to. But he's still fucking angry that I thought it was a good plan to kill the kid. He's still enraged that I put myself at risk like that. So, yeah, he's pissed. And this task will be a release of pressure for him. *Have at it.*

"When you do shit, Danny, you do it in style."

I look up and find Spittle kicking remnants of my terrace aside, his shiny shoes dull with dust. He looks up at my mansion. "You're lucky. They could have taken out the entire house."

Lucky? My private suite is obliterated and I nearly lost Rose. Rising to my full height, I turn away from him and head for the house. "You going to find out who did this?"

"I was hoping *you* might be able to enlighten *me*." Spittle follows me without invitation, taking a hanky from his suit pocket when he makes it inside. Sitting on the bottom step of the staircase, he wipes at his shoes.

"Do I look like an FBI agent to you?" I ask. "You think I would be here now if I knew who just sent a bomb sailing into my bedroom?"

He grimaces at his blackened hanky and folds it neatly. I head toward my office, my mind set on the Scotch awaiting me. I take the bottle and two glasses and drop into my chair, Spittle joining me on the other side of my desk. I hold up a glass and he nods, prompting me to pour. Passing him his glass, I sink back into my chair as Brad walks in, helping himself to the hard stuff after giving me a nod. It's going to be a bloody afternoon.

"Is your house being partially blown up anything to do with the shoot-out in Fort Lauderdale?" Spittle asks. "Because you may have cut CCTV, but I know you were there."

"Nothing to do with me."

He sips and nods his approval at the Scotch. "Not the shoot-out, no. Officers chased down the gunman a few miles away."

I hitch an eyebrow. "Oh?"

"He won't talk."

"Give him to me," I order. "He'll talk." I'll torture the fucker until he gives me what I want.

"Nothing to do with you? Come on, Danny. Why were you there?"

I sigh, bored of the twenty questions. "There's a kid there. Jepson. Parents just died in a plane crash. He survived. Someone wants him dead."

"A kid? Who? And why?"

"Just get the kid protection, Spittle, there's a good boy." I don't have time to fill in all the blanks. "The man, the shooter. Let us pay him a visit." They'll be no torture, but there will be threats galore. "And then maybe I'll give you something more to keep you busy." As soon as I find out who the fuck has strolled into my town wreaking fucking havoc.

"Fine, Black. You're a fly in my fucking ointment."

Yeah, yeah. I know. "His name?"

"Like I said, he's not talking. We've run face checks, fingerprints, DNA. Nothing. The man's a ghost."

Just like all those men in Vegas. "Get Brad into wherever he's being held."

"If you insist."

"I do."

Spittle regards me across the desk. "Since we're on the subject of explosions, your jet ski was found off the coast burnt to a cinder. What happened?"

"It was stolen."

"Then why didn't you report it?"

I shrug. "You know me, Spittle. Bigger fish to fry. Have it dropped off at the boatyard."

He visibly deflates, exhausted by the brick walls he keeps hitting. "It's beyond repair."

"I'm rather attached to it."

"Fine. And I have someone working on the phone."

"Forget about it." I strain the words. "Like I said, bigger fish to fry." I stand, my way of ending our impromptu meeting. "If that's all?"

"That's all. As ever, thank you for your time, Mr. Black." He bows, the sarcastic wanker. "I'll see you tomorrow."

Tomorrow. My father's funeral. Amid the rolling madness, I almost forgot. "He told me to shoot any FBI who show up."

Spittle laughs his way out of my office. "I'll be sure to wear my vest." Stopping at the door, he turns back, something close to concern marring his rugged face. "Someone is clearly determined to put an end to you, Danny."

"Is that your way of telling me to be careful?" What a joke. Me winding up dead would relieve Spittle of endless stress. "I'm touched."

He waves his hand flippantly. "I'm just pointing out that the whole of Miami, hell, the whole of America, knows you're burying your father tomorrow."

"I've got it covered," I assure him, pouring more Scotch. "See you there."

I'm left in peace for all of two seconds before my phone rings. I'm grateful. Silence leaves too much space to think, and I'm not thinking about shit I should be thinking about. I look down at the screen and smile. "Adams," I answer. "Called to tell me you're declining my invitation to visit me?"

"You tried to kill the kid."

My teeth grind impatiently. "I didn't try to kill the fucking kid. I got him out the firing line."

Adams is silent on the end of the line. I hope he's thinking carefully about his next move. He clearly is, but given his lack of a reply, I'm assuming he doesn't know what it is. "Perry, let me make this easy for you." I sit forward and rest my elbows on the table. "I have your girlfriend. I'm going to cut off her pretty face and send it to you in a pretty box if you don't tell me who the fuck wants my marina and why."

"I'm being blackmailed," he whispers.

"By who?"

"I don't know. They have pictures of me and Rose. God, I was so careful, but one of my staff . . ." He sighs. "I obviously wasn't paying him enough. It'll ruin me if they get out. My campaign will be obliterated."

Pictures of him and Rose? *Ignore the anger, Danny. Ignore it.*

Bigger fish to fry. "Are you telling me that you're trying to turn me over because you don't want America to know that you've been shagging behind your wife's back?"

"God, no."

"Who got the pictures? The member of your staff, I want his name." Let's start connecting some fucking dots.

"He's dead."

"What?"

"They sent me his head, Danny. They sent me his fucking head!" His voice is shaking terribly. His head. Fuck me, Adams probably vomited all over it.

"Yeah, well, I might be sending you a whole fucking body."

He's silent for a few moments, the gravity of his situation sinking in. "They've promised money. Said I could pay you back with it, but then you upped it to thirty-five million, for Christ's sake. They're not coughing up. I'm fucking cornered." Finally, the man gives in to his helplessness and crumbles down the line. "I walk away from you, you kill me. I walk away from them, they expose me and probably kill me too."

"I just threatened to cut off your girlfriend's face, you dick," I spit, disgusted by his lack of thought for Rose. "Does she feature at all in your dilemma?" I want to cut off *his* face now.

"You won't do it," he replies, too matter-of-factly for my liking. "There aren't just pictures of me and Rose."

"What?"

"Today I was sent some of *you* and Rose. Looking rather cozy on the shore at that boatyard of yours. And at an Italian restaurant downtown. For a man making threats on her well-being, you looked pretty smitten to me."

I stare blankly forward, my mind empty, leaving Adams to go on.

"My contact sent them and told me not to worry about my girlfriend. Told me she's safe, and I think she is, isn't she, Danny?

She's bewitched you too. But I know she means nothing to my contact. I know he'd rip her apart. You have to help me protect her."

Rip her apart? I'd like to see him fucking try. "She means nothing to me," I grate, so fucking angry with myself, seeing my dad shaking his head at me in disappointment.

"Really?"

"You want to test your theory, Adams?"

"I'm not surprised, Danny. Don't beat yourself up about it. She had the same effect on me."

"Let me spell this out for you, Adams," I seethe, starting to quake with anger. "If I don't get that marina, you, your wife, your kids, every living fucking relative of yours will be dead, and it won't be quick. They'll all know the reason why they're sitting on that chair with metal prongs in their thighs. They'll all know it's because of your dirty dealings. And as for Rose, you *will* get her pretty face in a box. You want that?"

"No," he whispers.

"Who is it, Perry?"

"I don't know! *They* contact *me*. I swear, Danny, I don't know who they are."

I slam my fist on the desk, out of control, standing and sweating on the spot.

Brad rushes into the office, his face alarmed when he finds me heaving down the phone. "The next time they reach out to you, you tell them to come see me." I hang up, reaching up to my throat, feeling my neck veins bulging.

"Do I want to ask?" Brad steps forward, nervous as shit.

"Get Adams and bring him to me." I slump into my chair, stressed as fuck. My only comfort in this moment is that Rose is here with me, so Adams's contact can't touch her. My head falls into my hands. That fucking missile came pretty fucking close, though. I don't know much right now, but I know whoever's pulling Adams's strings is playing for the win. And at this rate, he's going to get it.

If I could crawl into bed and stay there until today is over, I would. My bedroom being completely obliterated isn't the only reason why I can't. My father would haunt me for the rest of my days if I didn't show up at his funeral.

I fix my black tie in the mirror, wriggling it from side to side until it's perfect. Then I make my way to my office and have two straight Scotches, one after the other, before opening the top drawer of my desk just a fraction. I stare at the serpent ring, the emerald eyes glowing in the darkness. They could be my father's eyes, sharp and accusing. I ignore the ache in my stomach that tells me he's disappointed, pulling the drawer open the rest of the way and picking up the ring. I turn it between my fingers for a few moments. Then slide it into my pocket, unable to put the damn thing on my finger.

I look up when Brad enters, his black suit as crisp as his hair. "You find Adams yet?"

"Yeah." His eyebrow hitches, and for a moment I wonder whether he's going to tell me that yeah, they've found him. Washed up on the shore. Splattered on a sidewalk. A bullet in his head. "He's taken a last-minute vacation to the Hamptons. One of the men is on his way to offer him a ride back."

I laugh out loud, the sound unstoppable. He thinks he can leave the state and his problems will go away? Stupid fucker.

"You ready?" Brad asks.

"No," I admit, forcing my feet forward.

We walk together out of the office and down the corridor to the entrance hall, and Brad opens the front door for me. I pull the lapels of my jacket in, and then smooth my hand through my hair.

My skin heats, and everything tells me not to seek out the source. But I still turn, finding Rose standing at the top of the stairs. Our eyes meet, hers soft, mine hard.

I look away, refusing to be drawn into their dead depths. "Let's go," I say, even and strong, feeling anything but.

Brad gets into my car with Ringo, and two of my other men take the Range Rover behind. I watch them pull away, taking a left when they pull out of the mansion. I slide into the other Merc alone, wait five minutes, and then leave.

The entire drive to the quiet cemetery on the west side of town, I can hear my father voicing his displeasure, his ego dented by my intentions. I ignore him, keeping my hands firmly on the wheel. When I pull up at the ancient churchyard, the priest is waiting, my father's coffin laid by the side of a grave. I swallow and get out, making my way through the headstones to the spot I chose by a beautiful rose bush. The pink pompoms bursting from the green are the only flash of color in the cemetery, and the very reason I picked this spot.

"It's never too late to have some color in your life, Mister," I say quietly, reaching the edge of the pit that I'm about to have my father lowered into. The priest and the grave diggers remain a good distance away, leaving me to myself for a while until I give them the nod. I stare at the top of his coffin. "Don't be mad," I say to him, lowering to my haunches and resting a hand on the edge of the shiny wood. "I have an assassin on steroids after me. This was the only way." I fight down the expanding lump in my throat. "I know you wanted a show, to go out with a bang, but this time I've done what I wanted. Just me and you, Pops. How it's always been. Just me and you." My damn fucking eyes sting, and I reach up and roughly wipe them. "Things are changing, Mister. Power is harder to keep, people are harder to control, and my determination is getting harder to maintain. I just wanted you to know that." I stand and slip my hand into my pocket, finding his ring and feeling it. "Everything is uncertain, except one thing." I swallow and move back, nodding to the priest. "I miss you." It's only now I realize, all these years after he found me, that this moment was always in his thoughts. Because the reality is, who would miss him if I wasn't here? I feel like he's set me up for heartbreak. He succeeded. He's also made me wonder who the fuck is going to miss *me* when I'm gone? I'm the last Black. The legacy ends with me. I can't decide if that's a blessing or a travesty.

The priest approaches, his Bible across his hands, his white cloak dragging the dirt. I zone out while he bumbles on about The Lord, Jesus Christ, and how my father is at peace. I want to be at peace. I want the turmoil within me to fuck off. His coffin is lowered into the dark pit, and I move in closer to the edge, pulling out his ring from my pocket. I kiss it before dropping it to the wood. "Rest in peace, Mister," I whisper, tossing the priest a bundle of notes before turning and striding away.

The second I fall into the seat of my car, I pull the hip flask from my inside pocket and guzzle half, watching as the men shovel dirt into the hole in the ground. And I don't leave until they're done.

As I drive slowly up the lane toward the main road, I dial Brad, ignoring the endless missed calls from Uncle Ernie.

"Anything untoward?" I say as soon as he answers.

"You mean other than hundreds of people mourning a coffin full of bricks?"

"Yes," I answer shortly, my mood not interested in jokes.

"The son of Carlo Black was missing from his funeral. The whispers could be heard for miles." I hear footsteps, and then a car door slamming. "Your uncle Ernie knows something isn't right. He knows you wouldn't miss it for the world."

"I'll deal with Ernie. Anything else?"

"You mean anyone here to kill you?" He laughs lightly. "I doubt they'd be coming out of their hiding place to ask where the fuck you are." The engine starts and more car doors close, my men joining Brad. "We've had our eyes open. Nothing obvious. Spittle was here, too, asking after you."

"Spittle has a fucking death wish." I turn onto the main road and put my foot down. "I'll see you back at the house." I hang up and turn on the radio, shaking my head in wonder when one of my father's favorite tracks invades my hearing. Otis Redding sings *Sittin' on the Dock of the Bay*. I join him, cocking my elbow on the window and relaxing back in my seat.

New gates are being installed when I pull up, the new wall built, the cement still wet. The workmen move aside, letting me through, and I breathe out my relief as I roll up the driveway and park.

As I'm walking around the path toward the back, the quickest route to my office, I glance up, seeing Rose standing on her terrace, just meters away from the mangled remains of my own balcony. She's wrapped in a towel, her wet hair piled high, her hands braced on the metal railings. Watching me. I rip my eyes away and enter the house via the garden door in the drawing room, walking through to the corridor that leads to my office. I see Esther up ahead, a bale of towels piled in her hands. "Go tell Rose to get off that terrace," I snap, wondering why I'm bothering to even worry. The woman has complete disregard for her life. Why the fuck should I care?

Esther nods and leaves, and I break the threshold of my office, grabbing a bottle of Scotch and doing what I seem to be doing so well these days. I pull my tie loose, undo my top button, and drop into the chair. I open the bottom drawer and pull out a framed picture of Pops. "Don't look at me like that," I mutter, setting it down before me and putting the bottle to my lips, glugging down more than I should while he watches me. It kills me to think that he would be disappointed in me. He's been gone a matter of weeks, and it's all gone to shit.

More Scotch.

By the time Brad makes it back some time later, I've ignored dozens of missed calls from Spittle and Uncle Ernie and worked my way through nearly an entire bottle of Scotch, the alcohol dulling my senses perfectly, my body relaxed for the first time today. He takes one look at me and sighs.

"Fuck you," I mumble, taking another glug out of principle. "I buried my father today. I deserve a drink."

"How'd it go?" Brad asks, putting his hand out for the bottle. I reluctantly give it up and he knocks some back.

"I could hear him cursing my arse to hell," I admit, accepting the bottle back, liking the feeling of my mind becoming fuzzy. "What does Spittle want?" I point to my phone where the missed calls glow up at me.

"He's got me in. I'm going to find out who this shooter is and who the fuck he works for."

"Good." I shove my phone back when it rings again, Uncle Ernie's name flashing threateningly at me.

"He knows something isn't right," Brad says, giving me a look to suggest I'm deluded for thinking I can avoid my father's cousin. "He's already on his way here." Brad only just finishes speaking when I hear a commotion from outside the office, Uncle Ernie's booming voice sinking through the wood and telling me what to expect. My heavy eyes stare at the door, waiting for it to fly open.

"What the hell just happened?" Ernie bellows as he charges in, the door hitting the wall behind it.

"I'm not in the mood," I say calmly. "If you've come to toast the old man, then sit down and I'll pour you a drink. If not, fuck off and leave me in peace."

Ernie's nostril flare dangerously. I couldn't give a fuck. "Where the hell were you?"

"Burying my father," I snarl, my men moving in behind my uncle, ready for the nod to eject him. The wave of confusion that travels across Ernie's face is a novelty.

"He wasn't in the coffin," he breathes, realization dawning. The old man reaches for the doorframe to hold himself up. "I wanted to pay my respects, Danny. Say my goodbyes."

I ignore his hurt and get up on unstable legs, collecting a fresh bottle of Scotch before retaking my seat. "It had to be done."

"How could you?"

My fist meets the desk without thought, the bang echoing loudly. "Quite fucking easily. Someone wants me dead, Ernie, and today was the perfect opportunity for them to take me out. I know how this world works. The bigger, the more elaborate and daring the kill, the more satisfaction. No one knows that more than I do. So apologies if you're a little put out that I'm still breathing."

"You fooled them all. All those people there to see your father off."

I scoff. None of them loved him like I did. None of them really cared. I bet most were just there to make sure the old heathen was definitely dead and buried.

Uncle Ernie's face softens somewhat, and a rue smile slowly creeps onto his face. "You really are your father's boy, aren't you?" He shakes his head and limps over, his dodgy knee clearly giving him grief today. Slumping down in the chair, he points at the bottle in my hand. "Pour me one of those, for fuck's sake."

I pour some into two tumblers and slide them across the desk to Ernie and Brad, keeping the bottle for myself. "To Pops," I say, raising my bottle to their glasses. They mumble their acknowlededgements and neck their drinks with me.

"So hundreds of people just said their prayers to an empty coffin?" Ernie asks.

"Not quite," Brad chips in, thumbing over his shoulder. I take the opportunity of him explaining to chug down more Scotch. "Don't know if you noticed, but we're kind of overrun with bricks after some fucker went nuclear on our asses."

Ernie chuckles, thoroughly amused. "Well, I'll be damned. So where is he?"

"Somewhere quiet and peaceful." My words are becoming more slurred by the second, my eyes heavier, as I drink the Scotch like it's water. "I'll let you know where when the dust has settled."

Ernie scoffs. "If you keep getting bombs hauled at you, that's going to be a while." He stands, creaking his way upright. "Be safe, Danny."

"Always am, Unc," I mumble, glugging down a few more inches of the amber stuff. He shakes his old head, a fond smile growing. "Call me. Let me know if there's anything you need."

My nod is a little haphazard, the Scotch now on its way to controlling me completely. Good. I hope it knocks me out.

Ernie leaves, and my damn phone screams again. "Fuck off," I slur, turning off my mobile and struggling to my feet. "If anyone wants me, I'll be in my room." I'm slightly aware of Brad's poorly hidden amusement as I sway my way past him, my treasured bottle of Scotch held to my lips. I stumble to a stop just short of the door and frown, wiping at my mouth. "I haven't got a room. Some fucker blew it up." I turn toward Brad. "Who blew up my room?" I raise the bottle as he goes to speak. "Never mind. I'll find out who, and I'll shove my gun up their arse and rape them with it before I fire." Brad flinches but keeps quiet. "I'll be wherever I make it before I collapse." I reach for the doorknob, missing it, having to close one eye to focus. I hear Brad chuckling from behind me. "Shut the fuck u—" My demand is cut short when the door flies open and smacks me in the face, sending me stumbling back in a daze. I land on my back with a thud, the impact winding me, as well as sending my Scotch flying. "Shit," I curse, shuffling onto my side and grappling for the bottle rolling away from me.

"What's going on?"

The sweet, familiar voice has my hand pausing in its search and my body rolling to my back again. I blink as I look up, the swaying vision of two bodies making my head spin. "Rose?" I ask, my hands coming up to my head and cupping each side, trying to stable my vision.

"He's fucked." Brad's voice comes from behind, but I don't take my eyes off the blurry vision of her.

"I buried my dad," I mumble. "I have every right to be fucked. So fuck you. Fuck you all. Fuck everyone." I lift my head with way too much effort, pointing a limp hand at Rose. "And especially fuck *you*." The strength needed to keep my head up is too much, and it pisses me right off that I have to drop it back to the carpet. My brain rattles when my skull collides with the floor. "Fuck." I cough, clumsily reaching up to rub my head. I'm fucking plastered. I don't think I've ever been so drunk. Being inebriated is being vulnerable, but I'm not so steaming to know that I've been vulnerable for a while now. "And it's your fault," I spit, feeling some hands under my armpits. "Leave me here."

"How much has he had?" Rose's voice is concerned. Fucking joke.

"Not enough." I'm not unconscious yet. I roll, shrugging off their hands, and scan the floor for my bottle. "Where have you hidden it?" I ask accusingly.

"For fuck's sake," Brad mutters.

I'm suddenly on two feet, though far from stable. I feel weightless, and it's only when Rose yells and something collides with my shoulder that I realize I'm falling. "Fuck." I land on the

floor again with a thud. The curses coming at me tells my
drunken head that Brad and Rose aren't much appreciating my
state, but I couldn't give a flying fuck. I'm feeling great. The
sense of freedom, the relief from being so sloshed quite liberating.

"You're not very attractive when you're drunk," Rose mutters,
dropping to her knees next to me.

The cheek. "Well . . ." I point a finger at her, trying to focus
on the tip as it circles the air all by itself. On a sigh, she takes it
and holds it steady for me.

"Well, what?" she asks.

"Well." I draw a blank, rummaging through my head for what
I was going to say. "Oh yeah." I sniff, forcing my face into scowling. Or something close. "Well, I don't like you slicing your arms
open. A-a-and I don't like it that it doesn't hurt you, because it
fucking hurts me." I yank the sleeve of my shirt up clumsily and
rip the bandage off, as if to show her my agony. "I did this
because of you."

"For fuck's sake." Brad dips to get his face up close, and
probably a bit clearer for me too. His eyebrows are high. Accusing. "Time for bed."

"Fuck you. I don't have a bed." I throw my arm out and catch
Rose on the arm. "Put me in her room." Brad looks to Rose, and it
riles me. "Why you looking at her for? I fucking tol . . . old you,
put me in her room. In her bed." I start to scramble up, swatting
their hands away when they both move in to help me. "It's my
fucking house. My fucking bed. My fucking life." I stagger to the
door, smacking my arm on the frame. "And she"—I whirl around
too fast, dizziness sending me staggering a few paces before I
right myself and narrow my eyes on Rose as best I can—"is mine
too. Anyone got a problem with that?" I hear no protests, though I
can't see any faces clearly to gage reactions. So I start walking,
pin-balling off the walls as I make my way down the corridor.
Fuck me, I'm a mess.

I see Esther coming out of the kitchen across the hallway, a tray in her hands. "Mother," I sing, and she startles, stopping in her tracks and looking past me. I follow her stare over my shoulder and find not only Brad and Rose, but all my other men too. The fact that they are completely unaware as to Esther's true identity is escaping me now. I shrug and return my attention to my mum. "Today I buried the man who saved me," I declare. "The only . . . only fu . . . fucking person in this world whooooo had any t . . . ime for me." I sway forward, getting my face up close to Esther's. "Because you bloody didn't, did you, huh? My own fucking mmmmotherrrr leaving me to be beat . . . beaten, raped, and tortured." I think I hear a few gasps from behind me. I can't be sure. "Thanks a million, *Mum*," I sneer, blindly reaching for the handrail leading up the stairs. "I'm going to bed."

"Good idea," she says flatly, and I snort to myself, gazing up the stairs. There must be a million fucking steps.

I tackle the first, squinting, lifting my foot and settling it down on the same step. I hear a collection of gasps from behind me and swing around, a bit to quickly for my pissed head's liking. Down I go with a whack, my arse hitting the edge of a step hard, my body sprawled, spanning at least ten of the million steps. "When did I get so many stairs?" I ask no one in particular.

"Ready?" Rose's voice sounds thick and distant. Is she leaving? Fuck, she can't.

"Someone stop her," I demand. "She's my prisoner."

"Shut up, you jerk." She's close now, and I grapple thin air for her, feeling her breath on my cheek. "Ringo, get him under his legs. Brad, you get his arms. Esther, would you mind bringing some water to my room?"

"It's *my* fucking room," I spit, feeling my body leave the ground. "And I can walk." I'm a joke. I can barely talk. "Youuuu are my prisoner." My body starts to bob mildly, and Brad

chuckles his way up the million steps, his face suspended above
mine.

"What's so fucking funny?" I snipe.

"The only prisoner I see around here is you, Danny."

"Go fuck y—"

"I've fucked myself enough today, thanks."

I land on something soft, my sense of smell bombarded with
the sweet, stunning smell of her. I roll over and bury my face in
the pillow, getting as much of it as I can. My eyes become impossible to keep open, and my mouth dries quickly from hanging
open.

*Rose. Rose Lillian Cassidy. Oh, how you've fucked me over
good and proper. I fucking hate you. I hate everything. But I especially hate you.*

No, you don't.

Yes, I do.

You don't.

I do.

Don't.

Do.

"I don't hate you," I slur, my voice even more muffled, my
body on the move. I drag myself to the edge of the bed, tossing
my legs off the side and sitting up. The fucking room spins at a
hundred miles an hour, around and around, forcing my hand to
come up and cling to my head. "Fuck." Where am I? What the
fuck's going on? I hear the door close and peek up through
squinting eyes. The slim silhouette of a female figure approaches,
finally coming into view when she's just a foot away. I look up
and lift my hand, reaching for Rose and tugging her forward until
she's standing between my legs. My head falls onto her stomach.
I feel her hands in my hair. I settle against her. "I told you ev . . .
everything about meeee," I mumble. "And you won't tell me
anything about you."

"We'll talk tomorrow," she says, pacifying me, rubbing soothing circles through my hair with her fingers.

"No, now," I order, forcing my limp body away from hers. "Talk to me now."

She smiles. It's the smile that makes me truly happy. A rare and precious smile. And I put it there. Her hand cups my cheek and she dips a little, coming close to my slumped form. "You won't remember a damn thing if I tell you anything now."

"You wanted to die."

"I want the impossible, and that makes me want to die."

"Nothing is impossible," I argue. "Nothing."

"Everything is impossible." She rests her lips on my scarred cheek, and I seize her, pulling her down to the bed with me. I can do no more than hold her to me, my body now done for the day.

"One day, I'm going to prove you wrong." I close my eyes and fight my way through the room spin.

"I hope I'm here to see you do that," she replies, making me frown into my darkness.

"Why, where else would you be?" She's my prisoner. Why does everyone keep forgetting that detail? "You're going nowhere, Rose L . . . L . . . Lillian Cassidyyy. Unless . . . unless it's with me."

20

ROSE

I should feel great. I don't. I had to pry myself from his arms last night. Strip him down. Redress the cuts on his arms after he ripped the bandages off, knowing I caused those. Watch him murmur and whimper in his sleep. Seeing him like that—so drunk, so raw, open and vulnerable . . .

It hurt. He won't remember a thing. He won't wake up and recall any of the things he said, what he did, how he held on to me with all he had.

That's why I don't feel great.

And the message on my phone is the reason I have to leave. Now.

Stupid Rose

There's a picture of me. I'm with Danny. On his terrace. I close my eyes briefly. Nowhere is safe. Not even Danny's mansion. His lips are on my chest. The photo is taken from above.

From the sky. A drone? Here, in this moment in the picture, I'm a different woman. And to Nox, I am a dangerous woman.

He's texted me. He never texts me. He's taken a risk, and that alone shows his state of mind. The phone buzzes in my hand again, making me startle, and another picture appears. A low, broken sob escapes me when I see a photo of my son. He's getting on a school bus, a backpack being dragged behind him, some soccer cleats slung over his shoulder, joined by the laces. I don't have a second to appreciate him. This isn't a reward. This is the end. My thumbs work without thought, bashing the keys across the screen.

> I'll call you. Give me five.

I click send and squeeze my hand around the phone, crushing it so hard it could crack. I was so sure I could do this. So certain I could fix this mess with Danny's help. But as long as Nox plays his ace card, I can't fix anything. No one can.

I peer out of the bathroom, seeing Danny still unconscious on the bed. I softly close the door and dial Nox. He doesn't speak when he answers, leaving me to explain. "It's been impossible to get in touch," I say. "There's always someone watching me, and Black takes me everywhere with him."

"You're lying. You've betrayed me. You've betrayed your son."

"No," I sob. "I'll get you what you want, I swear."

Nox hesitates for a second, humming. He knows he has me. I hate him with every fiber of my being. *Hate him.* "You have one chance to redeem yourself. And if you do, I might make sure you're out of the firing line in future."

"You knew I was on the balcony?" The drone.

"I want to know when the exchange with the Russians is happening. I want a time and a place. Or the next picture you get will be of your son in a coffin. And then I will kill you and find myself another whore."

"I'll get the information." I assure him. "I promise."

He hangs up, and a ragged cry escapes, forcing me to cover my mouth to muffle the sound. I'm going to lead Nox directly to his prey. I may as well be loading the gun and pulling the trigger. This is it. I look up to the mirror, seeing my bottom lip trembling terribly. "Shit," I curse, rubbing at it, sniffing and generally trying to compose myself. I need to be together. I have no fucking clue how I'm going to get the information Nox wants. No clue. But I must.

Hiding the phone, I roll my shoulders and pull the door open. Danny's starfished, his body stretched and spread far and wide, his face rough, his hair rougher. I creep toward him. I don't know why, as I don't think an atomic bomb would wake him. As I near, I stare at his beautiful, scarred face, replays of our time together flipping through my mind—the angry times, the times we looked at each other and understood each other, the times we kissed, made love, comforted each other.

I breathe in some resolution and settle on the edge of the bed. I don't want to wake him. I don't want to disturb his slumber and bring him back to a place where his head is likely to feel like it's falling off. I don't want to set in motion what will be the end for us. The end of him.

I'm about to gently nudge him when the door knocks, and I shoot up, pulling my robe in. "Come in."

Brad pokes his head around the door, eyeing up his boss on the bed. "It fucking stinks like a distillery in here."

I hadn't noticed. All I can smell is my regret. "Everything okay?"

"Sleeping beauty needs to get his ass up. It's past twelve, for fuck's sake."

My curious mind gets the better of me. "You need to be some-where?" I ask, striving to sound as nonchalant as possible.

"You could say that." Brad walks over to Danny and pokes him in the arm, and something deeply protective inside of me rises.

I move in to nudge him away. "I'll deal with him."

"I bet you will."

I ignore his sarcasm and press more, being delicate and casual. "He's probably still drunk. I doubt he'll be up for anything today other than recovering."

"He hasn't got any choice. It's important."

Important. Like an exchange important? God, is it today? Brad moves in to poke Danny again, but I block his path, standing firm. He gives me a curious look. "I'll wake him. He's going to need the gentle approach, and you don't look like you're in the mood for gentle."

Brad winks, and it riles me, because I know something obscene and inappropriate is coming.

"Don't," I warn, turning away from him. "I'll tell him you're waiting for him." And as soon as Danny's gone from my room, I'll be making a call that I so don't want to make. Guilt is a vise around my heart as my gaze jumps across the sheets of the bed.

"You got it," Brad replies, almost mocking. "And Rose?"

I lift my eyes and stare at Danny's sleeping form, unable to look at Brad, worried he'll see my agony. "What?"

"You ever try to cut yourself again, it won't just be Danny all over your ass."

I pivot, a little stunned. His face is straight, as if he means for his blank, emotionless expression to contradict his soft words. "Danny doesn't give a shit about me," I say, knowing it's bullshit. We *all* know it. Especially after last night. But I go on, neverthe-less, maybe hoping that Brad might confirm what I'm wishing. "I'm here out of convenience."

"And that's why he tore his arm up with a knife, is it?" He doesn't give me the opportunity to refute him, bringing the wood between us.

I drop back down to the edge of the bed, my mind in turmoil as I stare at Danny's comatose form. The ache in my heart, the kick in my gut, the butterflies that have taken up residence in my tummy. It's love. I've fallen in love with the monster. I should ask myself how, but the answer is very easy. He sees me. Feels what I feel. Thinks how I think. And that makes what I'm going to do to him unforgiveable. Yet, I really do not have a choice.

Danny coughs, and for a split second, I worry that he might throw up. "Fucking hell," he mumbles, rolling onto his side and sinking his face into a pillow. I smile, a little amused, a little sad, reaching for his shoulder, but quickly retracting my hand. I shouldn't touch him. I shouldn't light the spark.

"You're wanted," I say, practically on a whisper, aware that every sound might be amplified by a million decibels, making it sound like I'm screaming.

One eye opens, and it squints. I can see his poor, battered head trying to locate the memories he needs to tell him why he's in my bed and why I'm here. And he obviously can't find them. Brusque Danny appears, though I can tell it takes some effort, his face bunched in disgust as he wrestles his uncooperative body into a sitting position. "What the fuck are you doing here?"

"You mean in this room?" I ask, standing and letting him take in the space. "Because you demanded it. Because I'm your prisoner. Because this is your house, your room, your life." I smile sickly sweetly, the natural feistiness in me that he spikes racing forward and smacking him around his hungover face. "That's why."

He looks down at his arm, taking in the bandages I wrapped carefully and lovingly. Then he scoffs and rips them off. It's a message. "I fucking hate you," he spits, wincing his way to the edge of the bed.

"Join the club, Danny," I retort, heading for the bathroom. I hate myself too, and his stunned eyes as he looks up when I'm shutting the door tells me he's grasped my hidden meaning. I slam the door and heave for a few seconds, my blood boiling. How does he do this? Get this rise from me? I suddenly feel like I have so much more to say, to remind him of every drunken slur that fell out of his stupid mouth last night. Why, I don't know, but the urge is there, and when I have urges where Danny Black is concerned, I can't seem to restrain them.

I yank the door open and put one foot in front of the other, charging right into his naked chest. I ricochet off his mass of muscles, forcing him to grab my wrist. The cuts on his forearm make me wince, and I drop my eyes, every word I had ready to fire disintegrating under his closeness. Under my guilt.

A firm grip takes my jaw, squeezing as he forces my face to his. I make it as difficult as possible, but he wins. I hope he always wins. Blue fire rains down on me through red-rimmed eyes, his torso subtly rippling from his labored breathing. Today is the day I'm sentencing him to die, and he's not even in full working order. He's not alert enough. If he was operating at full Danny Black ability, he might stand a chance. Yet, in reality, I know that the moment our paths crossed, we were both sentenced to death.

"I'm sorry," I whisper mindlessly, my voice groggy with regret.

His head tilts in question, his forehead weighed down with confusion. I see softness breaking past his sharp face, but he quickly reins it back in. "Get dressed." He drops my face and passes me, removing his boxers and getting in the shower.

My panic is instant. "Where are we going?"

"To the boatyard."

"But I . . ." But I what? Can't? "I'd like to stay here. I'm not feeling too well." It isn't a lie. I feel sick all of a sudden. I can't go. I can't watch everything unfold and know it's all my fault. I can't watch him die.

Danny's soaping hands pause on his stomach, an incredulous look passing over him. "You don't feel too well?" He snorts, turning away from me and continuing with his shower, his ass glistening like a perfect pair of hard, smooth rocks. "Join the fucking club, Rose," he retorts nastily, turning the spray onto his face. He trails his palms all over his cheeks, his arms, his stomach, his thighs.

He steps out of the stall, grabbing a towel and rubbing it over his hair, standing utterly bare and beautiful before me. "Didn't fancy joining me, then?" he asks, pure, infuriating malice in his tone. He steps forward and pulls the front of my robe away, exposing my breasts. I breathe in, searching for my veil of protection. It's lost with Danny. Lost forever. "Shame," he whispers. "A good fuck against the wall to let off some steam before my day would have been welcomed." I'm too angry to be turned on. He's trying to make me feel worthless, cheap, and I hate that he's succeeding. Any other man I wouldn't care. But Danny? After I've experienced him at his very best, I just want to slap his bastard face for being so hurtful. "Maybe I'll call Amber." He drops my robe and steps back, looking down at his cock. It's twitching. He pouts.

The heat in my veins might burn them to nothing. "Maybe you should do that." I grind out the words, ignoring how painful they are to say. I'm chasing myself in circles here, swaying between love and hate. I'm supposed to be getting information from him. Retaliating to his asshole behavior isn't the way to get it, but the man infuriates me. I square up to him, getting close, my face pushed up to his. I have to get on my tiptoes to do it, but it's worth the effort. "This *whore* is done with you." I pivot and get exactly two paces away before I'm tackled and thrown against the wall. I hit it with force, the impact dislodging a cry of shock from me.

"I decide who I fuck," he growls, ripping my robe open and pressing his naked front into mine. I turn my head away from his face, determined to stop the desire from surging forward and controlling me. It's too late. It's already taking pole position, but I *can* control it. I *must* control it. But surely I should want this. Surely having him surrender to me is for the best, because, make no mistake, as much as he's growling and spitting scathing words in my face, he is surrendering. Yet I don't want to do this. I don't want to strengthen the connection between us. It'll just make this harder, and it's already unbearable. I'm certain the exchange is happening today, and it's happening at the boatyard. I need to put the call in and run. Pretend that I never met Danny Black, but remember that what I've done was for my flesh and blood—the only flesh and blood I have.

"You won't touch me if I say no," I whisper, hitting him below the belt. I don't care. He's playing dirty. I'm playing dirty. We're both dirty. Perfect for each other. My hair is grabbed, his erection growing where it lies on my lower stomach. He yanks hard, demanding I look at him. I won't. "No," I say, simple and firm, and he growls, yanking my hair again, rolling his hips into mine. I bite down on my teeth, blinking back the sting in my eyes, trying not to embrace the sparks of life inside me. "No," I grate, jerking my head back until my hair pulls and my skull meets the wall.

"Rose . . ." His voice is full of warning, his cock now leaking pre-cum on the skin of my tummy.

"No." Now, I look him in the eye, forcing mine clear of the building tears. "No." I find my fists opening and clenching, over and over, the restraint needed becoming too much. "No. No. No. N—"

His mouth meets mine and my refusals are swallowed whole, along with my willpower. "Yes," he whispers, taking my mouth greedily, not letting me come up for air. I taste Scotch on him, and pure, raw Danny.

He is my utopia. My Achilles heel.

My downfall?

"Say it," he growls, his demand thick with need. "Say the fucking word, Rose."

My head and my heart argue, fight and throw different orders at me, and I sob through our kiss, so fucking torn. I can't. I can. Yes. No. *Help me!* He's losing, and he must sense it because he risks breaking our consuming kiss to find my eyes, holding my cheeks firmly in his palms. His expression is still cut, but the rare softness I love is lingering beyond somewhere. It only makes my challenge more challenging. Part of me wants to do this. To have one more time completely consumed by him. The other part is fighting it with all I have. Walk away now.

"I think you should call Amber," I tell him, ensuring I keep my certain eyes on him so he sees my resolution. I can't have this one more time. I hate Amber, hate her with a vengeance, because if Danny doesn't die today, I will, and then Amber will have him. Any willing Amber will get the man I love . . . *if he lives.*

His nostrils flare, ice filling his eyes. "I don't want Amber. I want you."

He wants me. No one has ever wanted *me* before. The real me. My closing throat starts to suffocate me, conflict tearing me apart. "No." I must be strong. I want him, so much, but I want something else more. "You really can't have me, Danny."

"Who fucking says?"

"Me," I scream, losing the plot. "Just leave me alone!" I try to push him away, my palms forcefully shoving into his chest. He tussles with them, our bodies becoming a mess of grappling limbs. I'm hysterical, shouting through my frustration and hopelessness as Danny fights to gain control of me. His hold of my wrists is strong, immovable, as is his full weight wedged into my chest, pinning me to the wall. "Please," I murmur pitifully, looking away. "Let me go."

He releases me in an instant.

"No!" I grab him, and he growls, spinning me around and pushing me forward into the wall. My robe is yanked down my arms and tossed aside, allowing his naked front to meet my naked back. By the time I locate the use of my arms, he's already spread the length of me, his lips at my ear, breathing slowly in and out, wreaking havoc on my nervous system to match the state of my head. His teeth graze my fleshy lobe, dragging wickedly. His hands come up and cup my breasts, his thumbs rubbing circles around my nipples. I whimper and bend at the waist to escape, pushing my ass into his arousal.

"You feel that, don't you, Rose?"

"Yes," I breathe shakily.

He pinches each nub harshly, and then swivels his hips, driving deeply into me. He gasps, and my forehead falls to the wall, my shaking world calming. Peace finds me. Ecstasy clouds everything. "You feel me." He thrusts once, pushing me farther into the wall, pausing and growling as my internal walls grab on, stroking him, encouraging him, begging for him. "Yes, you feel me." His hands clamp down over my boobs as he retreats and buries himself hard and high. I lose my breath, lose my mind, lose sight of my whole purpose. I bend my arms on the wall, using my forearm to cushion my head. There is nothing I can do. Nothing I want to do. "And I feel *you*." His advancements quicken, but every move is meticulously executed. I close my eyes and accept what needs to be accepted.

I feel him. Hear him.

And for my fucking sins, I love him.

My ass starts to sway, tingles take hold, and I'm a slave to his merciless taking of me. Not because it's hard or forceful, but because this moment, this intimate, understanding moment, will be lost in the carnage to come.

The sounds of his pleasure drowns out my helpless thoughts, and when he drops my breasts and takes my hips, I know he's looking for more leverage, ready for the home stretch. I build and build, get higher and higher.

My orgasm rules me when it hits, swallowing me up in its intensity and completely blanking my mind of everything other than how free I feel in this moment. I don't cry out, just tense. The surge of pressure from Danny's climax forces him forward, his body falling against mine and forcing me to the wall.

He takes a moment, panting into my neck, not letting one drip of his essence escape me. Then he abruptly pulls away, leaving me plastered against the wall, naked and exposed. "Get ready." He spits over his shoulder as he walks away.

"Fuck you," I snap in return, making him stop abruptly. He looks back and smiles. So I flip him the finger as I dip and pick up the robe, pulling it on to cover myself up, feeling dirtier than I've ever felt before.

Danny pivots and stalks toward me, but I don't back up. No way.

He reaches me.

Snarls at me.

And then smashes his lips on mine.

"Get the hell off me, you asshole." I shove him away, and he walks backward, obviously relishing my fury. This is so fucking toxic. His expression screams victory.

I go to the bathroom, shut the door, and grab the phone. I hate myself. I hate my fucking self so much right now. I'm condemning a man I love to death. Tears fall from my eyes, tracking past hollow cheeks. *This is the end.* I don't know if I'll even survive today, let alone whatever hell Nox has planned for me next. And I'm so fucking tired. I'm sick of being a pawn.

I punch out a message through a sob. It's done. *And so am I.*

> The boatyard today. I'm not sure what time, but it looks like we're leaving soon. He's making me go with him.

21

DANNY

I feel like someone has stamped on my skull repeatedly while I've been sleeping. Shit, I'm sure my head could fall off my neck at any moment. The Scotch is to blame, but Rose hasn't helped my sorry state. Neither have I.

I don't know what I just did. What I was hoping to achieve. A slow, painful death? I scoff to myself as I lean down to tie the laces of my boots. I'm pretty sure you can't get much more painful than this.

When I sit back up, I get a head rush, having to slowly blink to clear the black spots from my vision. "Fucking hell," I mutter, reaching up and feeling at my sensitive scalp. What a fucking mess. I'm sweating Scotch, my stomach is revolting every sip of water I take, and my brain feels like it's shrunk to half its size. Not the best shape to be in when I'm handing over millions of dollars' worth of firearms.

I look across to the bathroom where Rose is taking her time getting ready. "Hurry the fuck up," I yell, falling to my back, utilizing her dragging feet to my advantage. I close my eyes and flashes of last night come back to me, and with each one, I cringe myself the fuck away from it, not bothering to take the time to think about the finer details. The small flashbacks are hideous. The full picture will likely send me off the deep end. But there's one thing amid the hideousness poking at my memory that I can't cast aside so easily. Something she said. About dying. That recollection came to me the second I shot my load into her, falling against her back and nailing her to the wall. She doesn't care if she dies. That's been proven. And now she's actually said it.

And she's fighting me harder than she has before. A tiny bit of me thinks she's just being stubborn. The largest part of me is concerned it's more. But what?

I hear the door shift and drop my head to the side. She's in the doorway, wearing the British sweater I bought her and those perfect figure-hugging jeans. I scowl at her, stupidly moving my eyes up to her face. She's not wearing makeup. Why the fuck did she take so long if she's not spent that time applying makeup? And her hair's damp, all tugged up into a haphazard knot. She's made zero effort.

And she's still fucking perfect.

"About time," I grunt, cringing my way up to standing. My brain drops from my head into my boots as I walk to the door, feeling somewhat unstable. I hear a small chuckle from behind me and swing around, way too fast. The room swooshes, and I grab the door to stabilize myself, making Rose's chuckle break out into a full-on belly laugh. The sound would be wonderful if it wasn't so fucking loud and irritating. I level her with a pissed-off stare, and she quickly snaps out of her fit, straightening and entwining her hands in front of her.

"I guess fucking a whore against the wall didn't have the desired effect," she says calmly, her face deadpan. My mood takes a further nosedive as she walks forward, throwing a filthy look my way as she passes. "Maybe you would've had better success with Amber."

And like she's heard her name, the woman herself walks out of another room, probably after seeing to one of my men. A bit of stress relief before the exchange. I get it. Her eyes take in the scene. Me. Rose. Leaving a room that isn't mine. "What are you doing here?" I ask, cold and sharp, not that Amber's used to anything more from me.

"I was just . . ." She thumbs over her shoulder to the door she just came from. She doesn't want to say it. She doesn't want to tell me that her pussy was another man's for a while. What, does she think I'll give a shit? Stupid woman. "I was coming to find you." She smiles coyly.

I see Rose's stance noticeably straighten. "You're a few minutes too late," she says, walking away, leaving Amber staring at her back. "He used this whore instead." Her arms go up in the air above her head, her index fingers on each hand pointing down to herself like flashing arrows. "I'd like to say you missed out on something special"—Rose glances over her shoulder as she reaches the end of the corridor—"but I'd be lying."

Fuck me, hold me back before I throw her over the gallery landing. I leave Amber where she is, looking bewildered, and stalk after the woman who I think I could take the greatest *ever* pleasure in killing. Every step I take, my brain rattles and my mood worsens. I hit the stairs, a few steps behind Rose, noticing she's quickened her pace. She knows what's coming. I reach for her wrist, missing it when she stealthily moves, leaving me losing my balance and stumbling down the final few steps.

Fuck!

I hit the deck with a thud, and I lie on my back, blinking up at the ceiling. Rose appears, smiling smugly down at me. *Bitch.*

"All right?" Brad asks, offering his hand and pulling me to my feet.

My ears are red hot. I'm pretty sure they have steam coming out of them. I straighten as Brad's nose wrinkles and he moves away, looking me up and down. "You smell as bad as you look."

"Go fuck yourself." I turn, ready to tackle Rose, but get tugged back toward Brad.

"We have things to do." He cocks his head, screaming a warning at me to hold back on the pussy shit until we've gotten through the day. He holds up my phone, and I snatch it, turning it on. It dings, chimes, and vibrates in my hand when it comes to life.

"Spittle," I grunt, wiping the ten missed calls and ignoring his voicemail. I can't deal with him right now. I can barely deal with the exchange. "We all set?"

"All set," Brad confirms. "Ringo's gone fishing in his shit heap boat, and the rest of the men are scoping a mile radius." We start toward the car, and I pull Rose along with me. "Are you kidding me?" Brad stops in his tracks, pointing at her.

"What?" I ask.

"You are not bringing her. Why the fuck would you do that?"

I stall, searching for my reasoning. I never gave it much thought, really. Failing to think clearly is a huge red flag. I just told her she was coming and thought no more of it. Truth is, I don't want her out of my sight.

I don't get a chance to think of a response. Brad takes Rose and leads her back to the stairs, his look daring me to argue. And for once, I don't. He's being sensible. I am not.

"He'll be back before you know it," he says sarcastically.

Rose snorts, making her way up the steps. "I don't care if I never see him again."

Ouch. "Fuck you, Rose," I spit.

She meets Amber at the top, and the look Amber throws Rose should turn her to a pile of dust. Not my girl. It's water off a duck's back with my girl. Rose stops, looks Amber up and down, before getting on her way. "It's your turn tonight. He's in the mood for rough."

My jaw is tight as I gaze up at her, getting farther and farther away. That fucking woman has me straddling the line between fury and amazement.

"Come on." Brad nudges me in the arm, and I slowly cast my eyes to his. "Danny?"

"I'll be two minutes." I find myself running up the stairs after Rose, my vision now clear, my body now stable. My target is my only focus. She's a firecracker. *My* firecracker. I need to feel her one more time before I go.

"Danny, are you fucking shitting me?"

"Two minutes," I call, passing a stunned Amber who's forced to jump from my charging path. Rose looks over her shoulder, quickening her pace when she spots me in pursuit. "Don't run," I warn, only making her break into a sprint. "Rose."

She zooms down the corridor like a rocket, me on her tail, and when she reaches the door to her room, she bombs in and slams it. I snort in the face of the wood between us, disregarding the fact it's only just been repaired after I practically knocked it off its hinges only the other day. I shoulder-charge it and fall into the room, quickly locating her running to the bathroom. She doesn't get to slam that door. It bounces off the toe of my boot, and she squeals, all high-pitched and girlie, pricking at my delicate brain. I fill the doorway, legs wide, hands braced into each side of the wood. "Come here," I pant as she backs up toward the sink.

"Fuck off, Danny. You've got what you wanted."

"Have I?"

Her gaze jumps past me. She's trying to gage her chances of escape. Stupid woman. She doesn't want to escape. Not really, no matter how much she wants to convince me or herself otherwise. "What do you want then?" Her hands disappear into the sleeves of her sweater, like she's trying to cover up as much of her skin as she can. Then she folds her arms. She's mentally restraining herself.

"Come here."

She shakes her head.

"Come here."

"No."

"Do it."

"Fuck you."

I steam forward and pull her arms loose of her torso, shoving them to her sides. "Kiss me." I cage her in, one arm on either side of her against the sink. Her pretty face is taut, her lips pressed tightly shut. "You don't want to?"

"N . . ." She fades off, and I cock my head.

It's her that makes the first move. All her.

She grabs me and hauls me onto her mouth, going at me like a mad woman. Her moan contradicts her hands that are trying to push me away. The heat of her body contradicts her attempts to be cold. This woman is one huge bag of contradictions. But she needs to realize that she causes conflict in me too. She is the epitome of weakness for me. A weakness that I want. Because while she strips me of strength to some extent, she injects me with it in others. My heart beats stronger with her around. I have purpose like I've never had.

I loop one arm around her waist and tug her into me, my other hand taking her jaw, squeezing.

"No, please." She suddenly pulls away, turning her head, wriggling to free herself. "No more, Danny."

A little stunned, I step back, her rejection stinging. Because I sense something in her tone I've never heard before. Resolution. My headache is suddenly back, my body suddenly shaky again. Her resolve is a smack in the face. Her expression as fierce as she is. "No more games?" I didn't mean it as a question. It was supposed to be an assertive statement. None of this has been a game to me, not for a while now.

"No more anything." She stares me down, refusing to look away from me, strong and firm in her stance. "You and me." Her finger drifts between us. "We're impossible."

"Who says?"

"Me." She turns away and drops her eyes from the mirror, hiding from me. "We're toxic all on our own. Together, we're poison."

And explosive. And perfect for each other. I engage my muscles to approach, but hear footsteps coming from behind.

"Danny, for Christ's sake, we're late." Brad takes in the scene, but impatience won't allow him to take in the atmosphere. "Let's go." He reverses his steps, jerking his head. "Now."

"This isn't done," I tell Rose, backing up.

"No, Danny, it's done." She looks up, and I swear there are tears in her eyes. "Trust me."

I shake my head, not prepared to believe it. "I'll be back," I say, turning and leaving the room. I pull the door closed and take my keys from my pocket, locking it with the master. Something unsettling tells me that Rose doesn't plan on being here when I get back, so I need to ensure she is. And not only because we've got shit to iron out, but because, as Adams pointed out, his contact wouldn't think twice about killing her. "Not a word," I warn Brad as we head back downstairs.

"Fine."

"Talk to me."

"It's the shooter from the hospital. He's dead."

"What the fuck?"

"I went to the prison this morning. They turned me away. He was found in his cell. Twenty stab wounds to the neck. Worried he'd talk, I expect."

"Fucking great." I shake my head to myself.

"And Adams—"

"Don't tell me he's dead too."

"No, he's hiding. Somewhere in the Hamptons, but not at his own place. Don't worry, we'll smoke him out."

Amber is loitering in the entrance hall when we make it there. "Go home," I order without looking at her, striding down the steps and slipping my shades over my squinting eyes. "And stay the fuck gone." The men will have to find another in-house whore.

We get in the car and Brad starts the engine, putting his foot on the pedal, racing down the driveway.

All I can see in my mind's eye is Rose's tears. Rose doesn't cry. *What the hell is going on?*

The last of the shop staff is leaving when we pull up, and he waves out the window of his truck as he passes us on the mud track road leading up to the shack. The water is especially calm this evening, still and almost eerie. I get out and walk down to the shoreline, staring out at the sun dipping on the horizon. I hear the slide of the huge bolt of a container behind me, then the creak of the door being pulled open. Looking over my shoulder, I find one of the men pulling up to the container in a forklift, the telescopic arms extending into the metal shed and reappearing with one of the jet skis across them. "Ready to go," he calls, motioning out to the water.

The deep chug of a boat rumbles in the distance, slowly appearing around a rocky section of the bay. "You have to be kidding me." I say as the logo splattered down the side of the boat comes into view. "Miami Cruises?"

"You get a free trip." Volodya's Russian accent from behind tears my eyes away from the water, and I turn, finding him leaning on the open door of his Rolls Royce.

"What happened to the eighteen-wheeler?"

"It's a bit conspicuous. There's nothing strange about a tour boat loaded with jet skis."

"Very creative," I say, strolling over to him and accepting his extended hand.

"We're branching out into water sports." He motions to the jet ski still on the arms of the forklift. "Hope you don't mind a bit of competition."

"Sure I'll cope. All this will be a lot easier when we're operating from Byron's Reach."

"Hurry up that day." Volodya strides across to the forklift and runs a palm down the side of the Sea-Doo. "Beautiful machine. I bet some fun can be had on one of these things."

"Not that one, since it's a shell."

Volodya laughs. "How have you been, Danny? I hear the grim reaper is out to get you."

"*I* am the grim reaper, Volodya," I retort, reaching into my pocket when my phone rings. Spittle's name on the screen rattles me, and I slam my thumb down on the accept button. "I'm kind of in the middle of something here," I hiss, wandering away from Volodya .

"Yeah, I know. I've been trying to fucking call you all day, Danny. The FBI and half the MPD are currently heading your way. I'd say you have ten minutes tops."

My eyes immediately start scanning the area. "What?"

"Ten minutes, if you're lucky."

"Fuck." I hang up and find Brad. "Code fucking red," I grate. "Volodya, turn your boat around and get the fuck out of here."

"What's going on?" he asks, watching as I march down the dock to the forklift.

"Company is on the way. There's a hidden track halfway down the lane that'll take you onto the main highway. Find it."

He doesn't hang around to get details, going straight to his mobile and calling in a mission abort before rushing to his car. "Fuck's sake, Black," he spits, his Rolls Royce wheel spinning away, kicking up the gravel and dirt. The forklift screams its way back to the container as my men all work urgently to get it closed up. I pelt toward the shack, grabbing the first wetsuit I can find and getting myself into it. I hear the men land in the café, hear the tops of beer bottles being popped off and a pack of cards being shuffled. I fly into the workshop . . . and skid to a stop when I see the charred remains of my Sea-Doo. "Fuck," I curse, heading back into the store. "Brad, give me a hand."

He's with me in a second, taking the front of the Yamaha jet ski nearest the doors. "Lift," he grunts, going red in the face. "Fuck, where's the trailer?"

"No time." I shuffle toward him as he shuffles back, his eyes looking like they could pop out his head. "Come on, you fanny," I tease.

"Go fuck yourself."

We manage to get it down to the shore just before the sound of sirens drown the air. And then we both turn and take in the invasion of unmarked cars coming at us from all directions. "What a surprise," I say quietly, wading into the water and tugging the Yamaha in. I recognize the suited prick walking toward me as one of Spittle's colleagues, Harold Higham. He has resting smug face. "All this for me?" I ask, climbing onto the seat of my jet ski.

"You won't mind if we have a look around," he says, casting his beady eyes around the open space, his men doing the same.

"You can do what you like." I'm polite. It's sickening. "With a warrant."

"Of course." Higham drags a piece of paper from his inside pocket and waves it in the air.

My coolness waivers for a split second. "And what are you looking for?"

"We'll see, I guess."

Translated: I haven't got a fucking clue. I grit my teeth and get back into the water, wading my way back to the shore. "Will this take long? I was looking forward to my evening ride on the water."

Higham's shrewd stare is pinned on me, his jaw ticking. "You think you're so fucking smart, don't you, Black? Swaggering around town like some kind of fucking king. Leaving blood and death in your wake. Your time is coming, my boy."

My eyes must be glass as I hold his stare. "You're barking up the wrong tree, Higham."

"Not this time." He tosses the warrant at me. "Your days are like your father's. No more."

I'm forced to call on endless control before I grab the fucker and pull out his teeth one by one with plyers. "That's rather insensitive of you, Higham." My voice is unmistakably quivering with rage. "I only buried him yesterday."

"Sir," an officer calls from across the yard.

Higham snarls at me before stomping to the first container. "Get it open," he yells, prompting three officers to step forward, each holding a battering ram.

I remain where I am, watching as an army of agents charge down one of my container doors. I could tell them the doors are unlocked. But I won't. Fat bastards look like they could do with a workout. Sitting on a nearby rock, I watch as they ram-raid the first container and Higham comes out, his brow wet, his face twisted.

"Beautiful machines," I say. "Want to buy one?"

Higham hisses and stamps his way over to the next container, barking orders left and right.

"Fucking hell, Danny," Brad whispers out the side of his mouth. "This is a bit close for comfort."

"They don't even know what they're fucking looking for." The FBI is a constant ball-ache, but fucking clueless. They know we have money, but they have no idea where it comes from, and it's been their mission to find out for decades. I kick my feet out and get comfortable, watching Higham ordering the beating down of door after door. I can't deny it, I'm tense as they search the containers that are *literally* loaded. I can hear Brad's heart hammering ten to the dozen, his feet shifting in the gravel. "Be cool," I whisper, getting up and wandering over casually, being glared at by every cop I pass. I lean my shoulder on the side of one of the doors, motioning to the Sea-Doo that was hanging off the end of the dock not ten minutes ago. "If it's power between the legs you want to feel, I recommend that one."

Higham's up in my face quickly, steam billowing from his ears. "I'm onto you, Black."

I push my forehead to his, my eyes blazing. "I'm quaking in my fucking wetsuit, Higham."

Wisely, he backs up, his frustration obvious. "You're as arrogant as your father was."

"Don't get personal, Higham. You'll regret it," I warn, moving forward, prompting a nearby agent to reach for his belt. I throw him a death stare. "Calm down, Tackleberry."

Brad chuckles as he approaches, lighting a cigarette before offering me one.

"Are you done?" I ask, accepting and slipping it between my lips. "Unless you're in the market for a jet ski, I don't think you have any business around here."

"Get me a hammer," Higham spits, holding his hand out as he glares at me. I don't let my eyes waver from his as one of his minions runs to his car, returning a few moments later with an axe rather than what his superior requested.

Taking it by the handle, Higham swings it a few times, all cocky as he wanders over to the nearest jet ski. Which happens to be the one we just hurried back into the container. I sense all of my men tensing as Higham proceeds to smash the machine to pieces while everyone looks on. I glance across to Brad who's broken out in a sweat. Me? I smile, making my right-hand-man give me a *what the hell?* look.

"You done?" I ask as Higham heaves and kicks pieces of the jet ski away, looking for something he won't find. "Or are you going to smash up every jet ski I have?" I ask, motioning to the one beside it. "Feel free. Because with every one you damage, you're racking up I-owe-yous, Higham."

His nostrils flare, and he throws the axe down into the dirt, throwing his arm in the air in signal for his men to move out. "This isn't done."

I pout, lighting my Marlboro and pulling in deep. "Nice seeing you, Higham," I say, exhaling thick smoke all over him. It takes everything in him not to cough.

"Yeah," he mutters, marching away, frustration pouring from him.

As soon as they've fucked off, I take one last drag of my cigarette, thoughtful, before flicking it away.

"What the fuck?" Brad says quietly, joining me. "Where the hell are the guns?"

I step toward one of the containers and lightly tap the wall, looking back at him. "Always expect the worst."

"Jesus," he breathes, putting his cigarette out and immediately lighting another.

My phone rings, and I pull it out. "What?" I mutter down the line to Ringo.

"Why the hell has Volodya's boat just chugged past me with no jet skis?"

I head to the shack, pulling down the zip of my wetsuit. "FBI stopped by."

"What?"

"You heard."

"Was anyone gonna tell me?" Ringo asks, full of annoyance.

"I've been bobbing up and down on this broken piece of crap for hours. So far, I've caught a dead octopus, a pair of panties, a license plate, and a shark. A fucking shark."

I stop yanking my wetsuit down my body and dump my arse on a bench in the changing room. And I laugh, a proper belly laugh, my head thrown back.

"Fuck you, Danny," Ringo mutters, the sound of an engine spitting in the background. "You asshole. And now the fucking boat won't start. Fuck!" There's a loud bang, forcing me to pull my mobile from my ear. "The engine just blew up," Ringo says flatly. "The fucking engine just fucking blew the fuck up."

I'm off again, laughing, my amusement doing a damn fine job of dousing down the anger burning my gut. "I'll call the Coast Guard."

"What's going on?" Brad asks, eyeing up my amused form.

"Ringo's had a productive fishing trip," I howl, pressing my hands into my knees to help me up. "And the engine just blew up."

Brad snatches the phone from me on a frown that suggests he's truly worried about me. He should be. I'm feeling a bit unhinged, but if I don't laugh, I'm likely to go on a killing spree.

Brad tells Ringo that someone is on the way to rescue him while I strip out of my wetsuit. He hangs up and stares at me. "So what the fuck do we do n—" He pivots toward the door when we hear the sound of tires crunching the gravel, followed by a voice.

We look at each other. "Spittle," Brad and I mutter in unison, heading outside as he hands me my phone. I take the steps down from the cabin, my bare feet crunching into the gravel.

Spittle looks me up and down. "Having a slumber party?" he quips as I shift my bare feet on the cutting stones.

"What the fucking hell just happened?" I ask.

"They got a tipoff," he mutters, walking past us to the shack. "You got any beers in this place?"

After a quick confused and worried look thrown at each other, Brad and I follow him in, Brad going straight to the beer fridge and pulling out three bottles, twisting off the caps. "A tipoff?" he asks, setting one bottle in front of Spittle and handing me another.

Spittle takes a long, and what looks like a much-needed slurp, and drops it back to the table with a thud, breathing in. "I've been trying to get hold of you. I couldn't fucking stop them. I don't know what's going down with you and the Russians. I've made it my business not to make it my business, if you know what I mean." That's fucking bullshit. Spittle knows exactly what I deal in, the bent fuck. He casts serious eyes to me. "You have a mole."

My bottle pauses at my lips. "What?"

Reaching into his inside pocket, he pulls something out and tosses it on the table like he's glad to be rid of it. I move in, looking down at the photographs.

"Motherfucker," Brad breathes, slamming his bottle on the table.

I'm deathly still. A statue. But my insides are blowing up, all kinds of manic shit happening. My heart feels like it could be making a bid for freedom, ramming down the walls of my chest. An atomic bomb feels like it could have gone off in my veins. My eyes can see more clearly than they've seen before.

My arse drops to a chair and my numb hand reaches for the pictures, dragging them toward me until the images are blinding me. Rose is coming down the steps of a jet, a man behind her. I don't recognize him. "Who's that?"

"That, my friend, is Nox Dimitri."

My eyes fly up, and Brad curses under his breath. "Dimitri?" Flashbacks bombard me, my head pounding. I see Pops take out Marius Dimitri. I see me, just a boy, take out his son. I look at Brad, my forehead heavy. "The Dimitris are all dead."

"All except him." Spittle taps the picture, and I force myself to look at it. "Nox is Marius's illegitimate son. He's moved in and reformed the Romanian mafia, and it seems he has a beef with you. Why's that, Danny?"

"Jesus," Brad breathes.

I look up to Spittle. His face harbors a million concerns. "When were these taken?"

"The day before *she*"—his finger moves across to Rose's face —"found Adams in a hotel bar and seduced him. The phone you gave me. Hers?"

I close my eyes, trying to breathe.

"Tracked," Spittle finishes.

My fucking heart clenches. I didn't know it was capable of such . . . hurt? "She's spying for the Romanians?" My blood just surpassed boiling point, and I slowly rise, my balled fists braced against the table supporting me. My head is in tatters, realization dripping into my brain little piece by little piece. "Nox Dimitri." I let my thoughts roll out. "He planted Rose on Adams to get intel on me, and then I fucking took her in Vegas." Nox must have laughed himself out of town. She's bait. A trap. "Don't fucking look at me like that," I warn Brad, feeling his accusing eyes on my profile. "Just don't fucking look at me like that." I flex my hands and claw my fingers, dragging in the photos until they're screwed up balls in my fists. "I'm going to fucking kill her." I turn and steam out, feeling psychotic, every muscle vibrating with the strain to contain my temper.

Falling into the car, I slam the door and start it up, smashing my foot on the gas and roaring away as Brad makes chase. I lose control of the back end, the Merc swinging from side to side as I speed down the lane. She's played me. She's fucking played me. How could I have been so stupid?

The drive home is fast and furious, my anger worsening the closer I get to my mansion. I break every speed limit, cut up a million cars, and punch the steering wheel every few seconds. When I screech up the driveway, I don't bother turning off the engine, throwing the door open and sprinting up the steps, bursting through the door like a raging bull.

Esther is halfway down the stairs, a laundry basket in her hands. She stops abruptly, assessing me from head to toe. It's only now that I register I'm only wearing my boxers. "Where is she?" I can hardly speak, my throat burning with the strain of trying to catch a breath.

Esther's head tilts a little, and for the first time since I met her, I sense concern. If I had the energy, I would laugh in her face. She glances up the stairs.

Jesus, is this what panic feels like? My heart could have fallen out of my chest and splattered on the floor in front of me. My eyes follow Esther's stare up the stairs, my feet feeling like they're buried in cement. I can't move. Don't want to go up and find her room empty. Yeah, I locked the door, but I know Rose. That won't hold her back. I don't want this anger to take on another level, because it might very well burn me alive.

After too much mental encouragement, I slowly take the stairs, each step feeling like I'm climbing a mountain. The house is quiet as I pace down the corridor to her room, and when I get there, I find the door open. Something is missing before my eyes can scan the space and tell me she's not here. There's no soul.

No Rose.

My chest expands, searching for oxygen. I walk to the wardrobes and find it full of clothes. It doesn't reassure me.

Because her red dress is missing, and I know Rose well enough to know that if she was going to run, that's all she would take.

I blindly stagger to the bathroom, finding everything in its place. My breathing becomes more labored, by body revolting against my attempts to give it air, throwing out every modicum of breath I find on constant gasps. "No," I roar, turning and throwing my fist into the first thing within range. The shower screen shatters, my knuckles split, and I slump against the wall, a rage so potent consuming me.

"Danny?"

I look up. Esther is in the doorway, the basket still in her arms.

"I let her out," she says unapologetically, her chin high.

I stare at her for a long, long time, feeling a bit lost. She doesn't back down. What do I do? Punish her? And how? Scream at her? I can't talk.

I shake my head and brush past her, walking aimlessly through my house. It felt like the soul was ripped out of my mansion when Pops died. It came back somewhat when Rose was here, spirit filling this hollow brick shell. And now it's gone again.

I feel anesthetized, numb, unfeeling.

Gutted.

My steps become quicker, more urgent, and I barge into my office, swiping up the Scotch on the way to my chair. I drop. I glug. I swallow. And I eventually focus past the end of the bottle.

Red fills my vision.

I lower my drink, swallowing down the burning liquid. She's sitting on the couch by the fireplace, one leg crossed over the other, her own bottle in her hand, though she's opted for vodka. Her beauty swamps my mind. That red dress throws me back to the night I first laid eyes on her. Every kiss, touch, and word races through my mind. She caught me. Reeled me in. Blinded me.

And betrayed me.

I slam the bottle on the desk and slowly rise, the fading anger returning now I'm looking at her beautiful, deceiving face. "Nox Dimitri," I say simply. I'm surprised when she frowns, diverting her stare to her bottle of vodka in her hand. "What, did you forget that you betrayed me?" I round the desk, taking my Scotch with me for support. "The boatyard was crawling with FBI tonight."

Her eyes dart to mine. "What?"

Her ignorance makes me want to strangle her, and before I know what I'm doing, I'm pulling her up from the couch. My hold of her injured arm is firm, and she comes with ease, meeting my eyes without a wince of pain. I walk her back until she's pinned against the wall. "I had the pleasure of a photo-viewing session. Saw you and Nox Dimitri together. Heard of your expert qualifications in seducing men too."

Her eyes widen. "No . . ."

Her denial angers me more, my hold of her constricting. "You've been feeding information to that Romanian cunt and now I've got the FBI crawling up my arse." I push my forehead to hers, hard and forcefully. "The attempts on my life are because of you." I release her before I really hurt her, pulling myself back to a reasonably safe distance. "You lying, filthy whore." I say it with as much conviction as I feel, laughing on the inside when she appears to look insulted.

Her chin lifts in an act of pure Rose strength and she walks forward, brave and resolute. I can see her locking and loading that sweet palm of hers, and I don't stop it. She swings at me with a look of pure hatred on her face, landing me clean on the cheek with brute force. Her strike creates the most piercing sound, the echo probably carrying through the entire house. "I didn't tell Nox about the exchange," she says calmly. "I could have, but I fucking didn't. I typed out the message detailing where you would be and when, but I didn't send it."

I scoff. "Really, Rose? So if Nox didn't tip them off, then who the fuck did?" I spit back, cricking my neck before taking another soothing sip of the hard stuff.

"I don't fucking know. I was with you, Danny. Every time Nox tried to put an end to you, I was with you. Why would I do that?"

"Because you want to fucking die!" I roar.

"I don't!"

Lies. I grab her by the throat, flexing my grip. "Shame," I sneer, pushing my face close to hers, snarling. "Because *I'm* going to fucking kill you."

"No, you won't," she retorts as she, too, drops her bottle, her hands coming up to mine on her neck.

"You sure about that?"

There's that resolve in her again, and it makes me pause a beat as she pushes my hands into her throat, goading me to squeeze.

"Dead fucking certain, Danny Black." She forces her forehead to mine, her words virtually hissed in my face. "Because you love me."

22

ROSE

Danny drops me like I could be diseased, moving away quickly. He looks shell-shocked. "No." A shake of his head reinforces his lie.

"Yes." I swallow, rubbing at my throat, his anger seeming to have transferred to me.

"No." Now, he laughs, like my suggestion is the most obscene thing in the world. Sad truth is, it is. And that only angers me more. I shove my hands into his bare chest and send him staggering back.

"Yes," I spit.

His scar deepens with the irritated twist of his lips. "No."

"Fucking yes," I scream, charging and shoving him back again. This time, he crashes against his office door, the sound of his naked back smacking the wood echoing around us. My balled fists press into his pecs, my jaw sore with tightness. "I see you, Danny Black. I see you clearly. Just as clearly as you see me." I step back, freeing him, but he remains coated against the door, stunned into silence. I reverse my steps and dip to collect the vodka that was keeping me company, as well as feeding me some valor. "You can deny it all you like. I did." I release a huff of laughter, because this whole fucking situation is fucking laughable. "But for my fucking sins, Danny Black, I love you too, you sadistic, twisted asshole." I tip the bottle and take a healthy dose of courage. "I didn't tell Nox about the exchange today because I . . . love . . . *you*." I raise the bottle, face straight, and toast the air. "And if that isn't good enough, then kill me, because if you don't, he will." I finish the last inch of the bottle and toss it aside, feeling gravity working against me. I start to sway. "I've been held to ransom my entire life. Blackmailed to do as I'm told or face the consequences." I throw my arms in the air and let them plummet to my sides. "A punch to the back here, an invasion of my body there. Yes, you're right. I was made to seduce whoever fucking Nox made me seduce. And hated every minute of it. Everything at a cost. But I choose to face the consequences this time." I'm getting louder with each splurge of words, my hands more animated. "For you," I shout, making him blink a few times. I don't know who tipped off the FBI. I'm stumped. I tapped out that message and stared at it for an age before deleting it. Then I wrote it again after he left for the boatyard. And deleted it again. All I thought about was every moment between Danny and me that led to my realization. I couldn't do it. I couldn't do it to him. I wasn't sensible this time. I chose *him*.

Danny remains quiet, studying me. His nonresponsive form, his lack of emotion, tips me. "Why the hell would I still be here if I did that to you?" I scream. Still no reaction. "My fucking life and soul is on the line here because of my insane need to protect a man who apparently hates me, so you could at least say something."

"You want me to say something?" he murmurs.

"Yes! Fucking say something."

"I love you."

I inhale sharply, slamming my mouth shut and moving back. I knew it. Or hoped it. But hearing him actually say it? "What?" It feels surreal.

"I love you." It sounds as good the second time as it did the first. So why am I distancing myself from him? "I love you," he says it again, pushing himself away from the door by his shoulder blades. "Why are you wearing the red dress?" he asks, slowly closing the distance between us.

I look down my front on a frown, my head getting progressively woozier, the vodka replacing the blood in my hot veins. "To remind me of who I am," I admit, reaching down and feeling at the material. A whore. Cheap.

His bare feet appear in my dropped vision, and I look up when he takes my throat softly, walking me back to his desk. My swallows roll against his flat palm, his cold eyes looking down at me like he hates me. "You're mine. That's who you are, Rose Lillian Cassidy," he says quietly, with genuine conviction. "You're fearless. I'm fearless. The only thing we're scared of is each other." He dips and directs my mouth up to his with a light press of his hand against my throat. "Your scars are my scars. And my scars are yours." My bottom lip wobbles, and he presses his finger to it. "Don't cry, baby. It doesn't suit you." His lips replace his finger, and he kisses me with so much softness. So much love. It accelerates my emotions and has me sobbing through our kiss, my uncoordinated arms eventually finding his shoulders and clinging to him. He takes the hem of my dress and pulls it up, but only to allow me to crawl up his body and wrap my thighs around his waist. Unrelenting chemistry isn't fueling this. Unrelenting feelings are. Feelings neither of us have felt before.

Danny turns and walks us out of his office, his palm on the back of my head directing it to rest on his shoulder. No one has held me like this before. Like I'm the beginning and the end of the world for them. My mind is somewhat fuzzy with alcohol, but I will remember this moment, crystal clear, for as long as I live. It's a whole new world for me.

The sound of the front door opening up ahead doesn't prompt me to lift my head and look. I'm too calm. Settled. Heavy with drunkenness, but at peace with myself and the decision I have made. *I choose him.*

Danny stops, and I hear Brad. "She's still here?" There's no mistaking the shock in his voice.

"She didn't tip anyone off."

"But—"

"It wasn't her," Danny grates, his voice quiet but lethal. "We'll talk in the morning."

"What the hell am I supposed to tell the Russians until then?"

"Tell them I'm busy. We'll rearrange," he calls as he takes us up the stairs. I smile sleepily into his shoulder, using what energy I have left to hold him tighter. I don't open my eyes until he's laid me on the bed. Quietly and slowly, he strips me out of the red dress and then rips it apart at the seams, throwing it aside and crawling into bed with me. I'm pushed onto my side, he curls his body around mine, and tugs me back into his warmth. "No one has stood in your shoes before," he murmurs once he's settled around me. "No one has experienced me like you're experiencing me. No one has seen what you're seeing. No one has felt what you're feeling. No one has touched what you're touching." He kisses the back of my head gently. "I'm yours, baby. All yours." Warm breath coats my hair and spreads across every inch of my skin. "I love you. Because no one has ever loved me like you do."

When I wake, I momentarily panic that I dreamed everything. It's like Danny knew that might happen, so he's placed himself right in front of me to make sure he's the first thing I see when my eyes open. Bright, sleepy blues meet mine, his head on my pillow, the tip of his nose brushing mine. His breath is my breath. As every second of last night trickles into my brain, reminding me of where we're at, I sigh, each minute of my memory enhancing the peace. I reach for his face, framing his scarred cheek with my palm as my eyes dance across his beauty. This wicked, brutal killer is mine. I bite my lip as a soft smile creeps up on me, and he takes my hand from his face, kissing the tip of each finger.

"Come here," he orders, rolling to his back. I crawl my way onto his front and spread myself the length of him, my face finding his neck. He smells like man and freedom. He smells like he's mine.

"I love you," I mumble, nuzzling deeper into him, relishing the feel of his dangerous, rough hands working across my back.

"Are you still drunk?"

I nudge him and let the sound of his soft laugh wash over me. "Are *you*?" I'm moving, being pushed to my back, swapping positions with Danny. Framing my head with his strong, hard arms, he kisses me. "Only on you," he whispers, and for the first time in my life, I swoon. Danny Black made me swoon. The merciless, cold-hearted killer made me swoon. "We need to talk," he says around a nibble of my ear.

I fold, knowing it was coming and is needed, but expecting something doesn't make it any easier to tackle. "I don't know where to start," I admit, feeling his soft, chaste pecks of my neck easing me into a needed sense of security.

"Start from the beginning." He goes to pull out of my neck, but my hand on the back of his head pushes him down again.

"Stay there," I order quietly, needing him all over me, reminding me of why I'm doing this. Reminding me of why I've chosen this road. He returns to kissing my neck, each compression of his lips to my flesh injecting me with the strength I need to share my miserable story. "My parents died in a car accident when I was nine. My father was drunk. So was my mother." I close my eyes and zone out, forcing the memories back but bringing the words I need forward, reciting them robotically. "I had no other family so was fed into the foster care system. Three foster parents tried and failed to bring me under control. I was too angry at my parents for being so careless with their lives and leaving me all alone." Danny's lips falter for a split second, before he continues dotting my skin with his lips, weaving his fingers into my hair. As if his kisses have the power to heal. "I was teased at school. My pain wasn't my own. Everyone else seemed to control it—my mother and father for dying, the bullies for enhancing it. I started cutting myself because *that* pain I could control." My voice remains even and strong, but my grief returns, as strong as it was back then. "I was put in a children's home. The bullying went on and I continued to hurt myself. Every time someone was cruel to me, I cut myself. They put me in therapy. I did one session and ran away." I take a breath. I've never told this story. Ever. "A man found me in a homeless center where I used to go every Sunday to get hot soup. He was kind to me. Put me in a hostel with a dozen other young girls. Some were pregnant. Young girls who'd gotten themselves into trouble and had run away from home. Or so I thought." Danny's mouth stops again, and this time his body stiffens above mine. I smile sadly to myself, because he already knows what's coming. I should have realized back then, but I was young, naïve, and desperate. "The first week was fine. All hot meals, clean clothes, care, and attention. Then the men started coming. The first time I was raped, I just lay there, frozen. It was like an out-of-body experience. I remember telling myself that if I shut down, it wouldn't hurt so much. Just like I did when the kids at school teased me for being an orphan. That it would be over quicker if I didn't resist. I was pregnant by fourteen." Danny's on his way out of my neck again, and this time he doesn't let me stop him. His face is expressionless, though he can't hide the swirl of anger gaining momentum in his shrewd eyes. "It was a blessing and a curse," I continue quietly. "The men who came to the hostel didn't want the pregnant girls. I was left alone. Then one day I watched one of the other girls give birth to a little girl. I watched them pull it from her womb and take it away. A month later, she was back in the game. I realized then that the only thing I had that I loved was growing inside of me and the second it took its first breath, it would be taken. I didn't want to lose all over again. So I ran."

Danny's eyes close, his chest expanding from an inhale. Even his jaw is tight. "But they found you."

"I was in labor. Couldn't fight, couldn't run. They took me back to the hostel and I had my baby." For the first time, my voice cracks, and I fight fiercely to keep my emotions in check. "I held him for a few minutes, and they were the best minutes of my entire life. Then they took him away."

His head shake is mild as he scans my face. "How did you get away?"

"I didn't. After I gave birth, I hemorrhaged. I was broken. They had no need for me anymore. But . . ." I pause a beat. "But I still had my looks and my body, even if I'd lost my soul. Nox took a liking to me. I was given to him as part of a deal. Nox was young. He dealt in women and drugs but he had no money. No respect. No power. I helped change that." I take a breath. "He blackmailed people. I was his secret weapon. It was all I was good for. Dazzling men. Making them stupid. Distracting them. He's so hungry for power and respect, Danny. He's evil. Dangerous."

"And my family killed his family."

"What?"

"Fifteen years ago. Carlo went to Romania. He'd heard the Dimitri family were planning on moving into America. He went and killed the problem. He killed Nox's father. I killed his brother." He swallows, his eyes darting, and I don't like it. "He wants me dead. He wants my world."

I lose my breath. "Oh my God." This is worse than I ever imagined. This isn't only business. It's revenge.

"You could have run, Rose. Why didn't you run?"

"Because I want my son to live and be happy," I say, and Danny looks at me, the pain in his eyes unbearable to see. "Every time I needed putting in my place, if a good punch or slap didn't work, then a reminder that his happiness was in my hands did. That's how it's been. I crave pictures of him. I need to see how he's doing, that he's safe and happy, away from this evil world. Those pictures have been . . . my reward. I also get them as a reminder that failure to comply won't just result in *me* being hurt. So, you see, it's been very easy to do as I'm told. Because even if I am beyond hope, he is not."

Danny's stunned. It's not a look that suits him. But it tells me that he comprehends the true gravity of my situation. He comprehends the real risk I'm willing to take to be with him. He comprehends that I need his help. "I'm here," he says simply, like he is the answer to all my troubles.

"Can you find my son? Protect him?"

"Yes."

"Can you protect *me*?"

He sits up on his knees, pulling me up to straddle his naked lap. Both of his hands start in my hair and stroke their way down to the small of my back. "I can protect you from anything, Rose." He rubs his nose with mine. "Except me."

My smile is small as I slip my arms under his and cling to him, keeping our eyes together. "I'm not scared of you, Danny Black," I whisper, quiet but sure, as I push my lips to his, feeding off the heat that our touching mouths create.

His low moan is packed with an appetite I'm desperate to feed. "I won't rest until I have justice for you," he murmurs.

"Your dreams will be happy, I promise you." Breaking our kiss, he looks at me with serious eyes. There's a need in them. A need for vengeance. "Where was this hostel?"

"The east side of town. I can't remember exactly."

"And what happened? Tell me everything."

He wants more. Not just how I came to be me, but everything in between. I swallow, looking away, and Danny nudges me.

"Everything, Rose."

I dig deep for the strength I need. "After I was given to Nox, he took me to Romania. I was young, still growing into my body. He used me for himself for a few years. Then when I was eighteen, he took me to a charity event. The Romanian president at the time was there. Nox saw the way he looked at me." I swallow. "It was so easy to get what he wanted. So, so easy. And when he gave me a picture of my son as a reward, it became easier. Nox brought me back to the States a few years ago."

"The man's name?" Danny pushes, his jaw about ready to snap. "The one who gave you to Nox?"

I shake my head. "They only ever called him *sir*."

Danny's frustration is clear. "Do you remember anything, Rose? Anything at all that could lead me to him?"

I look away, racking my mind. "His ring. A horrible snake thing with evil green eyes that he wore on his little finger." The flashback of that dreaded ring sends a shudder through me, so much so, I jerk on Danny's lap. Only when I settle and toss the image away do I realize he's trembling too. I shoot my eyes to his. He looks like he's in a trance, staring straight through me. White as a sheet. "Danny?"

He shakes himself back to life, but his eyes dart. "A ring?" he murmurs, a million lines creasing his forehead. "When did this happen?"

"Ten years ago," I murmur, wondering where that time went. It's a blur of sex, abuse, and despair.

"And you've been with Nox since?"

I nod, remembering his face when I was handed over. I knew evil when I saw it. I knew in that moment my life was over.

"Anything else?"

I shake my head, my frown giving Danny's a run for its money. "Are you okay?"

Disappearing into my neck, he hugs me fiercely. "It's hard to hear. And that's a deplorable thing for me to admit when you're the one who's been through it."

"It hurt me when you shared your past too," I say to ease him, though it's nothing but the truth. Between the two of us, we've seen and experienced horrific shit, and that has molded us into the people we are today. Twisted people. Now we can be twisted together. But he needs to know why I bailed on him when his house was attacked. He needs to know I wasn't leaving him, but had simply lost all hope. "When I let go of your hand, when I wanted to die, it wasn't that I didn't want you. It was because I couldn't see a way out. A way for us. A way to keep my son safe. I didn't want anything to happen to you. All I'd brought was destruction and danger and—"

"Rose?" Danny says, my name hot against the flesh of my neck. "Our future together will make up for our torrid pasts."

I smile, though I'm not sure that Danny can be right. There will always be an empty space within me. I will always wonder where my son is and how he's doing. And in a sick way, I will miss my place in Nox's world, because there will be no pictures anymore. There will be no rewards. "He doesn't want me to have a future. I'm his property. He owns me."

Danny releases me and pushes me to my back on the bed, settling on his side beside me. "*He* is dead." A delicate fingertip draws a straight line between my breasts to my belly button and circles carefully, stemming the bullets of ice that broke out as a result of his promise. "This time next week, there will be no Nox."

Such a lethal vow shouldn't comfort me. It shouldn't fill me with peace and hope. But it does.

I might never meet my flesh and blood, but at least he'll be safe. Finally safe.

I glance down my body to his hand on my tummy. Gifted hands. Killing hands. My life is in them.

I turn and push him to his back, climbing on top of him and reaching for his arousal, stroking it a few times to full hardness. His arms splay limply on the pillow above his head, and he exhales as I sink down slowly onto him. Each inch I take, more peace finds me, until I'm flung into bliss that only Danny can help me find. I'm once again immune to the feelings my cruel existence has dealt me. There's no despair, only hope. There's no suffering, only gratification. There's no loss, only gain. There is only Danny.

And belonging to him is the best thing that could happen to me.

23

DANNY

With every advance into her body, I battled to find the calm I needed and not let the fuel fan the flames of my rage. I didn't want my soft and careful taking of her to turn into a brutal fuck. I forced myself to control the primal, animalistic need to reinforce to her, to me, to *everyone*, that she belongs to me. She panted down into my face, small, delicate wisps of air that added another layer to the heat burning me from the inside out. Her whimpers of my name held a need that physically pained me. My vulnerable, fragile warrior. She doesn't *need* to be strong anymore. But I want her to be.

When my climax hit, the earth moved, and Rose exploded above me on a cry that momentarily dented my anger and realigned my focus on her. I watched her face twist with pleasure. I suppressed my own roar, gritting my teeth, just so I could hear her nonsensical mumbles. I pulled her down and ran my nose through the glistening sweat on her neck, inhaling it in, feeding myself with everything I could get from her.

My life changed irrevocably in a heartbeat. Now I have two purposes.

Revenge.

And loving Rose.

I kissed her sleepy eyelids and let her settle into my side. She was asleep within five minutes, breathing softly and serenely. Breaking away from her warm curves felt like ripping our skin apart, but I forced myself, pulling on some boxers and leaving the room, closing the door quietly behind me.

And that's where I am now, still with my back to the wall outside her room, struggling to get my shakes under control and any decent amount of oxygen past the ball of fury blocking my airways. I can't fucking breathe. I sink to my arse and hold my pounding head in my hands, wrestling with the sway of my chaotic thoughts.

Abduction.

Rape.

Babies.

Human trafficking.

A serpent ring.

A fucking serpent ring. Rose's life was cruelly given to Nox Dimitri by a man with a serpent ring. In a deal.

I push out air and force myself to my feet, taking a moment to ensure some stability before making my way to my office. I slam the door behind me and take the picture of my father out of the drawer, my eyes falling to his little finger. I always hated that ring. Now?

I swallow, my head in fucking chaos.

"There you are," Brad says once he's barged in. "We found Adams. He'll be here any sec—"

"Have you ever wanted out?" I cast my eyes across to him, and he balks, stepping back. My rage must be embedded into my skin for the world to see.

"What?"

"You heard me," I say, returning my attention to my father.

"Never really thought about it."

"Well, think now," I counter shortly. "If you could get out, would you?"

"Danny, I don't like what—"

"Answer my question, Brad." My patience is thin at best. "Would you get out if you could?"

"I . . . shit, Danny, I don't fucking know." Out the corner of my eye, I see his arms launch into the air in exasperation. "Anyway, isn't it a moot point?" He joins me at my desk, pointing at the picture in my hand. "He left his legacy to you. His power, his reputation. You have an obligation to keep it all alive."

"I thought so too," I say, shoving the photo back in the drawer and slamming it. "But my obligations have shifted."

"The woman," Brad sighs.

"She's opened my eyes in more ways than one."

"Don't be a fool, Danny."

"I want out." I make the statement and watch Brad close his eyes as if to gather strength.

"You don't just walk away from this life."

"Who says?"

He almost laughs. "The dozens of assholes who want you dead, that's who. You think after what we've done we can retire and live out our days pretending we haven't bludgeoned hundreds of men?"

"They all deserved to die," I grate.

"Agreed. But there is always someone who doesn't agree. Don't lose perspective over a bit of ass."

I only just hold back my fist from sinking into his face. "She didn't tip off the FBI."

"You said. So who did?"

I ignore his question. "Call the Russians. Tell them I'll meet them tomorrow." I settle in the chair. "That'll be all."

His shock is clear at my dismissal. "Dan—"

There's a knock at the door, and Ringo pops his head round. "Adams."

I nod. "That will be all," I reiterate tightly to Brad, my stare a laser beam of threat. He backs out of my office, uncomfortable and unsure, as Ringo more or less tosses Adams into my office.

The man looks utterly beaten. "You've been on vacation, Perry. I expected you to look more chilled out."

He closes his eyes in despair. "Can I sit?"

"Sure." I point to the chair opposite my desk. "You look like you need it."

He flops down on an almighty sigh, his fingers digging into his eye sockets, rubbing hard. "Let's get this over with," he says, opening his eyes and looking at me.

"Rose was planted on you."

He balks. "Of course she wasn't."

The stupid fuck. Seven years of fucking college, twenty years working as a lawyer. He's done nothing but disappoint me at every turn. And he's the most popular candidate for the next mayor of Miami? He's not capable of organizing a fucking piss up in a brewery. How did I not see that? That he'd eventually be useless to me. "Does the name Nox Dimitri ring any bells?"

"What? No, no, it doesn't. Should it?"

"Romanian. Descendant of the Romanian mafia. He's shaking things up and reforming. He's the guy who's been blackmailing you." I get up and start pacing my office. "He's following in his father's footsteps. We're talking women trafficking, drugs, rape, and selling babies on the black market, to name a few of his inherited areas of expertise."

"What?" Adam's gasps.

For the first time this morning, I laugh under my breath. "Yes, he makes me look like a law-abiding citizen, right?" I reach up and pinch my nose. "He wants me dead."

"Then why does he want your marina too?"

"To start up a scuba diving business," I reply dryly. "You dumb fuck, Adams. He wants the most secluded part of the coast to ship women into the fucking country. He gets the best of both worlds. Me dead, and the perfect route into the country. He planted Rose on you to get intel on me. He knew you were dealing with me."

"The little bitch!"

There goes my last thread of sanity. I launch myself across my office to him, just holding myself back from kicking his head in. He sits back in his chair, wary. "Don't push me, Adams," I seethe. "I already want your death to be slow."

"She really has got under your skin, hasn't she?"

"It's not that simple." I push myself away and return to my chair.

"Wait," Adams says abruptly. "My contact, he referred to his partner. I don't think he's working alone. There's someone else.

"There was someone else, yes."

"Was? What do you mean, was?"

I look at the drawer where my father's picture is kept. "He's dead," I declare with the finality it deserves. I refocus on Adams and what I need to do. "Now, are you going to listen to me, because there's something you can do that might change my mind about murdering your corrupt arse?"

"If you don't kill me, he will."

"Not if I kill him first."

"What?"

"You heard. You can continue your campaign trail. The photos of you and Rose disappear. Your debt with me will be wiped clean."

"The money? I won't owe you?"

"If you pull off what I'm about to ask, then yes. You get your life back and you don't owe me. And for fuck's sake, stop cheating on your wife. Are you listening?"

There's just a slight pause. "Yes. Yes, I'm listening."

"Good, because I'm your only hope."

After I finished detailing exactly how Adams was going to redeem himself, I made a few more calls to various significant people, my accountant included. I hang up and breathe out, staring at the ceiling. I thought I knew everything. In fact, I know nothing. Enlightenment seems to have rained down, pelting me with purpose. Everything seems to make perfect sense to me now, even if it's hard to grasp. How can you be in this world for twenty years, think you know every depraved thing there is to know, and, actually, know nothing at all? *How is it possible I had no fucking idea?*

As I wander to the kitchen, I take a call from Uncle Ernie, nodding sharply to Esther as I start to make a pot of coffee. "Morning."

"Still alive, then?"

"I'm immortal, Ernie."

He laughs, the laugh that throws me back to my younger days when Pops and Uncle Ernie used to share cigars and brandy on the terrace. "We should do dinner," I say, the suggestion sounding odd, but I need to see him. Talk to him.

"We should." Ernie's easy agreement makes me relax somewhat. "Your father would want us to stay close."

"You're technically my only family."

"No technically about it, son. I never had kids myself. You're the closest I've got, and my asshole cousin will haunt me forever if we lose touch."

I falter in my motions before carefully setting two cups on the tray. "Tomorrow evening?"

"My place. It's private."

Private. Good, because what I'm going to say needs to remain private. "Looking forward to it." I hang up and brace my hands on the edge of the counter for a few seconds, thinking. Logic tells me I'm chasing a rainbow. Hope tells me I deserve respite from this world. Guilt slivers through my veins, my father's voice chasing it. He can go fuck himself.

I collect the tray and make my way upstairs. Rose is still snoozing, splayed on her front with the sheets covering her legs, the material finishing just shy of her arse. I smile and set down the tray as quietly as possible, easing myself down gently to the edge of the bed. Her arms are stretched above her head, buried under the pillow where her head rests. Blush lips parted, thick black lashes fanning her lids, a flushed glow painting her cheeks, her hair strewn all over the pillow. I touch the space between her shoulder blades and draw a perfectly straight, light line down her spine, following my path with my eyes until I reach the two cute dimples above her arse. I circle each lightly, flattening my palm and ghosting over the area that's now tinged yellow from the fading bruise. I blink back the sting of rage that makes my eyes water, making myself enjoy this moment of silently admiring what is now mine. How? How the fuck did she survive so many years of torture? Her life wasn't all that different to mine, yet I had someone step in and provide solace, a home, a purpose. Even if it stands for shit now. She was shafted from such an early age and *never* rescued. Always living a nightmare. Always in fear and pain. And yet, she gave the terrifying Angel-faced Assassin cheek from the minute she met me. Stood up to me. Didn't flinch. *A survivor.* And I'm going to make her a victor. Because it's about fucking time she won.

Supporting my upper body with my fists sunken into the

mattress, I lower and rest my mouth on one of the dimples, kissing it lightly, before trailing my lips across to the other, looking up when I hear a soft, sleepy moan. I smile to myself and reposition my body, straddling her upper thighs and dusting every inch of her back with my mouth. She smells like me, my scent ingrained into her skin, mixed with her own natural fragrance. It's a heady mix, a cocktail of fucked-up perfection. Me and her. Her back starts to roll each time my mouth meets her flesh, and I reach for her hair, pulling it aside to expose her neck.

She chose me.

And now I have to ensure that she didn't make the wrong choice. The wheels have been set in motion, my next moves meticulously planned, though I'm still operating on gut instinct. Have been since this woman charged into my life.

Lowering my chest onto her back, I lay one arm by her head and slip my other hand under her tummy, sliding it down until I feel the dark strip of hair just north of the gates to heaven. Her arse lifts, giving my hand space, and her tongue slips out and glides across her lips, wetting them. My fingers meet hot, swollen flesh. My lips part, as do Rose's legs, giving my fingers room, as well as my cock. My taut, aching flesh disappears between her thighs, and with one slight shift, I sink inside of her, my fingers scissoring and working as I lazily pump back and forth. Her sigh is peaceful, and I catch it when she turns her face as far to the side as she can, dragging her eyes open. My body hums with pleasure, tingles erupting with every careful stroke. The feel of her welcoming me into her body, pulling me in, her walls drawing me deeper, surpasses ecstasy. Her drowsy gaze screams a thousand words. We're both from worlds where actions speak loudest, and never more than now. The drives of my hips and the massaging of my fingers keep us balanced on the edge. Sweat is beading, blood is boiling, heartbeats are thrashing. The wild edge to her eyes kicks my pace up a notch. She's on the cusp. Her arms come from under the pillow, her torso lifting as much as she can, one arm supporting her, the other coming back and circling my neck. She tugs me down to her lips and cries into my mouth when my hips buck. My eyes close and my mind channels, the images jumping through all chaotic yet beautiful. All Rose.

The tip of my cock swells, shockwaves surging up my shaft, and I choke into her mouth when the pressure seizes me and I'm rendered paralyzed by my release. Calm. Peace. I never knew I could find it in pleasure.

I collapse, pinning her to the bed, her moans sounding painful. I sink my face into her neck and lighten the pressure of my finger, circling gently around her pulsing flesh.

"What happens now?" she whispers, her arm hooked over my head, stroking the hair on my nape.

Turning my lips into her, I kiss her like a man kisses a woman he loves. "Now, I save you," I whisper.

"Like a knight in shining armor?" She wriggles to turn over, and I lift, just enough to let her before settling on her front, every soft curve of her tummy and breasts melding into me.

"I'm more like a knight in rusty, tarnished armor." I kiss the edge of her mouth, working my way down her body while she strokes and feels my hair. I can't stop myself. My lips need to touch every part of her.

"I love rusty and tarnished."

Relinquishing my mouth from her chest, I peek up at her, my eyebrow growing into a curve. "And rusty and tarnished loves you." I crawl up her body and kiss her fiercely, rolling us until she's on top of me, the sheets all tangled up between our legs. "Tomorrow, I'm taking you out for dinner," I inform her around her tongue, making her withdraw in surprise.

"Will there be a murder for main course?"

Amusement tickles my lips as I push her up to sit astride of my waist. Flushed, hard nipples point at me. I smile and take my arms back under my head, propping it up to get the best view. "I want you to meet my uncle. Well, he's not technically my uncle, he's my dad's cousin."

Her head tilts in interest. "You want me to meet your family?"

"*Family* is pushing it. He's all I have."

"And you want me to meet him?"

"Yes." I can tell this thrills her, even if she's surprised.

Her teeth sink into her bottom lip, her gaze jumping across my chest. "Okay."

"I'm sorry, I should have been clearer. It wasn't a question."

A playful scowl hits me, followed by her palm on my pec. "And what should I wear?" Panic finds its way into her voice. It's endearing, if wasted.

I swing my legs off the bed and stand with Rose attached to my front. "Something pretty. It's a special occasion." I walk us to the bathroom and drop her on her feet outside the shower before flipping it on. When I turn to leave, I find her fidgeting on the spot, lost in thought. Is she really that worried about this? The possibility shreds my heart. Today is the first step to finding our true beginning. "Rose?"

Without acknowledging me, she approaches the vanity unit and reaches behind a drawer, pulling something out. A cell phone. Staring down at it for a few seconds, she turns it over and holds it out to me. "I found it in the silver purse I used in Vegas. I don't know how he got it in there. I only discovered it when we were back here. You can check the messages if you like. It's bugged too."

Regarding her carefully, I reach for the phone and take it from her hand. "I believe it wasn't you who tipped off the FBI, Rose," I confirm.

"I know." She shrugs. "But who did?"

My lips straighten, my eyes falling to the screen. "I have many enemies."

"And so do I. Nox knows I've turned on him. He won't let this go, Danny."

"Neither will I," I growl, stepping forward, holding the phone between us. I hate the look of utter dread distorting her beauty. The only thing in the world that she should dread is me. I want to be the only man who can hurt her. Because that means I get to be the only man who can love her. True pain, I've learned, only comes from within. It only comes from loving someone. I slide my hand onto her cheek, the tips of my fingers weaving through her hair. "I don't want you to waste one more thread of fear on anyone else, do you hear me? I am your master, your god, your lord, your fucking be all and end all." I kiss her hard on the lips. "He can't control you anymore because now you are mine. You got that?"

Her nod is jerky.

"Good." One more kiss before I turn her and direct her into the shower. "I have a few calls to make. We'll have lunch when I'm done." Leaving Rose behind, I throw on some sweatpants and head for the gym, slipping the cell phone in my pocket.

I'm looking forward to a little chat with the last man I'll ever kill.

24

ROSE

The next evening, I'm in a fluster, indecisive of what to wear, critical of everything I put on my body. Nothing seems suitable to meet the only family of my mafia boyf . . .

I pause mid-frantic think. "Boyfriend?" I say to myself, turning left and right in the mirror, taking in the simple black off-the-shoulder dress. Too formal? Too short?

Glancing across to the bedside clock, I note that I haven't got time to debate it. I grab my bag, slip my feet into some suede heeled pumps, and make my way downstairs. The hall is empty, so I continue to the kitchen. Esther's drying some dishes, humming to herself, and she stops mid-rub of a bowl when she spots me. "Hi." I wave a hand nervously at her, then immediately use it to pull down the hem of my dress. "Too short?" I ask, searching for reassurance. It's ridiculous. The red thing Danny tore up shattered the slut scale. This is nothing in comparison.

"Too lovely," she counters, a kindness in her eyes that I've not met before. Esther places the dish down along with the towel and clasps her hands together in front of her flat stomach. "Can I tell you something, Rose?"

I'm caught off guard, my hands pausing from fussing over my dress. I should embrace this moment of interaction, since it's never happened before. "Sure," I say, almost offhandedly, when on the inside I'm churning with curiosity.

"I just want him to be at peace."

My brow furrows before I can instruct myself to stop it. "You mean Danny?"

"He's full to the brim with resentment. I can't blame him, not after what I did to him." She smiles when my eyes widen. "I know he's told you, and just the fact he's found someone to confide in fills me with a comfort that you might not ever understand. I'll never forgive myself for abandoning him, Rose. For leaving him with that monster. Never." A hard swallow. "But—"

"Then why did you?" I can't stop myself.

"Sorry?"

"Why did you leave him?"

"Sometimes things aren't as simple as they seem. I was a young woman. Everything just seemed . . . impossible."

"I was fifteen," I say without thought. "I would have moved mountains to keep my son."

Esther recoils, surprised. Yes, I have a son, so she can't tell me I don't understand. I do. "Then why didn't you?" she asks gently, throwing my words back in my face. I suddenly can't breathe as I stare Danny's mother in the eye. She's not looking at me in disapproval or disgust. She's looking at me like she truly needs my answer.

"I—"

"There you are." Danny's voice joins us in the kitchen, and I turn to find my knight in rusty, tarnished armor, looks like anything but. He's wearing a fine black three-piece, his hair slicked back, his stubble neat. His piercing gaze assesses me, blazing a trail of appreciation up and down my body. "Are you okay?"

I pull myself together and push my shoulders back, glancing at Esther. She smiles at me before going about her business. "I'm fine." I strain a meek smile and approach him, slipping my arm through his when he cocks it out. We walk to the car, and I note Brad and Ringo getting in the Merc up front as Danny leads me to the one behind. "They're joining us for dinner?"

Opening the passenger door for me, he lets me lower to the seat, holding my hand. "I don't go far without them."

I wouldn't either if I had a target as big as Danny's on my back. I guess I have now, too, so their presence should reassure me. Danny slips into the driver's side and starts the car, studying me thoughtfully. "What?" I ask as I pull my seatbelt across.

"Tonight . . . it's going to be fine. Good," he tells me, laying his hand palm up in front of me.

I frown as I place my hand in his, looking at him in question. He doesn't entertain my curiosity. Just stares forward, squeezing my hand.

We pull up at iron decorative gates after a half-hour drive across town. The mansion is sprawling, easily on par with Danny's epic palace, and just like Danny's place, there are suited men at the gates. "I assumed we were going to a restaurant," I say as Brad opens the door for me and I step out, catching him looking across the roof to Danny. It might be me, but he looks pissed off. I follow his eyes to Danny and find a cold stare. Have they fallen out? Over me?

"Ernie suggested dining here with him." Danny rounds the car and collects me, leading me up the steps. "Given there's someone out to kill me, I took the offer."

"What's with all the men?" I ask, motioning to two more guys halfway down the driveway.

"Ernie's related to Carlo Black." Danny tips me an ironic smile. "Dad always insisted he have security, much to Ernie's displeasure."

I can understand his displeasure, but also the need. "Is Brad okay?" I ask, casting my eyes over my shoulder. He and Ringo are following us, though keeping their distance. "He looks tense. It's me, isn't it? He doesn't trust me."

"That's his problem. Don't make it yours." His words are final, daring me to ignore them. Brad looks around, his eyes high and low. Then his hard stare lands on me, and I shrink under his icy glare. Shrinking *isn't* me, but I hate the notion that he dislikes me. I don't suppose I can ask for anything more.

We're greeted by a maid, who dips her head and offers us wine. Danny takes a glass and hands it to me, and I accept on a smile of thanks. The entrance hall is stark white, a chessboard of black and white tiles under my feet. It seems cold and empty. The only furniture seems to be the loitering suited men. Danny nods to them in hello, placing a hand on my back. "Let me show you to the terrace." He leads me through a den that opens into a dining room, where an impressive table is set for three. Then we step out some doors to a large, well-kept garden with a pond.

I peek over the edge and see giant goldfish smoothly zigzagging through the water. "They're some big fish."

"In a little pond," Danny muses. "Or is it little fish in a big pond?"

I nudge him on a light laugh and wander down to a swinging chair, sitting on the cocoon of wicker and swaying gently. "It's nice here."

"I'll go find the old fool." He drops a kiss on my nose before wandering back toward the house, and I relax back in the swing, rocking myself gently as I sip my wine and listen to crickets and croaking frogs. The peace and calm within me is bordering overwhelming, and for a moment I let my mind wander to Nox. Where he is; what he's doing? They're not questions I can answer, but I can be sure of one thing: he'll be dead soon. Or is he already?

"Rose," Danny calls, and I glance up to see him at a set of doors in the distance, gesturing for me to come. I push myself up and head his way, a few butterflies lapping my tummy. Has he introduced a woman to his family before? I smile to myself, knowing the answer.

When I reach him, he encases my head in his hands and directs it down so I'm staring at his shoes. He pushes his lips to the top of my head. "I love you," he says into my hair, reinforcing his words with a borderline uncomfortable pressure on my temples. He kisses me again, breathing through it. "Rose, this is Uncle Ernie." Danny releases his hold and turns me as I lift my eyes from the floor, my mouth stretching into a friendly smile, ready to say hello. I make it halfway up a broad chest and see an empty Scotch glass wrapped in old, wrinkled, fat fingers. I frown when my blood turns to ice, an odd feeling of unease rippling through me. I try to shake it off. I can't. And when I look up and find his face, I realize why.

The ground disappears from beneath my feet.

My heart tumbles and rolls in my chest.

I step back into Danny on an irrepressible snag of breath, my heartbeat going from zero to sixty in one, overpowering and painful thump.

"Rose?" Danny's arm slips around my waist and presses my back to his front, his torso absorbing my quivers.

"I'm sorry." I shake my head mildly, yelling at myself to pull it together. "Too much wine too quickly," I mumble mindlessly, staring at the face that's haunted my dreams for years. I jolt once again, trying to pass it off as a wobble. Danny's uncle smiles. It's oozing malice. He recognizes me. In fact, he doesn't seem at all surprised to see me. I swallow down the bile in my throat repeatedly.

He ripped my baby from my arms. He callously gave me away when I was of no use to him anymore. I've been in living hell for the past ten years because of this debauched heathen.

My gut twists.

My head bangs.

My eyes sting.

Danny's family?

"Rose," Ernie chirps, extending his arms out to me. He captures me in his hold and hugs me to his chest, suffocating me. "Breathe one word and they're dead," he whispers in my ear. "My nephew *and* your son."

Panic immobilizes me, my brain spasms. Releasing me from his depraved clutches, he regards me carefully. "You must be pretty special for my nephew to bring you here."

I can only blink, stunned into silence.

"She is," Danny confirms, reclaiming me and slipping his hand onto the small of my back. "Which is why I wanted you to meet her."

"It's a pleasure, Rose." Ernie smiles, this time less wickedly. "Come, let's eat." He motions us to the dining room, and I glance up as I'm guided by Danny's palm. *Breathe a word and they're dead.* There are two men in the hallway. I saw two at the gate, and two more on the drive up to the house. I've no doubt there are more around, all here to protect him. But Danny said his dad supplied security. That Ernie was only in danger by association.

Ernie goes to a huge globe and lifts the lid, revealing a mass of bottles and an ice bucket. He plops two cubes in his glass.

"Where's Brad and Ringo?" I ask Danny quietly, forcing curiosity to mask my panic.

"They've gone to get something to eat."

Fear layers the dread as Danny helps me down to a chair. "I thought you never go anywhere without them."

He smiles at me, laying my napkin across my lap like a true gentleman. "I'm at my uncle's house. I think we're good." He motions to the armed men outside the dining room.

We're good? We're far from good. "Danny——"

"More wine, Rose?" Ernie asks, as if he senses my natural instinct to blurt out who he is. "Or would water be better?"

"Water, please." I swallow, ignoring Danny's inquisitive look pointing at my profile as he takes his chair. A maid pours for me, and I take my first sip with shaky hands, my eyes rooted to the glass.

"Tell me how you two met?" Ernie says casually, just making conversation.

I look at Danny, my mind blank. My dry mouth won't allow me to talk, even if I had the words to say. Not that Ernie needs them. He knows exactly how Danny and I met. What's going on? "Rose was my lucky charm in a game of poker," Danny speaks up, reaching for my hand and squeezing. "We met in Vegas."

Ernie's bark of laughter has me jumping in my chair. I'm skittish, hot, and sweaty. "You can't play cards for shit."

"Shut up, old man."

My shock and fear are getting out of control. I need to compose myself before I blurt out across the table what I know and get us both killed. Love's made me weak. How could I let this happen? I'd usually laugh in the face of threats. Contain my misery and fear.

I look over my shoulder and see the men still loitering in the lobby. "I need the restroom." I stand on shaky legs, placing my napkin on the table. "Please, excuse me."

Ernie pauses with his tumbler midway to his mouth as he watches me, and Danny rises from his chair. "Would you like me to show you where the bathroom is?"

I falter, glancing at Ernie who mildly shakes his head, a thousand death threats in his stare.

"Second door on your right through the lobby." Ernie points, resting back in his chair.

"Thank you," I say robotically, leaving my purse on the table and walking away on numb legs. I'm not surprised when one of the men lurking in the hallway follows me. I slip into the bathroom and close the door behind me, falling against the wood. "Oh my God," I whisper, looking around, trying to kick-start my brain. What the hell am I going to do? I try to straighten out my head, try to recall things I really need to remember. Danny's uncle? Or cousin. Or whoever he is. He's working with Nox. My hands come up, my fingertips pushing into my forehead. There's too much information bombarding my head, making it impossible to think clearly and unravel everything.

A tap on the door startles me. "Make it snappy," a man grunts.

I dash to the mirror to check my face. I'm flushed. My eyes are stressed. I frantically search my mind for a way out of this, coming up blank. Brad and Ringo aren't here. There's nothing I can do but hold my breath and pray. I need to be cool. Then we might just walk out of here alive. I've handled many situations over the years where I've held in my disgust, my fear, my anger, and let self-preservation and hatred for my situation fuel my confidence and bravado. And that's what I need to channel now.

Composing myself, I exit and make my way back to the table, being tailed again by one of Ernie's apes. Danny's laughing when I sit down, swirling his drink in his hand. His obliviousness kills me. I'm screaming at him in my head. It's all a waste. How can the man who's been dubbed evil and an assassin not know how much of the devil lurks beneath the skin of the man in front of him? *Because Danny isn't evil.*

Turning smiling eyes onto me, Danny motions to his uncle. "We're reminiscing."

"Yes," Ernie chirps. "I was just reminding Danny of the time he stole a cop car downtown."

I strain a smile as a bowl of tomato soup is placed in front of each of us. I don't see tomatoes. I see blood. "I don't feel too well," I blurt, desperation taking over logic. I turn to Danny. "I'm sorry, do you mind if we go home?"

His face falls somewhat, an epic frown creeping onto his forehead as he looks me up and down. "Now? You want to go now?"

"Yes, now."

"Nonsense." Ernie chortles. "You just got here."

"You're pale." Danny scans my face as he places his spoon down and reaches for my forehead. He retracts his hand when he touches me. "You're burning up." He goes to stand, pulling me up by the hand. "Sorry, Unc, I should get her home."

"Sit down," Ernie orders flatly, pulling Danny's attention back his way.

"What?"

"You deaf, boy?" he spits. "I said, sit down."

A confused half-smile creeps onto Danny's lips. "I'm sorry?"

"Sit down," I murmur, lowering myself and pulling Danny down with me. "Just sit down." Ernie had no intention of letting us leave tonight. None at all.

Danny's confused look passes between me and Ernie, and then he turns, looking over his shoulder. I follow his gaze, finding two handguns pointing our way.

"What the fuck is this?" Danny's confusion soon moves aside for anger.

"This, dear boy, is the beginning of your end." Ernie takes a condescendingly casual sip of his drink. "Cheers to that." He nods past us, an order of sorts, and I hear the sounds of safety catches disengaging. "Kill them."

My heart lunges.

"What the fuck?" Danny roars.

The first bang sounds, and I slam my eyes closed on a flinch, waiting for the pain to kick in, just as the second shot fires. But the sounds aren't nearly as loud as I've heard before. Silencers.

And I feel no pain.

I swing around on my chair to find the two men in the lobby face down, Brad and Ringo standing over them. Danny's men are looking past me. Cool as cucumbers. What the hell? I shoot back around and nearly pass out from shock at what I find. "Oh my God," I breathe, flying up from my chair, holding the table for support. Danny has a steak knife held at Ernie's throat. There's no confusion on his face now. There's not even anger. All I see is a calm, stable psychopath, with a whole load of crazy in his eyes.

"Actually, dear Uncle Ernie," Danny whispers, menace rife in his tone. My legs give, and I drop back to my seat, staring across the table at Danny looking positively murderous, and Ernie looking half-shocked, half-furious. "I think you'll find that this is the beginning of *your* end." Danny draws a neat line across Ernie's throat, not too deep, but enough to show he's not fucking about. Then he releases him, picking up a napkin and wiping the blade through the material before retaking his seat next to me. What is he doing? Danny picks up his spoon and stirs up the soup in his bowl, reaching for some bread as he does. "Tell me all about your plan to kill me off. I could do with some laughter in my life right now."

Ernie sneers, wiping at his throat with a napkin before inspecting the blood staining it. Then he knocks back his drink. The action stretches his neck, forcing the slice open, beads of blood trickling down and meeting the collar of his shirt. "You're nothing but a bastard," he spits.

I flick nervous eyes to Danny, seeing his hold of the spoon tighten to the point his knuckles are bloodless. "How long have you and Nox been friendly?" Danny asks. "Ten years? Or did you have dealings before you gave Rose to him after *rescuing* her from the streets and having her raped?" Danny sinks his teeth into the bread and rips off a piece, eyes trained on Ernie.

"He wants rid of you," Ernie states. "I want the boatyard and you gone too. Perfect partnership." He motions to me, smiling evilly. "You made it easier when your dick took charge of your brain."

"Except it's you who's sitting here now with two guns aimed at your head."

Ernie looks at me like I'm dirt. "As far as whores go, she's a good one, yes?"

I cry out when Danny literally throws himself across the table, taking Ernie from his chair and slamming him to his back on the floor. The knife is in his hand again, piercing another part of his uncle's throat. "Pops would be ashamed of you," Danny hisses in his uncle's face. "You filthy piece of shit. All this time you've been playing the good guy, the law-abiding citizen, the saint, the respected member of the family."

"He wasn't your father, bastard. You're not even blood. My cousin was weak and pathetic. If he wanted a kid, he should have just come to me." Ernie grins, and I flinch in my chair. "Picking up some fucking waif and stray off a London street. Signing everything over to a bastard kid. The man had lost his stupid mind." He looks at me. "And Nox assured me he could keep you to heel."

Danny smiles, taking the steak knife and dragging it deeply through Ernie's face, from his eye to his lip. Blood gushes from the cut instantly. "Now we match," Danny taunts.

"You won't get out of here alive. The moment I'm dead, the men out there will be coming after you. So go on, kill me. Do it."

"As much as I'd love to gut you and carve you up, I'm not going to kill you." Danny pushes himself to his feet, wiping his knife on the napkin once again. He's not going to kill him? Is he mad? Danny points to me. "She is."

She is? "What?" I turn back to Brad and Ringo, like I may have forgotten that they're both men. "Me?"

"I told you tonight would be good."

My gasp pushes me back in my chair, my fingers clawing into the arms. "You knew?" I ask, my eyes flicking to Ernie. "You knew he was working with Nox? You knew he was going to try and kill you?" He could have fucking told me! "You knew he was the man who took my son from me?"

Danny reaches for Ernie's neck, pulling out a chain that's tucked behind his shirt. I nearly choke when I see the serpent ring dangling from it, the green eyes as evil and bright as I remember.

It forces me farther back in my chair. "Oh my God."

"You mentioned this." Danny drops the chain. "My father had one too. A gift to them both from their grandfather. Ernie's fingers got too fat for it so he started wearing it on a chain a few years ago." Danny looks at him like he's filth. "You always hated living in Pops's shadow, didn't you, Ernie?"

"Fuck you, bastard."

That word. *Bastard.* I see it turn something in Danny, just like it has so many times before. But he doesn't go psycho. Instead, he calmly kneels and takes Ernie's hand, splaying his fingers on the floor. Then he rests the knife on his little finger and starts sawing back and forth, making Ernie squeal like a pig. I look away, sickened by the sight. The screams go on and on, piercing and shrill, forcing Danny to stuff a napkin in Ernie's mouth to muffle the sound, and Brad and Ringo to become extra watchful at their posts, looking out for any men who may come to investigate.

When I look back to Danny, he's pushing Ernie's little finger into his mouth to join the napkin. "Say goodbye, Ernie." Danny stands, his body trembling and sweating, and he holds the knife out to me. I stare at him, stunned. "Never hesitate to kill someone who's hurt you," he murmurs. His words are like a shot of life and purpose, and I slowly stand, walking forward. I take the knife from Danny's hand, adrenalin burning my bloodstream. "In the neck. The chest. Take your pick." Danny takes up position behind me, sliding his palm down my arm until he's at my hand, steadying it. His mouth falls onto my nape, kissing me gently. "I. Love. You."

I close my eyes briefly. He was telling me before. When he bowed my head and whispered in my hair, he was telling me that he had it all under control. I step forward, raising the knife.

Ernie spits out his mouthful of napkin and flesh. "You kill me, you'll never know where your son is."

My arm freezes, and my breath abandons me. A spark of hope threatens to light my world. "You know where he is?"

"Of course I know. Every baby I sold was filed. How do you think Dimitri got the photos?"

I swing around to face Danny, finding him shaking his head mildly. I step back as his lip curls at Ernie. "Don't you fucking toy with her." He snatches the knife from my hand, lunging forward. "Don't even fucking look at her." The knife plunges into Ernie's eye socket, and my stomach turns, my hand flying to my mouth as I pivot away. "Ever," Danny roars, the stabbing sounds constant and sickening. A choked sob falls into the palm of my hand as I tentatively peek over my shoulder. Ernie is unrecognizable. Danny's body is rolling, fury electric on his skin. I retch, making a mad dash for the hallway, jumping over the lifeless bodies of Ernie's men.

"Rose!" Brad whisper-shouts, but I ignore him, my freak-out not containable. Too much. *It's too much.* I've seen some things in my time. Endured many horrors. But this? This . . . I can't.

I make it to the front door and yank it open, but before I can put one foot outside, it's shoved closed from over my shoulder. "Be wise, Rose," Ringo says flatly, gently moving me to the side so he can block the doorway.

Wise? Danny has just bludgeoned his own family. There are

armed men all over the grounds. He's just killed the only man who knows where my boy is.

Danny appears, covered in blood, his face a picture of promised death. "You want to run away from me?" He heaves, tossing the knife to the tiles and grabbing a napkin. "The only man who sees you. The only man who would kill for you." He takes one step forward, wild eyes on mine, wiping the blood from his hands. "The only man who cares for you. The *real* you. The only man who understands you. The only fucking man who would fucking die for you." His eyes are pure, frightening white-hot heat. "And you want to run away from me?" He throws the napkin down with force, and I pin my back to the wall, aware of Brad and Ringo standing cautiously nearby, while Danny advances on me, his lips so twisted, like he could hate me. "You can't," he spits, slamming a fist into the wall beside my head. "You can't fucking go anywhere. Ever. Because when you said you wanted to be mine, you signed in fucking blood, Rose. Right across my fucking heart." His other palm slaps the plaster, caging me in. His face comes close to mine. His hair is damp on his fore-head. His scar is the deepest I've seen it. His eyes the wildest. "I. Love. You." His forehead meets mine and presses hard, forcing my head back into the wall. "So ask yourself just one question, Rose," he breathes. "Do you love me? Enough to trust me?"

"Yes." I exhale my answer into his face, no hesitation, my body going lax.

"Then don't run from me. Do you hear me? Don't ever fucking run away from me."

Right now he's fueled by hate, by the adrenalin of a kill of someone evil. Someone who stole from him. *He's right to be angry. And I'm right to be scared.* But not *of* him. I take a deep breath through my mouth so I can't smell the bitter, metallic tang of blood that's all around me. He's fulfilling promises to me, because he loves me. He's the first thing in my life that truly belongs to me. The first person to ever look out for me. To care for me. Why would I run?

I throw myself at him, and he holds me until both of our breathing is calm again. Then he turns. "You ready?" he asks Brad and Ringo, receiving two gruff confirmations. "I need you to use your own two feet, Rose." He sets me down, accepting a gun from Brad and placing it in my hand before taking another from Ringo for himself.

"What's this for?" I ask, turning it over in my grip and staring down at it.

"We have to get from here to the car. Don't hesitate." Stepping up to the door, he looks out of the peek hole as my dying panic rises again. "How many left?"

"Four that I know of," Brad answers, reloading his gun. "Two at the gate, two between here and there. Ready?"

"Ready." Danny pulls the door open and immediately fires, taking out a man who simply turns to look our way. The gunshot alerts another man, who's quick to reach for his belt, but barely lays his hand on the handle of his gun before Brad takes him down. I'm pulled along, two more shots sounding as I'm pushed into the back of the car, Danny following me in. Brad and Ringo jump in the front, and as we pull off, rather calmly given the circumstances, Danny lets the window down halfway, resting the barrel of his handgun on top of the glass. He fires, and I jump, covering my ears as Brad picks up speed.

"One more," Ringo says over his shoulder, pointing to the gates up ahead. I see a man in the distance running toward us, firing round after round, the bullets hitting the windshield. "Fuck," Ringo curses, ducking down. "Take him out, Danny!"

Bang.

The man catapults back, landing with a thud in the road up ahead. Right in the path of our car. I close my eyes and wince as the car jolts and jumps, running straight over him. "The gates?" Brad asks.

"Meh," Danny says, blasé, making Brad put his foot down. I plaster my back to the seat and brace myself for impact, yelping when I'm tossed around in my seat. Brad momentarily loses control of the car, and the back end sways back and forth a few times before he gets it under control. He curses his head off, and I close my eyes, breathing, focusing on only that.

When I brave opening them again, we're on the freeway. "Come here." Danny seizes me and pulls me onto his lap, settling me. "How was your date?" he asks, a certain amount of humor loaded in his question.

What the fuck? I blink into his chest. I think I'm in shock. "I had murder for appetizers," I quip mindlessly, absorbing the heat of his body.

"I wanted you to kill him."

"He knew where my son is," I say quietly, making Danny cuddle me closer.

"He wouldn't have told you. He would have killed you."

"Nox is still out there," I point out, feeling my steadying heart rate accelerate again.

Danny's face nudges me from his neck, encouraging my gaze up until we're eye to eye. "So am I," he whispers.

25

DANNY

Deep down, I knew. I knew when Rose mentioned the serpent ring she wasn't talking about my father. But I needed to know beyond doubt, even if everything was clicking into perfect place. And for my own peace of mind. Ernie wasn't mad that he didn't get to pay his last respects to Pops. He was mad that I foiled his plan to have me shot down at the funeral. He played a part in planting the bomb on my jet ski. He helped send a missile sailing into my fucking house. All to get rid of me? Get the Russians out, get me out, take control of Miami. Fuck, they would have been shipping in women from Europe on mass and selling them to the highest bidder. They had it all figured out. Pops would turn in his fucking grave.

I didn't take pleasure in leading Rose to Ernie. I didn't take pleasure in seeing the terror in her eyes when she came face to face with him. But I took the greatest of pleasure in slaying him. The best. That bastard played us all. Rose's reaction to him was the nail in the coffin. Ernie's coffin.

I look down at the mobile phone Rose gave me, slowly tapping out a text message to *"Mom"* as I pull a drag of my cigarette.

Game over.

I hit send, stub out my cigarette, and stand, making my way upstairs. I enter the steam-filled bathroom, the silhouette of her naked body holding my attention as I strip out of my blood-stained clothes. Her hands pause mid-soap of her stomach, and she looks up through a veil of wet lashes, tilting her head subtly. I wait on the threshold of the shower until she steps forward and offers her hand. Reaching for her, my eyes set on her fingers, I watch as mine lace through hers, playing for a moment. Then she takes the soap and starts to wash away the blood, slowly, meticulously, as if she's cherishing the time she's spending cleaning me. Cleaning me of dirt. Of death. Of our pasts. Her hands on me . . .

My skin heats, and I brace my palms on the tile wall before me, dropping my head, watching the red tinged water swirl down the drain until it's running clear. When her hands leave my body, I lazily turn to face her. She claims me and tugs me forward, sliding her arms over my shoulders and going straight for my mouth. I spin us and we crash into the wall, all teeth and tongues, groans and whimpers. Bullets of hot water hit my back, my hands sliding over her arse onto her thighs, pulling her legs up to my waist. Her muffled yelp mixes with my suppressed bark when her pussy skims the tip of my cock. *Inside her.* It's all I can focus on. Just getting inside her. Reaching between us, I grab my cock and guide it to her, nudging her face away when she tries to hide in my neck. "Look at me," I demand, hoarse and curt, pushing her up the wall on a scream with my first ruthless drive. Her jaw tight, she bores down, fiercely trying to match my approach to our union.

"You want to play, huh?" I tease, drawing back and slamming home on a grunt.

Her teeth grit, and once again she grinds down, taking every thick, throbbing inch of me until I growl. "Do *you*?" she asks, working her fingers up into my hair and giving it a brutal yank.

My smirk must be borderline cruel, my fingers digging into the backs of her thighs. "With you? Always." I ram home once more on a roar, and Rose hisses, gripping my hair harder.

"Then let's play." She slams her mouth on mine and moves her hands to my back, sinking her nails into my shoulder blades and dragging them down. I squirm, tensing and pushing my front forward, as I match the frantic, hungry pace of her tongue, our kiss crazy. I slam into her unforgivingly, pound after pound, eliciting scream after scream, and it feels so fucking good. We both need this. Crazy, uncontrolled madness amid the madness. Madness we're both in control of.

My torso presses her to the tiles, enabling my hands to reach up to her hair. I fist it and cling on, pinning her head to the wall and holding her eyes as we tumble down the void of never-ending pleasure. When we hit the bottom, it's going to hurt. My manic pumps become more urgent, Rose's yells into my face fueling me.

And when it strikes, it takes both of us out, bringing me to my knees on the shower floor, Rose clinging to me as I shout my way through the force. I mildly feel her teeth in my shoulder, her body rolling against mine. My arm circles her waist, and I lower to the floor, splayed on my back, my labored breathing not being helped by the hot, steamy air drenching us. "Was that dessert?" she wheezes, stuck to my front, her cheek on my pec.

"That was main *and* dessert." I smile when she looks up at me; she's a vision of soaked perfection. "Is madam satisfied?"

"No." She sighs, settling her head back on my chest. "I could binge on you forever and never feel full."

"Greedy."

She shrugs, unapologetic, and settles. "What now?"

I'm not burdening her with what happens next. Today was a gift. Sick as it sounds, but I know Rose, and I know she would want to see for herself that the root of her misery is dead. Now I need to kill off the stems of that root. "Now, you don't worry about a thing." I negotiate us up off the floor and place her under the spray, ignoring her indignant face. I shampoo her hair, rinse, and work through some conditioner, and all the while I can hear her mind working overtime. When I'm done cleaning her, I take care of myself while she dries off, and the moment I step out from the spray, I can see she's ready to launch an attack of questions. Her mouth opens and I slam my palm over it. "What did I say?" I ask, forcing her eyes into slits. I release my palm for her to talk.

"I want to know what you're going to do."

"No, you don't," I assure her, walking away. "You're not going anywhere near him."

"And I don't want you to, either." She makes chase, following me into the bedroom. "He'll hurt my son, Danny. That's his ace card, and Ernie gave it to him."

With my back to her, I close my eyes briefly, searching for calm. "He won't hurt your son," I assure her.

"How do you know?" She grabs my shoulder and yanks me back to face her. "That's what he'll do. That's his promise every time he thinks I need reminding of my place. Of who I belong to."

Talk about sending me over the edge. "You belong to me," I grate, my jaw out of control, ticking madly. The panic in her face could send me over the edge too, but I'm saving my barely contained wrath for someone else. I grab her wrist and squeeze. "Trust me." It's not a request, nor is it a plea. It's a demand.

And she can see that. Her mild nod as she swallows is almost subservient. My little warrior backing down. I don't like it at all, but it's what I need from her right now. I move my hand to her nape and bring her close, pressing my lips to her forehead. "Good girl," I whisper. "Tell me you love me."

"I love you."

"Tell me you trust me."

"I trust you."

"Tell me you're happy."

"I'm so happy."

I smile. So am I. "Tell me you'll marry me."

"What?" She dives away from my body, shock a blanket over her face.

"Not the reaction I was hoping for," I admit.

"Marry you?"

"Is it that outrageous?"

Her arms fly up into the air in exasperation, loosening the towel around her. It drops to the floor. She leaves it. "It kind of is, Danny."

"Rose, I can't have a serious discussion with you when you're standing there naked like that." I reach down and do the unthinkable. I cover her up, re-wrapping her in the soft white towel while she stands frozen and uncooperative. When I'm done, I move back, out of touching distance, forcing my eyes to her startled face. She looks utterly thrown. It's endearing, if a little worrying. "Well?" I ask.

"You want to marry me?"

"Yes."

"Why?"

"Because I fucking hate you," I quip dryly, making her huff a disbelieving puff of misplaced laughter. "With a passion."

Her lips purse. "I hate you too."

I move in, unable to refrain from touching what's mine any longer. Snaking my arm around her waist, I tug her forward, her palms lifting and resting on my chest as she leans back, keeping my eyes. "Then we're perfect for each other," I whisper, licking from one corner of her mouth to the other. "Don't you think?"

"I think you're crazy," she whispers.

"I think you're mine."

"I think you're a murderer."

"I think you're mine."

"I think you're depraved."

I take her nape and apply pressure, and she inhales sharply. "I think you're mine," I murmur, my gaze burning into hers. "So you'll marry me?"

"Do I have a choice?" she asks, a small curve lifting the edge of her mouth.

"What do you think?"

"I think I want a crazy, murdering, depraved husband."

"Whose name is Danny Black."

"Whose name is Danny Black," she confirms, jumping up to straddle my hips, attacking me full-force with her mouth. "I've never been so happy to not be given a choice."

It's the best *yes* I could have hoped for. If she's going to be mine, she's going to be mine in every way. "Forced my arse, Miss Cassidy." I return her kiss and carry her to the bed, ready to consummate our agreement. I toss her on the covers and crawl up to join her, pushing her hair back off her face and grabbing the box from the bedside drawer.

She stills when she spots it, her lip disappearing between her teeth. "What's that?"

I raise my eyebrows and nod at the box, silently encouraging her to open it. Her eyes flick constantly from mine to the small black box, her lip getting a punishing chew. "Hurry up, Rose. I want to fuck you with this ring on your finger."

Her lip slips from her teeth as a smile breaks, her hands tentatively reaching for the box. Gradually lifting the lid, I watch as she slowly pulls in air too. I'm mesmerized, but my dick is becoming restless. So I reach forward and yank the box open, pulling the ring free and shoving it onto her finger. "Done. Deal." I rip the towel from her body and shove her legs apart as she laughs, but it turns into a sigh when I slip into her. Jesus Christ, is there a better feeling in the world? I tense my muscles, ready to withdraw.

"Wait," she gasps, and I still, scowling at her. *Wait?* Smiling knowingly, she holds her hand up in front of her and studies the square-cut diamond that's sitting pretty on a platinum band. Her smile is epic.

"Is madam happy?" I ask sardonically, knowing damn well that any sane woman would love the ring I chose. And not just because of the price tag.

"Madam is very happy."

"Good. Then madam can open her legs wider and let her husband-to-be fuck her hard."

"With pleasure." She reaches for my hair and yanks it, her eyes narrowing playfully. "So what are you waiting for?"

She'll regret that. The first smash of my body into hers drenches the whole mansion with her scream.

There's never been room in my life for a woman. At least, that's what I thought. There's always been room, just never the desire to take on the responsibility of loving someone. Of protecting them. Of making them my life. Rose is very easy to love. She made me love her without me realizing. And protecting someone you love is natural instinct, therefore very easy. What's not easy is loving someone in *my* world. What's not easy to deal with is the fear that my life and how I've lived it could trump all of my intentions to keep her safe. And on top of that, her life and how she's lived it, though how Rose came to be where she is today wasn't through choice. She was forced into debasement, whereas I walked into it willingly.

With Rose's leg thrown over my thighs, her face nestled close to my neck, my arm holding her to me, I stare down at her hand splayed on my chest, the sparkles of the diamond ring twinkling madly everytime I inhale and make her hand rise slightly. Just seeing that ring on her finger does things to me that I could never explain. We're doing something neither of us ever imagined, and with it, we *get* everything neither of us ever imagined. Someone to love. Someone to keep. Someone to live for. Peace.

My mobile vibrates from the bedside table, and I reach for it, seeing a message from Brad asking if I'm joining him in the gym. I have no desire to work out. Here is where I want to stay, yet I know I need to talk to him. To update him. I fire off a quick reply telling him I'm on my way and start to gently negotiate Rose from my body, smiling when she clings to me in her sleep.

"I'll be back," I tell her softly, stroking her hair off her face and placing a light kiss on her cheek. I go to the wardrobe where Esther has stored my clothes and pull on some gym kit, slip my feet into my trainers, and head out to find Brad. On my way down the stairs, Rose's mobile rings, and I look down to see "Mom" lighting up the screen. I come to a stop and lower myself to a step, answering. But I don't speak. Neither does he. We're just breathing down the line at each other, wisps of air full of threats and danger. Just hearing the arsehole breathe prickles my skin, anger rising.

"So they call you The Brit?" he finally says, his accent thick.

"I prefer the Angel-faced Assassin."

"I prefer *dead*."

"Many do." I ensure my breathing in steady and quiet, tamping down the heightened rage just hearing his voice has instigated. "Shame many will be disappointed," I go on. "You've tried

and failed to kill me three times. I'm invincible, Dimitri. You're
out of your depth."

He inhales. "You killed my father. My brother."

"Why do you care? You're illegitimate. The baby of a whore
your father fucked."

"Yes, my mother was a paid fuck. No, Marius didn't know
about me. But we connected. He recognized my capabilities
before I did. Call me sentimental, but I'm really quite sad you
stole my chance of having a relationship with my father."

It's all I can do not to roll my eyes. He's out for vengeance?
Trying to keep his father's name alive while building his?
"Thanks for the sob story."

"The girl," he practically growls.

"You're not getting her."

"She has no choice if she wants her son to live."

Breathe. Breathe. Breathe. "And what would you say if I told
you I want to keep her?"

"I'd ask why."

I don't need to tell him. He knows. "You want the marina.
You want Adams. You want the Russians. You want my guns and
contacts." I wet my lips, noting his silence. "You want power,
Dimitri. But do you know what you *don't* want?"

He's silent, his ego not prepared to ask.

"You don't want me hunting you down, because if you don't
take what I'm offering, that's exactly what I'll do." My promise is
thick with malice that no wise man should ignore. "And it will be
my most brutal murder yet. Ernie is gone. His money is gone.
Your options are limited, you sick arsehole." Fuck, this kills me,
making a deal with this slimy, wannabe piece of shit, but I have to
face the facts. He knows where Rose's boy is. That's his ace card,
like she said. It's all he has. But it's all he needs. "It's just you and
me and the Russians. It could be only you if you make the right
choice."

"All for the girl?"

"All for the girl," I confirm, cementing the fact that he probably thinks I've lost my mind. "I want out. You want in. Do we have a deal?"

"Talk."

I glance up when I hear footsteps, delicate footsteps that belong to Esther. She stops when she spots me sitting on the stairs. Her blue eyes look sorrier each time I look into them. "Call me in an hour. We'll talk." I hang up and rise to my feet, though they seem rooted to the marble step, preventing me from walking away.

"Ernie's dead?" she asks, her hands joining in front of her midriff, nervously playing. "You killed him?"

I'm thrown, not just by the question, but because she's asked me a question. She never speaks unless she's spoken to. Hasn't since the day Pops brought her to the mansion. "Yes," I answer simply, instead of ranting at her for obviously listening in on conversations that don't concern her. "Why?"

She visibly relaxes, her tense shoulders lowering a good few inches. "He can't hurt me?"

I frown, taking the final few stairs down to the hall. "What are you talking about?"

Her eyes close for a long time, an obvious attempt to gather strength. "He took me."

My confusion keeps me still and silent. He took her? Who took her?

Opening her eyes, I see something that I haven't seen in Esther before. Grit. I back up, wary of it. "The day I walked out on you, I wasn't going forever. I was going to get drunk, maybe even high, just to ease the pain of my latest beating. And maybe to dull the one I'd get when I got home. But I didn't make it home. Because *he* found me."

I recoil and inhale sharply, blinking back my shock. Ernie

took her? In London? I step back, shaking my head, not wanting to accept the slow-forming understanding. I can't wrap my mind around this. "No." It's all my mouth will give me.

"I met a nice man in a back-street pub."

"No."

"The next thing, I woke up in a filthy bedsit."

"Shit, no."

"I spent months comatose on whatever they were pumping into my veins while man after man raped me."

My hands come up to my head and cover my ears, like the bombardment of truths can be blocked.

"For three years, I endured violation after violation until I was kicked out on the street because I didn't fall pregnant." Every word she speaks is delivered clearly and levelly. She's completely together, and I just know it's because she's prayed for this moment, for this opportunity, to tell me how it really was. After our initial reunion, we never spoke again about it. After she told me she never wanted to abandon me, I brushed off her pathetic claim and dismissed all her attempts to talk to me again. She was just here, cooking, cleaning, tending to me, without any gratitude or appreciation in return. It was a sick kind of punishment.

I think Esther sees that I'm struggling to unravel any words to speak, so she goes on. "I went back to our flat. You were gone. He was gone. Someone else was living there. I lived on the streets for two years. Then Carlo found me. I don't know how. I saw his ring, was scared to death, but when I looked into his eyes, I saw softness, not evil. He wasn't the man who took me from that pub. He never knew what his cousin did. He asked me about my past, and then, when he was certain *who* I was, he told me about you. Told me how he found you and what he did to your stepfather. He said you wondered where I was. Why I left. I just wanted to see you, be with you, to explain."

I look away from Esther, caught between shame, confusion, anger, and pain. "Why didn't you tell me?"

"I met Ernie before I met you." She smiles when I shoot a stunned look to her. It's a sad smile. "He recognized me. He told me that if I breathed a word, he would kill you. I wasn't prepared to risk that. I was just happy to see you every day, even if you hated me."

I wince, a vicious pain penetrating my heart. It's the kind of pain that only Rose has ever spiked. And my father when he died. And now my mother. I look down to the floor, my head tangled.

"I love Rose," Esther goes on. "She's like me in so many ways. A survivor." I look up as she backs away. "She deserves to be loved." And then she turns and disappears into the kitchen, leaving behind the lingering, hidden meaning of her final state-ment. If Rose deserves to be loved, then my mother does too. The pain in my chest doubles, and I reach for my pec, pushing my clenched fist into it. If I could, I'd bring Ernie back to life, just so I could fucking kill him again. This time even more slowly. Painfully. And with more satisfaction. I can't even comprehend the level of fear Ernie instilled into Esther for her to remain quiet all this time. It's the same level of fear he depended on with Rose to keep her mouth shut. To remain loyal to Nox. To not share her dirty past. Or was he depending on her shame? Either way, he underestimated her. He underestimated me. And he underesti-mated our trust.

Fuck, I need Pops here to explain this madness.

"Hey, you okay?"

I look up and find Brad with a towel draped around his neck, his face wet. I cough my throat clear, looking back to the kitchen doorway. "Yeah," I murmur, my mind spinning. I'm going to be fine. Everything is going to be fine. Returning my attention to Brad, I brace myself for the shock I'm about to encounter. "I asked Rose to marry me."

He's quiet for a second, though his eyes are wide. And then he starts laughing. "What?"

"You heard." I stalk past him, heading for the gym. I need to work off some of this lingering anger. Ernie? My mother? My girl? I blow out my cheeks, the shock growing.

Brad is quickly on my heels. "I think I heard."

"You heard," I confirm. "I want out. I want to wake up in the morning and not wonder who's going to try to kill me today."

"That's never going to happen." Brad laughs again. "Not while you have enemies."

I stop, forcing Brad to stop too. He looks at me, waiting. "I'm working on it," I answer, and keep moving, leaving Brad with a look of confusion and worry all over his face.

He should be worried.

I am too.

26

ROSE

After I get out of the shower, I find Danny on the terrace. He's straddling a chair, his forearms resting on the back support. He's deep in thought, gazing out across the gardens. I watch him for a time, unable to admire his sweaty form in his gym clothes, too worried about what could be running through his mind. Eventually, he notices he's not alone. Looks up at me. Smiles. But it doesn't light up his eyes. He pushes his hands into the back rest and raises, swinging his leg over the seat before tucking it back under the table.

He approaches me. Drops a soft kiss on my cheek. Then heads for the bathroom, pulling his black muscle vest off as he goes. Something's . . . off. He's quiet. Pensive and thoughtful. Part of me wants to ask what's changed his mood so dramatically. A bigger part of me doesn't. *Trust him*. That's what he said. And I do.

I listen to him shower as I dress, pulling on some thin gray sweatpants and my British sweater. As I look in the mirror, I can't help but think that the huge rock on my finger doesn't quite match the comfy clothes. I hold my hand up and inspect my ring. I could stare at it forever. Not only because it's beautiful, but because I can't believe I have a ring on *that* finger. And Danny Black gave it to me. But if there is a man in this world who I should be with forever, it's him.

"Still like it?"

I whirl around, finding Danny's rubbing a towel over his hair, his shoulder resting on the doorjamb. There's not a scrap of material covering any other part of him, and I fight to stop my eyes indulging in the vast beauty of his naked form. I have the rest of my life to do that. "What's not to like?"

He smiles and approaches, dropping a light kiss on my forehead before getting into his own comfy clothes, namely, a black T-shirt and gray pants. His feet are bare. His strong arms strain against the material around his biceps. Every muscle he has seems more prominent, even through his clothes. "Good workout?" I ask, pulling my hair into a ponytail.

A light nod gives me my answer, though something tells me it wasn't so good. I study him as he rakes a hand through his wet hair, pulling it off his face. "Ready?" he asks.

"What are we doing?"

"Watching TV." He claims my hand and pulls me along as I balk at his profile. "I just want to do something normal," he adds.

"What are we watching?"

"The Godfather."

I roll my eyes as he turns a dirty smirk onto me, nudging my shoulder playfully. "That's not funny."

He laughs lightly and looks down at his phone when it rings, coming to a gradual stop. "You go. I'll take this and join you."

"The theater room?"

He nods and ushers me on, turning and heading back to the bedroom. I hear him say hello to whoever's calling, his voice short and clipped, and then the door closes, and it takes every-thing in me not to press my ear to the wood to listen. *Trust him.* I breathe in and walk backward a few paces, eventually tearing my eyes away and turning. I take the stairs, the cold marble sinking into the bare soles of my feet, the slap of flesh on hard stone feeling good. When I arrive in the theatre room, I scan the cream space for a remote control to turn on the TV. Nothing.

"Lost something?"

I startle and turn, finding Amber in the doorway, her blonde hair secured tightly in a bun. It makes her face look sharp and unfriendly, her dark lips and black trouser suit adding to the hard look. "No, I—" I pull up, for the first time wondering why she's here. Again. "What are you doing here?"

Her unfriendly persona turns downright hostile. "I could ask you the same question."

"Well, that would be stupid, since you know the answer." And just in case she doesn't, or maybe just needs it confirming, I subtly reach for a loose strand of my hair and tuck it behind my ear, hoping the dazzle of my diamond blinds her. Her eyes widen, no doubt, but her body remains still, her face expressionless. "So, why are you here?" I ask again, this time moving forward, demonstrating that I'm not threatened by her. Not even when she's dressed to kill, and I'm dressed to veg out. "To fuck Danny, or one of his men?"

"He has feelings for me, you know." Her chin rises a little. It doesn't dent my confidence. The woman is deluded. "Before you, we were a sure thing."

"Clearly not such a sure thing," I reply, refusing to allow her animosity to get under my skin. Or her tall tales to worry me. I've had so much taken from me, I'll be dead before I let another woman try to take Danny. "Shouldn't you be leaving, since you have nothing here anymore?"

Her dark lips twist. "You're nothing but a whore."

"Maybe. But at least Danny wants this whore," I fire back, my irritation threatening to show. She will not get a rise out of me. "And at least he doesn't share this whore."

She can't disguise the shock on her face. "Will he want you when I tell him you're a rat?"

I smile. I can't stop myself. She's in it for the win, obviously. Shame she's already lost. "Do what you've got to do, Amber." I brush past her, set to go find out where Danny hides his remote control.

I get only a few paces before I have her claws in my back. Literally. Her nails sink into my shoulders through my thick sweater and haul me back, and she screeches something inaudible, slamming me into a nearby drinks cabinet. I'm momentarily disorientated, stunned that she would physically attack me, then I gather myself and wrestle her away, channeling my energy into shoving her back and using the time to compose myself. I refuse to have a catfight with a woman. Jesus, what on earth is wrong with her? "You're showing yourself up, Amber." I straighten myself out. "Have some self-respect."

"Fuck you. He would have been mine had you not seduced him." She stands and reaches behind her back, pulling a gun out and aiming it at me.

"Are you kidding me?" I stare at the black weapon in her hand, stunned. "You'd shoot me?"

"I've done worse than kill a whore."

I blink a few times, thinking I'm imagining things. Thinking the gun is actually a lipstick or something innocent. Yet five blinks later, I still have a 9mm pointing at my chest. I look up into her eyes, cold eyes, and shake my head in disbelief. "You think killing the woman he loves is going to win him over?"

She advances, her hand steady. "The chances of him loving me are a lot more likely without you around." She disengages the safety. "I need him. More than you do. I'm dead out there without him."

"You're insane."

"That's what happens when you hold out for years on a man. I will have him. No one will stop me. Not you, not him, and not—" Amber loses her line when she's barged from the side, taking a tumble to the floor on a loud thump. She drops the gun, and I watch as it's kicked away. I expect to find Danny when I look up. I don't.

Esther is glaring at Amber as she scrambles to her feet, a look of pure disdain tarnishing her usually clear complexion. "Get out," Danny's mother seethes, throwing an arm toward the door. "You've long overstayed your welcome."

Amber, her forehead heavy with a frown, pulls herself to her heels, never taking her cautious eyes off Esther, who is positively thrumming with anger. "Why do you care?" Amber asks, darting her eyes to me.

"Because if my son wants to keep her out of harm's way, then I do too. If my son wants you gone, then I do too."

Amber's shock is embedded in every pore. "Your son?"

Esther moves in, slowly and intimidatingly, backing Amber into the corner. "Be warned, you gold-digging, power-tripping slut. I will tear you to shreds if you're not out of this house in one minute."

"You're his mother?"

"Get out," Esther hisses, moving back. "Or so help me God, I'll—"

"What's going on?" Danny appears, and I drink in air, bracing myself for the extended showdown. His gaze jumps between the three of us, lines perfectly straight across his forehead. I'm quiet. Esther backs up even more, falling into the subservient mode I'm familiar with. Amber, though . . .

She's quick off the mark, quick to get her version of events across. She practically disintegrates on the spot, tears springing from her eyes like they were ordered on demand. Because they were. "Danny," she breathes, shaking her head in a really amazing display of despair. "I was just—"

"Shut up, Amber. I told you I wanted you gone." He doesn't give her a chance to spill her lies. Walking calmly across the room, he lowers to his haunches and picks up the gun, turning it over in his hand a few times, inspecting it closely. Anyone would think he'd never seen one before. Looking up, still crouched, he holds it out. "Whose is this?"

I keep my mouth shut. I'm not a squealer, and Esther seems to have taken the same road as me, because she's quiet too. Both of us still and silent, letting it play out without our input or intervention. Danny knows. Danny knows everything.

He slowly rises and wanders over to Amber. She's quaking now, her back against the wall. "Did you pull a gun on my mother? Or was it my fiancée?"

The beauty of that word doesn't get the chance to warm me. I'm too cold, too wary. Amber pastes herself tighter against the wall, fear filling her eyes and replacing the fake tears.

Danny shoves the gun into Amber's chest, his jaw vibrating with fury. "For the last time, get out of my house."

"She's a rat," Amber blurts desperately. "She was conspiring to take you down."

"She took me down," Danny breathes. "You're nothing more than a slut I used when I needed to fuck without giving a fuck. Now, get the fuck out of my house."

"But, Danny, I—"

Bang.

"Shit," I yell, as I hear a screech. Then I wait for the thump of a body hitting the floor.

It doesn't come. But my ears are suddenly ringing with Amber screaming.

"Out," Danny growls.

And then she's running. Because unless she's really stupid, by now she should know that with Danny Black, there are no second chances.

Danny stares at the gun for a short while, before flicking the safety on and placing it on the coffee table. He turns to me, looking impassive, like he hasn't just fired a gun at his ceiling. "About that TV time." He points to the couch. "Get your arse on there."

I'm moving faster than my self-respect should accept, sitting myself on the couch obediently and tucking my feet up under my ass.

"Can I get you anything?" Esther asks, heading out of the lounge. "Dinner?"

Danny pauses a beat, clearly thinking as my eyes bounce between mother and son. "We'll eat," he says curtly. "You'll join us."

"What?" Esther says what I'm thinking, though I choose not to make a big deal of it.

"You'll join us," he repeats, stoic. "Go relax. I'll take care of it."

I look at his profile as he studies his mother's uncertain form, silently wondering what's changed. My curious stare is concentrated; he must feel it, but I get nothing, no acknowledgement, so I turn my eyes onto Esther. She looks perplexed. "Who will cook?" she asks.

Danny shrugs, as if it's nothing. "Me."

I balk. Esther balks. "You will?" she asks.

"No man's a man unless he takes care of the women in his life." He says it with absolutely no emotion in his voice. But he doesn't need it.

Esther tears up, and Danny moves in and takes her in a hug. I swallow to shrink the lump in my throat as Esther melts into him, her body jerking from her quiet sobs.

"I'm sorry," he whispers into her hair. "For everything."

"Me too." She furiously wipes her tears away when he releases her, smiling through her sadness. Then she leaves quietly, and I turn into Danny when he settles on the couch. I see peace reflecting back at me. "What's changed?"

"Everything," he murmurs, slipping his arm around my shoulder and pulling me close.

27

DANNY

Forgiveness. It's a medicine that I've only just come to taste. One that I never once entertained trying. Not before now.

Music plays in the background as I sit at the table mindlessly chewing through the pasta dish I cooked, Esther and Rose chatting like I've never seen either of them chat. I try to comprehend the drastic change in direction that my life has taken. I'm struggling. I have priorities that I never once thought I'd have. I have a woman I adore. And a mother.

I even have a fucking conscience.

And . . . . a heart.

My life isn't about power anymore. I don't feel strong. But I feel alive. I'm weak because of Rose, but I feel so alive. Typical, when at this moment in my life, I need to be the strongest.

"Are you finished?"

I look up from my forkful of pasta and find Esther standing, an empty plate in her hand, and Rose watching me as she takes a sip of her wine. Am I finished? I look down at my bowl. My dinner has hardly been touched. But I have no appetite. Not for food. Just for freedom. I rest my fork down and hand her my bowl. "Thank you."

"You've hardly eaten," Rose says, setting her glass down and pinching the stem. "You should have some more."

I quirk an interested eyebrow at her, taking my own wine and easing back into my chair. "I asked you to marry me. That's not a free ticket to nag me."

Her scowl is adorable. So is Esther's light chuckle as she carries the dirty dishes to the dishwasher. Rose seals her lips, though the twist of them is evidence that she's finding it tricky to hold back her retort.

"I didn't know you could cook," Esther says from across the room.

"Neither did I," Rose adds.

"Or me," I admit. "Life's full of surprises." I level Rose with an accusing look. Another adorable scowl. Something stirs within me, and it's not the need to rush her up to the bedroom. Pushing my chair out, I pat my lap in silent order. Her scowl remains firmly in place as she slowly stands from her seat and leisurely makes her way to me. As soon as she lowers to my thighs, I kiss that scowl away. "Ease off with the dirty looks," I order, holding her around the waist as she links her arms over my head.

"You've made a woman very happy," she says quietly.

"You're welcome."

"I don't mean me." She looks across the kitchen to Esther, who's happily loading the dishwasher. "She has a twinkle in her eye."

She really does. And she's humming to herself while she potters around, a certain lightness to her steps. And she looks younger, far nearer her forty-seven years. "And what about you?" I ask, nudging Rose to win back her attention. "Do I make *you* happy?"

Her eyes are questioning, her smile unsure. "That's a silly question. I just agreed to marry you."

I shrug. "You could have been scared to say no."

"Actually, I was scared to say yes."

I nod mildly in understanding. We're both way out of our comfort zones. "I was scared to ask." I take her hand and bring her ring to my lips, kissing the diamond. "I've never been scared of anything in my life, Rose. Until you."

"You don't have to be scared of me." Her fingers slip into my hair at my temples, massaging gently. "I am just a woman who loves a fucked-up man."

"And I'm just a man who loves a fucked-up woman." My hand finds her nape and pulls her mouth onto mine. "Always be strong for me, Rose." I feel her frown through my kiss, though I try to kiss it away once more, limiting space for her to question my reverent words. It might only be Rose's strength that sees us to the end of this nightmare.

"I'll give you two some privacy." Esther's voice interrupts our moment, and we both break away. "Thank you for dinner." She smiles.

"Thank you for cleaning up my mess." My gratitude is a simple display of appreciation. But it's a first, and I can tell it means the world to her.

"Goodnight." She bows her head and slips out of the room quietly.

And now it is only us.

Us and need.

I stand and help guide Rose's legs around my back, and she smiles, her face close to mine. I walk us up to the bedroom as the speakers around the house keep our ears filled with music. The playlist moves to the next track, and The xx's *Intro* begins as I place Rose on the end of the bed, pushing into her chest with my palm to encourage her down to her back. She goes with ease. Of course she goes with ease. The music seems to enhance my want, the dulcet, almost sexy beat sinking into me. I take her sweats and drag them down her legs, dropping them to the floor. Then I strip her of the lacy fabric concealing her from me until all that remains is the jumper. I don't remove it, just push it up her chest until her bra-less boobs slip free. Her wounds are healing. Once they're gone, there will be no more.

I cup one boob in each hand and massage gently, and she sighs, the breathy sound stretching on and on, her arms settling above her head. The fire inside of me crackles and spits, and my hands pause in their feeling, my gaze drifting across her face. If there were ever two people who were meant to be together, it's us. It's undeniable. Life to this point now seems like a compulsory trek through a warzone. A fight for survival in a world that would conquer me if I didn't conquer *it*. It's ironic that now, with every intention of walking away from that world, I find myself more fearful of a life without looking over my shoulder. A life without blood, sin, and death. Loving Rose is far scarier than any of those things. Or letting her love me. Yet it's also unstoppable.

Together, we're a force. An inexorable force. A dangerous force. But there are only two potential sufferers.

Me.

And her.

"What's wrong?" she asks, looking up at me through heavy lids. Her question brings me back into the room. It also makes me think. Because how could there be anything wrong? My lightness is being weighed down with a heaviness I hate.

Instead of answering, I push my sweats down until my dick falls free, kick them to the side, and rip my T-shirt over my head. Taking Rose behind her thighs, I drag her down the bed. "Nothing is wrong." I lift her foot and kiss her ankle softly. She tenses, her chest starting to swell and subside with her deep breaths. Dropping to my knees, I pull her down farther until her arse is on the edge, her feet resting on my shoulders, my hands wrapped around her ankles. "You're here. I'm here. Nothing's wrong." My lips kiss their way up the inside of her leg, her body solidifying, and when I reach her inner thigh, she throws her head back on a whimper. "Good?" I nibble at her flesh, brushing my nose from side to side, relishing the smell of her skin. Of her sweet essence just inches away.

"This music," she breathes.

"Sexy, huh?"

"God, yeah."

I turn my mouth inward and growl under my breath when her scent hits me like a ton of bricks. I slide my hands onto her thighs and push them apart, opening her up to me. And I stare, watching the visible pulse in her clit thrum. Shit, she's not going to last. When I drop a chaste kiss on her wetness and she bucks, my doubts are confirmed. She needs to come down a little or this isn't going to last long. "Sit up," I order, reaching for her upper arms and helping her. I pull her jumper over her head, and then pull her down off the bed to my lap.

My skin blazes, my hand stroking over her hair, my mouth attacking hers. Her upper body pushing into my chest sends the blood flow in my veins into dizzying territory as I kiss her hard, exploring every part of her mouth I can find. Breath doesn't seem necessary right now. Taking in air seems pointless. Because Rose steals it all.

I growl as I wrench my lips away, pushing her back on my lap a little. Her eyes follow my hand to my dick, and I circle my girth with my palm, encouraging her back to me. I slide into her sweet heat, holding my breath and closing my eyes. Her nails find my shoulders and sink into my flesh. Her moan is broken, ragged, and caught in her throat. "I love you," I whisper, opening my eyes. The vision before me could be enough to call off my plan and stay here all night. The boatyard is the last place I want to be. But it'll be the last time. The last deal. Then it's full-steam ahead into a life I never dared dream of, with a woman I'd believe was pure fantasy had I not found her.

I retreat from her softness, clenching my teeth as I drive back up, using my hold of her waist to pull her onto me. My body shakes, and Rose increases her grip of my shoulders. "God, woman, you have no idea how good you feel." I ease her up and let her sink slowly back down, my head dropping back but my eyes sticking to her face. It's sweaty, flushed, and utterly fucking stunning. "You want me slow like this?" I ask, building and maintaining my pace, every drive sending bolts of harsh, intense tingles down my spine. "Or hard?" I lift her and abruptly pound up as I yank her down without warning, slamming into her hard. She cries out. It's the most indulging sound of want. "Is that my answer?" I ask, smoothly gliding forward. Now, she moans, her spine bowing, compressing her boobs between us. "She likes that too." Laying my hand on her breastbone, I drag it down between her boobs and come to rest on her stomach. "You need to speak to me, Rose. Tell me. Hard?" I power forward, hitting her deep and firm, shoving her upward on a shout of despair. "Or slow?" A few lazy grinds has her clawed fingers pulling free of my shoulder, her fists balling and slamming into me. "Tell me, Rose."

"Hard," she pants. "Slow. I don't care." Her drowsy, lusty gaze stops my moves, and she swivels her hips teasingly, my back teeth clenching when she pulls me deeper. Locking me in her arms, she kisses the scar on my cheek.

I turn my face and catch her lips, palming her bum and pulling her closer. Her gasp is my next inhale. "I'm sorry if I've ever hurt you," I whisper.

"I'm sorry for letting you." Her breasts press into my chest, warm and soft. "Or maybe I'm not. Because without pain, there is no you."

Never has something made so much sense to me. I grab her

neck and kiss her like it might be the last time. With her wrapped around me, my cock still buried deep, I rise and take us both down to the bed, crawling up a little way. My pace is sure and exact, our kiss becoming clumsy and rough, as we both climb to the point of no return. The pulse in my dick becomes a vibration, the walls of her pussy shaking around me. "I'm going to come so fucking hard." I bite down on her lip, growling through the heat blazing in my groin. My release is surging forward at an unstoppable rate, and when my orgasm strikes, I'm almost paralyzed by it, my body going into shock. "Holy—"

"Fuck," Rose shouts, jolting beneath me, being ambushed by a climax that must be matching the power of mine. Her head drops to the side, her muscles squeezing me, constricting, her strength unimaginable. "Oh my God."

Electric shocks hit me relentlessly, every single one almost agony in its intensity. "Christ." I've never been the victim of such merciless pleasure.

She sighs, relaxing a little under me. "I hate you."

"I hate you more," I counter, my lids heavy. I give in and close my eyes, my face settling on her shoulder. "Thank you for hurting me."

"Thank you for letting me." Her hold of me tightens. And my love for her grows.

"But where are you going?" The concern in her voice is undeniable as she follows me from the bathroom to the wardrobe, stark naked and wet. Our shower was just how I intended it to be. Intimate. Then I told her I was going out, and she's been like a dog with a bone ever since.

I pull on a pair of boxers. "Don't worry."

She scoffs. I get it. After everything, I get it. She remains before me, glaring at me with a look that could cut off my dick. "Tell me," she demands, folding her arms over her chest and pushing her boobs up high. I swallow and look away, reaching for some jeans. My hand just lands on them when they're swiped away. "Danny." My name is short, clipped, and drenched in warning.

I sigh and face her. "Give me my jeans."

"No." She takes them behind her back, as if that might stop me from getting at them.

Stepping forward fast, I grab her arm and swing her around, pulling her back into my front and locking her tightly in my hold. "Give me my jeans." I don't want to take them. I want her to surrender them.

"Only if you tell me where you're going."

"No." Fuck this. I haven't got time to play battle of the wills. I snatch them from her hand and release her, getting them on before reaching for a thin-knit V-neck jumper and pulling it over my head.

As I push my arms through the sleeves, I watch, amused, as her cheeks pulse from the fierce bite of her teeth. She's getting angry. It's sexy as fuck. "Fine." She reaches for her hand and pulls her ring from her finger.

I can't help but roll my eyes at her pathetic demonstration. "Put it back on," I order, slipping my feet into my boots.

"Being in a relationship is about compromising," she argues, placing her ring on the dresser nearby.

Did she read that in a book or something? I don't know, but she's seriously rubbing me up the wrong way. Stomping over to the cabinet, I snatch the ring off the dresser and swipe up her hand, shoving it back on her finger. Then I frame her cheeks with my palms, getting my face threateningly close to hers. "Ever take that off again, I won't be so nice next time." I slam a kiss on her lips and feel her go lax against me.

Her arms are over my shoulders in an instant, her body crawling up mine until she's hanging from my front. I know her game. Stall me. Or stop me leaving altogether. She hums, moans, and if I don't stop this kiss soon, she might claim a victory. "Enough." I pry myself away from her mouth, finding starry eyes and rosy, swollen lips. She's breathless. Her skin hot under my palms.

"I'm worried," she admits quietly. "I know you're going to see Nox. You are, aren't you?"

"I already told you, I don't want you worrying about that." I try to place her on her feet and get absolutely nowhere, every one of her muscles locking down. "Rose . . ." I warn.

"Promise me."

"Promise you what?"

"That you'll be safe."

I smile, even if I hate this unfamiliar uncertainty in her. "I promise," I reply softly, bringing her in for a hug. The wet hair on her neck tickles my nose, and I breathe her into me.

"I hate you." Her words vibrate with emotion.

I close my eyes and hold her tighter. "I hate you too."

"Come back to me."

"Always." It's an effort, but I rip myself away and leave her behind, walking out of the bedroom with purpose and grit.

"You're shitting me?" Brad's face is twisted with disbelief beyond recognition. "No way, Danny. No fucking way." He turns at the front door and marches out to the car, throwing himself into the driver's seat in defiance. The door slams with a thwack, and he starts the engine, revving it hard and loud.

Ringo slips his hands into his pockets and relaxes back on his heels. "I don't think he likes your plan."

"Tough shit." I go after Brad, pulling the door open. "I've made up my mind."

"You're fucking crazy."

"I told the Romanians I'd be alone. It'll be a bloodbath before we get out the car if they see you with me."

"Then I won't be in the car." He throws a hand out toward Ringo. "We'll take cover in the woods."

I sigh, working hard to keep my cool. "Don't you think Nox will have men covering every angle?"

His teeth grind, his brown eyes taking on an edge of psycho. "You're walking into an ambush. Alone. Who's going to cover you?"

"I won't need cover." I reach for his arm and manhandle him from the car, taking his place once he's out. "Besides, it was you who told me the Romanians were amateurs. Couldn't organize an orgy, remember?"

Brad grimaces. "Why the fuck didn't you tell me you're going alone when you detailed this plan of yours?"

"I was trying to minimize the fucking earache I knew I'd get." I slam the door and roar off down the driveway, looking to my rearview mirror. Brad looks like he's breakdancing on the gravel, arms and legs everywhere. It's an amusing sight, though I can appreciate his frustration and worry. I'm walking on dangerous ground, and I'm walking on it alone. I never walk alone. But to get what I want, I've got to do this my way.

I flick the radio on and rest back, working myself down, trying to relax. I *need* to relax. Be levelheaded. I can't let anything ruin my only opportunity to get out of this world in one piece *and* without the worry of my past catching up with me. This is the only way. Brad didn't like it, even before I told him I'd be going alone.

I watch the freeway disappear into the distance before me, the roads surprisingly clear for eight o'clock. The sun is dropping from the sky in the distance, casting an amber glow across the horizon. It's Miami at its finest. I think of Rose. I think about my prize. I'm pretty sure she would have tied me up had I told her my intentions. She would have done anything to stop me.

As I pull off the main road and hit the dirt track to the boat-yard, I'm watchful. I spy at least a dozen groups of men lingering in the overgrowth as I rumble down the divot-infested road. They're all armed. They're all monitoring me. They're all reporting back to Nox, telling him I'm alone.

When I roll to a stop, my car door is pulled open before I turn off the engine, and I'm hauled from the seat by a tall skinhead. One man checks the boot of the Merc, another pats me down. It takes everything in me not to head-butt the fucker manhandling me. It takes everything not to remove that machine gun from his hold and sink the bullets into him.

"Neînarmat," he calls over his shoulder. "Maşina?"

"Curat," another man replies as I'm shoved against the side of the Merc. My lip starts to curl, my fists twitching.

"The Angel-faced Assassin." Nox emerges from the shadows by the container, suited and booted, his head freshly shaved. His leer fills me with hatred, images of his bony fists getting friendly with Rose invading my head. So this is the fucker who's sent my world into fucking chaos.

"Tell your men to be more hospitable," I spit, pulling my jumper back into place. "Or don't, because I can't tell you how desperate I am to butcher each and every one of you bastards. Just like we did your father and brother."

Nox shows the sky his palms, smiling mildly. His move tells me something important. This is less about revenge and more about him finding his place in this fucked-up world. He couldn't give two shits about his dead family. "I would be a fool not to check you're meeting your end of the deal." His accent is thick, but his English perfect.

"I noticed." I point up the track, where his men probably still remain, poorly concealed. "If you're gonna have your men stake out, tell them to move farther into the bushes. I counted thirteen watch posts. Three men at each. You've certainly got me covered."

"You've always been ahead of the game, Black."

"Shall we get on with this?" My skin is starting to crawl in the presence of so much scum.

"You seem in a rush."

"I have a life to start," I reply coldly, heading toward one of the containers that's ram-packed with weapons that'll likely see Nox all right for some years, as well as shoot him up the ladder of power and wealth. I pull the keys from my pocket but pause from inserting it into the lock when I hear Nox call me. "What?" I ask.

"You're really giving up your empire for a woman?" I look at the metal doors of the container, nodding as he goes on. "I mean, Rose is out of this world, I admit. No one knows that more than me." I can't see him, but the satisfaction in his words must be all over his face. Which is why I won't look. I won't be able to hold myself back from murdering the sadistic prick. "I taught her everything she knows. I hope you're reaping the benefits of my lessons."

Don't kill him. Do not *kill him.* "Don't ever speak her name ever again. That's also part of the deal." I slip the key into the lock and turn it. "Good luck in your new business, Dimitri." I pull the door open fast, swinging it around to meet the side of the container and putting myself behind it, out of sight.

And out of the firing line.

When I hear the first shot, I smile.

The container jolts against my back from all the boots hitting the floor, all running forward and showing themselves. Then it's like a fucking firework display as machine guns ring out and the sound of a missile sailing through the air whistles loudly. I hear the panic. I hear Nox roaring at his men to run for cover. And then I hear the explosion. I close my eyes and relax against the metal of the container, like I could be listening to an opera with a cigar and brandy in my hand. My only regret in this moment is that I didn't get to see Nox's face when he found the Russians in the container instead of his guns.

"More," a man shouts, a Russian man, undoubtedly indicating the track where more of Nox's men are appearing, coming to investigate the bedlam. More shots. More explosions.

I pull my phone from my pocket and type out a text to Rose.

> I'm taking a break from the office. Let's get married next week. I hate you.

28

ROSE

The soles of my feet are sore from all the pacing. Upstairs, downstairs, into the kitchen, his office. My circling only got worse when I found Brad and Ringo. *Danny went alone.* Brad, like me, is furious. But he refused to tell me where Danny's gone *or* what he's doing. Seeing Nox, yes, but alone? Ringo had to pry my clawed fingers from the front of Brad's shirt when I lost my temper, demanding he tell me. He didn't.

Now, I'm staring down at a text message from Danny, and though it should make my pulse race with excitement, my heart has taken on a nervous thrum. Something doesn't feel right. My thumb finds its way to my mouth, and I chew my nail like a starved animal, thinking. *Thinking. Thinking.* I watch from the top of the stairs as Brad and Ringo cross the hallway, both quiet, heading for the kitchen.

I move quickly but quietly on light feet, down the stairs to Danny's office. As soon as I enter, I go to his desk and start tugging drawers open, rummaging through the contents. There

has to be something. A man like Danny Black, he must keep a . .
.

My thoughts trail off as my hand rests on something cold and
hard, and my breath tugs in my throat as I pull it from beneath
some papers. I stare down at the gun. It's heavy, feels alien, but I
have no time to waste getting used to it. I march to the kitchen
and enter, disengaging the safety. The sound silences the room,
pulling Brad, Ringo, and Esther to face me. Brad's face will be
one I'll never forget—somewhere between shock and disgust.
"What are you doing?"

"Take your guns from your belts and put them on the floor." I
aim at Brad's chest, my serious eyes on his face. "Do it."

"You're going to shoot me?" He laughs.

"If I have to."

"Rose, don't be—"

I aim above his head and fire, shutting him the hell up, before
re-aiming at his chest. His stare widens, all three of them ducking.
"Guns," I prompt.

Both men reach for their belts slowly, one hand up in surrender. Part of me is hurt that they clearly think I'm capable of such a
cold-blooded act. But part of me is thankful. They still don't trust
me. Right now, that's good.

They slowly lower their guns to the floor. "Easy, Rose," Ringo
says, kicking his to the side.

I gather up their weapons and slip them into my bag. "Now
take me."

Brad looks at Ringo. Ringo looks at Brad.

My patience begins to fray. "I know you know where he's
meeting Nox. Something isn't right. I can feel it."

Brad takes a moment. Shakes his head. Sighs. Pulls his phone
from his pocket and hits the screen a few times before tucking it
away. Then he stalks forward, passing me. "Fuck it, I wanted to
go anyway."

I blink, surprised by how easy that was. "That's it?" I question, running after him as Ringo follows me.

Brad sweeps the keys up off the table in the hall and opens the front door. "Yes, but I'm having my gun back." He swipes my bag from my shoulder and rifles through, pulling out his own and chucking Ringo's to him. "Fuck knows what we could be walking into. Get in the car."

I do as I'm bid immediately, aware that my plan could be foiled at any moment by either men swiftly and expertly disarming me and putting me back in the house. Yet, part of me knows that Brad is just as worried as me. He drives fast but carefully, and the silence is so fucking loud.

"He sent me a text." I move forward, putting myself in between the front seats and showing them my screen. "I'm worried."

Brad returns his attention to the freeway.

"He's not been right," I go on. "Lost in thought, saying things like he might not ever see me again."

"Like what?"

"He told me he needs me to be strong for him. Why would he say that? Why does he need that? The last time he behaved like that, he pulled a psycho on Ernie. Has he told you what he's doing?"

Brad's eyes meet mine in the rearview mirror as the car picks up speed, and I sit back, my unease increasing tenfold. Now, the more I think about Danny's need for me to be strong, the more I'm wondering why. And Brad's silence isn't helping. Does he know? Or is his mind racing like mine?

The rest of the journey is quiet. It's only when we pull off the freeway that I realize where we're heading. The boatyard. But when we reach the turning for the track, Brad passes it, continuing down the road. I notice Ringo look down the dirt lane that leads to the boatyard. "Saw nothing," he says.

"We'll take the back road anyway." A few more miles down the road, Brad slows and takes a right, and we immediately start jumping around, the Merc struggling with the huge potholes and rocks in the road. "Anything?" Brad asks.

"Can't see through the fucking bushes," Ringo mutters, his face up close to the window.

Brad slows to a stop, and they both get out the car, not bothering to close the doors. I remain in my seat for a few seconds, until the instruction I need finally falls into my head. I jump out, too, following and leaving the door open so not to create any sound. I jog after them, so damn tense.

"Get in the car, Rose," Brad hisses over his shoulder.

"No."

"Do it."

"No way."

"Fuck me, no wonder he's so stressed lately."

"Shit," Ringo curses, putting his arm out to stop me in my tracks. He starts looking around, as does Brad, both their guns appearing from behind their jackets.

I withdraw, scanning the space too. Then I see what's got them all twitchy. "Oh my God," I breathe, feeling Ringo reach for me and pull me close. His hand comes over my mouth, as if he senses my impending scream of panic.

"There's another." Brad motions with his gun toward a nearby tree where a body is slumped against the trunk, his throat cut. My eyes widen, breathing becoming increasingly difficult, not only because of the hand over my mouth. I recognize him. He delivered a picture of my boy to my room and a punch to my kidneys not too long ago.

I reach up, trying to yank Ringo's hand away. "Keep quiet," he warns, letting me win.

I swing around to face him. "They're Nox's men," I pant,

spotting yet another body only a few feet away. It's a fucking graveyard.

"Not that one," Ringo says, pointing his gun to a bush that's decorated with a man's brain, his body propped up against the dense foliage. "That one's Russian."

Russians? What are the Russians doing here? Nox hates the Russians.

I feel dread and fear arrest me. Everywhere I turn, another dead body is staring at me. I cover my own mouth, backing up until I slam into a chest and jump out of my skin.

"Easy," Brad whispers, holding me up. I could fall to the ground, my earlier grit when I held Danny's men at gunpoint vanishing. He takes my hand and starts to guide me through the trees, Ringo leading, both of them alert and tense. More bodies. More blood. More carnage. Tears prick at the backs off my eyes, my worst nightmare becoming more real with every step I take. We seem to trek for miles, my strength waning, and when we emerge from the bushes onto the road that leads to the boatyard, it's like a mass grave. I choke on nothing, scanning the faces of all the men we weave through, my eyes studying each face carefully. I don't know what I'll do if Danny's face is among the dead.

My cheeks wet, I blindly stagger along with Brad, tripping over small rocks as I go. Every beat of my heart hurts, to the point I wish it would just stop beating altogether. All these men. There are dozens, and Danny was alone, damn him. What was he fucking thinking?

"Rose," Brad says, tugging me in front of him and resting his hands on my shoulders. "Look."

I lift my eyes from the scattered bodies around me, and what I find has me falling back, needing Brad's chest to support me. A low, broken sob escapes me. Danny's up ahead, his back to me. He's shaking someone's hand. I don't know who. I don't care.

He's alive. I make to break from Brad's hold, a newfound strength injecting life into me. I just need to get to him.

"Wait," Brad orders, hauling me back. "Just wait. Let him finish."

"What's he doing?"

"Selling his soul to the devil."

"What?"

"That's Volodya. Russian mafia. Danny just handed the Romanians to him on a silver platter."

I inhale, my eyes falling to a body not far from Danny's feet as if a magnet is pulling them there. But this body is still breathing. "Oh God." I stare, enthralled, as Danny releases the Russian's hand and turns toward Nox's bloodied, limp body. He lowers to his haunches. Gets as close as he can. He smiles. Then he nods to a nearby man who steps in and drags Nox to his feet. He's battered, bloodied, and disheveled. But he's alive. At least, for now.

Danny's saved him for last. For himself. Nox spits at Danny, the move labored, leaving saliva dribbling down his chin as he heaves. "Any last words?" Danny asks, rising to his feet and holding his hand out. A machete is placed in it, the blade sparkling, freshly sharpened and glistening.

"Fuck you," Nox rasps.

And Danny grins. It's the dirtiest, most evil grin I've ever seen. Not just on him. On *any* man. He raises the machete and sweeps it through the air smoothly, taking Nox's head clean off his shoulders in one accurate stroke. The thud when it hits the ground is deafening, and I wretch, turning into Brad's chest and hiding, my stomach revolting against my swallows. There was so much pleasure on his face. So much satisfaction, and though I have wished Nox dead for years and years, triumph is hampered by my shock and nausea.

"Rose." Brad muscles me from his chest, and I turn, tears

painting streaks down my face. The Russian accepts the blade when Danny hands it to him, and he smiles, as satisfied as Danny. And they shake hands again before Danny turns to me. When he spots me, he stills, watching me from a distance. Mildly, he nods, his fist coming up to his chest and tapping over his heart. "For you," he mouths.

I crumble, wiping at my eyes, suddenly ashamed of myself for being so emotional. For being so weak. For letting him see me like this, but the relief that he's alive, the relief that Nox is dead . . . it's too much.

Danny starts toward me, his expressionless face slowly cracking, a smile growing as he comes closer. My surroundings blur and eventually vanish completely, the sounds dulling to nothing. In my world, my entire existence, there is only Danny.

But I'm abruptly yanked from my comforting place when Brad roars, "No!" Everything returns—sound and sight. It's chaos, men running and shouting around me. Confused, I look toward the container.

The Russian has a gun pointing at Danny's back.

"Danny," I scream, and he frowns, turning away from me.

"Goodbye, Black." The air is pierced by the sound of a gunshot, and Danny's body catapults back, landing with a thud on the gravel.

"Fuck!" Brad grabs me as more men appear from every direction, all brandishing guns. He fires round after round as I struggle with him.

"No," I yell, breaking free and running toward Danny. I can't feel my legs. Can't feel my heart pounding, though I'm sure it is. "Danny." I fall to my knees by his side, my palms instinctively resting on his chest. "Oh God. Oh God, please, no."

"I'm fine," he wheezes, his face screwed up. "I'm fine."

"Rose." I'm ambushed from the side by Brad, who hauls me to my feet.

"He's been shot!"

Ringo appears, taking Danny's arm and dragging him up. "Come on, you stupid fuck."

I watch as Danny struggles, his legs unstable, his face an unbearable picture of pain. "Fuck," he chokes, just as Ringo aims and fires at a man running toward us.

"The boat," he yells, dragging Danny toward the shore. "Get on the fucking boat."

I'm pulled along by Brad, as he and Ringo fire shot after shot, holding back the men coming at us. But the sounds are dull, my eyes nailed to the back of Danny, watching as he stumbles along with Ringo's help. "Rose, down!" Brad yells, shoving me to the ground. I land with a crash, my head hitting a nearby rock. Pain sears through me, and I cry out, immediately feeling hot blood trickling down my face. Disorientated, I look up, blinking, the gunfire still constant. I see Danny look back. I see him find me on the ground. I see him fight his way out of Ringo's hold and run back to me. He claims me and yanks me to my feet like I'm weightless, taking my hand.

"I need you to run, Rose."

His words, the sound of his voice, the feel of him holding my hand. I find life again, and I run, flinching with every shot that's fired around us. We hit the water, wading through, and Danny swoops in and lifts me. I practically fall into the boat as Ringo starts the engine, still firing as he does, his attention split between the men shooting at us and getting the boat moving. The engine roars as I scramble to the side, reaching over for Danny to help him up. But he turns away, catching a gun that Brad throws him and starts to wade back toward the shore.

What is he doing?

"Come on!" Ringo bellows.

"Danny!" I scream, watching, my fear multiplying, as he joins Brad, both of them up to their waists in the sea, firing non-stop. I watch as man after man drop like flies on the beach, the air pierced by the sounds of gunshots and shouts, the dusky sky lit up.

Brad turns and starts back toward the boat, and my heart kicks when I see Danny following. I mentally will them to hurry, their progress hindered by the water around them. *Come on. Come on. Come on.*

Brad reaches the side of the boat first and starts to pull himself up with Ringo's help. "Get Danny," he orders, his words labored. "Just get him in the fucking boat."

Ringo diverts his attention to Danny swimming toward us, leaning over the side, as Brad drops into the boat and reloads his gun. I watch as Danny gets closer and closer, it seeming to take forever, and when he's only a few meters away, Brad starts firing again. "Hurry the fuck up, Danny," he yells.

I lean over the boat too, and Danny locks eyes with me. He smiles. The sick fuck smiles as he reaches for Ringo's hand. I can only shake my head at him, caught between despair and fury. I'm going to kill him. For being so reckless and stupid, I'm going to kill him. The light in his eyes is blinding, and my panic starts to ebb, his fingers brushing Ringo's.

"Go!" Ringo yells, and Brad takes up position at the back of the boat by the engine, just as Ringo seizes Danny's hand and yanks him up on a grunt.

I jump as the boat lurches forward. Danny's eyes widen. Ringo curses, falling back to his arse, leaving Danny hanging off the side of the boat. "Fuck," he spits, grappling to hold on.

"Danny!" Brad roars.

I dive forward and grab his arms, adrenalin fueling me. "Get back, Rose," he yells, trying to shake me off. "You'll fall in."

"Fuck you." I fight to help him up, try my hardest, but he's too heavy. "Kick your legs!" I yell, finding his eyes.

He stares at me. Just stares. And he smiles again. And then the loudest bang erupts, and his body jerks, his smile falling. It takes me a few confused moments to realize what's happening. Then Danny's body becomes heavier, slipping from my grasp. "No," I mumble, searching his blue eyes. This time, I find . . . nothing. No light. No ice. No smile. Nothing. "Danny?"

He starts to slip down the side of the boat, his eyes closing, and I grapple and fight to keep him up as the boat speeds away.

"Ringo!" I scream, holding on to him for dear life. "Ringo, he's been hit again!"

But Ringo doesn't answer me, his gun firing constantly. I look up, seeing a few jet skis in pursuit.

"Oh my God," I breathe, realigning my focus on getting Danny into the boat. But he's slipping. Slipping. Slipping.

His eyes are closed. His body limp. "Please, Danny." I beg, but I lose my grip, and he slips away from me, dropping into the sea. "No!" I watch him getting further away from me. "Danny!" I scream, my heart tearing in two.

"Fuck, no!" Brad yells as I climb onto the side of the boat. "Rose, no!"

I'm yanked back and hit the floor hard. "I lost him," I sob, crawling to my knees, looking out. "We need to go back, Brad." A bullet hits the side of the boat, and I duck instinctively, covering my ears, the sounds unbearable. "We need to go back!"

"We'll all be killed," Brad shouts, and I break down, tears pouring down my cheeks.

Ringo curses, his body crashing down next to mine, his hand going to his shoulder, blood coating his fingers. "For fuck's sake." He looks at me. It's a look I'll never forget. Full of sadness. Of pity.

A wretched sob tumbles as I recklessly get to my knees and look back, searching for him, my eyes darting frantically across the dark water. And I see him. Floating. Just floating, face down. "No," I whisper raggedly.

"Get us out of here," Brad bellows, firing again taking out two of the jet skis.

My shout is carnal and raw and full of devastation, my body jolting as the boat hits the waves at high speed. But however much I'm being tossed around, my eyes remain steady and level, locked on Danny's lifeless body, growing smaller and smaller. Until the sea eventually takes him.

And I can no longer see him.

But I will always see him.

~

I stare down at the razor blade in my hand. Release. I need a release. I need to control this pain. I rest the edge on my arm. Close my eyes. Breathe in. And exhale as I drag it through my skin. My entire being relaxes.

"Rose!"

I startle, blinking my eyes open. Esther's face is a picture of raw disgust as she swipes her hand out, knocking the blade to the carpet. I stare down at it. Blank. She doesn't say a word. She doesn't take the blade either. She just turns and walks out, and I stare at the bedroom door for long after she's slammed it, until I feel the blood dripping from my arm onto the carpet. I look down, watching as the plush fibers soak up the thick red blobs.

Lost.

Flashbacks assault me, my hands coming to my head, trying to squash them. I can't. As long as I'm living, breathing, I'll never escape them. The boatyard was a mass grave.

Visions.

The blood. The destruction. The sounds. Danny's face before I lost my grip.

I drag myself to my feet and wander aimlessly through the silent mansion. I find Esther in the kitchen loading the dishwasher. She pauses. Looks at my arm. Then calmly goes to the cupboard and pulls the first aid box down. I take a seat at the island and rest my arm on the counter.

Empty.

She works silently, wrapping my arm carefully with steady hands. And when she's done, she looks up at me, her palm cupping my cheek. I know what she's going to say, and I absolutely cannot bear hearing it. So I start to subtly shake my head. It's been three days. I've sat in his mansion like a zombie for three days, waiting for him to walk through the doors. He hasn't, and with each minute that passes, my hopes are slowly dying.

"You need to prepare for the worst," she says gently, and my head shakes increase.

"He's strong," I reply, adamant. "Formidable. He'll come back to me."

She breathes in, swallowing, and starts to pack away the first aid box. I hate that she's so clearly humoring me. Where's her faith?

"He will be back, Esther," I reiterate, ignoring the part of my brain that's telling me to be real. That's telling me I am alone.

I hear the door to the mansion close, and I jump down from my stool and run to the main entrance. When I spot Brad leading someone towards Danny's office, I can't stop myself from following. The door is closed when I get there, but I don't knock. I walk in and find Brad with a man I don't recognize. They both look at me, both in pity.

"Who are you?" I demand. I've never seen him around here before.

He pulls a badge out and flashes it at me, and I withdraw. "Spittle. FBI. If you wouldn't mind giving us some privacy."

"She can stay." Brad says, catching sight of my bandaged arm before throwing me a look of pure filth. It doesn't affect me. He walks to the drinks cabinet and pours two glasses of Scotch.

"As you wish." The man, Spittle, takes a seat at Danny's desk, and Brad hands him one of the drinks.

"Do I need one of those?" I ask, motioning to the glasses held at their lips.

Spittle falters, setting his glass on the desk. "A body was dragged out of the cove earlier this morning," he says matter of factly, glancing at me.

The ground disappears from beneath my feet, and I reach for a nearby cupboard, clinging on for dear life. Spittle returns his attention onto Brad. "I knew Danny. But I need someone to formally identify the body."

A ragged sob rips my body in two, along with my world, and I fall to my knees. Spittle doesn't even look at me. But Brad does. And the wobble of his lip only makes it all the more real. *I knew Danny.* That's what he said. Spittle has already identified him.

"I'll do it," Brad replies, his voice shaky. He knocks back the whole of his drink and slams his empty down, his grip of the glass sending his knuckles white. He's angry. He's sad. He's lost. "I'll do it," he breathes, glancing across to me on the floor. I can't see him through my tears. But I know he's crying too. "Unless you want to," he adds coldly.

My head feels like it could explode. I don't know what happens now, where I'll go, how I'll survive. But I do know one thing. I can't see Danny like that. Never.

I jump up and run out of the office. Dead. He's dead. I see nothing as I race through the mansion, except the memories of him circling my mind. I don't hear a sound except him calling my name. I smell nothing but sea and driftwood and Danny.

I charge up the stairs, down the corridor, and into my room, slamming the door behind me. I find the blade on the floor. Pick it up. Rest it on my arm. And I slash repeatedly, over and over, screaming my way through it.

I'm not punishing myself.

I'm punishing him.

"Rose!" Esther knocks the blade from my hand, and I fold to the floor in a heap of devastation, my body racked with loud, jerking sobs.

I've never really felt. Not for years. Not before Danny and after my baby was taken.

But I don't think I've ever felt this numb. This broken. This hopeless. There was a small part of me that always hoped that maybe one day I would be reunited with my boy. That now seems impossible. The three people in this world who would know where or how to find him are all dead. I should feel free. Nox is gone. The man with the snake ring is gone. But so is Danny, and now I feel more trapped in darkness than ever before. And through my numbness, I'm in agony.

It's raining. Has been since Brad returned from the morgue and drank two bottles of Scotch two weeks ago. Dense, gray clouds blanket the sky. The ground beneath my heels is saturated and spongy. The air is thick with grief, and every fat raindrop that hits me hurts. I've declined Ringo's offer of an umbrella. Let the rain drown me. Let it pelt me until I'm bruised.

I stare as two men lower Danny's coffin into the gaping hole in the ground. I swallow when I lose sight of it. I close my eyes when the lump in my throat swells and lodges itself there, my measured breaths faltering. I try to breathe through my nose. I gasp for air, throwing my hand out to catch Brad's black-suited arm to steady myself. He moves quickly to catch me and hisses, his teeth gritting when he catches his shoulder.

"Hey," he whispers, pulling me close. I bury my face in his side, unable to watch as Esther steps forward and tosses dirt on top of the coffin. Her face has remained expressionless for the

two weeks since Danny was confirmed dead, though the devastation in her eyes is tangible. "Rose," Brad says, urging me from
my hiding place. I look at two sweaters in my hands, the British
flags facing me. My ring catches my eye. The diamond has
dulled. It hasn't sparkled like it once did.

Gathering strength, I step forward slowly, stopping at the edge
of the grave. Tears steadily drop and sink into the material of the
sweaters. One more time, I bring them to my nose and breathe
them in, closing my eyes. I see him. He's there, wild and beautiful. "I'll never forget you," I whisper, dropping the sweaters into
the grave.

I turn and walk away on unfeeling legs, but where I'll go
beyond here is unknown. I'm wet through, cold to the bone.
Distraught. Taking the handle of the Merc, I pull the door open.
"Rose?"

I frown at the voice I recognize, turning to find Perry Adams
behind me. "Perry?"

Stepping forward, his face drenched in sympathy that I just
don't understand, he hands me an envelope. "Danny asked me to
do something for him."

Tentatively, I accept the envelope, my frown growing.
"What?"

"Just read what's inside." He turns and walks away but comes
to a stop before he makes it to his car. Looking over his shoulder,
he smiles a little. "He really loved you."

Those words don't comfort me. They only remind me that
he's gone. I would rather Danny truly hate me and be here. Alive.
Living. A suppressed sob chokes me, and I shake my head. "Good
luck in the campaign race," I say, getting in the car before the
envelope is completely sodden by the rain.

I rip open the top and pull out some papers, my hand coming
to my mouth when I see a handwritten note from Danny on top.

Rose,

    If you're reading this, my plan for us didn't work out. But it still can for you. I asked you to be strong. Now, I'm begging you. I can't be with you, and that kills me all over again. I've enclosed a one-way ticket to St. Lucia. Go. Get out of that godforsaken city. There's a beachside villa all paid for. It's yours. Sell it if you must, take the money, but promise me you'll stay there for a while and remind yourself of who you are. My warrior. The woman I fell so madly in love with. You've lost me. I can't let you lose her too. Don't mourn me for too long. You've got a life to live. A life of freedom.

    But before you leave, there's someone I'd like you to meet. With the airline ticket is something else.

    I love you.

    Always will.

    Danny x

I blink, swallow, blink again. I can smell him. See him. The airline ticket underneath is for a flight the day after tomorrow. I pull out the paper beneath that, my forehead creasing when I see what it is. A birth certificate. "What?" I scan the page, seeing it belongs to someone called Daniel Christopher Green. I shake my head, my confusion growing. This means nothing to me. Was that

Danny's name before Carlo Black found him? My gaze falls onto the date of birth. It can't be. This person was born ten years a—

"Oh my God." I nearly drop the papers when the date sinks into my confused brain. A date I will never forget. But his name? "Daniel," I say to myself, feeling at my throat, massaging the swell of grief away. I urgently scramble through the rest of the papers, finding an address. My hand comes up to my mouth to contain my sob, my body convulsing. He found my son? In California. There's a plane ticket for there too.

I jump out of the car quickly. "Perry!" I yell, stopping him from pulling the door of his car closed. I hold all the papers up, fighting to find my voice. "Thank you."

He smiles again, this time not forced. But he doesn't say a word. He pulls the door closed and drives off.

And then the rain suddenly stops.

And the clouds clear.

I look up to the sky.

The sun is out for the first time since Danny died.

The house is perfect. White, spotless, and perfect. The front lawn is an unbelievable shade of perfect green and the white picket fence containing it looks like it's straight from a picture book advertising the most perfect family home.

"You sure you'll be okay?" Esther asks as I stare at the house from the back seat of the cab. "I don't mind coming with you. We don't know how they'll react to you." She looks at the house too. "Maybe you should have called first."

I shake my head and open the door. "Giving them notice of my arrival would give them time to stop me. I don't want to risk them blocking me." Reaching over, I kiss her cheek. "I'll get another cab back to the hotel. You don't have to wait." I get out and make my way toward the house, brushing down my black pants. I've never found it so tricky to decide what to wear. I wanted to look as together and presentable as possible, even if I'm anything but. Danny's note shook me to the core. When I started reading, he suddenly wasn't dead anymore. Then I finished the letter and it was like he'd died all over again. But he offered me hope. A savior. Something to live for.

I knock on the door and step back, listening for sounds from beyond. There's nothing. And then there's something. Footsteps. My heart starts beating double time, pounding fiercely, and Danny's voice drums in my head.

Be strong. Be strong. Be strong.

The door swings open, and all the words I'd planned abandon me as I stare at the woman before me. An attractive woman, with blonde hair and brown eyes, maybe mid-fifties. She's in an apron that's covering a pleated skirt and chiffon blouse. She's baking. Being a mom. Normal. She looks so normal. I cough my throat clear and search through the bedlam in my head for my lines. "Hello, my name is—"

"You don't need to tell me who you are." Her hand drops from the door, her eyes glazing. "He looks just like you."

I inhale, so sharply, I find myself staggering back.

"Careful, there." She rushes to catch me when my heel slips off the step, and I start plummeting backward.

I quickly right myself with her help, my head in even more chaos, trying to adjust to the unexpected direction this moment has taken. As I stare at the woman before me, I can't help but think that she was prepared for it. "You don't seem surprised to see me."

"I'm not."

"Why?"

"I've always wondered when you'd show up. How did you find us?"

I pull out the envelope from my purse. "My fiancé gave me these." Again, the notion that Danny had everything in place pokes at my mind. I don't want to believe he walked into his death willingly to save me, but everything I know suggests it. Ernie, Nox, now my son. He was willing to sacrifice himself for me. And I hate him for it. "Hilary," I begin, and she frowns. "It's on Daniel's birth certificate. It's fake, I assume. But that is your name, yes?"

Her head bobs on a light nod. "And your name?"

"Rose."

Looking at the house, as if thinking carefully, she motions to the door. "You should come in."

"Is Daniel there?"

She starts toward the front door, looking back. "He's at soccer practice."

It's weird. Part of me is relieved. Part of me is disappointed. I want to see him, and I don't. But only because I know that visual confirmation that Danny really did find my son might finish me off.

I follow her and enter a light, breezy hallway, letting Hilary direct me to the kitchen—a huge square space, with sofas, a dining area, and doors onto a huge yard. I see a soccer net at the back, a few balls scattered on the lawn before it. I keep my eyes on the balls as I lower to a chair at the table.

A glass of water slides toward me. I take a sip, feeling parched. "So what now?" she asks, joining me.

I look up from my glass, wondering the very same thing. "I don't know," I admit. "But I know I want to get to know my son."

"Get to know him?"

"Yes. You bought my baby on the black market. He was minutes old when they ripped him from my breast, and I never saw him again. Not a day has gone by, not a minute, when I didn't think about him."

She swallows, and I see the guilt she's probably been burying for years. She looks wholesome. A good woman. But she's not allowed herself to think about what I lost, only what she gained.

Hilary shakes her head. "You're misunderstanding. I expected you to come in here guns blazing, threatening to take him. But you want to get to know him?"

Guns blazing. I shake my head clear of the explosions of light bombarding my mind. "I'm not deluded, Hilary. I've never been a mother. Honestly, I wouldn't know where to begin, but I really want to try." I couldn't just rip him away from her. I've been there myself, and it was agony after a few minutes of nursing him. Hilary has had ten years with Daniel. She knows what she's doing. Look at her, all perfect. And look at me. Completely imperfect. My relief that for all these years my boy has been with someone who loves him so much won't allow me to turn his life upside down. "Does he know about me?"

She looks down, as if ashamed. "I've thought about telling him so many times. But then . . ." Her eyes swell with tears. "What if you never came? What if you were dead?" Her hand covers her mouth. "I wished you dead," she croaks, and I nod, oddly understanding. Sometimes I wished *myself* dead. Suddenly, she gets up and walks across the kitchen to the fridge. Opening the door, she pulls out a bottle of white. "I hope you don't mind."

I smile to myself. "I'll join you, if *you* don't mind."

She falters unscrewing the cap, regarding me carefully. "You're so calm."

"The storm's over," I tell her as she pours two glasses. "Now I'm trying to clean up the devastation it's left behind."

"I'm so sorry." Her lip quivers. "I never thought about you, I admit it. I told myself you were a no-hoper who didn't love him. A drug addict, a waste of space. I never thought of you as a mother, not even a decent human being. It was easier that way." She lowers to the chair, taking back at least half her wine. "I was so desperate to be a mom. Six miscarriages, a stillborn. Adoption was so complicated, and the red tape ridiculous. We got declined. Us." She laughs in disbelief, landing me with imploring eyes. "I just wanted to be a mom." Her hand meets mine on the table, squeezing pleadingly. "Please don't take him away from me."

"I'm desperate to be a mom too," I say in reply, and she inhales. That's all I need to say. All that *should* be said.

"Then you will be." She swallows, blinking back the tears. My son knows nothing but this woman who loves him. I could never take her away from him.

Silence falls for a short time, both of us thinking, both of us taking much-needed sips of our wine. "I'm scared," I admit.

"Scared?"

"What if he doesn't accept me?"

A knowing smile crosses her face. "Danny is the most level-headed, wise, gracious ten-year-old I've ever known. He's full of heart, Rose. He won't reject you."

Danny. They call him Danny. Pain slices me, and not only because of that. How much she knows about my boy hurts. How much I don't know hurts more.

I look past Hilary when I hear a car pull up. "Oh, this is them." She jumps up, brushing down her apron in a panic.

"Them?"

"Daniel and my husband."

I shoot up from my chair. "Oh, God." I place my wine down and follow Hilary's lead, fiddling with my own clothes. "I should go. Now isn't the right time. You need to sit him down and explain about me." I look around for a means of escape.

Hilary seizes my wrist to stop me fleeing, and I look at her in shock. "You should at least meet my husband." Her posture straightens, her inner strength growing. "I'll send Daniel upstairs so we can talk about what happens next together. I've stalled long enough. Will you wait in here?"

She heads to the front door, not seeming to give me an option, and I lower to the chair and push the wine away from in front of me, opting for the water instead. I hear the door close. I hear a man, and then the undeniable sound of him greeting Hilary with a kiss.

"Why don't you take a shower?" Hilary says to Daniel. "Get out of all that muddy soccer uniform. Take your cleats off first."

"Okay." His voice, young and sweet, tips my emotions as I hear the clunk of his cleats hitting the floor. The cleats I saw slung over his shoulder in a photograph. Then his thundering footsteps charge up the stairs.

I look down at the wooden table, shakes beginning to set in. I can hear hushed whispers from the hallway, Hilary obviously bringing her husband up to speed. I wait, tense, until he steps into the kitchen. His hair is silver, his glasses old-fashioned. Daniel's father. He says nothing. Just nods, breathes in, and then backs out of the room again. There were tears in his eyes. He needed visual confirmation of my existence.

Over the next fifteen minutes, question after question rolls around my head. I ponder what I'll do if Hilary's husband isn't as friendly and welcoming of me. I wonder if he'll send me packing. I wonder when they'll tell Daniel and how. I wonder how much longer I'll have to wait to meet him. I've heard his voice, and the ache inside has only intensified. I wonder if my son will completely reject me. Or even what I'll do if he embraces me. I don't think I really did prepare myself for this. I thought I had. Now I'm here, I'm a nervous wreck. So when I hear a door open, I'm up out of my chair like lightning, a stressed sweat breaking out, my heart going wild, hitting my breastbone hard, over and over again. I expect to see Hilary and her husband. I don't. "Oh God," I breathe, trying to force my heart rate steady.

A boy wanders into the kitchen, and my ability to breathe escapes me. I blindly reach for the table to keep myself upright as he regards me with an interest that I'm not sure what to make of. My head is demanding I say something, but yet again I'm mute. Stunned. Overwhelmed. Not just because standing in front of me is my baby—the boy I've dreamed of every night for ten years. But because there's not one person on this planet who could deny that he is mine. I've seen pictures, but they've always been at a distance. I never got the opportunity to marvel at his looks. Everything about him is me. The dark shade of his hair. The deepness of his eyes. His complexion, his jawline, his nose. Even his lashes are long and girlie. If I didn't know better, I would question whether there was even another human involved in creating him. And I'm filled with gratitude for that small mercy. *He doesn't look like a monster.*

My knees begin to knock together, the moment becoming too much. I lower to the chair I just shot up from, needing something to support my overcome form. "Do you mind if I sit down?" I've planned what I would say to him time and again. I've dreamed of finding him and taking him in my arms, kissing his head and telling him how much I love him. I'm capable of none of those things, and, actually, now it feels inappropriate. I wonder where his parents are, yet I can't find the words to ask. I wonder what he's thinking, yet *dare* not ask. He's put on pajamas, red ones emblazoned in Star Wars characters. His hair is wet, his skin so clear. I've never seen anything so beautiful. "Where are your parents?"

He shrugs, and I look past him, torn. Should I get them? Should I leave? "Who are you?" he asks.

I swallow, my mouth so dry. "Rose. I'm a friend of your mom's."

"I've never seen you before."

"You like Star Wars?" I blurt, frantically steering him off course.

His little mouth twists a fraction as he pads forward on bare feet and pulls a chair out. The legs scrape the tile floor loudly, and while I cringe, the sound seems to go over Daniel's head. "Mom says I'm a Star Wars whizz."

Mom. It hurts so much hearing him refer to the woman who bought him as *Mom.* Me. *I'm* his mom. He should be calling me that. "What else do you like?"

He considers my question as he regards me, closely and carefully. "What do you like?"

His counter question throws me, his little forearms settling on the table as he gets comfortable. "Me?" My mind blanks. What do I like? "The sun on my face," I tell him, smiling when his little brow furrows.

"Do you like Star Wars?"

Crap. I've never seen a Star Wars movie in my life. Silly, but I fear admitting that might destroy our relationship before it's even started. "I've never seen Star Wars."

His little face is astonished. "Never?"

I shake my head. "You could show me sometime. We could watch them all together." I see the excitement on his face.

"Cool," he chirps, as a woman's sob sounds in the distance. Daniel looks over his shoulder, and I shrink in my chair. I'm mute again. And for the first time, I try to comprehend the turmoil Hilary's in. How desperate she was for a baby, how she got that baby, and how she must feel now it's come to bite her on the ass.

"Why's Mom crying?"

I shoot my eyes to his. "I don't know." A lie. But it's not my place to tell him. It pains me, but I know that.

Daniel links his fingers on the table and starts studying his entwined hands. "So, you'll watch Star Wars with me? Mom and Dad are fed up with it now. They say there's only so many times they can watch the same films, but I could watch them every day for the rest of my life."

"I would watch them every day for the rest of my life too." I really would.

"Really?"

"Really," I affirm.

"But you don't even know if you like it yet."

"If you like it, I'm sure I'll love it."

He smiles, and it very nearly has me weeping. "You're cool."

"Does that mean you like me?"

"Yeah, I like you."

A ragged breath cuts my throat. There's only one thing that's ever been said to me that can compare to my son's words. The first time Danny told me he loved me. "I like you too," I tell him, compelled to extend my hand across the table. He doesn't hesitate to take it. I see all the qualities in him that should have been in me. Grace. Warmth. Honesty. For the first time in my life, I don't look back on my life and curl up in pain. Because everything I should have been is sitting before me. My miserable life seems acceptable now.

I squeeze his hand, looking up when we're joined by Hilary and her husband. Her eyes are red and puffy. Her husband's face is grave.

"Daniel, why don't you get your homework out?" his dad suggests.

He's up out of his chair quickly. I've never known a kid to be so eager over homework. "It's algebra," he declares, almost proudly. "I don't need your help."

"Then maybe you can teach me," his dad replies. "Say goodbye to Rose."

My time is up. For now, at least. "Bye, Daniel." I fight off the excruciating pain radiating through me. *Be thankful. Be grateful.*

He wanders around the table and offers his hand. Unsure, I accept, and he shakes it. "It was nice to meet you."

My heart breaks. "And you."

"One day, we'll binge-watch my Star Wars box set."

"I'd love that." I feel so warm inside. So optimistic. It's an odd feeling, but I like it. "Can I have a hug, Daniel?" I ask.

"Sure." He dives on me like it's nothing, when it is absolutely everything. His little body against mine feels like the best medicine. A lifesaving medicine. I embrace his cuddle and let my mind wander back to the only other time I held him in my arms. *I love you,* I say in my head, closing my eyes and cherishing the moment. "You'd better go do that algebra."

He's gone from my arms faster than he dived into them, zooming out of the kitchen at one hundred miles an hour.

Then it's just me and his parents. Worry is rife on their faces. "I'm sorry. He just walked right in here."

"Did you tell him?"

"Of course not." My face must be as offended as my tone. "I'm not here to ruin your lives. I'm here because I should be. I realize it'll take time and a gentle approach."

Hilary relaxes. "Thank you."

"How do we get hold of you?" her husband asks, pulling out his phone. I reel off my number and smile gratefully when he calls my cell, giving me his. "I'm Derek."

I nod. "I'm going away," I say. "But I'm still contactable. There's no pressure. But I need you to know that I'm not dead. I'm more alive than ever. And I'm here."

They both look away briefly, ashamed, because they have both wished me dead.

"Thank you," I say quietly, rising to my feet. "For looking after him, thank you." I can't hold back the tears. They're powering forward now, the gravity of the moment settling. "I just want to get to know him."

Hilary shoots forward and takes me in her arms, and it's now I realize what makes her such a good mother. Comfort and peace blankets me, just from being in her arms. "I'm so sorry."

"Me too," I admit, breaking free and brushing away the tears. "You'll be in touch?"

She nods, and I smile, moving past them toward the front door. When I make it there, I look up to the top of the stairs and silently tell him I love him once again. That I'll see him soon.

As I wander down the perfect pathway toward the road, I see Esther still idling at the curb in the cab. She smiles at my tears, and I smile in return. I should have known she wouldn't leave. "Okay?" she asks when I slip into the seat.

"It will be." I look to the house, zooming in on the window on the first floor that has Star Wars curtains hanging at them. "I met him," I say and Esther's eyes nearly pop out, making me smile. "He doesn't know who I am yet, but I saw him. He's the most beautiful kid I've ever seen." My voice quivers, a perfectly clear image of Daniel at the forefront of my mind.

Esther's hand reaches for mine and holds it gently. "I'm so happy you've found him."

My heart squeezes for Esther. She found her son, and then she lost him all over again. I lean across the car and take her in a hug, relaxing into her warmth. I don't say anything. I don't need to. We're both utterly devastated by the loss of her son. Had it not been for the gift Danny left me, I'm not sure where I'd be heading right now. Actually, I do. I'd be freefalling into nothing. I detour from my thoughts before I soak her shoulder with my tears.

She pulls away from me. "Where to?"

"The airport," I say, resting back and gazing out of the window. I need to do as I'm told. Remind myself of who I am. Strong. Fierce. And soon, I pray, a mom.

29

ROSE

Crystal clear waters. Golden sand. Space for miles and miles. Peace and quiet. It's paradise here. The beach house Danny left me isn't quite a beach house. More a giant villa. Eight bedrooms, four reception rooms, five bathrooms. What the hell will I do with eight bedrooms? My mind was blown when the cab driver pulled up outside the gated complex earlier today. I wandered around in a daze of shock and confusion, finding room after room. The garden is the beach, and that's where I'm standing now, looking out to the horizon as the sun sets. The breeze has loose strands of my hair whipping my face, and my toes are sunken into the wet sand, water swishing around my feet. There's not one cloud in the sky, and as I look up, closing my eyes, I breathe in the sea air, relishing the lowering sun on my face.

I remain there for an age, soaking up the rays and peace, looking out to sea. The colors here are vivid. My world isn't black anymore. And that was his intention.

I hear someone approaching behind me, and I turn on a

peaceful inhale, pulling my hair into a ponytail as I do. I see a short man, dressed in a white uniform. "Miss Cassidy?"

"Yes?"

He says no more and hands me an envelope before leaving. Looking down at the paper in my hand, my mind swirls. What is this? I look around the beach, for what reason I don't know. I'm just . . . thrown. Slipping my thumb past the seal, I peel it open, pulling out a sheet of paper. My heart gallops, wondering if this is another note from Danny. I don't want to read it if it is. He'll haunt me for the rest of my damn life.

Holding on to my breath, I unfold the paper, squeezing my eyes closed when I see my name in his handwriting at the top. "You bastard," I say out loud, wishing he was here to go psychotic at the mention of that word. Backing up from the shore, I find some dry sand and lower to my ass, knowing I'm going to need to be sitting.

Rose,

Isn't it beautiful? My dad used to bring me here in the winter. Where you're sitting is where I put my first wetsuit on and in front of you is where I rode my first jet ski. I cherish this place. I hope you will too. Up the road a few miles, there's a private hangar. Inside is a private jet. The contact details for your private pilot are on the table in the lobby. You'll want to visit Daniel as much as possible, and hopefully sometime soon his parents will agree to you bringing him here to visit you as well. The jet and hangar are in your name.

The papers for the villa are now in your name. I know I said you can sell it if you want to, but I really hope you don't. Because then I'll have nowhere to live . . .

My fingers tense around the paper, crumpling it in my grasp. My eyes are dry as I read the letter again. *"Where you're sitting now . . ."* I look down at the sand, my mind spinning. How does he know where I'm sitting now? The exact spot? My pulse rockets, and I dive to my feet, my eyes glued to his words. The note slips from my fingers, floating to the sand at my feet. And I stare at it. Trembling where I am, I just stare at it, my vision blurry from the onslaught of tears. Am I losing my mind? Have I got this all wrong?

I know I said you can sell it if you want to, but I really hope you don't. Because then I'll have nowhere to live . . .

My lungs scream for air as I spin on the spot. I can't see through the tears that are springing into my eyes, can't breathe through the blockage in my throat. Everything is a haze of yellow and blue. Except for one thing.

Danny.

"No." My muscles disintegrate, and I fall to my knees on the sand, battling with my logic and prayers. He's a mirage. I'm missing him so much, my mind is playing tricks on me. Yet the distant form of a man grows as he strolls casually down the shoreline, his hands in the pockets of his shorts, his chest and feet bare.

And then he's perfectly clear and perfectly here.

My head lifts as he nears until he's towering over me. His face is straight as he pulls his shades off. His skin tan. His black hair is longer than usual, his eyes bluer. More alive. At peace. His body sharper. My eyes land on a dressing just shy of his collarbone. A bullet wound.

He lowers to his haunches before me and reaches for my cheek, softly stroking away the trails of tears. "You remind me of someone I used to know," he whispers, smiling mildly.

I break down, covering my face with my hands and sobbing into them. He's not real. He can't be real. I'm dreaming, or maybe even having a nightmare. I sniffle and peek through my fingers. He's still there.

Astonishment.

Then anger.

I dive to my feet, knocking him to his ass. And I stare down at him as he looks up at me. "You bastard," I choke, diving onto him, finding his lips, kissing him, relishing the familiar feel, the smell of him, *everything*. My hands and mouth are in a frenzy, getting as much of him as I can, my mind telling me that he's going to turn to dust at any minute. That I'll wake up.

"I'm here," he murmurs into my mouth, rolling us so he has me trapped beneath him in the sand. Pulling back, he brushes my hair from my face and studies me for a few, quiet moments. He kisses me, a kiss like nothing I've had before. It's so deep, so intense. So *us*. "I'm sorry," he murmurs. "So sorry."

"How?" I ask, my mind a mass of questions. I saw him in the water. I heard the FBI agent. I saw Brad when he got back from identifying his body.

"I would never have been left to get on with my life with you, Rose. There would always be someone vying for my blood. As I hung off the side of that boat, as I looked at you, I knew what I had to do."

I shake my head, feeling like it could explode. Explode with happiness. With relief. "So you played dead."

"No, I held my breath for fucking ever and swam for my fucking life," he replies, full of sarcasm.

Good God, I've been through hell. Cried a thousand tears and more. Ached, hurt, and ached some more. "You could have told me, Danny."

"You had to be seen to grieve."

"But Brad . . ."

"He knows I'm alive, Rose."

"How?" He needs to tell me how he pulled this off.

He smiles at my wonder. "After I made it to the shore, I switched clothes with one of the dead and loaded him onto one of my skis. Rode out a way and dumped the body. Then I tracked down Spittle. Made him a few promises."

"Promises?"

"I was keeping hold of a few pictures." He shrugs. I don't need to ask what kind of pictures. "Spittle led the search and found the body. Paid Brad a visit, as you know." He reaches for my face, stroking my cheek, his touch full of apologies. "Poor fucker looked like he'd seen a ghost when he walked into the morgue and found me waiting for him."

I'm amazed. Speechless. The two bottles of Scotch Brad sank when he got back make sense for more reasons than one now. "And Esther?"

"She knows. But to everyone else, I'm dead." He stares down at me, thoughtful. "And it was all so fucking easy, Rose. All of it easy, except one thing."

"What?"

"Missing you," he whispers, placing a kiss on my lips. "It was fucking agony being without you. Not seeing you." He searches my eyes. "Feeling you." His hand drifts between our bodies, cupping me between my thighs. My breath hitches, and he smiles. "Hearing you. We have a lot of catching up to do."

My smile matches his, and with my hands in his hair, I nuzzle his scarred cheek, my eyes closing, my sense of smell taking a hit of his familiar scent. "I hate you so much."

He breathes in and lets out the air on a long sigh. "I love you too."

The story continues with James & Beau in
THE ENIGMA
book 2 of The Unlawful Men Series...

The Unlawful Men Series.
THE BRIT (Book 1)
THE ENIGMA (Book 2)
THE RESURRECTION (Book 3)
THE RISING (Book 4)

ALSO BY JODI ELLEN MALPAS

The This Man Series

This Man

Beneath This Man

This Man Confessed

All I Am – Drew's Story (A This Man Novella)

With This Man

The One Night Series

One Night - Promised

One Night - Denied

One Night - Unveiled

Standalone Novels

The Protector

The Forbidden

Gentleman Sinner

Perfect Chaos

Leave Me Breathless

The Smoke & Mirrors Duology

The Controversial Princess

His True Queen

The Hunt Legacy Duology

Artful Lies

Wicked Truths

The Unlawful Men Series

The Brit

The Enigma

The Resurrection

The Rising

The Belmore Square Series

One Night with the Duke

A Gentleman Never Tells

This Woman Series

(The This Man Series from Jesse's POV)

This Woman

With This Woman - Coming 2023

Book 3 - TBC

ABOUT JODI ELLEN MALPAS

Jodi Ellen Malpas was born and raised in England, where she lives with her husband, boys and Theo the Doberman. She is a self-professed daydreamer, and has a terrible weak spot for alpha males. Writing powerful love stories with addictive characters has become her passion—a passion she now shares with her devoted readers. She's a proud #1 *New York Times* Bestselling Author, a *Sunday Times* Bestseller, and her work is published in over twenty-five languages across the world. You can learn more about Jodi & her words at: JEM.Website